BADD BABY

A BADD BROTHERS NOVEL

Jasinda Wilder

BADD
BABY

ONE

Duncan

Oh, shit.

My mouth has gotten me into in more trouble than I'd like to admit. I've gotten in fistfights, been slapped on numerous occasions, thrown out of bars and clubs, arrested…all because I'm pathologically incapable of installing a filter between my idiot monkey brain and the runaway train that is my mouth.

I'm about to get slapped, I think.

The girl's eyes blazed blue fire, wrath and ire erupting with volcanic heat. Warning bells rang in my head—*danger! danger!*

"Never mind," she snarled. "You *were* hot…until you opened your mouth."

I blatantly checked her out while I racked my brain for a way out of this. And she was, in a word, a smokeshow. Five-seven or -eight, with glossy, thick, jet-black hair left loose in a wild storm cloud around her slender shoulders. Blue eyes, although to call them merely blue is a deep injustice. They're not just *blue*. They were twin sapphires, a deep, dark, vivid shade that captured my attention and refused to let go.

I only caught a glimpse of her body before she sat down at the bar, and that was a quick glance through the crowd. I'm not a betting man, but I'd bet she's got goddess curves for fucking days.

Right now, she had her arms crossed over her chest, her eyes sparking and spitting. "Nothing to say, huh?

"What's a week from tomorrow, and what's it got to do with me?" I said, after another few seconds of searching for a witty repartee and coming up empty.

"Nothing," she muttered, taking a sip of her drink—Seven-Up and white wine.

"It sounded like you need a date." I turned and snatched the ticket out of the printer, scooped ice into highballs, and started pouring well vodka for the six vodka Red Bulls for Tina's table of popped-collar golf bro douches at table sixteen.

"I don't," she snapped. "It was a moment of verbal diarrhea—it's a condition and I'm off my meds."

I cackled at this, shooting her an amused smirk. "Hey, guess what? I have that same condition."

She gave me a droll glare that said I might be getting somewhere with her. Not necessarily anywhere *good*, but somewhere. "Well, you need to up your dosage, then."

I waved a hand, blowing a raspberry. "Tina! Order up for sixteen!" To her, then. "I'm self-medicated."

"It's not working." She was killing that drink like it was the only thing saving her life.

I mixed another for her and switched it with her empty the second she set it down. "On the house."

"Is that your way of apologizing?" She sipped this one more slowly.

"Nope. I'm hoping if I keep you drinking, you'll tell me where we're going a week from tomorrow." Another ticket spat out and I scanned it, sighing— *more* goddamned Piña Coladas. Fucking frozen drink bullshit.

I couldn't spare any attention for the blue-eyed goddess with the sharp tongue as I set about making all the stupid Piña Coladas. All fucking eight of them. And I only have one blender, which only makes three—four if I stretch it, but if I stretch it, they complain there's not enough alcohol in them.

I was on my second batch when Elin tapped on the service bar with her book. "Dunc! My table is asking about their tequila shots."

I hold up the blender. "Sorry, Elin, one sec. I'm just making *eight* fucking Piña Coladas, *Arizona*."

Arizona, who put in the order, looked like she was about to cry—she's new, the Kitty was hopping, and she has the worst section, the poor thing. "I'm *sorry*, Duncan! What was I supposed to do? Tell them 'Sorry, you can't have those because my bartender doesn't like making them?'"

I hustled through the last batch and helped Arizona tray them. Her eyes were watery and red; I reached through the service bar to grab her wrist. "Hey, Ari, I was just fucking with you. You're cool. Just breathe, okay? You're doing great."

She nodded, sniffling. "Thanks, Dunc, I just…ugh. I'm about to have my period, and my hormones are whacked the fuck out."

I blinked at the overshare. "Um…yeah. No worries. And hey, remember, don't let customers take drinks from your tray again. They'll upset the balance and make you drop everything."

"The guy at fifteen just now took it before I could stop him." She winced. "I found that out the hard way at my last job."

I grinned. "I feel like there's a story in there."

She sighed a laugh. "Oh, there is. It involves a very wet US senator and a tray full of Irish coffees."

My eyes widened. "Oh. Oh fuck."

She widened her eyes back. "Yeah. However bad you're imagining it, it was way worse." She bent at the knees and lifted the tray. "I gotta drop these to my bachelorette table."

"Oh god, a bachelorette party?" I winced in sympathy. "Go with god, my friend." I faked a pious expression and crossed myself, kissed my fingers, and did a stupid waving gesture that was meant to evoke the pope but was more like Miss America.

This got me a snicker from Smokeshow. "So fuck Piña Coladas, huh? And bachelorette parties."

I took an order from a walk-up and pulled his beer while I answered her. "I've told Dad and Delia a million times the frozen drinks need to get cut. They just take too much time. So yeah, fuck Piña Coladas and every other frozen slushie bullshit drink."

"Dad and Delia?"

I tapped the logo over my left pec. "Badd?"

She shrugged. "I'm not from around here."

I'm tempted to point out that we have over a million followers on IG and another million on TikTok, but I don't. "It's a family business. My grandfather established the first and original Badd's bar over forty years ago. My dad took over when my grandfather died, and now my older sister is about to take the reins."

"So the name Badd Kitty…?" she prompted.

"Was named, in a fit of rash but inspired creativity, by my Uncle Rome, for the woman who later became my aunt. Who is named…wait for it…Kitty."

"So, your uncle, who I assume possesses the last name Badd, named this bar after a girl? And then married her? Not, like, the other way around?"

"Yup."

"So her name is Kitty Badd."

"Yup."

"And this place is Badd Kitty."

"Yup."

"Weird."

"Well, Uncle Rome is…"I laughed. "He's just Uncle Rome. It's the kind of thing he'd do. His identical triplet brothers weren't happy about it, I'm told. He didn't consult them, he just had the sign made and put it up without so much as a how-do-you-do to them."

"So you're following in your family's footsteps as a bartender."

I nodded. "Yep. Well, I feel compelled to point out that I'm not *just* the bartender. I'm the GM."

She coughed in shock, spluttering. "Wait, what? You're the *general manager*? Of a whole bar? By yourself? You can't be any older than I am."

I snorted. "Not taking the bait on that one, Smokeshow. I'm twenty-three."

"Smokeshow?" she asked, with a cute-sexy frown.

How can a frown be cute *and* sexy at the same time? Sorcery, I tell you.

"You haven't told me your name," I said.

"You first."

I extended my hand to hers. "Duncan Badd, at your service."

She took my hand, but instead of shaking it like a normal human being, some idiotic instinct made me bow over her hand and kiss the back of it as if I was in a fucking Shakespeare play or some shit.

For several long, awkward moments, the gorgeous

girl just stared at me and then at her hand in mine, as if trying to figure out how she felt about what I just did.

TBH, same.

She twisted our joined hands to a normal hand-shake orientation. "A regular old handshake would have sufficed, Lord Bridgerton."

I grinned at her. "Which brother am I?"

Her frown was surprised. "You've seen it?"

"I have a mother, a sister, and a shitload of female cousins. My family hosted watch parties. As in, Mom and Delia made actual tea and crumpets and little weird sandwiches with cucumbers and shit. I still don't even know what the fuck a crumpet is, honestly. But yeah, I watched it."

"And when you say you have a shitload of female cousins…?" she prompted.

I sighed. "My extended family is…let's go with fucking colossal. It doesn't quite cover it, but it's close." I pulled beers and mixed drinks while I talked. "My dad is one of eight brothers. All eight of them are married with at least one kid, although most have two or three. So just from my dad's brothers, I have twenty-three cousins."

She spluttered in shock. "Holy fuck."

I laughed. "I'm not done, though, so hold on to your tits, Smokeshow. The Uncle Rome I mentioned? He's not actually my uncle, technically." I frowned. "I… wait, what *is* he? First cousin once removed, maybe?" I waved a hand. "Who the fuck cares? Point is, he's my Dad's cousin—my dad's grandfather had a twin brother, Lucas. Great-Uncle Lucas, who we all call Papa Lucas, has triplet sons, Roman, Remington, and Ramsey. Uncle Rome and Aunt Kitty have six kids, Uncle Remy and Aunt Juneau have two, and Uncle Ram and Aunt Izzy have one, so that's another nine cousins."

"Oh my fucking god."

I held up a finger. "But wait, there's more!"

She blinked at me. "No. There's more? You're kidding!"

"Nope. So Papa Lucas and Mama Livvie got married late, like, second marriages for both of them kind of thing." I waved a hand. "The details don't matter. Point is, Mama Livvie has five daughters, who we—meaning the cousins—call our aunts even though, again technically, they're not actually aunts. They all got married and had kids, and between the five sisters and their husbands, I have another...shit, gotta think about this one...um? One, two, three...uhhh...fourteen cousins. Or what we call cousins, regardless of the actual technical relationship."

"And you, like, *see* all these people?" she asked. "Regularly?"

I nodded. "Absolutely. Uncle Xavier and Aunt Low don't live here in Ketchikan full-time, but we see them several times a year at least, depending on Aunt Low's shooting schedule and what Uncle Xavier is up to."

She rubbed her face. "Fuck me, I have *so* many

questions. But first, you're telling me you have, like…
what? Forty…six? Forty-six cousins? Or cousin-adjacent
relations? That you see regularly? Like, you *know* them,
not just a 'this person is my relation but I only see them
on Thanksgiving and Christmas' kind of thing."

"Yes, ma'am. I know them all, I love them all, and
I've grown up hanging out with all of them. Most of
them either live here or come back frequently. We're a
very close family, the Badd and Goode clan."

"No." She facepalmed herself. "Goode? *Seriously*?"

I nodded. "Mama Livvie is Olivia Goode. Her
daughters all took their husbands' names which means
they're all Badds, so we're all technically the Badd clan,
but we refer to Mama Livvie's whole side as the Goode
side, and we're the Badd side. And Goode is G-O-O-
D-E, by the way."

"A family with the last name Goode married into
a family with the last name Badd."

"Yep."

"And you have forty-six cousins and a number of
aunts and uncles I can't even begin to count."

I laughed, nodding. "Yep. Twenty-eight aunts and
uncles."

"And the cousins…these aren't multiples?"

"Well, I have two uncles who are twins—Canaan
and Corin, and they married twin sisters."

I had to pause the conversation to serve some customers at the other end of the bar, and then returned

to the service bar once the other bartender, Elias, came back from the bathroom.

"The more you tell me, the more unlikely this whole story seems," she said.

I rolled my eyes and laughed. "What possible reason would I have for making this up?"

"I'm not saying you are, I'm just saying it *sounds* made up." She eyed me, thinking. "When you say 'Aunt Low's shooting schedule...'"

I winced—I try not to mention my famous family members too much. People get weird about it. "Oh, well, yeah. She, uh...works in the film industry."

She frowned at me. "C'mon, Duncan."

"Hey, you still haven't told me one thing about yourself," I said. "Your name, for starters."

"Rune Rigby."

"Rune?"

She nodded, her eyes already glazing over as she anticipated the questions she must get. "Yes, Rune, as in the pictographs used by the Norse and Germanic tribes from antiquity."

"From antiquity, is it?"

"My mother is a historian specializing in...can you guess?"

"Runes?"

She laughed, the genuine smile illuminating her features with the warmth of amusement, snaring my breath and trapping it in my lungs. "Well, yes, but not runes specifically, but rather the history of Norse and Germanic tribes in general."

"Why Norse and Germanic? What's the crossover?"

She rolled her eyes. "You're lucky Mom's not here or you'd be in for a hell of a lecture. The short version is that the Germanic tribes migrated west and north into Scandinavia and eventually became the Norse. Sort of. Mostly. It's complicated." She waved a hand. "I honestly don't know too much about it, as I'm not super into history. If you are, I can get you a copy of Mom's book."

"What about your dad?" I asked.

"Oh, he's not a historian." I just stared at her until she blinked, and then burst into laughter. "Wow…that was dumb."

I laughed with her. "I mean, it was funny."

"He's…well, he teaches Brazilian jiujitsu, and he's also a strongman. He used to compete, and still does compete once in a while, but not professionally."

I shook my head. "Talk about unlikely. A college professor mother who specializes in an obscure branch of history, and a dad who's a strongman and BJJ instructor."

"That's not as weird as having five million people in your family."

"Sorry, I didn't realize this was a weirdness competition," I said.

"If it was, you'd win," she answered.

"Probably, and in more ways than you can probably imagine."

I turned away to snatch a ticket from the printer and pull the drinks; when I turned back, she was gone. Her drink was there with a napkin over the top to indicate she was coming back.

And when I saw her approaching from the bathrooms, my heart skipped a beat.

Yeah, total fucking smokeshow.

The only average thing about this girl was her height—she's *stacked*. Like, *damn*. I guess it makes sense considering her dad is a strongman, but it's obvious even wearing loose, ripped jeans and a baggy, off-the-shoulder T-shirt that she's built like a brick shithouse. Which is a weird phrase, now that I think about it. A brick shithouse is not a flattering object to which to compare someone. I didn't make it up, obviously, I just think it's odd.

Anyway.

Thick, muscular thighs pressed against the legs of her ripped, wide-leg jeans, glimpses of smooth, tanned skin peeking temptingly through the rips. Strong shoulders and powerful, toned arms. And again, despite the bagginess of the oversized T-shirt she's wearing, she couldn't entirely hide the fact that she had some serious cleavage happening.

I watched her weave through the crowd, blatantly checking her out. Mainly because I couldn't not stare at her—the bar was over max capacity and full of hot, single young women, since the Kitty is a bit of a destination bar for the cruise ship tourists who flock to and clog Ketchikan this time of year—yet I had eyes only for Rune.

I caught her eye as she approached the bar; I was about to say something flirty—only my mouth knows what it would have been since it didn't bother informing my brain what I was about to say, though. But before I could get a word out, I saw a big guy slide up behind her and casually palm her ass.

She whirled, instantly furious, and shoved him hard. "Hey, hands off, *asshole!*"

That's as far as she got, though, because I've vaulted the bar and was shoving through the crowd. I launched my fist past Rune's ear and smashed it into the douchebag's throat, slipping around in front of her in the process.

The dude gurgled, eyes going wide as his mouth flapped like a fish out of water.

I may have forgotten about his friends, though, because I found myself facing four very large, very beefy, half-drunk douchebags from the popped-collar table.

"Uh, Duncan?" Rune said from behind my back.

"It's all good," I said, knowing the ruckus has alerted Uncle Bax at the front—he never misses a trick.

"The fuck was that, bro?" one of the big, beefy, popped-collar golf bro douchebags said to me, bucking at me.

"He grabbed her ass," I snapped. "That shit doesn't

fly in my bar." I pointed at the exit. "You guys can get the fuck out. I don't care whether you've paid your tab or not, just get the fuck out of my bar, *now.*"

"Or what, *bitch*?" he bucked at me again, even though I didn't flinch or take the bait the first time. "What're *you* gonna do about it?"

"Me?" I said, with an innocent look. "*I'm* not gonna do anything. I'm just the bartender."

A massive, hard-as-granite paw latched onto the back of the cocky douchebag's neck. "The question is what am *I* gonna do about it," Bax said, in his deepest, roughest, most intimidating snarl. "And the answer is either you sad sacks of steamy shit get *the fuck* out of my bar *right* the fuck now," he squeezed hard enough that the douchebag's eyes went wide with pain. "Or I'll snap your scrawny little neck and throw you into the fucking Passage."

The other dudes paled when they took in the size of my Uncle Baxter. Who, not incidentally, is six feet and two-fifty of solid, brutal muscle. He also happens to be a world-class MMA coach and instructor, and a former underground bare-knuckle brawler. He's massive, terrifying, tattooed, and radiates don't-fuck-with-me energy.

Bax turned the douchebag around to face the exit, pressed a thumb into a trigger point in his side, and force-marched him out. A single threatening glance was all it took for the fucker's friends to make themselves scarce in a hurry.

"Who was *that* monster?" Rune whispered, still behind me.

"That's my Uncle Baxter," I answered. "He moonlights as a bouncer here on the weekends."

"Moonlight my ass," Bax growled, returning. "Who'd that taint-stain grab?"

I indicated Rune with a nod behind me. "Her."

Baxter faced her. "I'm sorry about that, miss. We don't tolerate that shit around here." He scanned the bar, which has gone silent, looking from face to face; you could hear a pin drop. "I can and will break faces, folks, so keep your hands to yourself, or make *really* motherfucking sure the person you're touching has consented." He glanced at me. "Her drinks are on the house, Dunc." It wasn't a question.

"I thought you were the manager?" Rune asked, watching Bax's broad, departing back.

"I am. But…" I gestured at him. "Like I'm gonna argue? And also, that's our policy in these situations anyway."

"I could've handled that myself, you know," she said, heading back to her seat.

"I'm sure you could have," I answered, climbing back over to the service side. "But you shouldn't *have* to. It's our job to provide a safe and welcoming experience. In our bars, *no one*, no matter what, will *ever* feel afraid. You should be able to leave your drink on the bar and go to the bathroom without worrying it'll be drugged. And you sure as fuck should be able to walk through the crowd without getting groped. And if you *do* experience something like that, we're gonna handle it with extreme prejudice. You gotta set examples of what's gonna happen when you cross the line in a Badd bar. Namely, you're gonna get hurt. That fucker is lucky he's not visiting the ER to have bones set."

She nodded. "Well, thank you. Unnecessary, as far as I'm concerned, though appreciated."

It took me a good ten minutes to get through the backlog of service tickets, at which point Rune was counting cash while standing behind her stool.

"Leaving me already?" I asked, clapping a hand over my heart. "Say it ain't so."

She rolled her eyes. "Don't be a diva."

"Rune, wait."

She tosses a small stack of bills on the table and waves without looking back as she heads for the exit. "Goodbye, Duncan Badd."

"Fuck," I muttered, hustling after her. I clapped Elias on the back, stuffing the cash into the tip jar on the way past. "I'm taking five. You good?"

Elias—short, burly, bald, and gay—was closer to my parents in age than to me and had decades of experience behind the bar, so the question was rhetorical.

He nodded as he poured a row of Jägermeister shots. "I'm good. Go get 'er, kid."

I ducked under the folding section of the bar rather than lifting it and jogged for the exit—Rune was already half a block away, walking while texting. "RUNE!"

She stopped, turned, and looked up. "You again." She said it with a teasing grin. "You're not kissing my hand again, weirdo."

I held up my phone, showing her the schedule for next week. "I'm off a week from tomorrow."

She blinked at me. "Is that so?"

"Yep."

"Can you get the whole weekend off?"

"Maybe."

"My friend is getting married here in Ketchikan—it's a whole destination wedding thing, and I need a date."

"I'm in."

She quirked an eyebrow at me. "Just like that? Don't need to know anything else?"

"Nah. Although I *am* curious—why do you need a date? You can't just go stag?"

She hesitated. "It's complicated."

I grinned. "What's his name?"

"Who?"

"The guy I'm making jealous."

"His name is Hayes Motherfucking Willoughby."

"Hayes Motherfucking Willoughby. Is that his official middle name, or...?"

She rolled her eyes. "Don't worry about it. You're just arm candy."

"I'm okay with that," I said with a grin. "I make *great* arm candy."

"As long as your mouth stays shut, I bet you do."

Don't say it. Don't say it. *DO NOT SAY IT, DUNCAN BADD*.

"If you think me keeping my mouth shut is gonna stop me from charming you out of your dress by the end of the night, you're wrong." I said it.

Damn.

There I go again.

Her eyes widened. "You cocky bastard," she breathed.

She's affected, though. Her eyes searched mine, and her tongue slipped slowly over her lower lip, and she was looking up at me like she had a thousand things she wanted to say all at once.

I stepped into her space, staring down into her sapphire eyes. Leaned closer, and closer, and closer—her lips parted and I didn't think she was breathing. "You've got a date, Rune Rigby," I breathed, my lips ghosting against hers in a whisper of contact.

I stepped backward out of her space, smirking at her, and shot her a wink, heading back into the bar without a backward look.

TWO

Rune

I WOKE TO THE INSISTENT BURBLING OF MY CELL PHONE, which, as I swam up to consciousness, I realized had been ringing for a while. I fumbled for it blindly, my eyes still refusing to open all the way.

" 'Lo?" I slurred.

"It's a FaceTime call, dork," I heard Lindsey's voice say. "Pull the phone away from your ear and look at it."

"No." I ended the call and flopped back to the bed, but I kept the phone on my chest.

A second or two later, it burbled again. I answered and held it at arm's length. "What?" I demanded, peering at the screen. "And why are you FaceTiming me at…six in the fucking morning?"

"Be*cause*," she drawled, dragging out the last syllable into a sing-song, "we have a major, major emergency. As in code red, all hands on deck."

"You forgot your vibrator at home?" I guessed.

"This is no time for jokes!" she yelled. "And no, I would never. Lady Clitoria goes everywhere I go."

I stared at her. "No."

"No, what?"

"You did *not* name your vibrator Lady Clitoria."

"It's not a vibrator, first of all, *sinner*. Vibrators are *so* Gen X. It's a clitoral stimulator. There's a difference."

I rolled my eyes at her, wiggling my middle and ring fingers at her. "Well, *whore*, my clitoral stimulators go with me everywhere, too, but I don't have a stupid name for them. They're just called *fingers*."

"You're missing out on seriously next-level orgasms, Rune. For real. I bought you one for your birthday—are you telling me you haven't even tried it?" She shook her head with a sad, disappointed sigh. "Rune, Rune, Rune. Try it, girl. For real. It'll change your sex life. You'll thank me."

"I don't *have* a sex life, at the moment, Linz. I haven't had sex since I broke up with Hayes Motherfucking Willoughby."

Cue the horrified reaction.

"You *what*? Not even a hookup?"

"Linz…that's what *no sex* means. It's on purpose, also."

"You've gone more than *two months* without fucking anyone…*on purpose*?" She shook her head again. "Girl. *Girl*. The Old Ones did get one thing right: the best way to get over someone is to get under someone else."

"The Old Ones?" I echoed. "Why do you hate on the older generations so much?"

"Because my parents are the worst, and so are all their friends. They ruined the Earth, the government, and everything else with it. They—"

"Save the political bullshit, Linz," I snapped. "You can miss me with that shit. It's not just them. It's a fucking group effort."

She rolled her eyes at me. "Fine. Keep your head in the sand. But for real, you need to get laid."

"Nevermind my sex life," I said. "What's the emergency that required a FaceTime at fuck-o-clock in the morning?"

She rubbed her face with both hands, groaning. "The hotel here in Ketchikan, where Hamish and Raquel were going to have the wedding, reception, and stay for their first night together, had a really bad electrical fire last night. The whole place is fucked. It all but burned to the ground."

"Oh…shit. That's not good at all. The wedding is in three days."

"Not good?" Lindsey repeated. "It's a fucking catastrophe! It was pure dumb luck they had a last-minute cancellation in the first place—they're normally booked at least a year out. And so is everywhere else! There is literally not a single hotel or event center in all of Ketchikan with any openings before next fucking July! And we have our entire friend group flying in tomorrow for a wedding…but we have no location and nowhere for anyone to stay."

"Fuck." I winced. "What am *I* supposed to do about it, though? I forgot my magic wand back in LA."

Lindsey sighed. "You know, Rune, you don't have to be sarcastic *all the time*."

"Yes, I do. It's a feature, not a bug."

"I…you…" she groaned. "Whatever. Anyway. I was calling because your fake date, Duncan? He's a local. I was thinking maybe he'd have an idea, or something."

I groaned. "Linz, come on. Really? I've already roped him into going to the wedding for the sole intention of pissing off Hayes Motherfucking Willoughby."

"Rune…it's Hamish and Raquel. Their wedding is ruined if we don't find a solution. Not to mention the fifty people who all bought flights and booked rooms. Can't you just *talk* to him? I know you've been texting him."

I've been at the Kitty every night, flirting with him, that's what I've been doing. We texted once, yesterday, and that was Duncan asking if he should have his tux dry cleaned or just wear a regular suit. I may have told him to wear his tux, even though no one else is going to be in black-tie; I'm funny that way.

"Fine. I'll get a hold of him later this morning."

"Rune—"

"Linz, he's a bartender. The bar closes at two, and he's the manager. He probably didn't get to bed until three. I'm not waking the poor man up at six in the morning."

"Ugh, fine. Be all nice and logical and shit."

"I'll let you know what he says the moment I talk to him, okay? I promise. I'll do what I can."

"You're the best, Rune."

"I know."

She vanished from the screen in a swirl of blonde hair, reappearing with a pink object in her hands. "Behold, Lady Clitoria, my second-best friend, giver of epic orgasms."

"When you say she goes everywhere with you…?" I said, as a leading question.

"Well, not *everywhere*. Like, I don't just carry her around in my purse." She tapped her lips, thinking. "Although…a nice little lunchtime O might not be a bad thing."

"Linz."

She flapped a hand. "Anyway. The point is…you need to try yours."

"I didn't pack it, Linz."

She grinned. "Check your suitcase. The zipper pocket of the flappy-thing between the halves."

I left the phone on the bed, crawled to the foot end, and leaned over to check where she said. Sure enough, the "clitoral stimulator" was there, still in the box.

"Linz. I don't *like* sex toys."

"Only because you haven't tried *that* one."

"Linz—"

"If you're not getting piped, at least treat yourself to a good orgasm."

"Piped? You're so crass, sometimes."

"And you're strangely prudish, sometimes."

"You take that back, Lindsey Noreen Buckley."

"Not the dreaded full name!" she gasped. "Rune No-Middle-Name Rigby, it's true. You're very un-sexually liberated. You still hold to the toxic patriarchal system."

"Ohmygod. LINDSEY! I am not. I just...I don't do hookups. Casual sex is not my thing. I've tried it on multiple occasions, and it just doesn't do it for me."

"And how is monogamy treating you?" she asked.

"Poorly! Thus, the hiatus from dick. Men suck. They're all cheaters and liars. Unfortunately, I know for a fact I'm not bi or lesbian—I've experimented enough to know that, too."

"Thus..." she held up Lady Clitoria. "This. Doesn't gaslight, cheat, or lie, never forgets to put down the toilet seat, always comes through with a solid release, and, bonus prizes, it doesn't leave you all drippy afterward."

I gagged. *"Drippy?* Gross, Linz."

She laughed. "Raw-dogging it feels great in the moment, but good lord is it messy."

"I'm hanging up now. I haven't had enough coffee to deal with your shenanigans."

"Fine, but answer one question, first."

"Maybe."

"Are you or are you not going to let Duncan Badd explore your cave of wonders?"

"Bye-*eeeeee!*" I sang, drawing out the last syllable, and then ending the call.

Curiosity is a nasty thing. It's subtle, but insistent. Once it gets its hooks into you, it's nearly impossible to resist.

"Lady Clitoria," I mumbled, ripping open the packaging. "Ridiculous. How good can it really be?"

Within the box is a purple device made of some sort of soft, rubbery material with a white oval opening.

"Fine," I say, talking to the thing. "Let's see what you can do. But I'm not giving you some stupid name."

I *am* talking to it, though.

I wiggled out of my underwear and kicked the sheets away, tucked my heels up against my butt, and held the button until the purple device started vibrating. Which means it *is* a vibrator...*Lindsey*. Whatever. I closed my eyes and summoned the usual mental fantasy or scenario or whatever you want to call it: A faceless sexy guy who wants nothing but to eat me out until my legs are Jell-O. Boring, sure, but it's what gets me off.

Only, instead of a faceless dude with big arms and a long tongue, my imagination supplied something more...concrete.

He has messy reddish-brown hair and liquid chocolate eyes that sparkled with wit, intelligence, cocky confidence, and wry humor. He has thick arms and a six-pack—because if there is a god, then Duncan Badd has a six-pack.

In my imagination, Duncan is at the foot of my bed, shirtless in nothing but a pair of tiny shorts, all golden skin and brawn. He prowls toward me, buries his face between my thighs, and...

I centered the vibe over my clit, unsure what to expect.

"FUCK!" I screamed, yanking the thing away. I nearly came, literally instantly.

I cycled through the settings until it was at a lower intensity and tried again. This time, it was merely like being struck by lightning rather than a nuclear apocalypse in my vagina.

Jesus, Linz, warn a girl.

Imaginary Duncan went to work, then, and I could almost feel his big hands on my thighs as he licked and suckled, and I found myself on the cusp of a megalithic orgasm. I'm not exactly sure what megalithic means, but that's what I'm going with, since this purple device was, as advertised, doing something miraculous to my lady bits. Usually, it takes me at least five minutes of start-stop bean-flicking to get to this point, and it's been literally less than thirty seconds.

I let go with a shrieked gasp—and accidentally hit the button again, cycling to a higher intensity. My orgasm splintered into something new and titanic, my thighs shaking and my channel spasming as waves of heat smashed through me.

Fuck it—I cycled to the highest setting as a wave of release crested within me, and now I couldn't breathe to even scream as the orgasm utterly incinerated me.

Holy shit.

Sweating, panting, and shaky, I snapped a selfie while holding the vibrator and sent it to Lindsey: IT'S A VIBRATOR, BITCH. BUT ALSO. HOLY SHIT.

She responded almost immediately: RIGHT? SEE WHAT YOU'VE BEEN MISSING OUT ON?

Me: YEAH, BUT WHAT HAPPENS WHEN A GUY CAN'T COMPETE WITH IT? I JUST CAN'T COME WITHOUT IT?

Lindsey: UM, YOU USE IT DURING SEX, DUH.

Maybe I *am* a bit sexually conservative, as I've never even thought of using a toy during sex. I enjoy sex, okay? In fact, I *love* it... a fucking *lot*. Hayes and I fucked three or four times a week, at minimum, our whole relationship. He may have been a lying, cheating, gaslighting asshole loser in the end, but the guy could *fuck*. I always got off with him, and if I didn't come during sex, he always made sure I did afterward.

But now?

I see what Lindsey has been trying to tell me the whole time; I can't go back to using my fingers now. Not after that.

I washed off the rubbery white oval piece and

put the device away, took a shower, threw on a sundress and flats, and headed out in search of coffee and breakfast.

I found a place on the boardwalk that wasn't too crowded and treated myself to some pancakes and an endless cup of coffee. By the time I cleared the plate, it was nearly ten. I don't know how late Duncan usually sleeps, but I know Lindsey, and if I don't get ahold of him soon, she'll be blowing up my phone. So I found a bench looking out at the Inside Passage and FaceTimed him.

It burbled a few times, and then there was the connection sound effect, and Duncan's absurdly handsome, chiseled face filled the screen. He was bleary-eyed, squinting at the screen. "Rune, hi."

"Sorry to wake you up."

"Eh, it's fine. I need to get up anyway. What's going on, hot stuff?" He scrubs his face, wipes sleep away from the corners of his eyes and sits up.

My eyes went to his bare chest, to his hard, powerful pecs. I may or may not have licked my lips at the sight, because the man was *ripped*.

"Rune?" I heard the amusement in his voice. "My eyes are up here, babe."

"Shut up." I sighed. "Um, so…"

"Yes, I have my tux dry-cleaned and ready to go."

"No, that's not it. I, umm, I have a favor to ask."

"A favor, is it? Another one?" He shrugged. "I live but to serve, my lady."

"Well, it's more of a request for information, really. The wedding we're supposed to be going to…the venue had an electrical fire yesterday."

His eyes widened. "Oh, shit. I heard about that. The Old Toby Inn, right? The whole place went up. They had to evacuate all the guests, and nowhere else has vacancy. Everyone was talking about it last night."

"Yeah, well, now Hamish and Raquel have nowhere to stay *or* get married, and nowhere for the guests to go," I said. "We were hoping you, as a local, might have some ideas."

He scratched at his chest, and then leaned out of the screen to grab something—the action bared more of his lean, shredded, muscular body—I count abs: two, four, six…*eight*? Fuck me. The blanket covering him slid away, revealing a dangerous expanse of male flesh…including the sharpest set of V-cuts I've ever seen, and let me tell you, I'm a sucker for those things. Nice arms, a good chest, a tight, hard cannonball ass? Yes, please. Gets me going. But V-cuts? They turn me into jelly. I can't explain it, I know it's dumb and shallow, but it just does it for me.

And Duncan's were fucking glorious. My pussy clenched, my gut flipped, and my nipples went tight and hard. *Just lean a little further,* I can't help thinking. It's obvious he was naked under that blanket, and now that I've seen this much, I needed more.

A *lot* more.

He came back onto the screen with a water bottle, which he took a long drink from. Even his Adam's apple was sexy.

Did I or did I not just have an epic orgasm? I did. So…why am I hornier than I was before?

"Do you always sleep naked?" I asked, and then clapped my hand over my mouth. "Sorry. Forget I asked that."

He grinned at me. "In fact, I do." He winked. "What about you, Rune? What do you wear to bed?"

"A T-shirt and underwear," I answered. "Nothing too exciting."

He smirked, shrugging. "I dunno…there's something hot as fuck about a girl in a tee and underwear. Especially if it's *my* shirt she's wearing."

"If I'm wearing my boyfriend's shirt," I said, letting my mouth run wild, "then I'm probably not wearing panties under it."

He groaned, covering his face. "Goddammit, Rune. Now I'm picturing you wearing nothing but my T-shirt. I won't be able to walk for a while. Thanks for that."

"Won't be able to walk?" I ask, momentarily confused.

He quirked an eyebrow at me.

"Oh. Ohhhh." I covered my face with my hand. "Shut up."

He just grinned. "So, moving on. I can make a couple calls and see what I can come up with."

"That would be amazing," I said. "I know it's a

long shot, but Hamish and Raquel are desperate for a solution at this point."

"No promises, but I'll see what I can do. I'll call you back in a bit," he said.

We said goodbye, and I headed back to my room at the hostel. An hour and a half later, he called back.

"I have news," he said by way of hello, "but I'll only give it to you in person. Meet me for lunch."

"Alright," I answered. "Where and when?"

"Now. I'm outside your hostel. Come down."

"Are you stalking me, Duncan Badd?"

He snorted. "You told me where you were staying yesterday. I can do this cool thing called remembering."

There aren't that many people who can match my snark-itude, but Duncan definitely gives me a run for my money.

It's so weird to be on the receiving end of sarcasm that I found myself unable to come up with a witty retort. I am ashamed.

"Be right down," is all I said, and hung up.

I grabbed my purse and headed down—Duncan was dressed in faded, distressed black jeans, white Nikes, and a fitted three-quarter sleeve raglan tee with the Badd Kitty logo on the left breast—the sleeves were gray, the torso black. It was a simple enough outfit, but he made it look like high fashion.

He's just so damned *attractive*. It's honestly annoying, because being around him is distracting. I keep getting lost in his eyes, or staring at his stupid, toned, girthy arms. Yes, I said *girthy*. Deal with it.

And now, thanks to our conversation, I know what he looks like naked…almost. And I've thought about him going down on me.

Not a great combo for staying focused.

Although, to be fair to myself, I'm not the only one. His eyes flared when he saw me, his gaze raking down my body, fixing on my legs, which my canary-yellow-with-white-flowers sundress left bare from mid-thigh. After a long, blatant moment checking out my legs, his gaze fixed next on my cleavage, and that's where this dress really shines. It gives me *fantastic* cleavage, especially with the pushup bra I'm wearing. His pupils dilated, and his hands curled into fists at his sides.

"Hey, Duncan," I said, stepping into his space and tapping the underside of his chin. "My eyes are up here."

"Yeah," he said, smirking, "but your tits are down there, and I'm not done appreciating them."

I faked an annoyed sigh, stepping back with a flap of my arms out to the sides and then down. "Well? Get a good enough look?"

He shrugged. "For now."

"You said you had an update."

"I did—I do. C'mon. I'm hungry." He took my hand and pulled me into a walk.

And in weird news, I continued to let him hold my hand as we strolled down the street. It's weird because I don't hold hands. I've never liked it. My hands get sweaty, and most guys tend to unconsciously squeeze too hard. Duncan's hands were large and strong and rough, yet dry and cool. And he didn't squeeze, only held in a gentle but firm grip.

It was…nice.

Weird, but nice.

He led me away from the main drag and the boardwalk where the crowds of tourists are thickest. He took me to a narrow side street not far from the main drag where the shops were mostly tattoo parlors, Mom-and-Pop cafes, boutiques, and the like. We came to a shop with a large window framing a two-seat high top. A cute sign, hand-painted in pastel pink letters on a piece of driftwood, announces that the shop was named Ella's. Duncan opened the door—a bell tinkled a merry, silver little sound to announce our entry. Inside, the floor was tiled in a classic black-and-white checkerboard pattern, with 50s style booths along the left wall and a soda-jerk bar facing the door, with plump vinyl-topped cushioned stools.

A blond girl about our age was behind the counter, rapidly assembling a sandwich. "Be right with you," she says, not looking up from her work.

"The service here sucks ass," Duncan said loudly. "The owner is a real bitch."

I gasped in shock. "Duncan!"

The blonde girl's head whips up, light brown eyes twinkling with humor. "Donkey!" She grinned at him as she finished the sandwich—which was a massive thing, a masterpiece of thick homemade wheat bread piled high with turkey, Swiss, and all the fixings—wrapped it brown parcel paper, tied it with a pre-cut length of twine, and handed it to the waiting customer with a smile and a "Thanks, come again!"

She wiped her hands on her apron and rounded the bar to give Duncan a hug. "Been a while since you've popped in here. I figured I wouldn't see you until the softball game for the Fourth."

He tweaked her nose. "I had a craving for one of your sandwiches."

She batted his hand away. "Leave my nose alone, jerk, or no sammich for you." She turned her bright gaze onto me. "And who's your friend?"

"This is Rune. Rune, this is my cousin Ella. You met her dad, Bax the first day we met."

"Hi, Ella, nice to meet you." I looked around. "This place is adorable."

"Thanks!" She looks around with obvious pride. "It's my baby."

I frown. "Wait...*your* baby?"

She nodded. "Yep! I own the space, and I did all the work myself." Duncan cleared his throat ostentatiously, and she rolled her eyes. "Fine. I had *some* help with the complicated stuff, like using saws."

I shook my head. "So Duncan manages a bar, you own a cafe...are *all* of you guys, like, super accomplished? Because you're giving me an inferiority complex."

Ella shrugged. "I mean, to one degree or another,

yes. Our parents all tend to encourage us to be financially independent." She waves a hand. "Anyway. Welcome to Ella's. What can I make for you?"

Duncan rubbed his hands together, excited. "That one with the bacon aioli and the avocado you made me last time."

"I have four sandwiches that have those on them," Ellas said, rolling her eyes. "You'll have to be more specific, Donkey."

"The one with the turkey and the spicy cheese." He turned to me. "Ella makes the best sandwiches you'll ever eat. She makes all bread herself in-house."

I scanned the menu—there's pretty much every combo you can think of, and a few new ones for me—there's one with brie, green apple slices, turkey, and raspberry jam that sounds fucking amazing. But so does the Elvis—peanut butter, bacon, and banana. In fact, the longer I looked at the menu, the less I know what I want.

"You know what, it all sounds amazing," I said. "How about you surprise me. I am partial to turkey, though."

"Any food allergies or hated items?"

"No allergies, no olives, and no feet cheese," I said.

"Feet cheese?" she asked, wrinkling her nose in confusion. "The fuck is that?"

"Bleu cheese, gorgonzola, that stuff," I answered.

She made a disgusted face. "Ew, no. On salads, maybe, but on a sandwich? Not in my shop. No ma'am."

"Glad we agree."

"Chips, drinks, cookies?" she asked, then waved. "Why am I asking? You know your way around, Donkey. Help yourself. I'll bring them out to you."

Duncan got an iced tea and a bag of Baked Lays, and I got a diet and Doritos, because I'm still technically on vacation. It's just a two-month vacation during which I've put on more weight than I did my first year of college; that's an exaggeration, obviously, but not by much. But I don't give a fuck—I'll go back home and have dad coach it off me; it's one of the luxury perks of having a fitness professional father.

"So. Donkey," I said. "Interesting nickname."

"Nope." He pointed at me with a chip. "Absolutely not. Ella's the only one who can call me that."

"Fine, but where'd it come from? You gotta share that much at least."

He rolled his eyes. "It started out as 'Dunky', like Dunc, but with a Y. Eventually, it became Donkey. I gave up trying to make her stop using it years ago."

"Only because I give you free sandwiches," Ella said from the counter. "What he's not telling you is that I've called him Donkey since we were twelve, and it still bothers him, which is why I do it." She laughed as she sets the halves of a sandwich into a red basket lined with wax paper. "He's adorable when he's pissy."

"I'm a man," Duncan grumbled. "I don't get *pissy*."

"And you're gonna deny you have a man period, too?"

"You're an annoying ass bitch, Ella-Smella," he mumbled.

She just laughed. "He tries to find nicknames he hopes will annoy me as much as Donkey annoys him, but they're all stupid. Like Ella-Smella."

He glared at me. "If you call me Donkey, I won't tell you the solution I found for the wedding."

"Wait, *solution*? You said you had an *update*!"

He shrugged. "The update is that I found a solution."

Ella stopped what she was doing at stared at us. "Wedding? You guys aren't…"

Duncan cackled. "Us? *God* no, we just met a few days ago. We're just friends." He quirked an eyebrow at me. "For now."

I rolled my eyes at him. "Dream on, Bullwinkle." To Ella, then: "It's my friend Raquel and her fiancé, Hamish. They were supposed to be getting married at The Old Toby Inn the day after tomorrow. And they have fifty guests coming."

"Oh," she breathed. "The Old Toby Inn that burned down yesterday?"

"That's the one," I answered.

"Wow, that's…they must be freaking out."

"They are." I glared at Duncan. "I asked Duncan if he had any ideas, and apparently he found a solution…which he *hasn't told me about, yet.*"

"It's called dramatic suspense—you may have heard of it," he said.

"It's called my friends are having panic attacks, so maybe don't keep the news to yourself."

"Fine, fine." Duncan took the red basket from Ella as she brought our food to the booth nearest the bar where we're sitting. "So, you may or may not be aware, but we have locations outside of Ketchikan. Salient to this discussion is the location in Anchorage, which is now, thanks to Dee and Hunter, a fancy sit-down place. I called Dee and explained the situation, and she's agreed to let your friends use the back room for the reception. It can hold at least a hundred people, and they use it for events all the time. As for the wedding itself, there's a hotel not fifteen minutes from the restaurant, and they do have rooms available, as well as a conference room where the wedding itself can happen." He shrugged. "I know it's not ideal, but there's just nothing available in Ketchikan, and I did ask everyone I know. Even the Airbnbs are all booked."

I covered his hand with mine. "Thank you for doing that, Duncan. Let me call my friends and see what they say."

I took my phone outside and called Lindsey, who then added Raquel to the call, with Hamish listening.

"Rune, you said you have a solution?" Lindsey prompted.

"Yeah, I do. Well, Duncan does."

"Who's Duncan?" asked Hamish in his thick Scottish burr.

"My friend. He's a local." I hesitated. "It is a good

news, bad news situation, though. The good news he found you a hotel with rooms and a conference room as well as a nice restaurant that can host the reception."

"And the bad news?" asked Raquel.

"It's in Anchorage," I answered.

There were a few moments of silence—I can almost see the couple trading looks, having a silent conversation.

"Anchorage, is it? How far is that from Ketchikan?" Hamish asked.

"Uhhh, I have no idea," I answer. "Hold on." I poked my head inside. "Duncan? How far is it from here to Anchorage?"

"Oh, it's not that far," he answered. "A five-hour flight, or maybe…a day and a half drive? Two if you're taking your time."

I relayed the answer to Hamish, who guffawed. "It's no that far? It's a thousand fecking miles! A two-day drive! You Americans have a bloody fucking warped sense of distance."

"What choice do we have, baby?" Raquel asked in her soft, sweet voice. "We've got all our friends coming. We can't cancel on them, and there ain't a single room available anywhere in Ketchikan."

"I'm no cancelin' the weddin' anyway," Hamish grumbled. "I'm marryin' ya, be it in a barn, a bar, or a bog."

"Baby, nobody knows what a bog is," Raquel said, laughing. "But I agree. Anchorage, it is."

"Guess we need to find a way to Anchorage, then,"

Hamish said. "I'll not be spendin' two bloody days in the bloody car, though, so I hope to fuckin' god there's a flight available."

"Hamish, baby, be positive." Raquel, as always, was the voice of positivity and hope.

"Fine then," Hamish rumbled. "I'm bloody fuckin' positive I ain't drivin' that fat fuckin' lorry of a hire car a thousand bloody fuckin' miles."

Raquel just laughs. "It's an SUV, baby. And not even a big one!"

"Aye, and I've *seen* the big ones. Bloody monstrosities, them things are. You could carry a whole footie team in one."

"Okay, well, I'm gonna go," I said. "I'll talk to Duncan some more, see if we have any options for getting to Anchorage without driving or spending a fortune on last-minute flights."

"Aye, and we'll have to tell everyone to change their tickets, too. Fuckin' bloody mess, this is."

"Hamish, baby," Raquel said. "You're not being grateful. We have a solution. We can get married. The rest is just details."

"Aye, aye, aye," Hamish said, on a grumbling sigh. "Right you are, love, right you are."

"We owe you big time, Rune," Raquel said. "And your friend Duncan."

"I'll pass along your thanks," I said. "We'll be in touch soon, okay? Love you guys."

I ended the call and went back in—Duncan waited to eat.

I took my seat. "You didn't have to wait, Duncan. You should've eaten without me."

He shrugged. "My mama didn't raise no mannerless oaf." He dug into his sandwich with a groan. "Fucking amazing."

I examined my creation—Ella piled on turkey, cucumbers, cream cheese, provolone, and tomatoes.

"So," Duncan says after he's devoured half of his sandwich. "What'd they say?"

"Well, Hamish is from Scotland, so he was a bit surprised when your 'not that far' turned out to be over a thousand miles. But they're grateful and would like to take you up on it. The only question is how they're getting there from here."

"They're here in Ketchikan? Or they're meeting the rest of the wedding party here?" he asks.

"I think they're here?" I said. "Or maybe they're at a campground in the general area? I'm not sure, to be honest. I haven't actually seen them yet, so I don't know where they are. They're doing their honeymoon first—a backpacking trip. The wedding was the grand finale."

Duncan laughed. "I guess a thousand miles is pretty far to most people, huh? When you're from Alaska, distances are different. Everything is farther away up here. To us, Anchorage is pretty close. Pretty much every decent-sized city is at least twelve hours drive from here, and most are over a day away."

"Will there be flights available?" I asked.

He frowned, shrugging. "Hell if I know. I don't fly anywhere commercial."

I blinked at this newest revelation. "Um, okay, big spender. Not all of us can afford to fly private."

He cackled at this. "No, no, no. My Uncle Brock is a pilot." His eyes widened, and he smacked his forehead. "Duh. Uncle Brock can fly us there. You, me, and your friends. Well, a few of them. His plane can't hold all fifty guests."

"Would he do that?"

Duncan nodded. "Sure. No problem. I'll call and ask right now." A few minutes later, he was hanging up. "We're good. You, me, the bride and groom, and your friend Lindsey. And Uncle Brock has a friend with a jet big enough to accommodate the rest of the guests, so they don't have to change tickets. He can't do it for free, the guy with the jet, I mean, but if they all pool their funds, it'll be a fraction of what it would cost them individually to fly here and then to Anchorage, or to change their flights from wherever. Last-minute tickets are gonna be expensive as fuck no matter which way you slice it."

We finished our sandwiches and drinks, and then Duncan thanked Ella and gave her a hug. I noticed he also slipped a $20 into the tip jar on the counter—I suspect because Ella would have refused it, otherwise.

We strolled lazily back toward my hostel, stopping to sit on a bench together.

I chewed on my lip a moment. "Duncan, thank you."

He had an arm resting across the back of the bench—not quite around me, but nearly. "Hey, you know… what are friends for?"

I laughed at this. "We're barely friends. For real, though. Seriously. Thank you."

He looked at me, nodding. "You're welcome."

We're close. Kissing close. I can't help but think about this morning, and my thighs clenched.

"Looking at me like that is dangerous, Rune," he murmured, his eyes on my lips.

"Like what?"

"Like you wouldn't mind it if I did this." He leaned closer, slowly, giving me all the time in the world to shy away. When I didn't, he growled wordlessly. "Don't say I didn't warn you," he breathed.

And then he was kissing me.

THREE

Duncan

Her mouth was soft and warm and inviting. At first, there was no response from her—just a startled hesitation. And then a quiet gasp slipped from her throat, and she melted into me. Her lips softened, her mouth opened, her tongue danced delicately against mine. Quick, clever fingers stole into the messy thatch of hair at the base of my neck, sending a thrill shivering through me.

For a few moments, then, the world telescoped down and down and down, becoming smaller and narrower until there was nothing in this whole universe except Rune and me, our fused mouths slowly dissolving together, my heart pounding wildly in my chest and thrumming deafeningly in my ears, her soft curves pressed against me.

In that moment, in which nothing existed but Rune and me, I caught a glimpse of a future—one of a thousand, thousand possible futures—wherein Rune and I began with a kiss and found forever in each other.

I felt my heart skip a beat and then resume slamming madly against the prison bars of my chest. More—I needed more. I needed to feel the hot silk of her skin under my hands, needed to feel her muscles contract as she arched beneath me, needed to hear her whimper my name as she came apart. There was no thought in my brain except *more*—more Rune, more of that soft quiet shocked gasp, more of her pressing into my hands as I curled my arm low around her waist and pulled her against me.

"Mommy, what are they doing?" I heard a little boy's voice ask.

"Shhh, Tommy," his mother responded. "Something they probably should be doing *in private.*" The last two words were hissed in emphasis.

Rune and I broke apart, both of us panting. Rune's sapphire eyes were wide and wild, stunned, searching mine as if looking for something specific. "Duncan," she breathed. "I…"

I heard her swallow—a literal, audible gulp—and then she tore herself out of my arms and up off the bench, one hand raking angrily through the loose chaos of her stormcloud hair, the other pressing visibly trembling fingers to her kiss-swollen lips. Her eyes, the precise shade of blue of fire flickering from a burning stovetop, fixed on mine, searching and shaken.

And then she was gone, disappearing into a

swarming thicket of tourists, leaving me sitting stunned and alone on the bench with tingling lips and a raging hard-on.

What just happened?

I felt like the world had tilted on its axis, wobbling uncertainly and with sudden, debilitating violence…all from a kiss; my cock was bent sideways behind my zipper, angled painfully, throbbing and hard as an iron girder…all from a kiss; my heart pounded and my breath came in quick panting huffs, and I felt almost dizzy…all from a kiss.

When was the last time I was this affected, physically, by a woman? How about never. Emotionally? Also never.

I didn't know what I was feeling in that moment. Stunned? Left verklempt? Numb and yet greedy for a repeat. Greedy for more—for privacy to rip her clothes off and discover her body, find out what makes her scream, what makes her thighs quiver and her eyes roll back in her head.

Fuck, I *needed* her with a sudden and unexpected desperation that had me every bit as shaken as she looked.

I made the short walk to the Kitty in a daze—we opened in less than an hour. I pulled down stools and chairs and high-top seats, but my mind was elsewhere…specifically back on the bench with Rune's mouth on mine. I had to count the till drawer four times before I was sure it was right, as I kept getting distracted by the memory of her curves gracing delicately against me, a thigh on mine, chest against my arm, fingers dimpling my nape.

Fuck.

I took inventory, restocked the bar fridges, cleaned the liquor bottles…god, whoever closed last night did a shitty job, left a bunch of bullshit busywork for the opener.

That's a joke—it's me. I'm the closer.

I eventually managed to mostly banish Rune from my mind as the day progressed, mainly by virtue of being too busy to spare a thought for anything other than serving customers. It was a long-ass motherfucker of a day, closing last night and then working open to close today, but I couldn't complain since I'm the asshole who wrote the schedule—Elias needed the day off, and in return, he was covering for me over the weekend so I could attend the wedding with Rune.

By the time I got home, it was after three, and I should be exhausted and ready to crash, but instead I found myself antsy, agitated, and wired.

Thinking about Rune.

About that kiss.

Just revisiting the memory had my cock hardening into a painful erection that I couldn't ignore. And all I could think about was her. Those soft, warm, wet lips melting against mine, her tongue sliding against mine. The swell of her tits against my arm and chest.

Fuck, I need her.

I need her naked.

I need her screaming my name.

I need those thick, strong thighs clamped around my face as I devour her essence.

My attempts to distract myself were futile. Xbox, TV, scrolling on my phone—none of it kept my attention for more than a few seconds before I found myself fantasizing about Rune all over again.

I open again tomorrow—I *have* to sleep. I can't be still awake at...fuck me. Four a.m.

Yet I couldn't sleep. I closed my eyes, and all I saw was her shocked face, those stunned sapphire eyes searching me as if looking for answers as to why that kiss was so much more than merely a kiss.

I saw her reaching for me, hands sliding down my chest, diving under my waistband. It was my hand gripping my cock as I lay in bed, not hers, but it was her in my mind. I saw her twisting her hair into a messy knot on the top of her head, saw her peeling out of her shirt to spill her full breasts into my waiting, greedy hands.

I stroked my cock slowly, envisioning her heavy, round tits in my hands, her plump lips swollen from our kiss, lips parting as she lowered her mouth to my cock—

My phone burbles on the bedside table, startling me out of my fantasy.

Who the fuck is FaceTiming me before dawn?

Rune.

Shit.

I answered, leaving the light off so the only illumination came from the bathroom, casting me in long, angled shadows. The screen flickered, revealing Rune in a similar scene: dimly lit, shadows bathing half her face. I only saw her from the neck up, the phone held close to her face.

"Hi," she whispered. "I couldn't sleep. I know I shouldn't call you at this hour, but I…"

"It's fine," I murmured, "I wasn't asleep, either."

My cock throbbed, ached, full and hard and heavy, my balls tight against my body with the release I had been so close to, now denied.

"Am I crazy," she asked, "or was that kiss…"

"Strangely intense?" I finished for her. "Yeah, it was." I sounded tense, even to myself.

"Are…are you okay?" she asked. "You seem…"

"I'm fine," I lied, my voice gravelly with arousal I couldn't hide.

"Duncan. I know you're lying. What's up?"

I shook my head. "Trust me, Rune, you don't want to know."

"Maybe I do." Her voice was low and raspy, her eyes sparking in the dim light.

"Thinking about you," I said, growling the words. "Supposed to be sleeping, but all I can think about is you. It's a fucking problem."

"Why do you think I'm still awake?" she murmured.

I couldn't stop a wince as I shoved at my

ramrod-stiff cock in a vain attempt to relieve the pressure, groaning. The movement was well off-screen, but Rune's gaze betrayed the fact that she knew exactly what my groan was about.

"Duncan," she breathed. "Are you…?" she trailed off suggestively.

"Wishing my hand was yours?" I said, the words tumbling free unbidden—that damn lack of a filter striking again. "Abso-fucking-lutely."

"You can't say something like that to a girl, Duncan," she whispered. "It's not fair."

"Not fair?" I snapped. "Not fair is that fucking kiss. Not fair is you leaving me turned on, hard as a damn rock, and having to work all fucking day while trying not to think about you. Had to fight a half-chub all goddamned day because of you and that *fucking* kiss."

"You're touching yourself?"

"I was thirty seconds from coming when you called," I admitted.

Her eyes went heavy-lidded with desire, teeth snagging her lower lip. "Fucking hell, Duncan."

"You've thought about me, haven't you?" I demanded. "You touched your pussy while thinking about me."

"Yes," she whispered. "Several times." Even in the dim lighting, I could tell she's flushing scarlet.

"Several times?" I said.

"Every fucking day, Duncan, is that what you want

to hear? I think about you and your stupid sexy face and your stupid sexy abs, and I flick my bean."

"Do you say my name while you come, Rune?" I asked.

"Maybe."

"Let me hear."

This was stupid. Foolish. I didn't need the distraction. I needed to be focused on work—I've only been GM for a few months, and I'm still on probation with Dad and Delia. If I mess up, they'll make Elias the interim GM until they feel I'm more ready. That's *not* happening. The Kitty is *my* bar, now.

But I can't deny myself this. I can't deny myself her.

"Duncan," Rune gasped. "I'm not doing that over the phone."

"Why not?"

"It's embarrassing."

"It'd be fucking hot."

"You first, then." She fumbled the phone, dropped it on her chest, and then picked it back up—in the process revealing her bare chest, stomach, and the upper swell of her sex.

"Fucking goddammit, Rune," I groaned. "Tease."

"That was an accident," she protested. "If I was gonna tease you, I'd do it more like this."

She eased the phone away by infinitesimal degrees, baring her tits to me slice by slice, inch by inch, until only the very tips were out of the screen, and then she brought it back to focus on her face.

"Fuck," I growled. "You have perfect tits. Show me more, Rune."

"You first," she whispered. "I have needs too, you know."

I angled the phone so she could see my bare torso, and then tilted it lower...and lower, until my abs, hips, and cock were in the screen. My cock, however, I had gripped in my fist, hiding it from her.

"Fucking hell, Duncan," she breathed. "Do it."

"Do what?"

"Touch yourself. Jerk off while I watch."

I tightened my grip on my aching cock and stroked it, the phone showing the movement of my arm but nothing else. "Like that?"

"You're gonna make me say it?" she grumbled. "Fine. I want to see, Duncan. I want to see all of you. I want to see you come." She clapped a hand over her mouth, shaking her head. "I know I'm loud and sarcastic and crazy, but I've never done anything like this before. I'm nervous and I feel weird."

"You're sexy as fuck, Rune," I said, slowly jerking my length just off-screen. "I want to see you. Let me see your tits. Let me see you finger your tight little pussy."

She moaned, eyes closing briefly—Her arm moved, and she gasped. "Oh....oh fuck."

"Let me *see*, goddammit," I hissed.

"At the same time, then," she said. "Together."

Heart slamming crazily in my chest, I let out a groan as my cock throbbed in my fist, demanding release. "Together. Ready?"

"No. Yes." She opened her eyes and mine through the screen. "Yes. Please, Duncan. I wanna see your cock. I need to."

I tilted the screen until my abs and core were in the frame and slowly slid my fist down my cock, the tip sprouting out of the top of my fist, inch after inch bared. Rune's face was still in frame, and I was gratified to see her mouth drop open, blatant and powerful arousal carved into every line of her face.

"Jesus, Duncan," she breathed. "Stroke it for me."

I jerked my length for her, once, twice, three times, slowly. "Like that?"

"Mmmm, god yes. Your cock, Duncan. My god. It's beautiful."

"Like it?"

"I need it."

"Where?" I demanded.

She panned her screen down, finally giving me a full-length glimpse at her curves. Draped to either side by gravity, her tits were big and full, plump and round with pale, nearly invisible areolae only a hint darker than the rest of her skin, with small, hard, pink nipples, erect and begging for attention.

"Jesus, Rune," I snarled.

She panned further, and now her sex was bared

to me—a low mound thatched with dense black pubic hair. "I haven't, um…shaved or trimmed in a long time."

"I fucking love it," I said.

"Wait, really?" she said, sounding skeptical. "Don't bullshit me, Duncan."

"Why would I lie about that? I love a full bush."

"It's embarrassing."

"The fuck it is, I argued. "It's hot. If you were here in the room with me, I'd have you screaming my name right now. My face would be buried between those thick, beautiful thighs of yours, and I'd be eating your pussy out until you can't fucking breathe."

"Ohmyfucking*god*, Duncan," she breathed, "do *not* tease me like that."

"Who's teasing?" I answered. "Eating you out is literally all I can think about."

She groaned, and I watched her fingers slip down over her belly and fit against her slit. Her other hand slid down as well, two fingers framing her pussy and prying it open so her fingers could swirl against the pert nub of her clit. My mouth literally watered at the sight as I anticipated the scent and flavor of her sex on my tongue, her essence tingling on my lips and smearing my mouth, the pungent perfume of her arousal filling my nostrils.

I couldn't help but stroke myself, then, sliding my grip down to the root of my cock, watching with rapt attention as Rune's fingers swirl her clit with increasing rapidity.

"Slow down, Rune," I whispered.

"I'm close," she said. "I need to come."

"Not yet. I'm not there yet."

"Then hurry."

"No," I answered. "I wanna take my time. Pretend that's my mouth on your pussy."

"My hand on your cock?"

"Fuck, please." I couldn't help speeding my strokes as she tweaked her pussy faster and faster. "What would you do to me, Rune? If you were here with me?"

She whimpered, hips flexing, bucking as she neared climax. "I'd…oh god. Oh god."

"Not yet, Rune."

"Faster, Duncan. Work that big, hard cock."

"What would you do to me, Rune?"

"I'd take my time," she said, "I'd tease you. Play with your cock until you were begging me to let you come."

"How would you make me come? Where would you take it?"

"Anywhere you wanted to put it, Duncan," she breathed. "All over my hands. Down my throat. On my tits. I'd drain that gorgeous dick of yours until you forget your own name."

I jerked faster, harder, and my hips started to buck, to rock, and all I could do was watch as her fingers blurred and picture my fingers there, my tongue.

Heat and pressure swelled in my balls, and grunts escaped me as I stroked myself hard and fast, relentless and rough.

"Duncan!" Rune breathed. "Oh god. Are you… are you there?"

"Yes," I growled, "I'm close."

"I…oh, oh, oh god, I can't stop it, Duncan." Her hips rocked, and her thighs quivered and pressed together as her climax seized her.

"Let go, Rune," I ordered. "Come for me. Let me watch you come."

She shook all over, magnificent tits swaying and trembling as she arched off the bed, fingers flying in fast circles. "Duncan!"

"That's right, Rune, say my name while you come."

"I…Duncan…Duncan—fuck!"

"Let me see your face, beautiful girl. Let me see your eyes when you come for me."

She panned the camera up, the frame capturing her face lost in the throes of ecstasy, tits bouncing and swaying as she fucked her fingers. "Oh god! Dunc! I wish—oh fuck, I wish it was you. Oh god—I—oh FUCK!" she whimpered, a soft but intense gasp of release as she came. "DUNCAN!"

Her cry of release triggered mine, and I could no more stop myself from coming all over my stomach and chest than I could stop the sun from rising.

"Rune!" I growled, squeezing my cock to slow the release. "Fucking hell. Wish my hand was your mouth."

"Yeah?" she whispered. "That's what you want? You wanna fuck my mouth?"

"So bad."

"How bad?"

"I fucking need you, Rune. Say the word and I'll be outside your door in ten minutes."

"What's the word?" She cupped a tit, offering it up to the screen. "I'll say anything you want me to say if it means I get you eating my pussy."

"Fuck. Don't...*move*. I'll be right there."

I ended the call with a stab of my thumb, rolled out of bed, cleaned myself up with a wet, soapy washcloth, dressed in a pair of workout shorts and a baggy hoodie, and was in the car flying to her hostel in record time.

FOUR

Rune

To say I was waiting with impatience would be an understatement. I was also more nervous than I'd ever been in my life, for reasons I couldn't pinpoint and wasn't about to try to figure out.

I lay in my bed in the hostel room, covered in a flat sheet and nothing else, naked as the day I was born, still shaky from the orgasm yet hornier than I'd ever been in my life.

A soft tap on my door brought me to my feet, and I tiptoed across the small room, pulling open the door while hiding behind it.

Duncan's tall frame entered the room, immediately filling it with his presence. His hair was messier than ever, as if he'd been raking his hand through it all the way here—even as the thought crossed my mind, he turned to look for me, saw me standing with my hand on the knob, hiding behind the door, and his hand scraped over his scalp, further mussing the red-dish-brown locks.

"Close the door," he growled, his voice low and dark with arousal.

I pushed it closed and turned the lock, and then crossed my arms over my body, hiding my breasts and privates. "Now that you're here, I…"

He flicked the light switch on, bathing me in sudden and blinding light. "Need to see you." His eyes raked my body greedily. "Rune." He met my gaze. "No hiding."

"I just met you," I whispered. "It was hot on the phone, but now you're here and I'm…"

He prowled toward me, reaching for me. His hands grasped my wrists and he applied gentle but insistent pressure. "Let me see you, Smokeshow. Please."

It was the please that got me. The way he said it—quietly, genuine, a soft entreaty. More embarrassed than ever about my unkempt lady bits, I slowly moved my arm to let him see my boobs—I'm well-endowed in that department, so I wasn't as shy about letting him see them. I hid my sex with both hands, though.

He stopped a few inches away from me, gazing down at me—into my eyes. "You're so goddamned beautiful, Rune."

My heart leapt in my chest—I've not always had the most confidence in my looks. I'm strong and fit, and I'm confident in what my body can do. I love my hair, and I'm confident in that. But my body? My curves? The men I've dated in the past haven't always been the most supportive. Most recently, Hayes. He wasn't exactly the type to shower praise on me. I knew he was attracted to me, if only because he wanted sex constantly, and he'd get an erection if a stiff breeze blew past him, let alone if I was naked. He just didn't *say* it. And he was the best boyfriend I've ever had— the others have been uniformly terrible. Thus, my two-month self-imposed dry spell; I have awful taste in men.

Duncan seems different. I don't know why. He has the air of a playboy, a player, a fuckboy. But in other ways, he seems genuine and kind and funny. The things he says to me, though? Oof. Fucking hot.

I don't do casual sex, as I told Lindsey. But this was temporary. It has to be. I'm going back to LA after the wedding, finding a job, and getting back to life. Maybe end up with a boyfriend at some point—preferably one who won't cheat on me. But right now? Duncan is here, and he's staring at me like I'm something delicious to eat and he's starving.

I can have fun with him. Mess around now and during the wedding weekend. And then I go back to my life, he goes back to his, and that's the end of it.

But when he says I'm so damned beautiful, especially in that soft, reverent tone of voice, I just don't know what to do, how to respond. It makes me feel beautiful. Desired. Appreciated.

It's a frighteningly addictive feeling.

"Duncan," I breathed.

He tugged my hands away from my sex. "Don't hide, Rune."

I let him pull my hands away, but my thighs pressed together, one lifting and angling to cover my core. "I'm embarrassed. I wasn't planning on…this."

He stepped into me, his big, hard body pressing against my smaller, softer frame, walking me backward until my bare ass met the cold hardness of the door. His hands settled on my waist above my hips, where he'd hold me if we were slow dancing. His lips ghosted against my cheek, his breath hot on my ear.

"Want me to leave?" His words seared into me, leaving panic in their wake.

"No," I whispered. "I do not."

"Tell me not to touch you."

"No."

It was all different, now that he was here. The frenzy of arousal that prompted me, in a moment of horny stupidity, to call Duncan Badd, had fled. I had an orgasm while he watched…and I watched him do the same. But now he was here, live and in person, and my nerves were screaming with insecurity. I was naked; he was fully clothed. He was jacked, ripped, shredded, every muscle rippling and toned, a warrior's lean, hard physique. I saw his body on the phone, and even now I want him. I want to rip that baggy hoodie off, yank his shorts down, and lick and suck and touch and taste every inch of him.

The intensity with which I want these things is, in

fact, what's holding me back. I've never wanted anyone this bad. What if I get attached? This is why I don't
do this. I have boyfriends; we develop a relationship,
a level of trust and intimacy, and *then* we have sex. Of
course, all of them, so far, have betrayed me, but that's
a different topic.

Not really, but I'm not going there.

"Hey, Rune," Duncan whispered. "Come back to
me."

I swallowed, looking up at him. "What? I'm here."

"No, you're not." A rough palm cradled my cheek.
"I can go. I don't want you to be scared of me."

"I'm not scared of you," I said. "I don't want you
to leave."

"Then what *do* you want?" he asked.

"I…"

He bent down, thumb pressing my chin up, and
nuzzled my lips with his. "This?"

"Uh huh," I breathed, all thoughts rapidly evapo-
rating. "I like that."

Instead of delving into a lingering kiss like I expected, he turned my face away, tilted it higher to bare
my throat, touching hot, slow kisses down the column
of my throat; each touch of his lips burned my skin,
scorched my nerves, lit dynamite in my core. Soft wet
lips danced over my breastbone, touched the ridgeline
of my shoulder. I gasped as his mouth sizzled down my
chest and over the twin swells of my breasts, tongue
sliding over the slopes, left side and then right, left and

then right. His fingers dove into my hair and toyed with the thick tresses, his other hand descending by increments to cup the outside of my hip.

I tipped my head back until it thunked against the door, sent my hands on a quest to find his flesh and muscle. Lifting the hem of his sweatshirt, I found what I was looking for—hard muscle and soft, hot skin at his belly. I pushed at his hoodie, and he yanked it off with an impatient snarl, hurling it aside.

"Thank fuck," I whispered, carving greedy, hungry hands over the rippling wonderland of his impossibly shredded eight-pack abs. "How the fuck do you maintain this while working the hours you do?"

"Hard work, a strict diet, and fucking fantastic genetics." He grinned at me. "To be honest, it's mostly just unfair genetics. I do work out a lot and watch what I eat and drink pretty closely, but it's mostly just the genes."

I pressed the waistband of his shorts lower, baring those razor-sharp V-cut grooves, gnawing on my lower lip as my lady bits sat up and took notice. "These things drive me bananas," I whispered, trailing my fingers down his abs and along the grooves, only stopping when I reached the boundary of the waistband.

"I know the feeling," he murmured, scraping his hands up my belly to gather the heavy, aching weight of my tits in his hands.

"Yeah, but I'm naked," I pointed out. "You're not."

His smirk was that maddening, cocky grin, as

infuriating as it was arousing. "If it bothers you that much, maybe you should do something about it."

"Maybe I should," I agreed.

I tugged his shorts lower, but they caught on something huge and hard and upright. Hooking my fingers inside the elastic at his hipbones, I pulled the shorts away from his body—no underwear. Lowering them past the hard bubble of his ass and the tentpole of his erection, I let the shorts drop to the floor, letting out a whimper of aroused surprise at the size of the organ waiting for me.

I met Duncan's eyes, watching greedily for his reaction as I curled my fingers around his hot, hard length. "It looked big on FaceTime," I whispered. "But in person…"

I stroked him from tip to root, a caress that took an improbably long time, watching his face betray his pleasure: his eyes shuttered, eyelids fluttering as his eyes rolled back in his head, jaw dropping open with a quiet hiss. I squeezed at his root, palming his heavy balls in my other hand, grinning as his legs bent helplessly at my touch.

"Fuck, Rune," he growled. "Feels too fucking good."

I glided my loosely-curled fist up to his plump, round glans, rolling my thumb over the tip now weeping precum, making him growl like a cornered predator.

And then he yanked himself out of my grip.

"Goddammit," he snarled. "That's not how this is gonna go, Smokeshow."

Before I could so much as squeak in protest, my hands were pinioned in his and pressed overhead against the hard, cold surface of the door, and his mouth was plundering mine, tongue darting and daring, sweeping against my lips and teeth and tongue. His other hand cupped my breast, squeezed, thumb grazing my erect nipple, and then his palm seared down my belly and his fingers scratched over my pubic hair, parted the tender flesh of my pussy, middle finger delving between my lips and pushing inside me.

I whimpered at the penetration, struggled against his hold. "Let me touch you, goddammit, " I said through gritted teeth. "Please."

"Hell no," he answered, that long finger curling inside me, withdrawing to smear the essence of my arousal over my clit, making me whimper again, making my knees threaten to give out, making my tits ache and my nipples throb into diamond erections, making all of me go hot and wild with the need to reciprocate—to touch, to taste.

I didn't play-struggle, then—I genuinely fought his hold, trying to free my hands so I could get them around his massive cock. It was futile—he was too strong by several orders of magnitude; he held me without effort, without having to grip too tightly. The reminder of how much stronger than me he was should have frightened me, but it didn't. I continued to thrash against his hold, growling like a trapped wildcat, but those growls and snarls and mewling, frustrated whimpers shifted to gasps and pants and huffs of ecstasy as he fitted his finger inside me again, withdrew, smeared it circles over my clit, and then thrust two fingers into me, once again giving my clit a single, teasing swipe of his fingers.

"Duncan!" I whispered. "Please."

He shoved my hands hard against the door, extended at arm's length overhead, dipping at his knees to suckle a hard nipple between his teeth. "Fuck, Rune. Your body is fucking goddamned perfect. *You're* goddamned perfect."

Another thrust of two fingers into my clenching channel, another single swipe of fingertips against my aching bundle of nerves. "Duncan, dammit," I hissed. *"Please."*

"Please, what, Rune?"

I didn't know what I was asking for—my need to have his cock in my hands warred against my need to be touched. I wanted both in equal measure.

He answered for me. "If I let you touch me, this'll be over before it starts. And I need to taste your pussy." He reared back to stare into my eyes as he slid his fingers out of me and put them into his mouth; his eyes shuttered, and he groaned with unfeigned, delighted arousal. *"Fuck."*

"Duncan!" I gasped.

I found myself airborne, squealing in shock as

gravity evaporated. Duncan had me in his arms, one around my shoulders, the other under my knees, and he was carrying me across the tiny room, mouth fusing to mine. I tasted my essence on his lips, and…I liked it.

"Is…is that how I taste?" I whispered against his mouth.

He stood at the foot of the bed with me in his arms, liquid brown eyes searching me. "Yes. Never tasted yourself?"

"No," I answered.

He lay me on the bed with exquisite gentleness, his big, hard body over mine radiating heat and demanding my hands. I feathered my fingers through the soft, cool silk of his hair and down the column of his neck, raking fingernails over his back, eliciting a shudder from him. One of his hands was fisted in the mattress by my ear, the other toyed with my breast, tweaked my nipple, carved down my waist to cup my hip, and then his fingers were inside me, thrusting deep and gathering my essence.

Withdrawing.

"Watch," he commanded.

My eyes flickered open in time to see him slip those fingers into his mouth, and my pussy spasmed at the way he licked them clean with aroused relish.

He dipped them inside me again, curling deep to press against my inner walls, causing me to jerk with a sudden blast of orgasmic heat; withdrawing slowly, he circled my clit—twice this time. My thighs squeezed together, and my knees did too, clenching around his hand.

"Open your legs for me, Rune," Duncan ordered.

Whimpering with arousal, I gradually relaxed, letting my knees sag away from each other, and then rolling my thighs apart.

"More." He cupped my pussy with his hand, covering it, palm grinding against my turgid clit. "Open up for me, Smokeshow."

"Why do you call me that?"

"Because it's what you are. A fucking smokeshow." He ground the heel of his palm against my clit. "Open up for me. All the way."

"Duncan…" I whispered. "I need to touch you."

"Not yet," he muttered. "Not till you come."

"Then make me come, dammit," I hissed. "I need you."

He laughed at this, a low rumbling of amusement. "Not in a hurry, babe. Gonna take my sweet time."

He lowered his shaggy head and kissed my lips, and then my breastbone, and then his teeth were sawing gently around my nipple, and his nimble tongue was dancing over the flesh where his teeth left me aching, and I could only gasp and whimper, press my hips up to beg for his touch.

While he was licking, biting, and suckling my tits, his palm was grinding rough, hard circles against my clit, and my ass muscles were forced to clench hard, pushing me into his bruising touch. Heat rose in my belly, boiled behind my clit, pressure pulling taut the wires connecting my nipples to my clit. The more he licked and lapped and laved and nibbled and teased my nipples, the harder my clit became and the more his rough, grinding touch sent thrills of need rampaging through me.

Ache built in my nerves, need burgeoned in my sex. Pressure swelled. Heat became incandescent, white-hot. I shuddered all over, clutching helplessly at his shoulders, scratching at his back, knotting fingers in his thick, shaggy hair.

"Duncan!" I gasped, as orgasm threatened. "Oh god."

"I can't wait," he murmured, more to himself than to me. "I need to taste you."

His weight was gone, then, and he was kneeling on the floor at the foot of the bed, and I was left shaking and achy and confused as he merely knelt there and stared at me, hot brown gaze raking my naked body.

"Duncan?"

"C'mere, Rune." I started to sit up, but he shook his head. "No." He pushed at the inside of my knee. "Open for me."

I knew what he wanted, but I was embarrassed to do it. Embarrassed to offer myself to him, to display myself for him. I'm not ashamed of my sexuality—far from it, but Duncan just did something to me. Made me aware of myself. Made me aware of my need, made me aware of my nudity, of my arousal. How wet I was.

But the need to come was stronger.

I scooted to the edge of the bed, gnawing on my lower lip in arousal and embarrassment. Slowly, I drew my legs up, knees together, until my heels pressed into my ass. Duncan just knelt there, eyes on mine, patient, heated.

"Let me see that pretty little pussy, Rune," he whispered.

Breath caught in my lungs, I bit my lip until it hurt, hyperaware that no one I've ever dated or slept with has ever spoken to me this way, has ever looked at me the way he was, has ever demanded these things of me. No one has ever stared at me as if I was his last meal. No one has ever drawn out my pleasure like this—for his own enjoyment. No one has ever delayed his own gratification for mine.

It was the last one that convinced me to obey.

Panting in equal parts fear, arousal, and mortification, I eased my knees apart inch by inch. Duncan's eyes were fixed on the apex of my thighs, a grin spreading across his face the more of me I exposed for him. When my legs were splayed all the way open, his grin was all teeth and arousal.

"Look at you," he breathed, awed. His finger trailed delicately down my seam. "Fucking perfect. Fucking gorgeous."

"Dunc," I pled. "Please. I...please."

He nipped a tender fold of skin on the inside of

my left thigh, and then smirked up at me. "Please, what, Rune?"

I grasped his head, fingers tangled in his hair. "Put your mouth on me. Eat my pussy. Please. Make me come."

"Thought you'd never fucking ask." He open-mouth kissed my pussy, then, lips on my nether lips, tongue sliding up my seam and pressing in. A raw, rough, ragged groan escaped him. "You taste like honey."

I could only gasp.

Another slow lick. My hips bucked. A string of firecrackers detonated inside me at the swipe of his tongue as it ended at my clit, swirling in soft circles.

"Oh-oh-oh—fuck!" I hissed, my grip on his hair going brutally tight as I held him against me. "More. More. Fuck, please, don't stop."

"Stop?" he echoed, his tone belying disbelief. "Try and make me. I'm not stopping until you've come so hard you don't know your own goddamned name."

I cried out loud as he slid a finger inside me, and then a second one, curling them against that spot high inside me, and his lips suctioned around my clit and his tongue drilled against me. I arched off the bed, thrusting against his mouth and finger as the first wave of climax cracked open inside me.

He tongued me through it, two fingers massaging my inner walls as they clenched around his digits, and then I collapsed to the bed, panting and whimpering.

Now his tongue fluttered and slithered against my clit in soft, slow, delicate licks, barely touching, teasing. His fingers, though—they fucked me. Plunging in and out hard and fast, he fucked me with his fingers while teasing my clit, and now that wave of climax morphed into a surging wall of ecstasy battering me into wailing, hip-thrusting abandon, my hands clutching his head, heels pressed into the bed.

The orgasm shattered, the wall and the wave dissolving and becoming a hurricane, a mad swirl of arousal and ecstasy. He fondled my tits with his other hand, cupping a breast, pinching a nipple, twisting and flicking, caressing and holding, and all the while his fingers plundered my pussy, squelching in and out hard and fast.

I thought I knew what an orgasm felt like. I thought I'd had generous, skilled lovers before.

I hadn't.

Duncan seemed to know my body as if he had some kind of user's manual. Every time I thought I reached the peak of climax, he did something else that made me come even harder. And then, just when I thought I couldn't come any harder, when I thought for sure I'd come as hard as I possibly could, he backed away and let my body settle, and then...

He did something new.

A change in pace, slowing his fingers as they slid in and out of me, speeding the swirling of his tongue.

Or he'd marry the pace of both, slowly licking

my clit while plunging his fingers in and out of me just as slowly.

And then, without warning, he'd change it up again.

And I'd come even harder.

Or come again.

I'd lost track—there was no time, anymore. There was no me, no here, no now. There was only Duncan; there's only ever been Duncan.

His mouth. His fingers. My orgasm.

I came apart on a scream—my third? Fourth? I don't know. More than I thought was possible. Every muscle quivered, and the heat was impossibly potent, the pressure titanic. The more he made me come, the more I needed to come—yet I was overwhelmed and exhausted, shaken and shaking, hypersensitive, breathless and disoriented, and full of a million thoughts and sensations and needs.

When yet another orgasm splintered through me, I twisted away, curling into a ball with my knees together, shuddering helplessly. "No more, no more."

I felt his weight settle onto the bed behind me, and then I was in his arms, cradled against his chest with his heartbeat under my ear.

"I got you," he murmured.

When I could breathe, when I was no longer shaking uncontrollably and near tears from the intensity of so many orgasms so close together, I opened my eyes. Looked up at him, his eyes dancing with pleased, self-assured confidence. With arousal. With sheer, transparent joy at…well, me. At the shuddering, breathless, crazed desperation welling up inside me—for him.

"Fucking beautiful," he murmured. "So fucking perfect."

I uncurled, then, breaking his hold on me. I sat up and twisted to face him, straddling his thighs with his erection sprouting between us. Keeping my gaze on his, I grasped his cock in both hands and caressed his length slowly from tip to root, twisted at the base, and then cupped his balls in one hand while gently caressing his shaft with the other.

He rested his head on my shoulder, breathing deeply to control his reactions, his hands grasping my ass. "Rune, fuck. Feels good."

I couldn't begin to explain what came over me, then, but I nuzzled the top of his head, inhaled his scent. He looked up at me in naked shock at the tender gesture, but I was committed and could do nothing but keep kissing. Keep nuzzling. My chest was full of heat, of some emotion so potent I couldn't encapsulate it, couldn't fathom it, couldn't name it—it was so powerful and so big it only registered as desperation. I nuzzled his forehead. Kissed his cheekbone. The bridge of his nose. The corner of his lip.

And all the while, I pleasured him.

Caressed his hot length, luxuriating in the hard thickness of his shaft, the rigid silk of him sliding through my fingers. The sticky slide of his precum smearing my hand. His hot, tight balls so tender and delicate in the cup of my palm, pulsing with his nascent release.

He was panting, now, gasping raggedly as I jacked his length with slow, plunging, twisting touches, and with each successive stroke, his hips began to buck and his stomach tightened and his breath came in faster and ever more ragged gasps.

"Rune," he breathed. "Fuck."

"Yeah?" I teased, now giving him rapid, shallow pumps around the fat glans of his huge cock, the plump, round head blossoming out of the top of my hand, leaking precum from the pink tip. "You like?"

"I need," he breathed. "Need more. I need to come."

I sped my touch, then, pumping him faster. "Like this?"

"Y-yeah," he panted. "Oh…fuck. Rune, Jesus. The way you touch me."

I felt him rising, then. Felt his balls pulse and tense. Felt his cock throb thicker and harder.

"Gonna come for me, Duncan?" I asked. "Gonna come all over my hands?"

He was bucking into my touch, or trying to—I was sitting on his lap and he was sitting upright, hunched forward, gripping the upper swell of my ass in greedy, clenching hands.

He growled savagely, and then suddenly I was

beneath him and he was kissing me and thrusting into my fist with rabid, furious intensity, groaning into my mouth as his orgasm built and bloomed and burgeoned.

"Rune, I'm—oh god." He slowed, then. Fucked my hand slowly, but hard. "Gonna come, Rune."

I clutched his cock in both hands and pumped his length, then, but it wasn't enough. I needed more of him. I needed his orgasm. I needed his heat, his cum, his release, his desperation.

I needed more.

Not just his cum bathing my belly. Not just his cock pulsing in my hands.

I needed him inside me.

"Tell me you have a condom," I whispered.

"God...*dammit.*" He stopped thrusting, then, with a frustrated growl. "I don't. I left in such a hurry I forgot. And I was only planning to make you come. This part was...hoped for but not planned for."

"You think I'd let you eat me out and then just leave?" I said, laughing. "I won't be insulted because we haven't known each other that long, but I'm not that type of girl, Duncan."

"And I'm not the type of guy to assume a girl is gonna do anything." He hung his head, on his hands and knees above me, cock throbbing in my fist. "Just... let me come, Rune. However you want."

I heard myself speaking, but couldn't believe what I heard myself say. "What if I wanted to watch you jack off?" I asked. "What if I wanted you to jack off onto me?"

He levered upright, kneeling tall astride my hips, and took his cock in one big fist, roughly jerking his length. "Then that's what you'll get."

I bit my lip and watched as he jerked his cock with rough, hard, squeezing strokes.

But it wasn't enough.

I needed to touch him. *I* needed to make him come. *I* needed to make him break. *I* need to make him lose control.

"Duncan," I whispered. "Stop."

He let go and stared down at me. "Now what?" He was frustrated. "What do you *want*, Rune?"

I shook my head. "I don't fucking know. Just… *more.*"

His cock bobbed above me, angled slightly toward me, the head swollen and leaking clear precum, the sticky liquid coating his tip and glistening on his shaft.

I licked my lips, looking at his gorgeous cock, then met his eyes. "Dunc…"

He shook his head. "Don't do that."

"Do what?"

"Look at me like that. Lick your lips like that." He closed his eyes. "I've dreamed of that pretty mouth on my cock so many times, Rune—you don't even fucking know. So if you're not gonna give me your mouth, you can't look at me like that and lick your damn lips."

"You want my mouth?" I asked.

"Fuck yes, Rune. Yes, I want your mouth." He shook his head. "I need it. I need to come."

I rolled into him and he let me dislodge him so he fell to his back on the narrow bed, bouncing before going still. "Then you better not move."

FIVE

Duncan

HEART HAMMERING IN MY CHEST, COCK ACHING painfully, I fisted the comforter and tried to remember to breathe as Rune straddled me, sitting on my thighs with her stormcloud hair loose and wild around her shoulders, frizzy and staticky and thick as the night beyond the windows, framing her face and setting her blue eyes to blazing.

Her tits hung heavy and swayed with her breathing as she gently caressed my cock. Moving slowly, she leaned toward me. Her tits nuzzled my chest as she claimed my mouth, and then her hands released my cock and slid up my abs, palmed my pecs, and then framed my face as she kissed me, kissed me, kissed me. My stomach lurched and my heart floated, cracking open and soaring at the hot, wet wonder of her mouth sliding against mine, her tongue stealing into my mouth and demanding my own. And just when

I thought the kiss couldn't get any more intense, she moaned and rubbed her pussy against my cock, her wet seam slick against my shaft.

I whimpered helplessly, pushing against her, so close to coming right then and there that I had to break the kiss and grit my teeth and force myself away from the edge.

"*Fuck*, Rune," I snarled. "Don't tease me, goddammit."

She let her forehead hit my chest with a thud, whining in her throat. "I'm *sorry*. I'm not trying to tease you. I just...fuck. I need you. I want you inside me."

"We can't."

"I know." She slid her ass down my legs, palms raking over my torso. "We'll have to settle for this."

She lengthened her body onto mine, laying on my legs and gathering my aching, pulsing, throbbing cock in both hands, pulling me away from my body. Anticipation raged inside me, and I stopped breathing, heart crashing madly, abs braced, legs tensed, panting.

I pushed stiffened fingers into her hair, gathering the thick black mass of tresses in my fist. "Please, Rune. I'll beg if you want. Please."

"Begging is unnecessary," she whispered. "But don't let that stop you."

"Please, Rune. Have mercy. Suck my cock." I thrust into her hands. "Please. Make me come. Hands, mouth, I don't care. Just...*please* make me come."

"I shall be merciful," she said, stroking my

cock with both hands, her eyes on mine. "Very, *very* merciful."

Her lips parted, and she wrapped them around my cock, and my eyes closed, and a long, hoarse groan escaped my throat. Her mouth was hot and tight around the head of my cock, her hands still pulsing short little pumps at the base of me, and then she palmed my balls again, and that was nearly my undoing. I barely managed to hold off yet again, eyes shutting as I hissed, tensing and thrusting against her mouth.

"Mmmm," she hummed, "mmm-hmmm."

"Fuck," I snarled. "You like that?"

"Mmm-hmmm," she responded, humming around me. "Keep going." This was a whisper, the words huffing hot against my saliva-slick tip.

I clutched her head and thrust again, and she hummed another affirmative sound, gulping around me. "Oh fuck, Rune. Your mouth. Goddamn, girl. So fucking good."

She slid backward until she slipped off the bed, kneeling in the same place I'd knelt to eat her out. She pulled me with her until I was sitting on the edge of the bed with her kneeling between my legs, and she went down on me, taking my length with a loud gulp and a hard swallow.

"Oh...*fuck*," I hissed. "Rune. Jesus."

"Take it," she breathed, pumping my root with one hand while licking my leaking tip with her tongue. "Take my mouth, Dunc."

I wrapped her hair around my fist and stood up, and she gazed up at me, grinning. "Take your mouth? That's what you want?"

She caressed me with both hands, nodding. "Yes. Take me. Give it to me."

Unable to believe what she was telling me, I groaned as I thrust into her mouth. "Like that?"

Her sapphire eyes went wide, and she nodded. "Mmmmm-hmmm!" She kept her eyes on mine, pulled away to whisper against the tip. "Harder. More."

"Ahhh fuck, Rune. Are you real?"

"I hope so." She took me in her mouth and slid wet lips down my shaft, tongue swirling and sliding. "*Love* your cock. I need more of it. Give it to me. Give it to me, Duncan. All of it. I can take it."

"You want it all?" I asked.

"Uh-huh." She licked the tip, then palmed my ass in both hands as she wrapped her lips around me. "Take me, Duncan. Give me your cum. Give me your cock."

"Fuck." I gripped her hair in one hand and palmed the back of her head. "You're too fucking good to be true."

"Try me," she whispered, and then bobbed around my pulsing cock-head a few times, teasing me into helpless thrusting. "Let go, Duncan. Trust me."

Trust her. That's what was holding me back—I didn't want to hurt her or do anything she wouldn't like, no matter how good it might feel in the moment. I didn't trust myself—I was rabid with need, aching with the urge to let go, snarling and groaning and growling with the orgasm boiling in my balls.

I didn't trust myself; did I trust her?

Yes, I did.

Maybe I shouldn't have, but I did.

With a groan of relief, I let go of my self-control. "Take my cock, Rune."

I thrust into her mouth, and she mewled softly as I filled her mouth, drilling into her throat. She gulped around me, swallowing hard, but instead of pushing me away, she grasped my ass in two clawed hands and pulled me to herself.

Oh, *fuck*.

I sank into the tight wet heat of her throat, throbbing madly. "Fuck! Holy fuck, Rune. *God*, you feel good."

She answered with a moan of pleasure, as if I tasted good, or as if she loved the way I felt. I don't know—she didn't say. She just moaned again, pulling at my ass and pushing her mouth down my length, lips stuttering and sliding on my cock. She backed away, my cock popping free, and she gasped for breath, wiping her lips with the back of her hand.

"Come for me, Duncan," she whispered, caressing my length again with one hand. "Give it to me."

There was no option but to give her what she wanted—it was what I needed to. I couldn't hold back anymore, no matter how badly I wanted to drag this out, make the pleasure last forever.

My orgasm was boiling inside me, now, delayed for far too long.

The taste of her pussy lingered on my tongue, and it was exquisite, like the finest honey. Her moans were erotic, driving me mad. I'd nearly come just from the way she sounded when she came, the way she looked—a goddess made flesh, cutting loose and giving me her pleasure.

But now I was the one shuddering at the cusp, and she was kneeling in front of me, and her lips were plump and swollen, her tongue running along them as she gazed up at me with wide, wild sapphire eyes.

I captured the mass of her black hair in my hands and guided her to me. She opened her mouth, eyes not wavering away from mine for a split second as she took me into the hot, wet heaven of her mouth. My legs shook, then, as my orgasm built to an impossible frenzy, and it was all I could do to not fuck her throat.

She sensed I was still holding back—or holding back again, after a brief instant of having given over to desperation. She took control, then.

She clutched my cock in one hand and pumped slow strokes around my root, cupped my taut, hard, aching balls in the other, and slicked her mouth around my cock, wet and hot and suckling and slurping. Her bobbing mouth was wet and messy around me, then, saliva coating my length and lubricating her sliding lips, her pumping fist.

The ecstasy I felt then was unparalleled, pleasure

beyond anything I've ever felt in my life as she worked me to a grunting, panting crescendo of desperation. Her mouth slopped and slid and slurped noisily, wet and insistent and hot and tight, at odds with the way one hand pulsed at my root with slow, almost tender touches, the other massaging my balls. She slid a finger along my taint and pressed in, shocking me with a sudden rush of renewed intensity.

That finger teased further, her eyes dancing with mischief as they met mine, daring me to stop her.

I couldn't.

Didn't.

I held her gaze and gripped her hair and guided her motions, thrusting into her mouth with bent knees, hunched over.

There was no stopping the release, then.

I felt it hit me like a runaway freight train, the surging boil of need in my balls exploding up through my shaft.

"*RUNE!*" I snarled. "*Fuck!* I'm coming, oh fuck, holy shit, Rune…fuck, fuck, fuck."

She groaned low in her throat, took my cock deeper into her mouth, to the back of her throat but not any further, pumping my cock at the root as fast as her hand would go, bobbing on my length slowly and with wet swirls of her tongue: the juxtaposition of slow and fast and hard and soft made me lose any semblance of self-control. My thrusts were mad and helpless and wild, and she took them with eager hunger, whimpering and moaning as I fucked her mouth and hand.

The flood exploded out of me, then, and I shouted my release. As I started to come, Rune slid her finger inside me, pressing in up to the first knuckle, and something inside me shattered irrevocably as my orgasm went nuclear. My legs gave out, and I sagged to the bed, leaning against it for support as I collapsed, boneless and jellied and helpless. I heard Rune gulp as I came, swallowing the flood of my cum and pumping my length for more. The finger inside me vanished, and the release of the pressure sent another spasm through me, another hot flood of cum shattering out of me.

Rune took all of that, too, but then she had to back away with a gasp, panting for breath even as yet more cum spurted out of me and dribbled down my length. Grasping my cock at the base, she licked up my shaft, greedily licking away the rivulet of cum before suctioning around my head again, tongue swirling my tip, one hand cupping my balls with a tender squeeze. I couldn't come anymore, then, but she didn't stop trying to elicit every last drop, pumping and sucking and licking until I was going slack in her hands.

Only then did she release me, and I sagged to my ass on the carpet, sweating and panting. "Holy shit."

She sat astride me, sex on my now-flaccid cock, grinning at me. "Hi."

I could only stare. "Holy shit," I repeated.

She giggled, which did unholy and incredible things to her tits. "You said that already."

"Bears repeating," I said. "That was…holy *shit*."

"That's how I felt after you were done," she answered. "Turnabout is fair play."

"I don't think that's what that phrase means," I said. "But I'll take it."

I cupped her cheek, pulled her close. "Kiss me."

She resisted, pulling away. "I have cum-breath."

I grinned. "I know."

"It's not—" She frowned. "You don't think it's gross?"

I leaned into her, cupping the back of her neck and claiming her mouth in a long, hard, scorching kiss. I tasted myself on her, yes. But I tasted her on my own breath, as well. Tasted her on my lips. Tasted our mingled essences. I scoured her mouth with my tongue, kissed her until she drew away with a gasp.

"Gonna turn me on again," she said.

"That's the point." I relented, however, sensing she had something on her mind. "Did someone say something to you? A boyfriend or something?"

"About what?"

"About not kissing you after you've gone down on him."

She looked away, tried to pull away, tried to slide off me. "Don't worry about it."

I held her in place. "Hey, no. Nope. Talk to me."

She shrugged, still looking away. "Doesn't matter."

"It does to me."

"I just…" she sighed. "Historically, I have absolutely terrible taste in men."

"So that's a yes. Some jackass said something." I

tilted her face so she had to look at me. "Rune, listen to me."

She pulled away forcefully, and I had no choice but to let her go. "It doesn't matter. Old news." She sat on the floor beside me. "Men just suck. Present company excluded…so far."

I laughed. "Considering some of the stories my girl cousins have told, I'm inclined to agree that men do seem to suck."

She shrugged. "You're different, so far."

I scooped her onto my lap and stood up, went to the side of the bed, and sat down with her on my lap. "Tell me. Please."

She shook her head. "You don't want to hear about that shit."

"Maybe I do."

"Then you're a weirdo."

"I am a weirdo, and I do want to hear about it, if only so we can agree about what a fucking loser that guy was."

She sighed. "If we talk about this while I'm all…" she wriggled her shoulders. "Into you, or whatever, I'm liable to cry."

"That's okay. I'm not afraid of a few tears."

She sighed again and slid off me, but I captured her again and nestled her on my chest.

Eventually, she groaned in annoyed capitulation. "Fine. He was a jackass. End of story."

"Rune."

"We just had the hottest not-sex of my life, and now you wanna talk about old painful shit?" She snorted. "This was fun, Duncan, but you don't need to pretend it's something it's not."

I hated the sudden rush of complex feelings her words riled up inside me—hurt, anger, pride, curiosity, jealousy.

"Hottest not-sex of your life, huh?" I asked, faking a lightness I didn't feel.

She shrugged, rolled away from me, and sat up, pulling the sheet up and tucking it under her arms. "Yup."

"What's not-sex?"

She didn't look at me. "Well…that." She gestured with a flip of her hand at the edge of the bed. "Messing around. Sex, but not actual sex."

"I see." I sat up and turned toward her. "It's not gross."

She rolled her eyes. "You don't need to prove anything."

"I'm not." I paused, frowning. "But actually, I do."

"No, you don't."

"Yes, I do." I tapped the side of her chin. "Look at me."

She rolled her eyes again, but did meet my eyes. "*What*, Duncan? He was an asshole. It's fine."

"It's not fine!" I said, my tone heated. "It was the first thing you thought of when I went to kiss you after. You still think about it now, however long it's been since he said whatever the fuck it was he said."

"Of course I do!" she said, not quite yelling but speaking intensely. "I was on my period, and Hayes was horny. I'm not into period sex, so I went down on him."

"Lucky motherfucker," I muttered.

She hesitated. "I did it to be nice. I cared about him." Another hesitation. "I loved him. Or I thought I did, at least."

I sighed. "I'm already pissed off on your behalf."

She snorted. "I'm plenty pissed off on my own behalf, for that and for so many other reasons, but mainly for wasting so much of my time, attention, and love on Hayes Motherfucking Willoughby."

"So...what did he say?"

Her voice was small. Hurt. "I...you know. Gave him a B-J. Admittedly, it wasn't my best work—definitely not on par with what I just gave you, but I still did my best to make him feel good." She swallowed hard, audibly. "You have a sister, right?"

I nodded. "Two, sort of."

She frowned at me. "Sort of?"

"Well, my sister Delia's best friend, Emerson, is... well, it's complicated. She grew up with us. She had a very broken home situation, and my parents took her in as one of our own. She's always been like a sister to us. But then two Christmases ago, she took our last name, and my parents officially adopted her."

Rune sniffled. "So unbeknownst to each other, Emerson took your family's last name, and your family adopted her?"

I nodded. "Yup."

"That's the most adorable thing I've ever heard."

"So, when I say sort of, I only mean that I have one biological sister and one adopted sister. Sunni is my sister in every way that matters."

"I thought her name was Emerson?"

I laughed. "Oh, yeah, it is. We just all call her Sunni, S-U-N-N-I. Her last name is Day, plus Emer-*son*…Sunni. I dunno, Delia gave her the nickname years ago and it just stuck." I squeezed her. "You're not fooling anyone, by the way."

She gazed up at me with wide, innocent eyes. "I have no idea what you're talking about."

"You asked about my sisters. But we're not getting away from the real topic at hand—what Hayes Motherfucking Willoughby said to you."

She sighed, a long, angry, bitter sound. "My point in asking about your sisters wasn't to distract from the answer. Although I wouldn't mind if it did. I don't want to talk about this."

"Too damn bad," I said.

"If you have sisters, then you're probably aware of the reality of what periods are like. Men who don't grow up around girls often have no fucking clue about periods."

I nodded. "I do understand, as much as a dude can, obviously. Delia and Emerson have always been *very* open about it. They'll complain about their cramps and describe in *way* too much detail how it looks like a cat got shot in their underwear."

She cackled. "So you know a period isn't exactly fun."

"Uh, yeah. It's a week of hell and misery every month, by all accounts."

"Right. Hell, misery, blood, and pain." She shrugged. "I've always had heavy periods. Lots of blood, lots of cramps. Not a sexy thing to talk about, I know, but you insisted."

"I did," I said. "And it's fine. This is pillow talk. It doesn't have to be sexy."

"You're such a weirdo." She sighed again. "So anyway, that day, I was feeling particularly shitty. Heavy flow, bad cramps, all the fun stuff. But he'd been whining for *days* about how horny he was, how long it had been since we had sex, blah blah blah."

I scoffed. "Had it been longer than a month?"

Rune snorted derisively. "A *month*? Try less than a week! We'd just had sex the day my period started. It made it start as a matter of fact."

"Fucking hell, what a selfish tool."

She shook her head. "I really, *really* didn't feel like it. But he was just so fucking whiny and pathetic about it, and I did love him, and I figured I'd do something nice. Take care of him. You know?"

"What the fuck did he say, Rune?" I demanded.

"After I was done, he patted me on the head like

a fucking dog and said, 'That was great, babe, thanks. I feel better now.'"

"I literally cannot roll my eyes any harder."

"Right?" She scoffed again, disgusted. "I'd have been fine if that was the end of it. The head pat? Condescending and massively shitty, but at least he said thank you when I did something I very much did *not* want to do just to make my boyfriend feel better."

"But that wasn't the end of it."

"Oh no. No, no, no. It was not. I got up, intending to go, you know, rinse my mouth out. Maybe brush my teeth. Not that he tasted bad or anything, I just—"

I touched her lips. "You don't need to explain or justify a damn thing, Rune."

She playfully nipped at my fingers, and then continued. "I went to kiss him. I wasn't, like, gonna open-mouth French kiss him or anything, just a quick little kiss on the way to the bathroom." Again, the small, hurt voice. "He turned his face away. Denied me the kiss. He said, and I quote verbatim, because I'll never fucking forget it as long as I live, 'You just swallowed my cum, Rune. That's gross. Why would I kiss you after that? Who wants to kiss a girl with cum-breath?'"

I blinked in stunned silence. "Bullshit. There's no fucking way he said that out loud."

She laughed, but it was bitter. "Oh, but he did. He absolutely said that to me."

"And he's still alive?" I asked, not really faking the disbelief. "The girls in my family? Some dumbfuck says something like that, he ain't walking away. If she didn't murder him, the rest of us would. Do *not* fuck with the Badd Clan. You come for one of us, you get all of us."

She regarded me cautiously. "I don't know if you're entirely joking, Duncan."

"Me either," I said with a laugh. "He wouldn't be murdered, but it wouldn't go well for him. Case in point, my cousin Lena dated this dude a couple years ago. She came home late, after curfew, but she was upset. Uncle Canaan was pissed at first because she was seriously late for curfew—she'd just graduated from high school. She didn't want to tell him what happened, at first. Eventually, Aunt Aerie got her alone and got it out of her. They'd been messing around, and he got a little rough with her. And not in a consensual way—in a borderline sexual assault kind of way."

"Bastard," she muttered. "What did your uncle do?"

I could only grin at the memory. "Well, he called the cavalry. Meaning, everyone."

Her eyes went wide. "Ohhhh shit. That's a *lot* of people, huh?"

I cackled. "Remember Uncle Bax?"

"How could I forget?"

"He's the biggest of my uncles, but he's not the scariest."

Rune boggled at me. "Um? Incorrect?"

"You haven't met Uncle Zane. He's not as jacked as Uncle Bax, but he's a retired Navy SEAL. And he keeps his skills sharp to this day."

She winced. "Oh boy."

"Let's just say I've got a lot of uncles, and they're all big, and none of them tolerate even a hint of someone mistreating women. We take that *very* seriously." I paused, thinking. "We also brought some of the girls in on it—Delia, Sunni, Emerson, and Ella, all of whom are legit badasses in their own right, trained in all sorts of martial arts and self-defense styles by Uncle Bax and Uncle Zane. We hunted that punk-ass bitch down, kicked in his apartment door, dragged him outside to the parking lot, surrounded him, and let the girls fuck him up."

She laughed. "What? For real?"

"Oh yeah. We got some shots in for sure, but we let the girls kick his ass to kingdom come. The little bitch-ass motherfucker didn't stand a chance against *one* of them, let alone all four. Once he got out of the hospital, he skipped town."

"H-hospital?" She squeaked.

"Cracked ribs, broken nose, shit like that—nothing major or life-threatening. We wouldn't have let things progress to the level of serious injury. We just taught him a lesson."

"Jesus. When you say don't fuck with your family, you're not kidding."

"Absolutely not. He's lucky all he got was a little roughed up. If he'd have done anything worse? Well, it wouldn't have stopped at a few busted ribs and a broken nose, let's just say that." I looked at her. "I still can't believe your ex said that to you."

"I couldn't either." She sighed, squeezing her eyes shut. "I know it's stupid, but I just…I've never been able to let that go. He did and said a lot of dumb, hurtful shit in the years we were together. He cheated on me, and that's what made me break up with him, but he did a lot of other stuff before that. I honestly forgave him for way too much, let way too much go. I should have broken up with him over that alone, but I didn't. I don't even really know why."

"Rune, it's not stupid."

"It just…it hurt, you know? Like, why is that gross? It's gross to you? I put your penis in my mouth. I swallowed your cum. You let me do it, and you certainly enjoyed it. But then it's gross?"

"Did he ever return the favor?" I asked.

She shrugged. "Sometimes. It wasn't his favorite thing, but he'd go down on me once in a while."

I shook my head. "There's nothing gross about it. It's an act of generosity, Rune. If you don't think it's gross, neither should he. He should be grateful you did it at all."

"I certainly never did again," she said, "I can tell you that. And guess what? Not a month later, I found out he cheated on me."

"Wow. What a fucking tool."

She looked up at me. "I haven't done that to anyone since then, Duncan. After he cheated on me and

I found out, I broke up with him, kicked him out of my apartment, and left LA. That was over two months ago. I've been on a self-imposed celibacy kick ever since. Until now, at least."

"Rune, I—"

"You don't have to say anything, Duncan. I know you're not him. It's okay."

I shook my head. "It's fucking not. I would never have let things go there if I'd known."

She rolled her eyes at me. "Duncan, I chose to do it. I *wanted* to. I don't mind doing it. Under the right circumstances, I even enjoy it." She sat up and hugged the sheet to her chest, regarding me intensely. "And these were the right circumstances, Duncan, I promise. I wouldn't have done it if I didn't want to. It was just when you wanted to kiss me after that I…I got in my head, a little bit. I heard him say that all over again, and I…I guess I sort of felt like it must be true. I don't mind the taste, but—"

"It shouldn't be an 'I don't mind it' situation, Rune. If you're not totally into it, then you shouldn't do it. Not for anyone."

She looked away from me. "I *was* totally into it, Duncan, I promise. It was just you wanting to kiss me after, that threw me for a loop. After what Hayes said, I guess I unconsciously or maybe even consciously assumed all men feel the same way. I mean, I guess I get it? Straight men wouldn't want to taste cum, I suppose."

I laughed. "I mean, no. But it's my own cum, for

one thing. And after you did something that intimate for me, how could I possibly be anything but grateful? How could I *not* want to kiss you, even just to try to show my gratitude?"

She shrugged. "I don't know, Duncan. Don't ask me." She looked at me. "I enjoyed going down on you. While this whole wedding thing is happening, I'm totally down to keep hooking up with you, and I'll absolutely want to do that again. I appreciate you taking my side, but you don't have to work so hard to convince me that you're not a piece of shit like Hayes Motherfucking Willoughby. I see it very clearly."

I frowned. "I'm not trying to *convince* you of anything. If I have to work to convince you that I'm not a piece of shit, then I've already failed at not being a piece of shit. It should be really fucking obvious."

"It is," she said. "I promise." She leaned toward the bedside table, tapped her phone to check the time. "It's super late. We both need sleep."

I heard what she wasn't saying: she wanted me to leave. I felt a little hurt, if I was being honest with myself. I thought we'd shared something more than just a hookup. I didn't expect her to let me stay the night with her, but I guess I hoped for more than an "okay, that was fun, bye-bye."

Nonetheless, I slid out of the bed, stepped into my shorts, shrugged on my hoodie, and stuffed my feet into my slides, checked that I had my phone and wallet, pausing at the door. "Rune—"

She left the bed, leaving the sheet to walk naked toward me. She touched my chest with the fingertips of her right hand, gazing up at me. "Don't, Duncan."

"Don't what?"

"Say anything else sweet."

"Why not?"

She didn't answer, just stared up at me silently.

I sighed. "Fine." I couldn't help myself—I bent, caught her jaw in my hand, and kissed her. "Y'know what I taste?"

"Duncan...*don't*."

I stepped closer, palmed her belly, slid my fingers lower—she gasped when I slipped my middle finger inside her. "This." I withdrew the finger, stepped away from her, opened the door enough to admit my body, and paused in the opening long enough to make a show of popping that finger into my mouth. "Sweet as honey."

Her gasp was equal parts amused and scandalized, leaving me chuckling to myself as I left the hostel and went home.

SIX

Rune

SLEEP WAS SLOW IN COMING. MY THOUGHTS WERE RACING, chaotic, and confusing.

That was just a fun hookup…right? Duncan and me, it's not a thing. It can't be a thing. I don't want it to be a thing.

But my *god*—the orgasms the man gave me were seriously next level.

I'm not sure what time I fell asleep, but out of long habit, I woke up not much past seven. I dozed off again until nine, and then my bladder made me wake up all the way. I showered, put on some black stretchy booty shorts, a tank top, and flip-flops, and went in search of caffeine.

I found it at the breakfast place I'd been to previously. Once I was fed and caffeinated, I strolled the boardwalk and tried not to think about Duncan, his wicked mouth, or his big, fat, beautiful cock.

Or how sweet he was afterward, wanting to kiss me, to hold me, talk to me.

My previous boyfriends were starting to seem more and more like unmitigated assholes, and I blame Duncan…who isn't my boyfriend, nor even a friend with benefits.

He's just a hookup. That's it. Just a hookup.

My phone rang then, Lindsey's name and face appearing on the screen. "Hey, Linz," I said, accepting the call. "What's up, bitch?"

"So you and this Duncan dude."

"We're just friends," I lied.

Lindsey just guffawed. "Ohhhh-*kay*," she mocked. "You got laid. I can hear it in your voice."

"I did not, and you cannot."

"Something happened. I know you, hooker. You can't keep anything from me."

"Ugh. Are you in Ketchikan, yet?"

"I was about to be, but then the hotel burned down and I decided to just fly directly to Anchorage tomorrow."

"And where are Raquel and Hamish?"

"I think they were planning on arriving there today sometime. The flight is tomorrow, right?"

"I think so? I don't know." I huffed. "How did I get stuck planning this, anyway? I didn't even want to come."

"Since you're in Ketchikan and hooking up with a local hottie."

"We're not hooking up."

My phone burbled, indicating she wanted to switch from voice to FaceTime; I accepted the invitation, and her face popped up on the screen. She took one look at me and squealed. "You *liar!* You're totally hooking up with the boy. Tell me everything."

"Linz, I'm not—"

She held up a finger. "Nope. Do *not* try to lie to me, Rune Rigby. I *know* you. You're smiling. You haven't smiled once since you found out about Hayes Motherfucking Willoughby cheating on you. You've been positively *dour.*"

I rolled my eyes at the screen. "Did you buy a thesaurus?"

"Fuck you, no. I have an excellent vocabulary, thank you very much." She brought the phone so close all I could see was one big eyeball. "Now. *Details,* slutty-buns."

I sighed. I knew she wouldn't let it go. "Fine. We messed around."

She waited for a good thirty seconds, and then huffed. "Well? *And?* What does *messed around* entail? Did you come? On a scale from cocktail wiener to kielbasa, how big is his sausage?"

"My god, you're such a nosy lunatic, you know that?" I said, sighing.

"Yes, but you love me. Now. I'm currently in the middle of a horrible dry spell. I haven't so much as laid eyes on a real-life dick in *weeks,* so I'm going to have to live vicariously through you. Which means I need *details*. Now spill it, sister."

I spilled. I related every salacious detail—the phone sex, him showing up, the multiple orgasms, a detailed description of his dick, going down on him, my reaction, his…

When I was done, Lindsey was quiet for a long time. "Interesting."

I frowned at the screen. "Interesting? What the hell does that mean?"

"I don't know yet. My spidey senses are tingling, but I can't pinpoint why just yet. I think there's more to this with you and Duncan—and his donkey dick—than you're willing to admit to yourself."

"No, there's not," I argued. "He lives in fucking *Alaska*."

"And? You have no idea what you're doing with your life, girl. Maybe Alaska is in your future."

"You take that back, Lindsey Snelling. I do too have an idea. and it does *not* include Alaska."

She laughed. "Oh, so you suddenly know what you're doing when you get back to LA, do you? That would be what, exactly?"

I cleared my throat. "Things. And…stuff. Get a job. And do…things. And…stuff."

She just laughed. "Girl, you're in *trouble*."

"He's sweet, and hot as fuck, and gives good orgasms. But my foreseeable future does *not* include men.

This is just a bit of fun before I go back to real life. That's it."

"You don't do casual sex, babe. That's the one hard and fast rule you've never broken. That and always using protection."

"We came *so* close to doing it without a condom, Linz," I admitted. "Like, scary close."

"And you weren't drunk?" she asked.

"Not a drop. Just crazy horny."

"H-M-W really did a number on you, mentally, emotionally, *and* physically," Lindsey said, sighing. "I was honestly worried you'd turn into a spinster after that. I'm really glad to hear your libido is back."

"Me too, to be honest," I said. "If nothing else, I'll have to thank Duncan for flipping that switch back on."

"You can thank him by giving him lots and lots of hot monkey sex," she said, laughing. "Maybe even throw in a few spontaneous, just-because blowjobs."

"Do you do that for your boyfriends?" I asked.

"You know, I haven't had a real boyfriend in almost a year. Not since Damian. I've had a few longer-term situationships, but I haven't dated anyone seriously since Damian."

"That's understandable. That was messy." I paused. "But it doesn't answer my question."

"Everyone is different, Rune," she said.

"Linz."

She sighed. "I'm weird about B-Js, okay? I talk mad game, but I'm actually kinda shy about it."

"You are a terrible liar, Lindsey."

"I'm not lying! Like I said, I talk a lot of shit, but it's all shit."

"You're all talk, you mean."

"No! I like sex. I *love* sex. But…" she trailed off with a sigh. "Why are we talking about me?"

"Because we've done nothing but talk about me since everything happened with Hayes. I care about you. I don't want to talk about me anymore. I want to put the Hayes Motherfucking Willoughby chapter of my life behind me."

"You know my stuff, Rune. Everything that happened with Danny when I was twelve. Acting out afterward. Going to therapy. I'm doing better, but I'm just…I'm still messed up. It's hard. I like sex, but I still get hung up. Especially about oral stuff. I know I should be past it by now, but I'm not. And it's not something I can talk to people about. Especially not guys." She went quiet. "That's why Damian left me, actually."

I gaped at the phone. *"Lindsey!* You told me it was mutual!"

"I lied," she admitted on a sigh. "I was embarrassed. He broke up with me because I'm weird about sex. He's a big oral guy. He loves getting B-Js, almost more than sex, and loves going down on girls. We'd spend hours on foreplay."

I coughed. *"Hours?* I call bullshit."

"Maybe not actually hours, but a long fucking time. An hour at least, and I did time that, once. It can be fun, but it's exhausting. Sometimes I just wanted to fuck and go to sleep, but all he wanted to do was play around all night. I got tired of the foreplay. And while I was mostly okay with the oral stuff, after a while it'd... it'd start to mess with me. Because that's what Danny used to make me do to him. I've done a *lot* of fucking therapy to get past it. Faced my issues. Learned how to block the memories out so I can enjoy intimacy. I didn't want to let what Danny did to me keep me from enjoying every aspect of sex, and I've mostly succeeded. But I'm still weird about it. So the short answer is that no, I don't typically go down on guys until I'm comfortable with them. Because sometimes I still freak out. Not often, but it happens. And if I'm with some random dude from the bar or whatever, and I freak out because I have a flashback or something, it gets messy and awkward. He thinks he did something and how do I explain that it's not him without dumping my whole cargo ship full of trauma on the poor unsuspecting schmuck?"

"God, Linz, I'm such a shitty friend. I'm sorry."

"Oh for fuck's sake, Rune, don't be an idiot. I didn't talk about it on purpose."

"But I'm your best friend, Linz. You should be able to talk to me about this stuff. I tell you everything."

"Rune, I love you. You're my best friend, and the only person I truly trust. I mean that. But the whole 'I was molested' thing is something I don't talk about to *anyone* except my therapist. It's messy, painful, and talking about it doesn't really do anything. I have coping strategies. I'm okay."

"Linz, babe. You lied to me about why you and Damian broke up. How would you feel if the situations were reversed?" I sighed. "Look, you have the right to handle it however you want. I know that. You don't owe me anything. I won't bring it up. But know that I'm here. I love you. I'm here for you."

She sniffled. "Gah, dammit, Rune, I just put on mascara, so don't make me cry." Another sniff. "I love you too, Rune. I'm sorry I lied. I just…I didn't know how to explain the whole thing. I mean, it sounds pretty bad when I say my boyfriend dumped me because I wouldn't suck his dick as much as he wanted."

"That sounds bad because it *is* bad, babe."

"I know. But it was more complicated than that. Damian isn't a bad guy. I'm not mad at him. I don't hate him. I won't shit talk him. I was hurt when he broke up with me, but I got it. It was…it was more of a misalignment of what we wanted out of sex. We were super compatible in pretty much every other way. Our issue was sexual—we just weren't sexually compatible, and honestly, looking back, Damian was right to break up with me. It just hurt. It was hard to not feel like it was my fault. Like I should be able to get past my hangups."

"Says who?" I asked. "You were molested by a twenty-two-year-old man when you were twelve. And not just once. No one in their right mind should expect you to just 'be over it,' as if you could wave a magic wand and erase that trauma. That's not how it works, babe. *You* decide what you're comfortable with. No one else."

"That's just the thing, Rune—I *want* to be over it. I *want* to be comfortable with every part of sex, especially giving oral sex. But I'm not. And it's sort of random, which is the maddening part. I'll be fine and dandy, going down on a guy, *gluck-gluck-gluck*. And then suddenly I'm not fine and I have no idea what triggers it."

"I wish I had an answer or advice, but I don't."

"I'm glad you don't, Rune. If you did, it'd be because you had experience with it, and you don't. So I'm *glad* you don't have any advice for me." She shook her head, sighing. "We're done with this, now. Okay?"

"Okay, but please know you can talk to me. I'm not a therapist, but I *am* your best friend."

"I hear you," she said. She grinned, then. "And for the record, I'd like to live vicariously through you, so do us both a favor and give hunka-hunka burnin' love Mr. Duncan Badd some sloppy head and report back to me, okay?"

I saluted the screen. "Yes, ma'am. Private Rigby reporting for duty."

She frowned at her phone. "Oh, it's Raquel calling me. Lemme merge the calls, hold on."

A second later, Raquel's face appeared on the screen next to Lindsey's.

Lindsey and I actually look a lot alike, except she

has platinum blond hair. We both have bright blue eyes, similar facial features, and a similar build; we're often mistaken for twins.

Raquel is our other best friend. Lindsey and I were roommates all through college, until my parents surprised me with a condo at the start of my senior year at USC. By then, Lindsey was already living with Damian, so I moved Hayes in with me, and the four of us often went on double dates together. Raquel entered the scene junior year and quickly became a consistent third in our friendship.

Raquel was Black, with hair that changed styles every couple of months, big brown eyes, smooth, beautiful, dark brown skin, and a dancer's lean, lithe body. On screen, she was rocking her natural hair—cropped short in tight, close curls with the sides shaved, a style that highlighted her absurdly perfect facial structure, huge almond eyes, and perfectly red lips. In the background, I saw Hamish struggling to tie gear down onto the roof of a Ford Explorer, his wild red hair shaggy and messy.

"Ya'll, Alaska is *crazy!*" Raquel announced. "We camped by a river a few days ago, and this big ol' mama brown bear walked right by our tent with her little cubs. I about died, but they didn't do nothing. They just stopped, looked at us, and kept on going."

"Raquel," I said. "How the hell do you look so damn good after weeks in the fucking Alaskan wilderness?"

"Girl, I always look good," Raquel answered, tossing her head. "Real talk, though? I need a shower, like *bad*. Wet wipes and river baths can only get a bitch so clean, you know what I'm saying?"

Lindsey gagged. "River baths? You can miss me with that. Fish pee in rivers."

Raquel snickered. "It's refreshing. You're never as awake as when you jump into a glacier-fed river at six am."

"She's a nutter," Hamish said, leaning over his fiancée's shoulder to address the phone. "For a city girl, she loves the wild places even more than me. If it was up to her, we'd fly in a priest and get married on the riverbank."

"I grew up in Compton, Hamish. Until I met you, I never left LA. So yeah, I love the wilderness. It's…I dunno. It's just so *alive*—it makes *me* feel alive. Makes me feel connected to something larger than me."

Hamish gave her a loud, smacking kiss on the cheek. "And I love the shite outta you for that. You see everythin' with a delirious sort of wonder that makes me appreciate everythin' all the more."

I rolled my eyes. "You two are so adorable it's fucking ridiculous."

Raquel turned and licked Hamish's cheek, and then dissolved into gales of shrieking laughter as he returned the favor, the screen flailing wildly as they playfully fought to out-lick each other.

"OKAY!" Lindsey shouted. "WE GET IT! YOU

LOVE EACH OTHER! CAN WE HAVE AN ADULT CONVERSATION NOW?"

Raquel appeared on screen again, wiping at her face with her hand, panting. "Sorry, sorry. We're heading back to town, now, Rune. We don't have anywhere to stay, though, and the flight's tomorrow."

"I'll have to talk to Duncan, see if he has any options," I answered." I'd let you stay with me, but I'm in a hostel and the room barely fits me."

"Worse comes to worst, we can just sleep in the car," Hamish said.

Raquel gave him a "the hell you say" look. "Hamish, my love, I will sleep in a tent, and I will sleep in a sleeping bag on the bare dirt ground by the fire, and I'll sleep in a ratty ass log cabin a hundred miles from the nearest human. What I will *not* do is sleep in a car. You wanna know why, Hamish?"

"You'll be tellin' me anyway, won't you?" Hamish said.

"Damn right I will. Number one, you don't sleep in a car—you *try* to sleep in a car. And you fail. Number two, I spent six months living in a van with Mom and Ricky when I was fourteen. I swore when Mom finally got us an apartment that I'd never sleep in a car as long as I lived, and I don't plan on breaking that promise."

Hamish wrapped his arms around her from behind. "That's one I've not heard yet."

She glanced up at him, frowning. "I never told you about that?"

"No."

She shook her head. "Oh. My bad. I'm sorry, baby. I thought I'd told you everything."

Hamish only squeezed her harder. "I only care because I'd not have suggested sleepin' in the car if I'd known. I promise you, my love, you'll never have to sleep in a car again, even if I have to sell a kidney."

She shook her head. "Hamish, baby, the only way one of your kidneys is leaving your body is to give it to me. You ain't sellin' *nothin'*."

"No one is selling anything and no one is sleeping in a car," I cut in. "I'll find somewhere for you guys to sleep tonight, I promise. Just get back to Ketchikan. I'll have something figured out by then."

We said our goodbyes, and then Raquel dropped out, leaving Lindsey and I on the line together once more.

"I love them," Lindsey said. "They're couple goals."

"For real." I met Lindsey's eyes via the screen. "I am glad you made me come up for this. I would have regretted missing it, especially over Hayes Motherfucking Willoughby."

"Facts, babe, facts," Lindsey said. "Okay, well, I gotta pack. My flight leaves at the perforated colon of dawn tomorrow."

"The what?"

"Perforated colon of dawn."

"Gross."

"The only accurate way to describe a five a.m. departure."

"Ew, that *is* gross. I don't believe in being awake before six."

"Me either! I'm a cocktail waitress. I'm usually still *awake* at five."

"So will you still be awake when you board, or…?"

"Sadly, no. I tried that once when Damian and I went on vacation to Cozumel. The only flight we could find was a six a.m. departure, and I figured what the hell, I'll just work my usual shift, stay awake, and sleep on the plane." She laughed, shaking her head. "Spoiler alert, that did *not* work. I was crashing out in the lounge before the flight and then completely failed to sleep on the plane. I wasted the whole first day of our four-day vacation fucked up from jet lag, and we only went to Mexico."

"But how will you fall asleep?"

"Drugs."

"How will you wake up?"

"Willpower."

"Linz. That's not gonna work. You'll oversleep."

"Do you have any other suggestions? I've been awake for thirty-six hours, Rune. I *will* fall asleep. I've got six alarms set on my phone, two alarm clocks in my room, and my next-door neighbor who gets up for work at four is gonna pound on the wall when she wakes up for her shift."

"You're a nutter, babe," I said, sounding like a demented version of Shrek.

"You're not Scottish, so you don't get to call me a nutter."

"Fine, you're a fucking lunatic."

"Better."

"I gotta go," I said. "I need to get ahold of Duncan and figure out somewhere for Raquel and Hamish to stay tonight."

"Tell you what, though, that boy is earning his BJs."

I glared at her. "Sex is not transactional, *Lindsey*."

She rolled her eyes. "No, it's not. But B-Js do make an excellent boyfriend motivator. Offer a boy some head and he'll do just about anything you ask."

"But then you have to follow through," I pointed out. "And isn't that a little manipulative?"

She shrugged. "Maybe? Only if he thinks so. I did it with Damian, once. The man was *not* motivated to help around the apartment, so I used that to motivate him. I made him that offer—do some cleaning so the apartment isn't a disaster when I get back from work, and I'll blow you. Let me tell you, Rune, I got back from work that night, and that apartment was spotless. *Spotless*, I tell you. That boy cleaned his skinny ass off."

"And?"

"And I sucked his soul out through his dick, because I didn't have to vacuum or do the dishes or anything when I got home. He even did laundry. You know how I am."

I did—she was fastidious to the point of obsession. She hated mess, despised clutter, and loathed doing laundry. She would come home from class or work and be dead tired, but she'd spend an hour or two cleaning because she just couldn't relax with a mess. And to Lindsey, anything out of place or even slightly dirty was a disaster—there was no middle ground between clean and filthy. It worked for us when we roomed together, because my parents are both equally obsessed with cleanliness, so I tended to be pretty neat.

"Did that become an ongoing thing?" I asked.

"I mean, no. It's not something I'd do, like regularly. If someone is living with you, they should help out with the cleaning. I'm a neat freak, and I get that no one else is going to do what I do, but I just wanted him to help *at all*. He did help out more after that, even without the motivation. I think he was hoping for a reward, though."

I snickered. "Seems a little cruel, Linz. Make him think he'll get rewarded every time he cleans?"

"He's not a dog, Rune."

She laughed. "I mean, you met him."

I spluttered. *"Lindsey!* Mean."

"I say it with affection. He was goofy. He was a yellow lab in human form. Cute, funny, goofy, affectionate…but spazzy and not always the smartest crayon in the tool drawer."

"You just mixed, like, so many metaphors."

"I know. I'm funny that way."

"I'm hanging up now, Linz."

"Good. Because you know I won't. I'll just keep on yakking at you unless you hang up on me."

"Which must make you one of those little yappy dogs that are always barking, if we're comparing people to dogs."

"Excuse me! I am not a yappy little dog."

"You're one of those Chihuahuas with missing teeth so their tongue hangs out all the time. With yapping."

She gasped. "Rune Rigby! How dare you!"

I cackled. "Love you, byeeee!" I hung up before she could clap back.

Of course, she's not one to let anyone have the last word—she sent me a GIF of a pug looking demented and inbred, and while she didn't include anything else, the meaning was clear.

The bitch.

I sent her a selfie of me doing a kissy-face. She responded with a selfie of her flipping me off.

If I didn't just stop responding, though, we'd be doing this for hours, so I just ha-ha'd the image and called Duncan.

My heart shouldn't have gone pitter-patter at the thought of talking to him, but it did.

My lady bits shouldn't be moist at the mere thought of hearing his voice, but they were.

He's trouble, I tell you. Trouble with a capital T, and I've had my fill of troublesome boys.

Good thing this whole thing with him has a built-in expiration date—in three days' time I'll be back in LA and he'll be here, and that'll be that.

He answered on the third ring, sounding groggy. "H'lo?"

"Hi, Duncan. It's me. Sorry to wake you up... again."

"Mmm. Time's it?" A rustling. "Oh, shit. Good thing you did call—I'm gonna be late opening." More rustling. "You're on speaker while I get dressed. What's up?"

"Oh, well, this whole 'the hotel burned down' thing is causing all sorts of issues. Raquel and Hamish are coming back into town from wherever they were camping, but now they have nowhere to stay before the flight to Anchorage tomorrow. You know how small my hostel room is, or I'd let them crash with me. I, uh...don't suppose you have any more ideas?"

He laughed, sounding like he was halfway across the room. A moment later, he spoke again with the phone off speaker. "I might have an idea, let me make a call and get back to you...fuck me; *after* I get the Kitty open. Like an hour?"

"No hurry. I'm gonna hang out with them when they get here. I'm just hoping you'll come through again. I'm really leaning on you a lot, and I'm grateful."

"Hey, it's all good. I'm glad I could help. I really

gotta go now, but I'll call you back when I can. And hey, thanks for the wake-up call."

"Least I could do after all you've done for me and my friends."

"I mean, it's not like I'm not getting anything out of it," he said, his voice low and rough and intimate. "Not that that's why I'm doing it. Just saying. It's not *purely* out of the goodness of my heart. Just mostly."

"I the appreciate the honesty, Duncan. Now hang up and go be a manager. We'll talk later."

He hung up and I headed back to my hostel room to pack, and tried not to think about all the delicious ways I could repay Duncan for helping us with Raquel's and Hamish's wedding.

SEVEN

Duncan

I REALLY NEEDED TO START SETTING MY ALARM. I'VE ALWAYS been able to reliably wake up in time to open the Kitty without one, but since I've met Rune, even if I'm not up late with her, I can't fall asleep on time because I'm thinking about her.

Fantasizing about her.

Those fucking amazing tits. Her big blue eyes wide and fraught as she comes all over my mouth. Her lips sliding down my cock…

Fuck.

I tried like hell to put her out of my mind as I opened the Kitty, wiping down bottles, putting down chairs and stools, counting the till drawer, checking inventory, preparing the deposit from the previous day's take, going over the schedule for the week, rotating the stock in the beer fridges…yet even while doing all of this, my mind kept returning to Rune, her lush, gorgeous body, her wit and sarcasm, the way she sounded when she came.

I got the Kitty opened and ready for business, handled the first few customers, and then stepped into the office to make the promised phone call.

It rang three times before she answered. "Dunc! My favorite nephew!"

I laughed. "Hey, Aunt Low. I bet you say that to all the boys."

She faked an outraged gasp. "Why I never!" Her tone returned to normal. "So, to what do I owe the pleasure of this call, favorite nephew?"

"I wish it was purely because I love talking to you so much, but I do have a favor to ask you."

"Hit me with it, bub."

"So, I have this friend. It's a whole big story, but—"

"Whoa, let me stop you there," she said. "If you're gonna ask me for something, you have to give me the whole scoop or I say no."

I peeked out of the office to make sure I didn't have any waiting customers. "Okay, fine. So, her name is Rune."

"And she's definitely *just* a friend," Aunt Low said, her voice sarcastic.

"I, um. No. I like her. I don't think it's gonna *be* anything, but I do really like her. And she has these friends who were planning on getting married at the Old Toby Inn. They had their whole wedding party coming and everything. Tickets bought, rooms paid for, everything."

"Didn't the Old Toby just catch on fire?" she asked. "I saw a headline about that on one of my news feeds."

"It did. Like, pretty much to the ground, less than three days before the wedding. No one was hurt, thank god, but the place is just gone, and with it their entire wedding plan."

"Oh god. That's awful, Duncan. I'm so sorry to hear it. But I confess I don't really know what I could do to help."

"Well, Delia offered them the back room up in Anchorage for the wedding and reception, and the hotel nearby has rooms for everyone."

"But?"

"The bride and groom, Raquel and Hamish, have been out camping or hiking or whatever out in the bush. I have flights to Anchorage set up for everyone tomorrow, but Raquel and Hamish don't have anywhere to stay tonight, and Uncle Brock is taking us up pretty early tomorrow."

"And you're hoping Raquel and Hamish can use the yacht," she guessed.

"I know it's a big ask, Aunt Low. Especially because these aren't even *my* friends. I haven't even met them yet. So I totally get it if you don't feel comfortable with it. I just promised Rune I'd at least see what I could do, since there aren't any rooms available in Ketchikan."

"One sec, baby, let me talk to your uncle real quick." The line went silent for a minute or so, and then she was back. "We're okay with it, but we'd like to have a video call with the bride and groom."

"I have a feeling that can be arranged," I said. "Are you sure?"

"Dunc, that big dumb boat sits empty more than it gets used. We're more than happy to lend it to the happy couple for the night."

"You're the actual best, Aunt Low," I said.

"I know. We'll have the marina crew get the yacht ready. Shoot me a text when the couple is in town and ready to check into the S-S Loveboat."

"I, um, I was planning on just saying it belonged to a family member," I said. "I didn't want to get into who you are."

"Where's the fun in that? Just don't tell them anything before we video call them. Use the screen in the main saloon. You know how to work it?"

"Yeah, I do." I peeked out again and saw that I had a couple people waiting at the bar. "I gotta go, but for real, thank you."

"If this Rune girl turns out to be more than just a friend, I demand to be the first family member she meets. That's my payment for the favor."

"Deal."

"Okay. Love you with all my heart, favorite nephew."

"Love you with all mine, favorite aunt."

I ended the call and shoved the phone in my back pocket as I headed out to the floor to do my job.

For some reason, my idiot brain kept conjuring images of Rune sitting on my lap on the couch at home with the whole Badd clan around us, as if this limited-time-only situationship with Rune could ever be more.

I know the score. I see her keeping me at a certain emotional distance. And to be honest, I'm doing the same thing. I just…I really like her. And I don't want to; I know she has a life elsewhere, and as soon as this wedding is over, she's gonna go back to it.

And it's not like I have the time or space in my life for a relationship anyway—I work open to close most days managing the Kitty. This is what I want to do—I've grown up in the family bars, watching Dad, Mom, and most of my aunts and uncles pitch it and help out around the bars at one point or another. I've watched Delia work her way up to being the Vice President of the Badd's Bar company, and the next in line to be CEO when Dad finally steps into something resembling retirement…not that any of us expect him to ever totally retire.

None of my friends get it. Of the dozen or so guys I was close to from school, eleven of them chose colleges in the lower forty-eight and jobs down there after graduation. The twelfth, Rodrick, joined the Marines and is looking to make a career out of it. Of my entire football team friend group, I'm the only one who chose to stay in Ketchikan and not go to college so I could work at a bar for the rest of my life.

The point is that I take this seriously. I want my dad to know that I'm ready to do this, that this isn't just a job while I figure out my real plan. This *is* the plan. Just like Delia. I want this life. I want what Mom and Dad have had.

And that means I don't have space for distractions. Managing a whole-ass bar isn't easy. In fact, it's pretty damned hard. I can't afford the distraction of a girl right now, however much part of me may secretly wish the situation with Rune didn't have a built-in expiration date.

I handled the lunch rush. It was after two by the time I got enough of a lull that I could step away long enough to call Rune.

"Duncan, hi," she said, after answering on the second ring. "How is work?"

"Busy morning, which is why it's taken so long to call you back. I do have a place for Raquel and Hamish to stay, but I'm gonna keep the details a secret for now. I get off at six, so could I meet up with you guys once I'm done?"

"Raquel, Hamish!" Rune said, loud and excited. "Duncan found a room for you. We're meeting him at six—where, Duncan?"

"I'll call you when I'm done and we'll figure it out then."

A group of cruise ship tourists swarmed in then,

which meant I had to go, so I said my goodbye and went to work.

Six was more like six-thirty by the time I actually was able to leave the bar, but I'd shot Rune a text saying I was running behind. They were sitting down at a restaurant near the marina, and I joined them just in time to order dinner. Despite having never met me, Raquel gave me a warm, friendly hug, and Hamish gave me a back-slapping hug as well.

"So," Rune said, once our food had arrived, "where's this room?"

I grinned. "I had to get creative, but I think you'll really like it," I answered. "It's actually really close to here. But I'm gonna keep the details a surprise. It's more fun that way."

Hamish frowned. "There're no hotels anywhere near here, and nothin' in Ketchikan at all with vacancy," he said. "So I admit I'm a wee bit confused." The man's Scottish accent was thick as a concrete mixer from DQ, and his appearance—brawny, red-haired and -bearded, wearing flannel and denim—matched the accent perfectly, in my head, at least.

I just grinned. "You'll see."

We chatted through dinner, mostly about trivialities—music, movies, books, things like that. Once we'd paid the tab, we left the restaurant and I led the four of us on a leisurely stroll through the marina—seemingly at random but in reality heading toward Aunt Low's yacht, which was berthed at the far end of the marina, a location which afforded her some semblance of privacy when she and Uncle Xavier were in town. For the uninitiated, my Aunt Low is Harlow Grace, one of the most famous human beings on the planet. And my Uncle Xavier owns one of the world's foremost robotics and technology corporations.

We reached their yacht; it was only a few years old, as they'd just recently replaced the one Aunt Low had owned for over twenty years. This one was state-of-the-art, having been designed by Uncle Xavier. It wasn't a massive boat, certainly not a super-yacht like some celebrities own; only seventy feet or so, it boasted the main quarters, a saloon—the boat version of a living room—a gourmet kitchen, several guest suites, a diving platform, a workout space, an office, and every piece of technological wizardry Uncle Xavier could pack into the thing. Which, Uncle Xavier being who he is, means it has things not even NASA does.

When we stopped in front of it, everyone seemed confused. The yacht doesn't look like a traditional yacht, looking more like a Chinese Junk than a luxury yacht, because Uncle Xavier is kinda weird and Aunt Low usually just goes with it. It's a hell of a sweet boat, though.

Rune blinked at me. "Um. Duncan? What's... what's going on?"

I gestured at the boat. "This is where you guys will be staying tonight."

Raquel, Hamish, and Rune exchanged stunned, baffled glances.

"Is this yours?" Raquel asked, looking at me.

I cackled. "God, no."

Hamish cast a critical eye over the craft. "Never seen the like of it."

"Because it's one-of-one," I answered. Stepping onto the gangway, I waved them after me. "Come aboard."

I led them directly to the main saloon, which occupied the center of the boat's floor plan. Both of the starboard and port side walls opened to create an open-air living space. The bow-side wall featured a floor-to-ceiling entertainment screen with surround sound built into the walls and ceilings. The stern wall was a full bar and kitchenette, and the center of the space boasted a U-shaped sectional that could seat ten people with room to spare. Aunt Low and Uncle Xavier, being the type of people they are, all the materials and finishes were comfortable, cozy, and homey rather than ostentatious. A narrow hallway led past the right side of the screen and to a full bathroom; another hallway on the left of the screen led to the main bedroom with its own en suite bathroom. The kitchen—or galley, as boat people call it—is in the lower level, along with the guest suites, workout space, and office.

The trio took in the saloon, the glimpse of the

bedroom beyond it, the view out either side, and then the bottle of Dom Perignon and crystal flutes on the coffee table.

Raquel stared at me. "Duncan, what is this?" She indicated the champagne. "That's a three-hundred-dollar bottle of champagne."

I just grinned. "Have a seat, you two." I gestured at the couch facing the screen.

Hamish eyed me. "Why, though? This is all highly irregular."

"Just...trust me. Have a seat."

Rune stood next to me behind the couch, facing the screen. "What's going on, Duncan?"

"You'll see."

Hamish and Raquel gingerly sat down on the couch and waited, visibly impatient, while I withdrew the tablet device that controlled the yacht's central operating hub. Xavier had designed the ship so that it could be operated almost entirely from this tablet. For now, though, I used it to turn on the screen and then connect to Aunt Low and Uncle Xavier's matching setup in their primary home in Malibu.

The screen winked on, showing an empty white couch with the Pacific Ocean rippling and winking in the background. Just when I could tell Hamish and Raquel were about to be even more confused, Aunt Low entered the screen from the left and Uncle Xavier from the right, and they sat down in unison, as smoothly as if they'd practiced it.

Aunt Low grinned, waving. "Hi! You guys must be Hamish and Raquel."

Uncle Xavier gave a stiff, awkward wave and a polite smile. "Hello." He held his hands out, palms up, in a gesture he'd clearly—to me at least—practiced. "Welcome aboard The Argo. We are pleased to host you in our Alaskan home away from home on this penultimate night before your nuptials."

Hamish cleared his throat. "Ahem. Ah…pardon, but…you're Harlow Grace and Xavier Badd, are you not?"

"You are correct, Hamish," Uncle Xavier said. "I am pleased to make your acquaintance."

Aunt Low leaned into her husband. "Xave, baby. Relax."

He squared his shoulders. "I *am* relaxed. But I believe a formal introduction is not inappropriate in circumstances such as these." He gestured at my aunt. "As you have surmised, this is my wife, Harlow Grace Badd, and I am Xavier Badd."

Raquel was covering her mouth with one hand, reaching behind her to grip Rune's hand while vibrating with barely contained excitement.

"I, um, well I'm Hamish Campbell, and this is my fiancée, Raquel Ellison."

Aunt Low leaned toward the screen. "My god, you two are just gorgeous together! How did you meet? I need the love story."

Raquel turned to look at Hamish, then cleared her

throat. "Well, um, it's kinda boring. We met at USC. I was there on a scholarship studying journalism, and Hamish was there studying film. We met our freshman year in the cafeteria and just sort of...gradually fell in love."

Hamish laughed. "*You* fell in love gradually. I was besotted the moment I laid eyes on you."

Raquel rolled her eyes. "It was only gradually because I had no idea what you were saying, at first. I'd never met a real Scotsman before."

"Well, that's fair, I suppose," Hamish answered. "My accent *was* a wee bit thicker than it is now." *Than et ez noo.*

I choked on a laugh. "You're shitting me!"

Raquel turned and gave me a droll look. "When I first met him, it sounded like he was speaking another damn language."

Hamish shook his head. "It's no even Doric. Not even I can understand them lot. My uncle had a mate who was from Aberdeen, and that man's accent was tot'ly mad. Even his best mates just nodded and laughed when he spoke."

Raquel held up her hands. "Okay, I'm tryna play this cool, but I'm freaking out. Duncan, what the hell is going on?"

I shrugged. "They're my aunt and uncle."

Rune pinched my arm. "The Aunt Low who 'works in the film industry,'" she used air quotes here, "is Harlow freaking Grace?"

"Jesus, woman. The pinching!" I rubbed my arm. "Yes. I'm sure you can guess why I don't go around announcing it, though."

She sighed. "Yeah, I guess."

Hamish glanced at me, and then back at the screen. "And…this is your boat?"

Aunt Low nodded. "It is. My brilliant husband designed it himself."

"And…we get to stay on it tonight?" Raquel asked. "But…*why*? We don't even know you. We just met Duncan barely an hour ago."

"Well, we heard about the Old Toby burning down, and Duncan mentioned you needed somewhere to stay tonight. We're not using the Argo at the moment, so why not?"

Hamish shook his head. "I just…are you sure? When Rune said she'd ask Duncan to see what he could do, I thought he meant like a friend's flat or somethin'. I didnae think it would be…*this*."

"We're happy to be able to help, you guys," Aunt Low said. "We love a love story, and you guys are adorable. So please, make yourselves at home with our blessing. Congrats, Raquel and Hamish, and please accept our wishes for a long and beautiful life together."

Xavier smiled, as well, this one more natural. "I echo my wife's sentiments." He blinked, thinking. "I heard a toast at a wedding in the Highlands, once. I believe it goes like this: 'May the road rise to meet you, may the wind be always at your back, may the sun shine warm upon your face, the rain fall soft upon your fields, and until we meet again, may God hold you in the palm of his hand.'"

"Thank you," Raquel said. "For real, I…when they told us the inn was gone and refunded us the whole thing, I was…I thought…"

"We were determined to make the best of it, but the way things are turning out is better than we could have imagined." Hamish squeezed Raquel's hand. "We really can't thank you enough."

"It's really no problem at all," Aunt Low answered. "Dunc, honey, we love you."

"Love you guys too, Aunt Low, Uncle Xavier," I said. "Thank you for being so awesome about this. You guys are the best."

Aunt Low's gaze fixed on Rune. "You must be Duncan's friend Rune. I have to say, I love your name. It's really cool."

Rune flushed. "Thank you? I…it's so cool to meet you."

"Likewise." She glanced at the smartwatch on her wrist. "Oh, shoot, I have a meeting with Chris in a few minutes, so I'm going to have to go."

I rolled my name. "Smooth name drop, Aunt Low."

"Chris is a very common name, Duncan Badd," she answered.

"But you're not talking about any old Chris," I said.

Aunt Low grinned, putting her finger over her lips. "I'm not supposed to talk about it, but I'm meeting with Christopher Nolan. We're putting together a project."

Hamish clutched his hair in both hands. "You're not really, are you? As an aspiring filmmaker, he's one of my greatest inspirations."

Aunt Low shrugged, smiling. "I really am. We worked together before on—"

"Antony and Cleopatra," Hamish cut in. "You were brilliant in that, Mrs. Grace. Just brilliant."

"Thank you, Hamish. It was a fun project." She glanced at her watch. "I hate to cut this short, but I really do have to get ready for my meeting. It was absolutely wonderful to meet you all. Hamish, Raquel, congratulations, and please, enjoy your evening. Duncan, I expect you to call us again soon, you hear me?"

"I will, I promise. And not just when I want something."

Aunt Low just waved me off. "That's not what I meant. You know we're here for whatever you need." She kissed the tips of her fingers on both hands and blew kisses at the screen. "Okay, we're off. Goodbye! Congratulations!"

"Congratulations, indeed," Uncle Xavier said. "Duncan, excellent to see you again, however briefly. Goodbye."

I waved, and then ended the connection.

There was a moment of stunned silence, and then

Raquel turned to look at me. "Is this for real? You're not pranking us?"

I laughed. "That would be the cruelest prank ever pulled, I think." I gave her slender shoulder a friendly squeeze. "It's for real. They're really my aunt and uncle, this is really their boat, and you're really sleeping here tonight." I moved away from the couch. "C'mon, let me give you the tour."

Later, after I'd given them the tour of the yacht and they'd brought their luggage aboard, Rune and I were lounging together on the bow, sipping beer from the stocked galley while Raquel and Hamish got settled— they'd insisted we stay so we could all keep hanging out together.

"So," Rune said to me. "Any other famous family members?"

I laughed. "Um, well?"

"C'mon, no." She gave me a wide-eyed stare. "For real?"

"I mentioned Uncle Canaan and Aunt Aerie, I think…"

Rune blinked. "Wait…no. No! You're kidding."

I shrugged. "No?"

"Canary? Your *other* aunt and uncle are Canary?"

"Aunt Eva is a pretty well-known photographer," I said.

"Eva..." She frowned. "Evangeline Badd is *also* your aunt?"

"Yes."

"My mother is obsessed with her work. They have at least four framed original prints at their house." She sighed, shaking her head. "Anyone else?"

"My sister Delia is married to Hunter Hawkins. Not sure if that counts."

She facepalmed herself. "Yes, Duncan, it does. Is he as hot in real life as he looks in photographs?"

I laughed. "I mean, I'm a straight dude, but yeah, he's pretty freaking good-looking. Cool as fuck, also. He gives pretty rad gifts at Christmas."

She giggled. "Can I be super nosy and ask what he's gotten you?"

"Well, last year he took all of us cousins up to the Asgard for three days, which was, obviously, really fucking wild."

She boggled at me. "Shut up. You're lying to me."

I laughed. "I'm not! Look!" I pulled out my phone and scrolled back through my photos until I found the section from the trip. "Swipe left."

She swiped slowly through my photos—of the Brynhild that took us up, the Asgard from a distance, floating in the blackness of space, and then various views of the Asgard, the Earth, the sun, the moon.

"What was that like?" Rune asked.

"Unbelievable. Hard to describe, actually. I mean, the takeoff was kinda scary, to be honest. And then being weightless? Nothing can prepare you for that." I sighed, thinking about it. "If you want the embarrassing truth, I actually got kinda choked up the first time I saw Earth from the outside. Like, it's…there aren't words, Rune. How beautiful it is. But also how terrifying it is to *not* be on Earth."

She shook her head. "That's the craziest gift I've ever heard of."

I laughed. "Yeah, I'm not sure how he's gonna top that. Although, I gotta say, Uncle Xavier's gifts are usually pretty fucking baller, too, for obvious reasons."

Rune frowned, shaking his head. "I admit I don't know much about him. I know he's a famous tech guy, and he does a lot with robotics, but that's about the extent of my knowledge."

I snorted. "He's sort of the world's leading expert on robotics. As in, there's Uncle Xavier, and then there's everyone else. He pretty much single-handedly invented the modern approach to nanotechnology, especially as it applies to medicine. But most people know him for what he calls his gizmos."

She clapped a hand to her forehead. "Oh! All those little toy sets? The modular bots?"

I nodded. "Yeah, that's him."

"Holy shit. I had a set when I was little. My cousin Tilly was obsessed, though. She had every set they made. She was actually a front-runner in one of those contests they did, the whole open-source competitions."

"That's awesome. Growing up, all of us cousins were basically his beta test group. He'd give us all sets that weren't on the market yet and watch us play with them and ask us questions and stuff. In fact…" I got up. "Stay here, I'll be right back."

I went down into Uncle Xavier's office, found what I was looking for, and took it up to the lounge area. I set the giant plastic bin on the deck and flipped the lid open—within was a jumbled assortment of bots from Uncle Xavier's lines of toys from over the years. These were mostly parts he'd built himself as prototypes and test products, mixed in with some production pieces. He'd made sure that every new line of bots was back-ward compatible with all the rest, so even though some of the bots in the crate were pushing twenty years old, they still worked perfectly with the newest ones.

Rune picked up a bot, a spider-like one with eight limbs that could articulate in every direction. "This was the set I had." She found another one and pieced them together, and immediately the bots came to life, the legs moving and swiveling and seeking purpose. "God these were fun."

We spent a while playing with the bots and talking idly about not much of any importance. Eventually, she set the pieces aside and looked at me with an expression that said she had something serious on her mind. "I re-ally can't thank you enough for this. For everything."

"Hey, no problem."

She shook her head, resting her hands on mine.

"Don't downplay it. Without you, Hamish and Raquel wouldn't be getting married. You're basically a hero."

I laughed. "That might be overstating the case a bit, Rune. My family has been incredibly fortunate. We have a lot of resources, and we believe in using them to help people when we can. I'm happy to have been able to facilitate Hamish and Raquel getting the wedding they deserve."

She nuzzled my jaw, rested a hand on my thigh. "Well, I, for one, am very, *very* grateful."

I huffed a laugh. "Oh yeah? I don't mind admitting I like the way you say thank you."

Her fingers teased over my zipper. "Is that so? I could thank you right now, if we had somewhere a bit more private to go."

I was about to suggest one of the guest cabins, but Raquel's and Hamish's voices filtered to us from the main saloon, putting a kibosh on that plan.

As the couple approached the bow, the bottle of champagne and four flutes in hand, Rune met my eyes. "Later. Promise."

Later never came, though—the four of us ended up getting clobbered, and we all passed out in the saloon together as dawn stained the sky pink.

EIGHT

Rune

OH FUCK.

Ow.

I considered opening my eyes, but even moving my eyeballs behind closed eyelids hurt like a bitch, and so I opted to leave them closed. Fuck—this is why I don't party like this very often. This part is just not worth the fun from the night before.

Eventually, after who knew how long trying to convince myself I could go back to sleep and abjectly failing, I had to get up. As always, it was my bladder that forced the issue.

Except, when I cracked my gritty, pulsing eyes open, I was not at home and nor was I at my hostel—oof, right. The yacht. Raquel and Hamish and Duncan, and I partied here last night. I have only vague memories of the night—flashes and glimpses of moments.

Raquel and Hamish falling on each other laughing,

Duncan nearly toppling over the side of the boat, yet somehow managing to not spill a drop of his drink, playing some wild drinking card game. Duncan chasing me around the boat trying to pin me down and tickle me.

I assessed myself—clothed, so nothing happened between Duncan and me. My hair is loose, wild, and tangled. My makeup was probably smeared to hell and gone.

I stumbled to my feet, blearily peering around in search of the bathroom. Duncan was conked out on the couch with his head angled toward where mine had been—he was shirtless in a pair of black jeans, barefoot. His hair was messy and draped over his face, fluttering with his soft snoring exhalations. One door beside the giant screen was closed, the other open; the open door led to a bathroom, and I lurched toward it, unsteady on my feet.

After taking care of business, washing my hands, and splashing cold water on my face, I felt marginally less like warmed-over death. Now I just needed caffeine. The kitchen was in the basement of this boat—well, lower level, not a basement; I don't know shit about boats. But there was also a kitchenette up here; maybe there was a coffeemaker. I rounded the bar and poked around a bit, and found a pod coffee machine, a box of coffee pods, and a jug of distilled water.

A few minutes later, I had sweet, blessed coffee in a mug—there was no cream or sugar that I could find, but fuck it. I don't need it, I just prefer it. Right now, I was definitely a beggar and thus couldn't be a chooser. I found bottles of water in the fridge as well, and I took my coffee and a bottle of water out onto the deck, soaking up the early morning sunshine. I spent the next several minutes lounging in the sun, sipping coffee, trying to coerce memories from last night out of my alcohol-addled brain.

Mainly, I wanted to make sure I hadn't done anything stupid with Duncan.

It seems unlikely I'd have gotten re-dressed afterward if we had, but you never know—booze makes you do weird shit, man.

At some point, I heard noises from the saloon—a male grunt of pain, followed by a rough, raspy voice grumbling, "Ohhhh fuck me. Ow—too loud." A few minutes later, I heard the toilet flush, and then. "Oh, thank god, a coffeemaker."

I felt him approach from behind, and then he was gingerly lowering himself into the chair beside me, a mug full of coffee in one hand, a bottle of water in the other. He set the bottle between his thighs and opened his palm, revealing six pain reliever gel capsules.

He tossed three into his mouth, chased them with a long, gulping glug of water, and then proffered the other three to me with a wordless grunt.

I grunted back as I took them from him.

He sipped coffee, I sipped coffee, the sun shone

too brightly, and somewhere a seaplane droned and a motorboat hummed.

After tossing back the last of his coffee, Duncan glanced at me. "You remember much of last night?"

I shook my head. "Bits and pieces. You?"

"Same." He tugged at a belt loop. "I'm still wearing pants, and you're fully dressed, so I don't think we did anything. Did we?"

"Don't think so. I'm not sure how, why, or when you lost your shirt, though."

"Eh," he said, waving a hand dismissively. "My shirt always vanishes when I drink. Dunno why."

I snickered, and immediately regretted it, wincing and closing my eyes as a wave of hangover headache surged through me at the noise. "Oh god, don't make me laugh."

"I…didn't? I dunno what's so funny about what I said."

I looked sadly into my empty mug. "Coffee all gone. I has a sad."

Duncan snickered, and then mirrored my groan and winced. "Oh, fuck. Laughing does hurt." He took my mug and shuffled back into the saloon, and I heard the noises of coffee being made, and then he returned with full mugs. "Here."

I accepted the mug with a grateful smile. "Thank you, Duncan."

He nodded. "Welcome."

"I was laughing because you're the shirtless guy

at the party," I said. "There's always one guy who ends up shirtless after a couple of beers."

He snorted softly. "Yeah, that's me."

Not long later, Raquel and Hamish appeared on the deck, looking as ragged as Duncan and I did, clutching coffee and water and wincing at the sunlight.

No one said anything for a while, as we each tried to rouse ourselves into something resembling life.

A phone rang somewhere in the saloon.

"That's no *my* mobile," Hamish grumbled.

"Mine's in my purse in the room," Raquel said.

"My phone's been on vibrate since the day I got it," I said.

Duncan groaned. "It's mine. It's just so far away." With a heaving sigh, he lumbered to his feet and staggered into the saloon. "Hello? Oh, hey Uncle Brock. Uhhh...forget? Forget what?"

Raquel sat bolt upright. "The flight!"

Duncan held a hand out to silence her. "Yeah, we sorta celebrated a bit last night, so we're dragging ass. Sorry, Uncle B. Yeah, we can be there. All right, see you then. Bye."

"We tied a bit of one on last night," Hamish said. "I've no been that pissed in an age. Jaysus, I'm hungover."

"Is your uncle mad?" Raquel asked, sounding worried. "I feel bad. He's doing us a favor, and we don't show up."

Duncan shoved the phone in his back pocket,

shaking his head gingerly. "Nah, he's cool. He figured it was something like that. He's running a couple errands instead, so we have a couple hours to get our shit together and meet him at his dock."

"I need some greasy-ass food pronto," Raquel said. "So we need to drag our hungover asses to breakfast."

"Word," I said, levering myself out my chair. "And in my case, I need to retrieve my luggage from my room."

Ninety minutes later, we'd eaten said greasy-ass food and drank several buckets of coffee, retrieved my luggage, and were buckled into Duncan's uncle's seaplane as he piloted it away from Ketchikan.

Brock Badd was a silver fox. I'm not into old dudes, but this old dude was handsome as hell. Brown hair shot through with silver cut in a neat, classic, Old Hollywood side part, wearing mirrored aviators, he had chiseled, angular features, day-old stubble shadowing his rugged jaw, and a physique a man twenty years his junior would be jealous of.

I see now why Duncan claimed his physique was largely the result of unfair genetics—I saw the resemblance, as well. Duncan definitely favored Brock, especially in the jawline and the lean, hard build.

Brock greeted Raquel and Hamish with gentle handshakes and congratulations, waving off Raquel's profuse apologies for oversleeping our original departure time.

When he greeted his nephew, he did so loudly, effusively, with a lot of rough, unnecessary back slapping—giving him shit for being hungover, in a teasing way.

Me, he greeted with a speculative look, a gentle hug, and a knowing grin. What he thinks he knows, I couldn't have said, but he obviously thinks he knows something about me, or about me and Duncan. I smiled back as if I was clueless and took my seat on the seaplane.

You couldn't really hear anything over the drone of the propellers, so all four of us opted to close our eyes and try to rest on the flight.

I jolted awake with a mortifyingly porcine snort as the seaplane touched down. "Wha—?"

Duncan's shoulder was a firm, warm support under my left ear. He patted my thigh. "We just landed in Anchorage."

"Oh. I fell asleep, huh?" I said, sitting upright.

Duncan chuckled. "Yeah, you were out for the count." He grinned at me. "You, uh, have some…" his thumb slid over the corner of my lip.

I groaned, even more embarrassed. "I was *drooling*? Someone shoot me."

He just laughed again. "Hey, drool happens. Don't worry about it."

I rolled my eyes. "I fell asleep on you, drooled on you, and snorted like Babe the pig when I woke up. I think that's plenty of grounds to be embarrassed."

His deep brown eyes danced with humor, and he pinched my chin. "You're adorable, Rune. Drooling and snorting and all."

"Adorable," I muttered. "Lovely. Every girl longs to be adorable because she drools and snorts in her sleep." The noise of the engines, however, meant Duncan didn't hear this part.

Brock taxied us to a dock, where a dockworker moored us to a pylon. After thanking Brock, Raquel and Hamish went in search of a taxi to the hotel while Duncan and I hung back to talk to Brock.

"My friend with the jet has confirmations from everyone," he said. "So that's all set. Duncan, when you two are ready to come back to Ketchikan, just let me know and I'll come pick you guys up."

"It'll just be Duncan, actually," I said. "My flight back to LA is out of Anchorage, now. I switched it around the other day."

Brock frowned. "Oh, really? I was under the impression that you two were an item."

Duncan coughed in surprise, glancing at me with a shrug. "I have no idea where you'd have gotten that impression, Uncle B. We're just friends."

Brock smirked—and again, I saw where Duncan

got his propensity for devilish smirks; Brock's was every bit as debonair, mischievous, and tempting as Duncan's. In an old guy to whom I'm not attracted sort of way, I mean.

Geez, get a grip, Rune.

"Right, right," Brock said, his voice dripping with teasing sarcasm, "just friends."

"Uncle B, come on." Duncan was blushing furiously, giving his uncle a *don't do this to me* glare. "For real. We're just friends."

"OH LOOK," I said too loudly, "RAQUEL AND HAMISH HAVE A CAB."

I scuttled away, hauling my hard-sided roller suitcase behind me, my carry-on duffel smacking the small of my back, while my purse flounced at my hip; I'm not running, you're running.

Duncan and Brock did the manly handshake-and-hug thing, and then Duncan slung a sleek black leather duffel bag over one shoulder and followed after me. He caught up as I was heaving my bags into the trunk of the taxi van.

"Sorry about Uncle Brock being nosy," he murmured to me. "My family has no sense of personal boundaries."

"It's all good," I said. "No worries. I've got nosy family too."

He caught my hand after I closed the hatch. "Hey. About us being just friends…I hope you understand I only meant—"

"Duncan," I said, cutting in over him. "It's the truth. We're just friends. We may have, um…messed around a bit," I leaned closer to him, "and probably will some more before the weekend is over, but we both know this is…" I trailed off with a shrug.

"It has a built-in expiration date," Duncan answered, although he didn't sound entirely thrilled.

"Exactly." I took one of his hands. "Look, Duncan. I…I do like you. A lot. I just…I've been away from LA for more than two months. After finding out about Hayes, I sort of left town and never went back. But I… my family is there. My condo is there. My life is there. I have to go home."

He sighed heavily, nodding. "I know. I get it. And it's cool. I mean, a part of me does wish we could spend more than just this weekend together, but you have to go home. And I need to focus on running the Kitty. Dad and Delia took a risk trusting me as the GM, and I'm not about to let them down, especially not because I'm getting distracted." His eyes widened. "Not that you're a distraction, I just meant—"

I laughed, putting a hand over his mouth. "Relax, I know what you meant, Duncan. It's okay. We both know this is what it is, and we both have lives to get back to. In the meantime, we can have fun with each other and know that when it's time to go our separate ways, it's with mutual respect and understanding. Yeah?"

He grinned. "Yeah. Exactly."

Raquel leaned out of the open sliding door. "Hey, you two. C'mon. We need to check in and then go meet the manager of the venue."

The hotel was either newly built or freshly remodeled—there was a strong smell of fresh paint in the lobby, and men in construction gear wandered around in pairs and groups. Raquel and Hamish were already at the check-in desk, conversing with the receptionist.

"Our manager heard about the reason you guys are here," the receptionist said—she was a young woman, possibly Inuit or the like, based on her skin, hair, and facial tattoos. "He has upgraded your reservation to the penthouse suite, on us."

Raquel seemed like she was about to start crying. "Oh my god, that's so kind of you. Thank you so much!"

A few minutes later, a bellhop or whatever they're called these days was escorting the couple up to their room, and Duncan and I took our place at the desk.

"What's the name the reservation is under?" she asked, addressing us both.

"Oh, um, it should be two separate ones," Duncan answered. "One under Badd, B-A-D-D, and the other under Rigby." He glanced at me. "Right? R-I-G-B-Y?"

I nodded. "Right. I made my reservation the same

day as they did," I said, indicating Raquel and Hamish where they waited at a bank of elevators.

"I made mine the day after," Duncan said. "If it matters."

There was a long moment of silence punctuated only by sporadic typing, and then the receptionist frowned at us. "Um, hmm. I see your reservations here, but there's been a bit of an issue."

Duncan sighed. "I see. And what is the issue?"

She waved at the construction workers swarming the lobby. "We're finishing some renovations, as you see, and with the rest of the wedding party all making reservations at the same time…" she typed some more. "We've oversold, unfortunately. A whole floor is under construction at the moment—it was supposed to be done by now, but there's been some delays."

"So…what?" I asked. "You're saying there's not enough rooms?"

She gave a simpering, apologetic smile. "Unfortunately, yes. We only have one room available."

Duncan and I exchanged glances.

"So…" Duncan raked a hand through his hair. "There's no other solution? You've only got one room left in the whole hotel? When I called, no one said anything about renovations. I was told there would be plenty of rooms."

She sighed unhappily. "Well, sir, as I said, it was supposed to have been done by now, but there was some sort of delay. The information you were given was supposed to have been true, but unfortunately no longer is. I'm sorry for the inconvenience."

Duncan opened his mouth, looking like he was about to ream her out. I squeezed his hand. "Duncan, it's fine. We can share. We're both adults. It's fine, I promise."

The receptionist looked relieved. "The room I have available is a single king bed suite. It's actually one of our nicest rooms and has a window facing the bay. I can give it to you for a pretty significant discount, as well, to make up for the inconvenience."

A single bed?

I looked up at Duncan, and saw that he was likely thinking the same thing I was—it's not like we would have spent too much time in our individual rooms anyway, considering how combustible our physical chemistry is.

Duncan nodded, flipping a hand. "Yeah, that's fine. Thank you."

We barely had time to set our bags down and take a quick peek at the room—which was, as advertised, a nice one, with a stellar view and a spacious bathroom. No sooner had we both sat down on the bed with nearly-in-unison sighs than Raquel was blowing up my phone, wanting to know when we could meet in the lobby and go see the venue.

I patted Duncan's rock-hard thigh. "C'mon, then. Raquel is a little excited, if you couldn't tell."

He chuckled. "Yeah, I noticed. But she's getting

married, and Hamish seems like a great dude. It's good she's excited."

"Hamish is as great as he seems," I said.

He glanced at me. "You're okay sharing a room?"

I shrugged. "Not like we have much choice." I grinned up at him. "I doubt we'll be getting much sleep, though."

His answering grin held promises of long, sweaty, delightful nights to come. "No, I don't think we will."

My phone buzzed with another incoming message from Raquel. "Come on," I said, dragging myself upright. "We'd better go before Raquel has an aneurysm."

We headed down to the lobby together. It was so crowded that Duncan had to take my hand so we didn't get separated, and then once we were through the crush around the elevators, neither of us seemed inclined to let go.

Raquel's eyes flicked to our joined hands, and a small smile flitted across her face—I immediately let go of Duncan's hand and put a bit of distance between us.

Duncan informed us that the restaurant was within walking distance from the hotel, so we set out on foot.

"Sorry about the state of the hotel," Ducan said as we walked. "I had no idea it was being remodeled. They didn't tell me that when I called. I don't visit this location much."

"Hey, I'm grateful, Duncan," Raquel said. "Our room is amazing. I'm happy."

"How are your rooms?" Hamish asked.

I snorted. "You mean *room*, singular. They ran out, so we're sharing."

Raquel didn't even try to suppress a snort of laughter. "I bet that's gonna be a hardship."

"We're just friends, Raquel," I said. "Don't make it weird."

"I'll tell you what, though," Hamish said, grinning, "I've never kissed any of my friends the way you two were snogging last night. It's a bloody miracle you didn't end up fornicatin' right there on the bloody fuckin' deck in front of us."

Duncan and I traded glances. "Um, what?" I asked.

Raquel cackled. "You guys were *so* wasted, ya'll. I'm not surprised you don't remember. I do, though."

"Yeah, well, you're annoying, because you never black out," I said.

She just shrugged. "I can't help that I remember everything. Trust me, Rune, there've been a few nights I wish I *could* forget."

"Like that party at the Kappa Kappa Gamma house?" I said.

Her eyes narrowed. "We won't be discussing that." Her tone was arch and prim.

I laughed. "But why ever not, Raquel?"

She looked sidelong at Hamish, who was watching his fiancée with amused curiosity. "Rune, don't."

"Something I should know, my love?" Hamish asked, grinning. "I feel like there's a story here."

"You were back home in Scotland, visiting your family over the holidays, before we were serious." She shrugged, waved a hand. "I got a little messy. No story."

I cackled at her response. "No story? I beg to differ."

"Well then?" Hamish said, covering Raquel's mouth as she tried to protest. "Do tell."

I spent the rest of the walk telling a truthful but embellished version of the story, which involved Raquel, Jell-O shots, and a dance-off, which ended up with Raquel covered in body paint, glitter, and nothing else except her underwear. The more I told, the harder everyone laughed…except Raquel, who was laughing while also protesting certain embellishments.

"Okay, first of all," she said, pointing a finger in my face, "I had pasties on! And second, I *did not twerk*. I'm a *dancer*. There's nothing wrong with twerking, as a thing, but that bitch challenged me to a dance-off! I brought my A-game, and my A-game does not include twerking."

"The only thing I'm no exactly clear on," Hamish said, "is how a dance-off led you to being body-painted and covered in glitter." *Glitter* ended up sounding more like *gl-IH-rrr*, with a curling roll of the r-sound.

"Don't worry about it, baby," Raquel said. "The reason is I was wasted and making damn fool choices. And my *friends*, instead of stopping me, thought it'd be funny to egg my drunk ass on."

I slung an arm around her shoulders. "Raquel, you

know we wouldn't have let you do anything too bad. You did indeed have pasties on, and underwear, and even though you were three sheets to the wind, you still kicked that girl's ass in the dance-off."

"Damn right I did," she muttered.

We arrived at the restaurant, then. It was designed to look like a hunting lodge, with lots of heavy live-edge logs, a green metal roof, and lots of glass. Inside had the feel of an upscale steakhouse—low lighting, deep booths of rich leather, tea lights on the table, a quiet, slow-moving atmosphere, and a live pianist playing tinkling covers of top pop hits. Servers in all black with long aprons glided this way and that, carrying round trays of drinks and oval trays of food. Conversation was a low hubbub at best.

Raquel's eyes were gleaming. "This place is *gorgeous*, Duncan!"

He shrugged. "Feels weird to say thanks, since I didn't have anything to do with it. I was only a year or so out of high school when Delia moved up here to revamp this place." He looked around, assessing, and nodded. "It is very nice. Looks like it's running well, too." He paused. "Ah, here's Rebecca."

A woman in her early thirties approached us— she had black hair, blue eyes, and was wearing a black pencil skirt, low pumps, and a silk maroon blouse; she had a clipboard in one arm.

"Duncan! Great to see you again!" She greeted Duncan with a professional handshake. "And you must be Hamish and Raquel. I'm Rebecca, the manager. Welcome to Badd's Fine Dining, you guys. I have to say, we're *so* pleased to host your wedding. We have everything ready to go. Would you like to see?"

Raquel nodded eagerly. "Yes, I would, very much."

She showed us the kitchen and introduced us to Anton, the head chef, and then escorted us to the back room—a capacious space big enough to hold at least a hundred people. Long tables lined a far wall, draped in spotless white tablecloths, topped with trays waiting for burners and food. A dozen large round tables dotted the middle of the room, also draped in white, and a temporary parquet dance floor took up a quarter of the space at one end of the room, with the DJ booth nearby. A set of double doors led out to the back patio, which was where the wedding itself would be held. The restaurant was at the edge of town, on a large lot with a wide swath of verdant lawn behind the building. An arch wreathed in white roses stood at one end of the green space, with several rows of folding chairs facing it, an aisle running between the blocks of chairs to the double doors.

Raquel stopped at the arch, looking around with watery eyes. "It's perfect! It's even better than our venue in Ketchikan. Isn't it, Hamish?"

Hamish nodded, his expression shuttered and serious—hiding his emotions, I think. "Aye, it is. It's right lovely. You've done a fine, fine job, Rebecca, and our thanks to you and your staff for puttin' this on in such short notice."

Rebecca beamed with pride. "For a long time, the back room was wasted space—it was originally designed to be an extra dining space, but no one ever wanted to be this far from the main room. It was my idea to host weddings here. The fortunate thing for you is that we had a last-minute cancellation, beyond the point of refunding and returning everything, so we had all of this on hand already. It was just a matter of setting it up." She looked around, taking in the space. "Is there anything you'd like changed, removed, or added?"

Raquel shook her head, sniffling and swiping a finger under her eyes. "No, no. It's absolutely perfect. The centerpieces are just adorable."

Each table, back in the event room, held a glass jar filled with tiny twinkling white string lights, baby's breath, and a live lily, surrounded by pink rose petals. Once evening had fallen and the lights were dimmed, the effect would be magical, I was sure.

Raquel, Hamish, and Rebecca headed to the kitchen to go over the menu, which left Duncan and me to our own devices.

It was awkwardly silent for a few minutes.

"Uh, you…you don't remember making out, do you?" Duncan asked, eventually, sounding sheepish. "Because I don't. Sadly."

I shook my head, wincing at him. "No, I don't either."

He sighed in relief. "Glad I'm not the only one. I'd have really felt like a dick."

I glanced at him. "Duncan, be real with me. Why are you doing all this for people you don't know?"

He shrugged, but spent a few moments thinking before answering. "To be honest, you."

"Me?" My heart twisted and clenched at his answer. "Meaning?"

Another shrug. "I dunno, Rune. It all just sorta… snowballed. You needed a date to the wedding, and I had nothing going on this weekend. I'd probably have ended up pulling an extra shift or two."

"I really don't mean this as a dig, so please don't take it as one, but you don't have much of a social life, do you?" I asked.

He laughed ruefully, shaking his head. "Nah, not really. All my friends from school and football moved. I go out once in a while. I date."

I snickered. "Date means hookup, though, right?"

He arched an eyebrow at me. "Sometimes. Is that a problem?"

I held up my hands in a gesture of surrender. "No! Not at all."

"Rune." His tone said he didn't believe me.

I sighed. "Fine. I'm judging a little bit, but only because my experience with men is that they're all players. I guess…I…" I paused and thought. "Maybe I'm unfairly judging you based on my own experiences, but I've learned that players are gonna play. A guy who's

smooth and charming and experienced…like you…
doesn't usually have much of a relationship with truth,
honesty, and fidelity. That's my experience. I'm not
saying you're like that, Duncan, I swear. Although that
was my initial impression of you."

He didn't answer for a minute. "I'm not smooth."

"Yeah, you are. You've got lines, Duncan."

"They're not lines, Rune. I'm just saying what I
think." He rubbed the back of his neck, and my stupid eyes couldn't help watching the way his big, thick
bicep shifted and rippled as he moved his arm; yum
yum. "I understand the impression you may have gotten, though. It's true I don't typically do relationships,
but honestly, it's only because I haven't met anyone I've
been interested in enough to give a real relationship a
try. I'm not a player. I'm really not."

"Have you ever had a serious girlfriend?" I asked.

He shook his head. "Nah. I dated a girl for six
months my senior year, but that's it. We graduated,
and she moved to Chicago for school."

"Since then?"

"Since then there's never been anyone I was serious about. There was this girl who worked at the
Kitty over the summer last year, before I was the GM.
Shannon. I really liked her. But it was a summer job,
and she made it clear she wasn't staying past the sea-
son." He glanced at me, his expression curious. "You
think less of me because I've never been in love?"

I thought about this. "No, I don't. I just personally

have always liked being in a relationship. I've hooked up randomly here and there between relationships, but…" I trailed off.

"But what?" Duncan pressed.

"But in my experience, hookup sex isn't as good as relationship sex."

He frowned thoughtfully. "Really? Why, do you think?"

"Hmmm. That's hard to answer."

"But you've clearly thought about it some. Or talked to one of your girlfriends about it," he said.

"Yeah," I agreed. "Both. I talk to my friend Lindsey about pretty much everything. I guess…" I thought some more. "I guess it's about emotions, for me. I'm not a prude—clearly. But I just…in a relationship, there's an emotional connection. I can enjoy sex without that, but it's better with it. It's deeper, and that's not an innuendo or anything. When you're with someone for a longer period of time, in my experience, at least, your sexual relationship changes as your emotional one does, naturally enough. It grows. You learn things about each other. There's a certain…comfort, I suppose, in sharing that with the same person for a long time."

Duncan was silent for a long time, processing this. "Honestly, Rune, no bullshit—with you and me…is it hookup sex?"

My heart did a somersault. I swallowed hard. "I don't know, Duncan. That's the honest answer. We haven't had actual sex yet, for one thing. But…" I sighed. "If I wasn't going back to LA, yes, I think you and I could have something. Which I think is what you're getting at."

He sighed at this. "I appreciate the honesty. I guess a lot of me wishes you didn't have to go back to LA. At least, not so soon."

I swallowed hard. "Duncan, god. Don't go there. Please? Can we just…can we not?"

He nodded. "Yeah, I got you." He stood up. "I'm gonna go check on…um. Things."

I watched him go, trying to ignore the way certain non-physical parts of me ached at the obvious conflict in Duncan. At the fact that part of me wished the same thing.

I let him go, though.

And I wondered if sharing a room and bed for the next two nights might be more problematic than I'd originally expected.

NINE

Duncan

RETURNING TO THE HOTEL AFTER VISITING THE restaurant was significantly more eventful than our initial arrival. Raquel and Hamish preceded Rune and me—walking a bit apart, the air between us a bit tense—into the lobby, and were immediately greeted by a cacophony of wedding attendees swarming them. Rune was swept up in the mayhem since these were her friends as well, leaving me standing awkwardly alone at the outer edge of the fray, watching with bemusement as fifty-some people all tried to hug and back-clap and air-kiss each other all at once.

Most of the attention was on Raquel and Hamish, naturally enough—they couldn't move for the crush of humans all trying to get to them. I noticed, however, that once the appropriate greetings and congratulations had been extended to the happy couple, Rune was the next stop—every direction she turned saw her hugging someone, laughing, answering questions, and trying to extricate herself from one conversation only to be dragged into another.

There was one anomaly in the scene: a pretty-boy, preppy nerd type dude standing by himself off to one side, his eyes glued to Rune as she lit up the lobby with her charismatic presence, her bell-like laugh ringing clarion-clear throughout the lobby, sapphire eyes bright and joyful, ink-black, stormcloud hair a thick, plaited cascade over one shoulder. He was about six feet tall and lean—a distance runner build—with sandy blond hair carefully coiffed in a less classy version of Uncle Brock's neat, classic side-part. He was clean shaven, with a weak jaw and an expression of sour longing that curdled my stomach.

As I watched him watch Rune, the sour longing went briefly bitter and angry and jealous: she was hugging a tall, built Black guy who I assumed was Raquel's brother—he resembled her pretty obviously, for one thing. I could only snort to myself in cruel amusement though—it was obvious enough to me, someone with pretty real feelings for Rune, that her relationship with Raquel's brother was platonic and brotherly. Yet the preppy dick-waffle was jealous.

I couldn't help myself. I sidled over toward where Rune's ex was wallflowering, endeavoring to appear casual and unassuming. Hayes noted me idly and dismissed me immediately—he didn't know me, didn't recognize me, and so I wasn't worth his attention. I pretended to follow his obvious stare for the first time.

"Wow, she's hot, huh?" I said, pitching my voice low, conspiratorial. "That ass, amiright?"

He shot me an annoyed look. "Huh? You talking to me?"

I jutted my chin at Rune, who was clutching Raquel's brother's hand with obvious affection, listening as he related a story that had Rune cackling. "Her, with the black hair and blue eyes. Rain, I think her name is?"

What was I doing? Why was I fucking with this tool?

Because he was a tool, that's why. Also, I didn't like the way he was looking at Rune.

"Rune," he muttered. "Her name is Rune."

"Ah, right." I hesitated. "You friends with her?"

He shot me a glance that said he'd rather eat a live cockroach than have this conversation with me. "You could say that."

"Maybe you could introduce me, then."

He turned to face me fully, then, angry. "Do I know you, bro?"

I opened my mouth to answer—I wasn't even sure myself what was about to come out of my mouth—when Rune happened to glance this way and saw Hayes and me standing near each other. Her features went slack at first, and then raw, naked fury suffused her expression. She met my eyes, confused.

I winked at her, and then turned to Hayes. "Wow, she *really* doesn't like you, does she?"

He opened his mouth to answer, clicked his jaw shut, tried again. "Fuck you," he managed, eventually.

I snickered. "Hey, man, I'm just observing, here. You *do* know her, don't you?"

The douche-turd's face went through a series of emotions, most of them a form of embarrassed anger. "Used to. Now, if you don't mind, I see someone I'd like to talk to."

"It's probably not Rune, I'm guessing," I said. "Going off the way she looked at you just now."

He whirled on me mid-step. "You got something to say to me, bro?"

I just laughed—this skinny little punk was about as much of a threat to me as a wet kitten. "If I did, I'd say it...*bro*."

I pushed past him, "accidentally" bumping him with my shoulder—I was more than half hoping he'd try something just so I could break his sad sack of shit jaw. He didn't, though, more's the pity. I felt his angry glare on my back, but he didn't otherwise do or say anything.

I beelined through the scrum of people to Rune, knowing he was watching. I stepped right into her space. "Play along," I murmured, giving her a mischievous grin.

"Play along with what?" she answered, keeping her face carefully neutral.

"This." I grabbed her by the hips and yanked her flush against me; she gasped in shock at the move, stiff at first, and then she melted against me.

I cupped her face in one hand, tilted her mouth to mine, and kissed the everloving fuck out of her. All tongue, no chill.

She whimpered into the kiss, momentarily forgetting our surroundings as our natural chemistry took over. Shit, I lost track of everything myself as she stabbed her tongue into my mouth and shoved her chest against mine, rubbed her pussy against my thigh, and stole her hands into my hair.

She was the one to come to her senses first, yanking free with a shake of her head, stepping back and dragging her wrist across her mouth. "What the *hell* was that, Duncan?"

"Check out your ex before you lay into me," I said.

Her gaze flicked over my shoulder, and I knew my ploy had had an effect. She bit her lower lip in an attempt to not burst into laughter. "Oh. Oh god."

"That was gloriously done, sir," I heard a woman's voice say from my left elbow. "I applaud you. Bravo, bravo." She even clapped; the speaker, except for having white-blond hair, could have been Rune's twin sister—their facial structure was damn near identical, as was the shade of their sapphire eyes. "You must be Duncan Badd."

I extended my hand to her. "I am. I'm guessing you're Lindsey, the best friend?"

"Yup." She covered her mouth with one hand, spluttering a laugh, and then shook my hand. "Oh man, he *big* mad."

If looks could kill, I'd be dead—Hayes was glaring daggers at me from across the room; hate wouldn't be too far from the truth.

Rune, however, was looking at me, not Hayes, two fingers pressed to her lips. She looked like she was about to say something to me, but someone tapped her on the shoulder, and the moment was gone.

Lindsey leaned close to me, murmuring so only I could hear her. "How's it going with her?"

"No idea what you mean," I said.

"That was a hell of a kiss," Lindsey said. "She was shooketh."

"Things are weird," I admitted.

"She's a tough nut to crack," Lindsey said, watching Rune navigate three different conversations at once. "Her luck with men hasn't been the best."

"So she said."

"She likes you."

I sighed. "Maybe. But she's going back to LA. Once this wedding is done, that's it. She's established pretty clear boundaries."

Lindsey shrugged. "There are ways around that boundary."

"No, there's not." When she looked at me with an arched eyebrow, I shrugged back at her. "She set a boundary. Whatever this is between us, it's over when the wedding is over. She's clear on that. Trying to fight it isn't going to get me anywhere."

"I've never seen her react like that. To anyone, ever, let alone from a public kiss." She looked at me. "There's something there."

"Maybe there is," I said. "But there's no point in thinking about it."

She looked at me with disgust. "And you're just... giving up?"

I stared back at her. "Sorry, but I was raised to respect the boundaries a woman establishes. She's acknowledged there could be more, but she's also made it extremely clear that's not happening."

Lindsey sighed, a frustrated sound of resignation. "She doesn't know what she wants. She's run as far as she can for as long as she can from the damage that turd-sucker Hayes Motherfucking Willoughby did to her, and now she's going back to what's familiar."

"I get that," I said, "But I can't make her want something. We've known each other barely a week. Sure, there's killer fucking chemistry, but it takes more than that."

"Well, I'm not giving up. It takes a lot to shake Rune, and I'm telling you she's all shook up from that kiss." Lindsey patted me on the bicep, paused, frowned at my arm, and then blatantly felt up my bicep. "Damn, son. You got a permit for those guns?"

I snorted, pulling my arm out of her grip. "Okay, we're good."

"Oh, relax. She's my BFF, I'd never poach her man. I'm just appreciating a nice set of arms."

"I'm not her man."

"You could be, if you had balls." She cackled. "I'm kidding, I'm kidding. Jesus, relax. You're so wound up, Duncan."

I blinked at her. "You're a lot, you know that?"

She nodded seriously. "I do know. Trust me. There's a reason I'm single. Being a mouthy, sarcastic, know-it-all, pain in the ass is that reason, to be clear."

I laughed. "You'd get along great with my sisters."

"I would. Why?"

"Because they're both mouthy, sarcastic, know-it-all pains in the ass."

"And they're both still single?"

"Nope. Delia is married to Hunter Hawkins. Emerson is married to a computer programmer who gives serious Clark Kent vibes."

"Excuse me?" She turned slowly to face me. "Sorry, sorry, but it sounded like you said your sister is married to *Hunter Hawkins*?"

"That is what I said, yes."

She blinked up at me. "Pardon me, but the fuck you say."

I laughed. "It's true. He tried a corporate takeover of our family business a few years ago."

"Tried?"

I shrugged. "He ended up marrying into the family, funding the revamp of the restaurant Raquel and

Hamish are getting married at tomorrow, and now they have a kid together."

"Your sister snagged the world's most eligible bachelor?"

I got out my phone and pulled up a photograph of Delia, Hunter, and me together from a weekend trip I took to NYC to see them over the spring. I swiped to show her a pic I took of Hunter, Delia, and Sebastian, my nephew. "That's them with their son."

Lindsey sighed, disgusted. "Well there goes my fantasy of Hunter Hawkins sweeping me off my feet and taking me to his private island estate in the Mediterranean for a week of swinging-from-the-chandeliers sex."

"He sold that estate off last year," I said.

She frowned at me. "That was a joke."

I cackled. "Well, he really did have a Mediterranean estate, and he *did* have a habit of bringing girls there, before he met Delia."

"So I could have had a week of hot monkey sex at Hunter Hawkins's Mediterranean estate, but I'm too late?"

"Yup."

She shook her head. "There's no justice in this world. I swear." She eyed me speculatively. "You have any brothers?"

I stared back blankly. "Yes, one. He's an ugly old troll who lives under a bridge."

"I can't tell if you're joking or not, Dora."

Rune crashed our conversation, then. "Stop gossiping about me, you two."

Lindsey flipped her off. "You could have told me his brother-in-law is Hunter Hawkins. You know how I feel about that man."

Rune rolled her eyes. "I only found out myself recently. And you were never gonna get with him, babe."

"I could have, you don't know. I can be very alluring, I'll have you know." She tossed her hair with a funny little bob-and-shake of her head and a faux-prim expression.

Rune just laughed, wrapping her friend in a side hug. "Never change, Linz. I really do love you, even though you're a crazy woman."

"SHOTS IN THE HOTEL BAR!" someone yelled, and the wedding crowd herded into the hotel bar, swarmed the bartender, and then it was off to the races.

To say mayhem ensued is to vastly understate the case.

Rune's friend group could seriously drink, and this is coming from someone who grew up in bars, with a family that took partying to a whole other level.

Even though no one knew who the fuck I was, they included me without question, especially after I beat their reigning chugging contest champion. I tried to behave myself at first, but by the time the fourth round of tequila shots had been passed around, there was no holding back.

My shirt came off, as usual.

I watched Rune throughout the evening—she was obviously avoiding me, choosing to spend most of her time flitting from person to person, group to group. She was one of the most popular people in the group, too, along with Lindsey and Raquel. Those three, at some point in the evening, took up spots together at a round high top near the center of the bar and held court there.

In some ways, it was fascinating seeing Rune in the context of her friends—she was loose, wild, effusive, loud, funny, and charismatic. And by loose, I mean free and uninhibited, not loose as in free with her sexual mores. I couldn't look away from her.

Specifically, I found myself staring at her mouth. Her plump red lips, moving as she spoke, wide as she laughed. I couldn't stop thinking about how soft they were, how they felt slicking against mine. How they looked wrapped around my cock....

Fuck.

"You're pinin', lad," A Scottish-accented voice said to me.

Startled, I turned and saw Hamish beside me, a fresh pint of beer in his hand, looking as tipsy as I felt. "I'm not pining."

Hamish laughed into his beer as he took a long swig, lowering the glass to show foam sticking to his bushy red mustache. "You are so." He gestured at the trio of girls. "You haven't taken your eyes off our Rune the whole night."

I rubbed my upper lip. "You've got foam on your stache."

He took another swig, letting even more foam coat his upper lip. "Aye, and dinna try an' change the subject on me."

"I'm not pining. She's avoiding me and it's annoying."

"She hasn't seen her friends in two months. Don't read too much into it."

"Yeah, but it's not just that. She's definitely avoiding me."

Hamish snorted. "She is no."

"Watch." I took my pint glass and wandered casually across the floor, dodging people.

I reached the table where Rune, Lindsey, and Raquel were camped out, pretending to not realize who was at the table until I made a show of noticing.

"Oh, hey," I said. "Lindsey, Raquel, Rune. Having a fun night, ladies?"

Raquel, who at some point had acquired a bride-to-be sash and a plastic-and-glitter crown, lifted a rocks glass toward the ceiling. "Best night ever!"

Lindsey lifted her glass in support. "So far!"

Rune, however, chewed on her black cocktail straw, eyeing me warily, as if I were a wild beast she wasn't sure it was safe to approach. "I need the ladies' room," she said. "Linz, you coming?"

Lindsey allowed Rune to haul her away, leaving me alone at the table with Raquel. I tried to think of something to say to Raquel, but I was saved when a cluster of four drunk blondes accosted her. I left the table and wandered back to Hamish.

"See?" I said. "Avoiding me."

Hamish pulled a face, nodding. "You may have a point, anyway." He had wiped clean his mustache at some point and was already on a fresh beer. His gaze narrowed, anger clouding his features. "That hackit wee jessie's got our girl cornered."

I stared at him. "The fuck does that mean?"

He gestured with his glass at the hallway where the bathrooms were—Hayes had one hand braced against the wall, blocking Rune from exiting the hallway. Whatever he was saying, it was only pissing her off.

I started toward the hallway, but Hamish's blocky big fist caught my arm and held me in place. "Nae, lad, let the numpty dig his own grave. This is a confrontation two months in the making. He's been spoutin' shite about her since she left him, and now it's all come due. It's her fight, Duncan."

"Maybe so, but I'm gonna be there just in case." I jerked my arm out of his grip and pushed through the crowd, taking up a spot near the hallway mouth where I could watch and listen without being obvious.

"…Didn't give me a chance to explain, Rune!" Hayes was saying. "You popped off and threw my trophies at my fucking head!"

Rune growled in frustrated rage. "Hayes, you fucking moron! There's no explanation you could *possibly* give that would make anything better!"

"But—"

"No, stop—just fucking stop. Did you or did you not put your penis in that girl's vagina?"

"Well…we…I…"

"It's a very simple question, you lumpy sack of fucks. *Yes* or *no*?"

"Yes, but—"

"Ohmy*god*, Hayes! Just fucking *stop*! The cheating was just the last straw, you do realize that, don't you?" She got in his face, shouting. "You are a terrible human being! You were a terrible boyfriend. Yes, you have a pretty face, but you're a pathetic piece of shit! You know how many different mental and emotional hangups you gave me?"

I noticed a distinct reduction in the volume of the bar; a quick glance told me people had noticed the confrontation and were tuning in.

"What are you talking about?" Hayes demanded. "I loved you!"

"Oh *fuck you*! Fuck you till the end of time, Hayes Mother*fucking* Willoughby. If the way you treated me when we were together was love, then I shudder to think how you treat people you don't like. You fucked me up, *bad*."

Rune hadn't noticed that everyone was watching and listening, and something told me she wouldn't want this kind of attention. I had to do something.

I shoved through the crowd, climbed up onto the bar, and held my pint glass up. "I'd like to propose a toast!" I shouted, drawing everyone's attention to myself. "We're all here for two people! Raquel and Hamish!"

Everyone cheered, and glasses were lifted to the ceiling.

"I just met you guys yesterday, but I can already tell that you're my kind of people. My toast is simple, you two. Here's to a long and happy life together."

I hopped down, ignoring the dirty look from the bartender, and stole a look around the room—I spotted Rune exiting the hotel bar and vanishing into the lobby, her keycard for our room in hand.

I set my nearly-empty glass down on the nearest table and hustled after her. She vanished into a full elevator, the door closing on her; she was breathing hard, visibly upset. I couldn't tell by her face if she was crying or not since her head was ducked, chin to her chest, but judging by the way her shoulders were heaving, she was definitely crying.

I snagged the next elevator and rode it up to our floor, arriving at our room right as it the door clicked closed.

I opened it with my card and stepped inside. Rune was facing away from the door, shoulders shaking. "Go away, Duncan."

I halted behind her, close enough to touch, to wrap my arms around her—I didn't, yet. "'Lumpy sack of fucks' was a truly inspired insult. I'm for sure stealing that one."

She sniffled a laugh. "Thanks. Doesn't do him justice, though."

"No, it certainly doesn't. What did you ever see in that putz in the first place?"

"I wish I could say. I don't remember. He's not even as good looking as I used to think he was." She inhaled, held it, and let out a long shuddery breath. "Why did you do that, Duncan?"

"Do what?"

"Oh, I dunno, bait Hayes? Kiss me like that in front of the whole bar? Jump up and do a big toast when you don't even know anyone?"

"Well, answering in order..." I cleared my throat and started over. "Number one, I baited Hayes Motherfucking Willoughby—"

"I think we can just call him Hayes at this point. The whole name thing is getting exhausting, and I'm tired of giving him my time, attention, or energy."

"Fine by me," I said. "So, to continue. I baited him because I saw him glaring at you like he was pissed at you for even existing. It made me angry on your behalf, so I decided to fuck with him. Number two, I kissed you like that for two reasons. One, because I'm fucking obsessed with kissing you. Number two, because I knew it would really get that bitch's goat seeing me kiss you. And then as for the toast thing, that was for you."

"Um, you're gonna have to explain that one? How was it for me?" She finally turned around and looked up at me, her big blue eyes wet with tears.

"Well, after you ran away from me in your haste to avoid me, Hayes followed you. I saw him corner you outside the bathroom." I held up a finger. "Actually, I gotta give credit where it's due—it was Hamish who saw it first. I could tell you were getting upset, so I went over and listened, in case you needed backup."

"I can handle Hayes on my own, but thanks."

"Handling Hayes wasn't the issue, Rune." I dropped my voice to a murmur. "You guys were shouting at each other. The whole bar had gone quiet."

Her face paled. "What?"

"Everyone was watching and listening, Rune. *Everyone*. I…" I sighed, shrugged. "So I drew their attention to myself. I didn't think you'd like that kind of attention, especially not on the, um, *conversation* you were having, so I did something about it. The toast was the first thing I thought of."

"Oh." She sounded small and miserable. "I just don't get him, Duncan. Even after having months to think about it, Hayes *still* doesn't understand why I'm so angry at him. It feels like gaslighting, but I think he's just so narcissistic, he just genuinely doesn't see the problem."

"Rune—"

"I just feel so *stupid*," she whispered. "How could I have ever loved someone like that? I look back and all the signs are *right there*. Our first date, he never held a door. I paid for my own food. He was rude to the server."

"Well, there you go. Alongside the shopping cart theory, how someone treats service workers says everything about who they are."

Rune frowned up at me, tugging at the end of her braid. "Shopping cart theory?"

"It's a psychological, social thought experiment thing. Basically, it posits that the greatest litmus test of what kind of person you are is whether or not you return a shopping cart to the corral. I mean, think about it. There is absolutely no consequence whatsoever to not returning a cart. No one is going to yell at you. It's not illegal. It's not even really immoral or unethical or whatever. So, are you someone who returns a cart or not?"

She frowned, looking away in thought. "I always do. But Hayes never did. He'd leave it in the middle of the parking lot. It drove me nuts. Like, it takes all of sixty seconds, and it makes life that much easier for the poor assholes who have to round up the carts."

I laughed. "I was that poor asshole, as a matter of fact. My first job was at Safeway, collecting carts."

"I figured your first job would've been washing dishes for your parents," she said.

I snorted. "Oh I did that, I just didn't get paid for it. I actually got the job at Safeway so they couldn't keep making me wash dishes for free. Although looking back, I think that was their plan all along. I *hated* that job at Safeway. I lasted all of a month and a half before I was begging Dad to officially hire me as a dishwasher."

"Did it work?" she asked.

I nodded. "Oh yeah. I washed dishes at the original Badd's all through high school for pocket cash. Once I turned eighteen, they trained me in other jobs. They just had to see me develop my work ethic and drive."

"Your parents sound pretty cool."

"They are." I brushed a thumb under her eyes. "Why are you crying, Rune?"

"I'm just…angry. At Hayes. At myself. I'm also a little drunk, which makes me weepy sometimes."

I swept another tear aside as it fell, caught another at the corner of her mouth. "Don't cry, Smokeshow. He's not worth it."

Her wet blue gaze lifted to mine, and she nuzzled her mouth against my palm. "Don't, Duncan."

"Don't what…Rune?"

"Look at me like that."

"Can't help it."

"I'm going back to LA. My life is there."

"I know."

She pushed her lips into my palm, and then nuzzled her cheek against my hand, and her eyes slowly drooped closed. "I wish like hell you hadn't kissed me like that," she whispered.

"Why?" I asked.

"Because I can't stop thinking about it."

I shifted closer to her, and her breasts crushed against my chest, and her thighs pressed against mine. "Me either."

Her eyes snapped open, blazing brightly. "This doesn't change anything."

"What doesn't—"

Her lips slammed against mine, cutting off my words and stealing my breath. I growled, surprised, and then her tongue was sweeping against my lips and her hands were in my hair, pulling me down, and she was lifting on her toes and gasping and tilting her mouth to deepen the kiss.

Need took over, then, and I dipped at the knees, filled my hands with her ass, and lifted her. She immediately and instinctively hooked her legs around my waist, and her arms circled my neck and her hands clutched at my hair, and she kissed me with everything she had.

I walked us toward the bed, supporting her with one arm and peeling her shirt off with the other. She broke the kiss long enough to toss the garment one way, unhooking her bra and flinging that the other way.

With both of us topless, her heavy, lush, beautiful

tits swaying between us, she cupped my face in her hands and stole a soft, delicate kiss. "Tell me you have condoms, this time, Duncan. Please."

"In my toiletries bag," I answered.

She unhooked her legs and slid to the floor. "Go get them."

I went to my bag and ripped the zipper open, grabbed my leather toiletries case, and withdrew the new box of condoms, ripped it open, and tore free a few squares from the string.

When I turned back to the bed, Rune was wriggling out of her jeans, taking her panties with them. My eyes caught at the apex of her thighs, at the dripping honey of her arousal, and I stalked toward her.

She kicked her jeans and underwear aside, putting a palm to my chest as I reached her. "Wait."

"I'm no mood for games, Rune," I murmured in a low grumble. "I need to taste you."

She yanked at the fly of my jeans, roughly shoving them down. The waistband of my boxer briefs caught on my erection, and she pulled them away, dragging both garments down past my hips. I stepped out of them and kicked them aside, growling as Rune's hand wrapped around my cock.

"Rune, wait. I need—"

She spun us so my back was to the bed, stepping into me so I had to step backward. She took the condoms from me, tore one packet free, tossed the rest

toward the head of the bed, and ripped the packet open
with her teeth.

I opened my mouth to speak, but she lifted onto
her toes and shut me up with a kiss, rolling the condom
onto me hand over hand, eliciting a soft snarl from me.

"I don't want that right now, Duncan," she
breathed.

She clenched her arms around my neck and
gave me her full weight, forcing me to pick her up—I
palmed the soft warm flesh of her ass and lifted her,
and those strong thick legs circled my waist once more.
This time, there were no layers of clothing between
us, just the hot wet cradle of her sex against my belly
and the grip of her thighs around my hips. Clutching
my neck with one hand, Rune reached between us and
gripped my dick in the other, guided me to her opening. Pushing up with her thighs, she fit me into the
slick press of her seam.

"All I want is this." She claimed my mouth, demanded my tongue, and then broke away again as she
sank onto me. "Holy *shit*," she gasped as I slid a few
inches inside her. "Duncan, oh god, holy shit."

I lost my breath as she pulsed around me, hot and
tight and slick and wet, and my legs shook, and my eyes
squeezed shut and heat billowed through me. "Rune,
fuck, fuck, oh god fuck!"

I heard her whimper, a soft, quiet, almost broken sound.

"You okay?" I asked.

She pressed her face into the side of my neck and nodded. "You're just..." she tilted her hips subtly, and I slid a little deeper, drove a little further inside her. "You're fucking *huge*, Duncan."

I laughed, but it came out as more of a rough, ragged groan. "You...you really know how to..." I trailed off into a wordless, huffing growl of shocked ecstasy as she sank onto me further yet, taking me deeper, and now I was buried fully inside her, aching at the rippling squeeze of her vise-tight pussy. "Oh god, Rune. You really know how boost a man's ego, saying shit like that."

"I..." she had her arms cinched tight around my neck, face buried in the side of my throat, and she used her grip on my neck and shoulders to lift herself, dragging my cock back out through the hot clutch of her pussy, groaning at the slide of me through her rippling, spasming channel. "Oh my *god*, Duncan. Holy shit. Holy shit." She sounded like she could barely breathe, her words thin and breathless and shaky. "I knew you'd feel amazing inside me, but...oh god, oh god. I didn't know it would feel like *this*."

Words failed me. I needed...my god, what did I need? Her. All of her. More of her. I needed to move, to take her. To feel her slide and feel her come.

"Rune," I gasped. "I need to move."

She slid wet, stuttering kisses from my throat to my chin, to my jaw, to my mouth. "Duncan," she whispered. "Just...be gentle. You're a lot."

I growled into her mouth, tasted her whisper of need as I tilted my hips away to slide out of her.

"Ready?" I asked.

She nodded, her forehead touching mine, hair coming loose from the braid to waft in inky clouds around our faces.

I adjusted my grip on her ass, held her apart and let gravity ease her down around me as I drove a thrust up into her, moving slowly, gently.

She whimpered, shaking all over, and her fingers clawed into my neck and shoulders with a sharp, painful bite. "Duncan—holy *shit*." She let out a feral, keening, high-pitched wail as I bottomed out inside her, throwing her head backward.

"Again, Duncan," she pleaded, pulling back to stare into my eyes, hers wet and blue and bright and wild. "Do that again. Please."

TEN

Rune

I WAS BEING RIPPED APART BY DUNCAN'S COCK.

It was glorious.

I couldn't breathe for the fullness of him inside me, the aching, burning stretch sending pulsing throbs of wild arousal searing through me. My pussy couldn't possibly take any more of him—I thought. And then he slackened his claw-grip on my ass cheeks and let me fall while thrusting into me, and I realized I was wrong: I *could* take more of him. *So* much more.

My lungs seized, my blood boiling and my heart hammering, and the only sound I could manage was a shocked, whimpering gasp of ecstatic wonder as he filled me to a glutted, spasming ache without end, ecstasy without limit.

"Dunc," I hissed between gritted teeth. "Again. "

He nipped my earlobe, growling wordlessly as my throbbing, clenching pussy swallowed his shaft, his hips pressing against my ass when he finally drove to the hilt inside me. "You okay, Rune? I don't wanna hurt you."

"So good. So fucking good."

He paced across the room with me, pressing my back to the wall between the desk and the TV, pinning me there with his hips. Locking my feet together at the small of his back, I trusted him to hold me, fitting my fingers to my clit as need billowed through me with wildfire intensity. I rested my head against the wall and clutched the back of his head with my other hand, circling my clit as he rolled soft, slow thrusts into me while still buried fully within me.

My orgasm rose in waves, then, each successive wave of pleasure building on the last as he pulsed inside me, driving so deep with each thrust that my attempts at sucking in a full breath were foiled, each thrust stealing my breath and leaving me shuddering and keening—the ache of him was almost too much. Tears burned in my eyes—overwhelmed, gutted at the scorching burn of accepting his huge, hard cock, I could barely function, could barely find the rhythm I needed to help myself to orgasm.

Duncan leaned into me, crushing me against the wall, his fingers digging into the meat of my ass as he lifted me and drew back his hips.

"Tell me you can take me," he growled, his words so low and rough and strained I could barely hear him. "Please fuck, Rune, tell me you can take me."

I let my head fall forward so my brow rested on his

shoulder, my eyes fixed on our union, where his cock disappeared inside me. He was panting hard, shaking all over—the strain of holding back.

I nodded against him, circling my clit faster. "I can take you, Dunc. Give it to me."

He drove up into me, hard, my pussy accepting the thrust with a wet squelch—I screamed as his rough thrust sent me freewheeling into ecstasy, the slide of his cock stuttering against me, spearing my G-spot so unerringly I could almost believe he knew exactly where mine was and how to thrust to reach it.

"Rune?" he panted.

"Again!" I gasped, tears trickling down my cheeks—I wasn't crying, I was just…overcome. Glutted. Shattered. And I hadn't even come yet.

"Ah god, fuck," he snarled, and slammed into me again.

And again, a hoarse scream was ripped out of my throat as a white wave of hot, crushing ecstasy exploded inside me. "DUNC!" His name was all the sense I could make, the only word I could form as he withdrew his cock.

I clawed at his nape with my fingers, using my legs to lift up, panting quick, shrill, half-screamed breaths of anticipation, feeling his cock nearly slip out of me, just the plump fat head spreading my pussy open.

I slammed myself down on him, biting his shoulder around a wailing cry, his huge, hot, hard cock squelching into me and his hips slapping against my ass.

I released his neck and knotted my fingers in his hair, crying out in a loud, shuddering voice as orgasm reached a crescendo. "Duncan!" I shrieked, shattering, heat smashing through me, white light pulsing behind my tight-shut eyes, my pussy spasming around his huge pulsing cock. "Oh god oh god oh god, Dunc, I'm coming!"

He only grunted in response, slamming another slow, hard thrust that sent my climax into a whole new plane of existence, screams ripping out of me—staccato, gasping, and breathless.

I clung to him, my arms around his neck, my lips against the hot column of his throat, my legs locked around his waist, feet digging into his ass, tits crushed against the immovable wall of his chest.

He staggered away from the wall, and he was so deep inside me that it almost hurt, but a hurt so fucking good I wept from the wonder of it, sobbing as my orgasm kept destroying me in wave after wave.

He set me on the foot end of the bed and lay me onto my back. I wriggled backward, losing him in the process. I whimpered at the loss of him, reached for him as he crawled up onto the bed after me. I greedily clutched his cock in my fist, squeezing the thick shaft that was wet and slick and sticky from our mingled essences.

Duncan moved over me, his broad shoulders occluding the world beyond him. I notched his cock inside me, brought my heels up against my ass cheeks and let my knees splay open.

"Fuck me, Duncan," I breathed. "Take me. Come for me. Come inside me."

He eased into me slowly and gently, and his eyes never left mine—my jaw dropped open as he filled me all over again, the wonder of his improbable, almost-too-big cock spread me apart, stretched me, set me to shaking, burning, aching.

"Rune, holy shit," he whispered, his words huffed against the shell of my ear. "You feel so fucking incredible."

"Dunc," I breathed. "Take me, baby."

I stopped breathing even as I heard the word leave my lips—whoops. I hadn't meant to say that.

He didn't remark on it, but I felt him go tense and still for a second before need resumed control.

He pulled back in a slow, wet slide, paused, and drilled in just as slowly. "Fuck—Rune. Jesus, you're so fucking tight. So wet for me."

I could only whimper breathlessly as he split me open and tore me to pieces with each successive thrust, each one a slow, full slide, giving me every last inch of him from tip to root. I felt my body responding to his thrusts, aching around him, pulsing around him. Another climax spread through me in a slow, seeping rise, like floodwaters rippling down a river, imperceptible at first and then with increasing violence until I was shaking all over helplessly.

"Faster, Dunc," I begged. "Harder. I…oh god, Dunc, I'm gonna come again. But I…oh god. I need—I need—" I lost the thread as he gave me what I was begging for.

I clawed my fingers into his hard, flexing ass and pulled at him, meeting his thrusts with my own, and I was desperate, now, shuddering on the cusp of another violent, shattering release. "Dunc! Fuck! Fuck, please, oh god please don't stop, don't stop!"

He was fucking me in earnest now, each rough, wet, hard, squelching thrust dialing up the inferno of orgasmic heat inside me, until I was all aflame with it, panting shrill screams every time he bottomed out inside me, wailing in desperation when he drew out of me, when I lost, even for an infinitesimal moment, the fullness of him inside me.

"Rune!" He groaned, his lips pressed wet against my breastbone. "Oh god, I…oh god. Oh god, baby."

Baby. He said it too. Because I did? Or was his utterance an accident, too?

The question evaporated as he braced one hand beside me and used the other to scoop my breast up to his mouth, suckling my nipple and flattening it between his tongue and the roof of his mouth. The hot squeeze of his mouth on my aching, sensitive nipple sent me into paroxysms of bliss, toppling over the edge into an orgasm so wildly potent I couldn't even scream, could only shake and shudder and spasm helplessly, spine arched to press my breasts into his face, heels digging into the mattress.

"Duncan!" I whimpered. "Come! Please, please, please, Duncan. I need you to come. I can't take any more."

"Yes, you can," he snarled. "You can take it all."

He wrapped his arms around me, under my neck and around my shoulders, lifting me as he sat on his shins. I was impaled on his long, thick, upright cock, speared by his pulsing shaft, held immobile and still coming as he thrust into me, rising up tall on his knees as he shoved me down into his thrust.

I screamed—and came.

He sank to sit down again, draping me backward and sucking my other nipple into his mouth, biting it, licking it, making my orgasm smash into pieces, each shard of orgiastic release blossoming, like a hydra, into renewed waves of release, through which I could only scream and shudder and tremble.

I ground my pussy on him, writhing desperately, panting in his ear. "Come for me, come for me, come for me," I chanted. "Give it to me, baby, give it all to me. Fuck me and don't ever stop."

He thrust hard, harder than ever, faster and faster, driving up on his knees and sinking down in powerful, athletic, violent rhythm. "Love you begging for my cock, Rune," he growled.

"I need you to come," I panted. "Please, Duncan. Come for me. Fuck me. Give me your cock. Please,

Duncan. Please. Please. Please fuck me as hard as you can."

"Am…am I hurting you?" He breathed, fucking me exactly as I was begging for—hard, fast.

I shook my head and clawed at his back, raked my nails down his skin, met his wild thrusts with my own ragged, desperate, grinding ones. "It's perfect, Duncan. Just…just don't stop. Don't stop."

I felt him reach his endpoint, then. His thick, heavy cock pulsed inside me, throbbing against my tight-stretched lips, and his rhythm faltered.

His grip on my shoulders failed, and I fell back to the bed. I pulled him down after me and clutched him to my heaving breasts and hooked my feet at his ass and jerked him against me, silently begging for him to keep going, to keep fucking.

He groaned raggedly, drew his knees up against my thighs, and started fucking with utter, glorious, violent abandon.

"YES!" I screamed, shattering into yet another orgasm as he fucked me. "YES! YES! YES!"

His grunts were rough and guttural, then, and each hard, fucking thrust shook my whole body, made my tits jounce violently. He was hunched over me, ass pumping desperately, his fat, throbbing cock slamming into my pulsing, spasming pussy again and again and again.

I felt him come. Felt his cock pulse inside me, and he shouted in a rough, ragged voice, his trembling mouth pressed against my shoulder. Legs locked tight around the backs of his thighs, I clawed at his ass, gripped it hard and tight, and pulled him against me as I thrust with him, took him as deep as he could and squeezed my walls around him as hard as I could, clenching and clutching with every ounce of strength in my body.

His orgasm lasted for an eternity, it felt like, and my own release left me shivering and panting with him. His wild, desperate, pumping thrusts slowed at long last, and then he went still, gasping hard as if he'd just sprinted a hundred meters full out, and our sweat mingled and our breathing was mated, synched, and I was weeping helplessly, wrought and wracked by so many crushingly intense orgasms that I was limp, boneless, and shattered.

I ran my hands all over his body, smearing his slick sweat from shoulders to back to ass to waist in a circuit of affection. "Duncan," I whispered. "Holy shit."

He was heavy on me, his face buried in my throat, fists planted in the mattress to keep the worst of his bulk from totally crushing me.

I looped my legs around the small of his back, scratching his back with my fingernails, shaking with him as we descended from the endless heaven of united ecstasy.

"Holy shit, Rune," he breathed, eventually. "Holy motherfucking shit."

"Holy motherfucking shit," I agreed.

He angled away, intending to roll off me, but I clamped down on him. "No. Not yet," I whispered. "I like this."

And so we breathed and sweated and held each other for a time I didn't even try to measure, blocking out thoughts that threatened to take over my brain.

Idiot thoughts. Foolish, reckless thoughts.

Things like, how will I ever have sex with anyone else after this?

Things like, no one has ever or will ever fuck me like that again.

Things like, I had no idea I could come that hard, that many times.

Things like, I might be in love.

I shoved that last one away savagely, and that was what finally made me relinquish my grip on Duncan. That, and feeling him go slack inside me, knowing the condom could slip off and cause a truly unfortunate accident neither of us wanted or was ready for.

He rolled away from me to the edge of the bed, sat up, and levered to his feet. He took one step and his legs gave out, and he staggered like a newborn foal to the window, bracing one hand on the glass.

"Jesus," he muttered. "Never in my life have I been fucked so good my legs don't work."

"Me either," I said, laughing. "I know for a fact I can't walk right now." I wasn't sure I'd be walking at all any time soon, based on the burn in my jelly legs.

I watched Duncan shuffle into the bathroom. He

didn't close the door, and I watched as he stripped the condom off and wrapped it in toilet paper, tossed it in the trash, and then wetted a washcloth, wrung it out, and wiped clean his long, heavy, dangling cock.

He swaggered back to the bed, and I was hypnotized by the sway of his cock, the flex of his shredded abs.

My god, the man was beautiful.

And that was the best sex I'd ever had, hands down. The next best sex of my life—with the guy I dated before Hayes, actually, a hot but vain, vapid, jock from USC named, I shit you not, Brutus—wasn't even close to this. Not even by half.

I was ruined.

Duncan flopped to the bed next to me, scooped me in his arms, and cradled me against his chest.

Oh, no. No, no, no. This isn't good. This isn't happening.

I can't do this. I have to go back to LA. I have to go back to my life. I can't get cozy with Duncan Badd. My life is in California, not Alaska. My future is there. My family. Everything and everyone I know.

But this just feels...*good*. Right.

I wormed away from him. "Need to pee."

I did close the door, if only so I could freak out properly in private.

Duncan Badd was a sex god.

His cock was divine.

His hands were clever and talented.

His tongue was devilish and wild.

His body was perfect.

How many times did he make me come, just now? Four? Five? I lost track. Some of them seemed to be almost an extension of the previous one, each building on the one before.

I've never come so hard I cried.

Sex has never felt so fucking good I couldn't even breathe. God, I'm still breathing hard.

I finished peeing, wiped, washed my hands, and then stared at my reflection. "You're not falling for him," I ordered myself. "It was just sex."

Just the most mind-altering, world-tilting, body-wrecking sex of my life.

"It was a one-time thing," I told my reflection. "A fluke. It can't *always* be that good."

Can it?

Fuck. Now I need to know.

We're sharing this room through tomorrow night. My flight leaves at ten the day after tomorrow. We can have all the sex until then. I can test the question until it's time to leave: can the sex with Duncan continue to be *that* good?

Thank god—when I exited the bathroom, Duncan was asleep and snoring.

I snagged the robe from the bathroom, wrapped myself up in it, and tiptoed with my phone out onto the balcony.

I texted Lindsey: *911! Need to talk. NOW.*

She hit me back immediately: *Call, text, or IRL?*

Me: *What's your room number?*

She was on the same floor as me, but at the other end. I took my phone and a keycard and snuck out of the room and then scuttled to Lindsey's room.

She let me in, hiding behind the door as I slipped past her. She was naked, and several vibrators were scattered on the bed, one of them still lit up and humming.

"I'm...interrupting something?" I said, smirking at her.

She shrugged. "No, I'm done."

I pointed at the rogue vibrator. "She's not."

"Oh, shit. My bad." Lindsey turned it off, scooped up the various devices, dumped them in the bathroom sink, and slipped on a robe. We sat on her bed together, and she clapped her hands. "So. What's the 9-1-1?"

I grabbed her hands and squeezed hard. "I'm ruined, Linz."

Her eyebrows flew high. "Oh dear. You fucked him, didn't you?"

I nodded slowly, my eyes wide. "Oh lord, yes."

"And you're ruined?"

"Totally and completely."

"That good?"

"Better," I whispered. "He fucking *destroyed* me."

Lindsey clapped a hand over her mouth. "Girl! Spill!"

So I spilled. And with each new detail, her eyes

got wider and wider. "Rune, boo-boo, you are in *major* trouble."

"I know!" I shrieked, and then clapped a hand over my own mouth to quiet myself. "I know. It's bad, Linz. Bad, bad, bad."

She frowned at me. "I mean, just playing Devil's Advocate, here, but…what if you didn't go back?"

My entire being revolted. "How can you even *ask* me that, Lindsey? Of course, I have to go back. My whole life is there."

"Yeah, but…is it?" She held out her hands. "You're done with school. You don't have a job yet. You're not with anyone, obviously. If there was ever a time to reconsider your future, this would be it, babe. I mean, can't you even let yourself *consider* it? Just, like, ask yourself what if?"

Panic at the very thought had me shooting to my feet and shaking my head. "No, I can't. Not him. Not now. Not Alaska."

"But why?"

"I don't know!" I shouted. "Sorry. I just…I don't know, Linz. I'm freaking out."

"Clearly. You just had the best sex of your life, and you sneak out to my room to have some sort of existential crisis? The man fucked you into another dimension, Rune. If it were me, I'd be climbing that boy's dick like a tree and I'd never get down, if it was as good as you say it was."

"It was better."

"So what are you doing here?"

"FREAKING OUT! It wasn't supposed to be that good! It was supposed to be *casual*!"

She snorted. "If you thought for a single second you were capable of casual sex, you're delulu, sweetie. You have never had casual sex in your life. You do this—or a version of this—every time you try. You get some kind of a feeling and you freak the fuck out, and then a few weeks later, you find some tool to date so you can have your so-called *guilt-free* sex. This is the worst episode yet, by far, though."

"What's *wrong* with me, Linz?" I asked. "Why can't I just hook up with a dude like a normal person and not develop stupid fucking feelings every time? I just…I had to get my mojo back. Seeing Hayes, it…"

She sighed, patted my cheek. "Rune, my darling, you're nuts. I love you to bits, you know I do, but you're not being self-aware. This isn't about your mojo. This isn't even about Hayes. It's about that boy asleep in your bed, he of the magical dick."

"What do I do?"

She shrugged. "You only have so many options. One, just go with it. Fuck his brains out while you can and then go home and try to move on. Or, don't. Try to hold out. Don't have sex with him again, and go home and try to move on. Or, stay here with me. We can share a bed. Wouldn't be the first time, obviously. Or, fuck his brains out, and just…don't stop. See where it leads. Be brave."

I shook my head. "If I'm in that room with him, I'm gonna fuck him again. There's no question."

"You want to," she guessed.

I nodded. "I have to know if it was a fluke. Like, just built-up tension, you know?"

"It wasn't, I promise you, but go on."

"Linz, you don't know that."

"I'm pretty sure. Sex that good doesn't just happen. And girl, you're still high from it."

I showed her my hand, which was trembling. "What do I do?"

She shook her head. "You're not gonna listen to me."

"I'm not staying."

"I know. So just...let yourself have the moment, at least. Get through the wedding. And just...be prepared that when you go back to LA, you're gonna be a mess."

I groaned, palming my face. "I'm already a mess—*still* a mess."

"Like I said, Rune, if it was as good as you say—and you led with 'I'm ruined'—then you're gonna have a hell of a time moving on. If you insist on ignoring your feelings, then you have to be aware of the consequences. You'll be walking away from the best sex of your life, on purpose. Because you're scared."

I shot to my feet. "Fuck you, Linz."

She laughed. "I tell it like it is, babe. Don't shoot the messenger."

"I have to get back," I said. "I don't want him to wake up and think I bolted."

"Which you did?"

"Absolutely. But he doesn't need to know that."

"Good thing you're not looking for a relationship with him, then, because that's not a great place to start things from—lying to him and keeping things from him."

"Good thing," I agreed. "Okay, I'm going back. Thanks for hearing me out and making it that much worse with your shitty advice."

She only laughed again, the traitorous bitch. "Go get him, tiger."

I flipped her off as I left her room.

Back in our room, I unlocked it and eased in as quietly as I could.

Duncan's eyes were open, and laser-focused on me.

Shit.

ELEVEN

Duncan

SHE FROZE WHEN SHE SAW ME AWAKE, EYES WIDE LIKE A deer caught in headlights; the door swung slowly shut, clicking closed behind her.

"How's Lindsey?" I asked.

"Um, fine?" She swallowed hard, otherwise still motionless. "Duncan, I…"

"Told you, I have sisters," I said. "I know girls gotta tell their friends everything."

She relaxed a tiny bit. "I just…"

"Weird that you snuck out to do so, though. Weirder yet that you tried to sneak back in."

"Dunc, I'm—it's…"

"You gonna tell me the truth about what's going on in that head of yours?" I asked.

She didn't answer.

I knew she wouldn't. I felt her tense up when she called me baby, and again when it slipped out of my mouth. I hadn't meant to say it any more than she had. I'm fine chalking it up to the intensity of the moment, but deep down, I know it's more than that.

For her and for me.

I also know she's not about to admit to that—even to herself. I see the writing on the wall. She's scared shitless. She felt the same things I felt, and the second she realized I was asleep, she ran to her friend for commiseration or sympathy or whatever it was she needed. Because she's scared shitless.

"Take the robe off," I said, lounging low in the bed with my head propped up on a couple pillows, the blanket draped low over my hips.

Her nostrils flared, and she swallowed hard again. "Duncan—"

"You ready to sleep?" I ask.

"No, but—"

"So take the robe off."

She slid her phone and the keycard out of the pockets and held them in one hand, hesitated a moment, and then unknotted the belt. The edges sagged open, baring a slice of her lush, nubile body down her centerline—throat, breastbone, the inner swells of her breasts, belly, navel, and a hint of her pussy.

She hesitated again, licking her lips. "Duncan…"

"Off." This was my way of putting emotional distance between us.

Keep it hot, keep it sexy, keep it physical. Give her orders, keep her off balance. In a way, this was for her.

She wanted the distance. She wanted to keep this casual and fun.

So that's what we'd do.

Rune searched my face, sucked in a deep breath, and then slid the robe open, letting it slip down her arms to pool at her feet. Her heavy, teardrop breasts swayed subtly with her slow but deep breaths, flat belly tensing and relaxing. Her nipples peaked as I watched, pebbling to hard points.

She took a step toward me, but I held up a hand. "Stay there."

"What is this?" she asked.

"Pinch your nipples."

"Duncan—"

"Trust me." I slid the blanket down an inch or two. "Do it."

Shifting her weight from foot to foot, she searched me, swallowing hard, eyes dancing, flicking to my abs, the low rise of the blanket over my burgeoning erection.

Her hands drifted up to her belly, hesitated. Licking her lips, Rune cupped her breasts. Finger and thumb of each hand gently seized her nipples and squeezed. Her eyes widened and she sucked in a short, sharp breath. "There, now what—"

"Hard."

I waited, face blank, a slight smirk on my lips—the smirk I knew annoyed her and turned her on in equal measure.

"Duncan, I don't under—"

"Pinch your nipples for me, Rune. Hard. Really hard."

Her thighs pressed together, and she caught her lower lip in her teeth, brow furrowing as she considered my demand.

And then she did it.

She pinched her nipples hard enough that she squealed out loud in a shrill gasp, thighs squeezing together against her pussy.

"Touch yourself." I slid the blanket lower, showing her the upper couple of inches of my hardening cock. "Touch your pussy, Rune."

Gnawing on her lip, Rune trailed her right hand down her body, fit her fingers over the dark triangle of her sex.

My heart hammering, I lifted my chin. "Touch your pussy, Rune. I want to watch you finger your clit."

Her middle finger dipped inward, and she sucked in a breath and her eyelids fluttered.

"Keep going."

She pressed her middle finger against clit again, and she whimpered, her knees dipping and her shoulders hunching. "Duncan, why—?"

"Don't stop, Rune. Finger yourself."

She swept her finger in a slow, exploratory circle, and her eyes closed as pleasure flooded through her. "Oh god," she whimpered. "Duncan."

"Open your eyes, Smokeshow," I ordered. "Look at me while you touch yourself."

Sapphire eyes met mine, then, confused, aroused, needy. "Oh god, oh god." Her finger circled, circled, and her knees dipped in time with the movement of her finger. "Dunc—oh—oh, oh god. Oh god."

I tossed the blanket aside totally, then, baring my fully erect cock. She bit her lip and whimpered at the sight of my arousal.

"Duncan, I…I want—" her words cut off as a shudder rippled through her, forcing her to hunch forward and bend at the knees, gasping. "Oh—fuck!"

"Don't come, yet, Rune."

"I—I can't stop it."

"Not yet," I said. "Hold it off."

She whimpered again, her finger flying over her clit, now, knees dipping, tits swaying and bouncing, hair loose and wild and kinked from the braid, mouth open, eyes wide and locked on me. "I need to come, Duncan. I can't—I can't hold out anymore."

"Yes, you can." Her eyes closed, and I growled. "Eyes open. Don't look away from me."

She hissed, locking those big sapphire eyes on mine, her whole body bucking and hunching and dipping as she fingered herself to orgasm and yet fought off the release.

"Dunc, please," she whispered. "Please. I need to come. I can't—Oh god, oh god, I can't—I can't stop it!" Almost crouching now as her legs threatened to give out, she threw her head back and keened through gritted teeth. "Duncan! Please!"

"Come here."

She ran across the room, crawling up my body, grasping my cock in one hand and reaching for the condoms on the table beside me.

"Ah ah," I scolded, gripping her hips and lifting her away from me, dragging her up my body as I scooted down flat. "Not yet."

She knelt astride my chest, inky black hair wild around her face and shoulders, staring down at me as I guided her over my face. She fell forward, catching herself on the headboard.

I swept my tongue up her seam, and she gasped, bucking at the initial slide against her sensitive flesh. When I drove my tongue against the hard nub of her clit, she lost it, throwing her head back and letting out a low, guttural groan of bliss.

"Yes, Duncan," she growled. "Yes, oh god, *yes*."

"*Now* you can come, Rune."

My words were a trigger.

She came with a scream, bucking against my mouth as I fused my lips around her clit and thrashed her with my tongue, rubbing my stubble against her thighs as I shook my head from side to side. Honey essence flooded my mouth as she came, release soaking through her. She screamed again, both hands gripping the headboard as she rode my mouth, grinding on my face.

"Fuck!" she hissed, as the orgasm kept her shaking and riding, bucking on my face as I clutched her ass and helped her move. "Duncan!"

I thrust my tongue inside her dripping entrance, tasting her juices and growling at the flavor of her. She screamed again when I slid two fingers inside her, hooking them to massage her G-spot, and now she sat upright, back arching, tits thrusting forward, head thrown back as she rubbed and ground and bucked against my mouth and fingers.

"Holy fuck, Duncan!" She wailed, the orgasm wrenching her into helpless paroxysms. "Duncan! Oh god, oh god."

She collapsed forward, gasping and panting and sweating as she shuddered through the aftershocks. I grabbed a condom and ripped it open with my teeth.

"Rune."

She forced her eyes open. "Hmmm?"

"Put this on me."

She took the latex ring from me and slid down to sit on my thighs, fitting the rubber to the tip of my cock and then rolling it down onto me. She didn't wait for any more commands, then—she grasped my shaft and fit my tip to her folds, hesitated. Locking eyes with me, balanced over me, palms flat on my chest, she slid onto me, filled herself with my cock. Her mouth hung open as I stretched her tight, hot, wet pussy.

Bending over me as she slowly eased herself down my length, her tits brushed my chest and her mouth found mine, lips to lips, not kissing but just touching as she gasped, taking inch after inch of me.

Her big, beautiful, round ass settled onto my thighs, and I ached for being so fully inside her. "Rune," I growled. "Fuck, you're so goddamned tight. Jesus."

I filled my hands with that plump, perfect ass, then lifted her almost off of me, and then yanked her down, thrusting up into her, hard.

She screamed.

Came.

Every last inch of her curves shook, then, as she spasmed above me, pussy squeezing hard around my cock, and she dug her nails into my chest, gasping a shrill, desperate cry.

"Oh fuck, Duncan!" Her orgasm released her, and she collapsed forward, arms circling my neck as she gasped.

For a moment, she only lay there on top of me, my cock buried inside her, and panted.

And then she levered up onto one hand, covering my mouth with the other. "My turn."

I nodded, thrusting into her.

Bracing both hands on my chest, she lifted her ass high, until my cock was about to slip out...and then slammed down onto me, hard. I shouted at the rough slap of her ass against my thighs, the ache of being driven so deep my balls throbbed.

Another slow grind on me.

A third.

Faster.

Faster.

And then…she was mercilessly riding me, slapping her against my thighs so fast it sounded almost like applause, taking control and taking what she wanted. I couldn't even begin to keep up—there was nothing I could do but lay beneath her and let her have her way with me, and it was beautiful.

I groaned and grunted as she rode me, pushing hard, desperate thrusts into her as she slammed me deeper and deeper and deeper with each wet, slapping thrust.

"Oh fuck, fuck, oh fuck," I grunted, "Rune, I'm gonna come. Oh god—Rune, oh fuck!"

Buried to the hilt, she stopped moving. "Not yet."

I tensed every muscle, trying like hell to hold back. "Fuck—I'm trying."

With my cock as deep as it could go, Rune rolled her hips, dragging her slick lips against me, tilting back and forth and then circling. Tilt, circle, tilt, circle, and my balls ached with the need to release, but I held it back.

Titling faster, now, she ground herself on me, bringing me back to the edge of climax. "Duncan?"

I snarled wordlessly, thrusting into her, pushing deeper. "What?"

She sat upright, kneeling tall so I was about to slip free. "Come."

With that command on her lips, she slammed

down onto me, and I had no choice but to obey. Shouting, guttural and hoarse, I emptied myself into her, thrusting up into her downstroke. She cried out as well, her pussy rippling around me with her own orgasm. And then she was riding me again, rising on her knees and slamming down, sitting tall with her head thrown back, hands cupping her big, bouncing tits, rising and crashing down harder and harder until her orgasm ripped her into weeping, whimpering shudders, collapsing forward.

Still coming, I palmed her ass cheeks and pulled her open so I could fuck deep, hard, and fast, and she wailed into my chest as I took her, each thrust almost brutally hard, slapping and squelching and crushing as deep as her body would allow.

I came so hard I saw stars, then, and my body was out of my control, and all I could do was fuck Rune through my orgasm.

Gradually, sense returned to me, and I slowed my thrusting, loosening my grip on her ass. Unable to help myself, I cracked my hand against her ass hard enough that she shrieked in shock.

"Duncan!" she protested. "What the hell?"

"This fucking ass of yours," I snarled through gritted teeth, her pussy spasming around me at the smack. "Fucking *love* it."

She whimpered as I feathered a slow thrust. "How are you still hard?"

I spanked her again, and she cried out, pussy

spasming again. "I could make you come like this." I smacked her yet again, and now she jerked, wailing, as a mini-orgasm sheared through her. "You love that, don't you?"

"Dunc…" she breathed.

"Don't you?" I demanded, spanking her ass again. "You like being spanked."

"I—oh. Oh god." Smack, smack. Hard enough to make her jerk and gasp, not hard enough to actually hurt. "You love it. Say it, Rune. You love it when I spank this sexy ass."

"*YES!*" She cried. "Okay? Yes! I love it when you spank me, Duncan."

I was subsiding then, even as I was still so turned I could fuck her all over again, if my dick would have been able to cooperate.

I slid out of her, wincing and hissing as I lost her tight, wet heat. I left her on her belly on the bed, nuzzling her ear. "Don't move."

"I couldn't if I wanted to," she mumbled.

I took care of the condom, cleaned up, and went back to her. Her ass cheeks were bright red from being spanked, so I caressed each generous bubble with my palms, kissed and nuzzled the reddened flesh until she was moaning in delight.

"Dunc," she breathed, eventually. "I can't stay awake anymore."

I pulled the blanket up over her, settled in beside her on my back. "Rune, I…"

She reached out blindly, patting my chest and then my chin before finding my mouth and clapping her palm over it. "Shushy-time."

"I know this doesn't change anything, but I—"

She clapped her hand over my mouth again. "Duncan...we can talk in the morning."

I groaned in frustration—my head was swirling with thoughts, my heart pounding with emotions.

This wasn't just the best sex of my life.

This was more.

This was everything.

She was my everything.

Fuck.

Fuck, fuck, fuck.

It was true, and I knew it. Now the cat was out of the bag—a horrible saying, honestly—and there was no going back.

Delirious, in love, still wild with need for Rune's incredible body, desperate to have her feel the same way for me, I hovered at the edge of sleep for a long time before finally dropping into slumber.

And when I did, my sleep was filled with dreams of Rune.

I woke slowly, to heat.

To a soft, warm body nestled against mine. I was the little spoon—Rune was curled behind me, naked hips against my ass, breasts against my back, breath hot on my neck, one hand draped low on my hips.

I tried to go back to sleep, but couldn't. I was too aware of Rune.

I did doze a little, and must have actually dropped off again despite myself, because the next time I woke up, I was on my back and Rune was laying on my chest, and she was playing with my cock.

I swallowed hard, gruffly huffing as she stroked me to an erection. "Rune?"

Her hand covered my mouth. "Shhhh."

I shushed.

She took her time playing with me. For a long while, she wasn't even stroking me, just thumbing my weeping tip, cradling my balls in her hand, twisting the root. Toying with me for her own purposes.

Even this attention eventually made heat rise in me, and she knew it. She began stroking me lazily. Slowly. With a loose grip, teasing, toying. For long, agonizing minutes, she played with me, bringing me to the point of needing to move before stopping again.

Paying me back for last night.

Growling as need barreled through me, I thrust into her hand.

She jacked my length with her soft, small hand, twisting at the top, giving me a few quick twisting pumps around the head and then stroking my full length until I was in a frenzy of arousal.

"Rune!" I groaned.

"Hush, Duncan," she whispered, "Don't move. Don't make a sound."

I clenched my teeth together and held myself immobile.

I was rewarded immediately—she drew her wild, tangled mass of jet-black hair away and slid her cheek down my belly and took me into her mouth.

I groaned involuntarily and lost her mouth.

"Not a sound or I stop," she murmured.

I wrapped her hair around my fist, palming the back of her head, waiting. When she was sure I was silent, she gave me her mouth again.

This time, I gritted my molars together and watched, rapt, as she gave me long, slow, tonguing, slurping strokes of her mouth, each one taking an eternity, never stopping, never changing her pace, and I dared not so much as blink or twitch or breathe.

Panting as orgasm rose within me, I clutched the cool silken mass of her hair and watched her mouth slide down my shaft, heat shearing through me, pressure building, pleasure shattering me until I was gasping raggedly from the exertion of not moving, of keeping silent.

She knew when I was about to come—she cupped my balls, squeezed hard around the pulsing root of my cock to prevent me from releasing even as she bobbed on my cock faster and faster, her hot mouth wet and tight and heavenly around me.

The heat and pressure built as she continued to

squeeze my root to keep me from coming. I was a mad-
man, then, needing to come and unable to—knowing
if I made a sound or moved at all, she'd stop.

Without warning, Rune released her grip on
my base and took my cock down her throat, gulping
around me and cupping my balls in gentle hands.

I came, shouting helplessly as my orgasm detonated inside me, and she gulped my cum and slid her
mouth up my shaft and swirled her tongue against
my tip, swallowing my cum as it poured out of me,
and then bobbed around the head of my cock while
pumping my length and base, and I just kept coming
and coming and she swallowed and gulped and licked
and suckled through it all.

Even when my orgasm had run dry, Rune was unrelenting, suckling, bobbing, and slurping at my cock
until I was utterly limp.

Only then did she release me and return her cheek
to the nook of my arm.

I held her there for a few minutes, and then rolled
her to her back, brushed her wild hair out of her face,
stared down at her. "Good morning, Smokeshow."

She searched me, her expression fraught and intense. "Hi."

Just to prove the point, I cupped her cheek and
dipped, kissed her, sweeping my tongue through her
lips and scouring her mouth, demanding her tongue,
tasting myself on her. She whined into the kiss, her

hand stealing into my hair, the other splaying over my cheek, temple, and ear.

A fist rapped on the door, fast and sharp. "Rune! We need to go to Raquel's room." It was Lindsey.

She broke the kiss with a gasp, turning away. "Okay! Be right there!"

"Hi, Duncan!"

"Hey, Lindsey," I called.

Groaning, Rune thudded her head onto my chest. Paused like that for a few seconds, and then rolled away and out of bed. I watched her dig in her bag for a clean red thong and wiggle into it, and then find a plain white bra, hook the clasps at her diaphragm, swivel it around, fit her breasts into the cups, and shrug on the straps.

I've always found it almost as unbearably sexy to watch a woman dress as the other way.

"Don't look at me like that, Duncan," she muttered. "I'm late. I have to go."

"We were gonna talk," I said. "I have things to say."

She yanked a short, pastel pink sundress out of her bag and slipped it on, settled it to drape just right, and then shoved her feet into black ballet flats. "I have to go, Duncan."

I growled, annoyed. "I know."

She snagged her phone and keycard from the nightstand paused to stand over me, gazing down at me. "There's nothing to talk about, though."

"Yes, there is." I hooked a hand around her bare

thigh beneath the dress. "There's a lot to talk about. You know what that was last night as well as I do."

She bent, kissed me, and pulled out of my reach. "I'll see you later, Dunc."

And then she was gone in a swirl of scent—woman, sex.

"Fuck." I forced myself to sit up, raking my hands through my hair. "I fell in love with a girl who doesn't love me back." I thunked myself in the forehead with a fist. "Smooth move, Ex-lax."

I let myself wallow for a few more minutes, and then got up to shower the sex off of me.

Yet, even clean and dressed in my best suit, I couldn't erase the scent of Rune, the memory of the night we shared from my skin.

I am fucked. So very, very fucked.

TWELVE

Rune

LINDSEY HAD ARRANGED FOR A GLAM SQUAD TO PAMPER the three of us. I opted to use Raquel's shower to rinse off while Lindsey got glammed up first, since I had been, um…rather busy last night. And this morning. I felt Lindsey's eyes on me as the effusive gay man doing my hair chattered on and on in a relentless patter about some ongoing personal drama with his boyfriend. And while the man's prattle annoyed me, it also provided a nice cover for me not to have to talk about Duncan.

Because I just couldn't handle talking about it. I'd bolted at the first opportunity rather than engage in a rational, adult conversation about our feelings.

Fuck that.

I know damn well that the sex last night was not just world-class fucking, I'll never forget. It altered my emotional chemistry. It shook the axis of my very existence.

Which is exactly why I'm not discussing it. I'm *not* in love with Duncan Badd. I can't be. I met him not two weeks ago. I barely know him. I haven't met his parents or his siblings—although I have met two of his uncles and one cousin. My life is in LA and his is here—well, here Alaska, not here Anchorage.

No, the best thing is to pretend it was just the hottest sex any two human beings have ever had, never to be repeated.

Except maybe tonight.

No.

I can't.

If I let myself fuck Duncan again, it'll only screw up my emotions even more. I need to make sure I get nice and drunk and pass out in Lindsey's room.

To that end, the three of us start day drinking with a pitcher of mimosas. Raquel was in hair and makeup, sipping her drink and actually engaging with Robbie's endless nattering, leaving Lindsey and me to finish getting ready.

Lindsey leaned toward me as I sipped my mimosa, doing so delicately in an attempt to smear my lipstick as little as possible. "You fucked him again, didn't you?"

I choked on champagne and OJ, coughing and gasping. "Dammit, Linz!"

She cackled. "You did!"

"So?"

"Was it as good the second time?"

I felt myself flushing like a 13-year-old discussing her first crush. "No." I cleared my throat, dabbed at my lips with a napkin. "It was better."

She boggled at me. "You said the first time, and I quote, 'ruined you', and that it was the best sex of your life."

"Yes. That's still true. And round two was even better. Quite literally, round two was the hottest thing that's ever happened to me."

"What did he *do*?" she demanded in a hiss.

"He was awake when I got back from your room. He ordered me to take off the robe, and then made me masturbate while he watched." I was whispering so quietly that Lindsey had to put her ear nearly to my lips.

Lindsey clapped a hand over her mouth. "Holy shit."

"But he wouldn't let me come until I was riding his face. Linz, I'm telling you, I've never come so hard or so many times in my life." I swallowed hard, shaking my head. "It was…epic. That's what it was."

"Which is why you were still asleep when I knocked on your door? And why you didn't answer any of my six texts or three calls?"

I glanced at Raquel—not that I didn't trust her, but my relationship with Lindsey was deeper, and this was very, very personal. "I didn't oversleep. I actually woke up kinda early and spent a good hour freaking out while Duncan slept. And then I, um, I sort of woke him up with a blow job."

"As in, he woke up in your mouth?"

"Uh, no, not exactly. I sort of played with him first."

"So when I knocked?"

"I'd just finished blowing him and he was kissing me."

"You let him kiss you after you blew him?" Obviously, she knew about my hangup and where it came from.

"We talked about that, actually, and…yeah."

She blinked at me. "Rune, that's a big deal."

"No it's not," I lied.

"You're still in denial!" she said, way too loudly.

Raquel glanced at us in the mirror. "You think I don't see you two whispering about Rune's fucked-up situation with Duncan?"

"Uh-oh! Drama!" Robbie sing-songed.

"It's not a fucked-up situation!" I argued.

Raquel and Lindsey shared a look and then burst into identical cackling laughs.

"Oh, sweetie," Lindsey sighed. "You're so far into denial you don't even realize it."

"It's just good sex!" I insisted. "That's all it is! That's all it ever will be!"

"You told me he ruined you." Lindsey arched an eyebrow at me. "I dunno about you, Raquel, but if I had sex with someone and it ruined me, I wouldn't be walking away so easily."

Raquel grinned. "I *did* have sex with someone who ruined me." She paused for dramatic effect. "I'm marrying him in a couple hours."

"Okay, but can we talk about that, though?" Lindsey said. "What is it about sex with Hamish that's so good?"

Raquel sighed dreamily. "It's the connection. He just…he *gets* me. It's like he knows my body. It also doesn't hurt that…" she trailed off, glancing at Robbie.

Robbie, prepping her scalp for the custom wig Raquel was going to wear, flipped a hand. "Don't mind me, girlies. Anything you say in here is covered by a doctor-patient confidentiality clause. Or something like that." He winked at Raquel in the mirror. "So spill it, sister."

Raquel snickered. "Fine. It doesn't hurt that Hamish is hung like a horse." She bit her lip, gaze twinkling with amusement and love. "He knows how to use it, too. But it's not just that. When I first started hanging out with him, I was sort of…I didn't expect to feel the way I do about him. He's the first and only white guy I've ever dated, and I wasn't sure what to expect… in that department. But it turned out it didn't matter. We took that *slow*, ya'll. We didn't sleep together for almost three months. By that point, I didn't care what he was packing, I just *wanted* him." She looked at me in the mirror. "I knew I loved him, even though on paper our relationship made no sense. We're from two totally different worlds. But he gets me. I dunno how, but he does. He shouldn't understand me, you know? He's from a little rural town in Scotland, and I'm from Compton. But…that shit don't matter—*at all*. We both worked our asses off to escape where we were from. His culture may be totally alien to me and vice versa, but who he is? The man he is? How he treats me? *That's* what matters. He doesn't need to know anything about Black American culture to love me. And I don't need to know anything about Scottish culture to love him. We love each other—the rest is just details."

"I love that for you, Raquel," I said.

She rolled her eyes. "I'm saying, Rune, that you and Duncan aren't even that different."

"I know we're not. That's not the problem."

"Then what is?" Raquel asked.

"She's scared," Lindsey said.

"I am not!" I lied.

Lindsey nudged her forehead against my temple. "Bitch, I love you. But you're a terrible, terrible liar. You're scared shitless. You *know* that the chemistry between you and Duncan is way more than just physical, and after everything that happened with Hayes, you're scared. I get it. But Duncan isn't Hayes."

"I know he isn't."

"So? Woman up, bitch!" Lindsey said. "Take a chance on the man."

"I'm not *moving to Alaska*!" I shouted. "My life is

in California! Everyone I know is there. What do you think is gonna happen? I'm gonna stay here forever because of some really amazing sex? That's stupid. It's irresponsible. I can't abandon my entire life because of some boy, no matter how good the dick may be."

"It's not about the dick, honey," Robbie said. "It's about what the dick does to your heart."

"The dick isn't doing anything to my heart."

Robbie sighed. "It's a lost cause, girls. She's so far up denial you can call her Pharaoh." All three of us stared at him until he scoffed. "Denial? The Nile? Oh come on! That was a good joke!"

Lindsey patted me on the shoulder. "We'll let it go because you're obviously not willing to listen to reason, but mark my words, Rune Rigby—you're making a mistake. Duncan Badd is more than just a big dick and nice abs. You have feelings for him and he absolutely, one hundred percent, not a shred of doubt about it has feelings for you. And yet you're committing to running away from that before you've even given it a chance just because of his zip code."

"*Zip code?*" I screeched. "He damn near lives on a different continent! I am *not* cut out for Alaskan winters. It's not happening, and I *do not* have feelings for him. It was the best sex I've ever had, yes, but that's all it was. And Linz, I'm crashing in your room tonight. I plan on getting wasted so I can't do anything stupid with Duncan before my flight tomorrow."

Lindsey sighed. "Whatever you need to do, babe.

You know I've got your back, even if you are being an idiot."

The rest of the day was a whirlwind of preparation, mimosas, brunch with the gang, more mimosas, re-touching makeup, photography behind the venue...

By the time four o'clock rolled around—with the wedding scheduled to start at four-thirty—I was well on my way to tipsy. Or...y'know, something. Tipsy... drunk, whatever. I was functional, and happy to be spending quality time with my friends—I'd missed them in the last two months of wandering north from SoCal to the Pacific Northwest. Hayes, in a wild burst of intelligence, avoided me like the plague, opting to stick to hanging out with Ricky and the other guys. Even when we did toasts with the whole group, he made sure to stay as far away from me as he could get, even going so far as to avert his gaze if I happened to look his way.

Duncan may as well have been adopted by the crew—he seemed to get along with everyone. He shot Hayes dirty looks every chance he got, but otherwise left him alone. He tried to corner me a few times, wanting to talk about last night, but I managed to escape every time.

He was getting frustrated, if not outright pissed off, but I was committed. We had fun, and now the fun was over, as planned: come to the wedding, find a guy to hook up with, make Hayes jealous, go home.

Success on all fronts.

Raquel and Hamish had opted to forgo having a best man and maid of honor, since the wedding was so small and rather informal, which meant Lindsey acted as the flower girl while Raquel's brother Ricky carried the rings and held them through the officiant's opening remarks and the couple's vows.

Sitting front row, I watched Raquel's eyes tear up and her voice choke as she promised to love, honor, and respect Hamish for the rest of their lives, even if she didn't always understand everything he said. That got some laughs. When Hamish started his vows, he did so in a Scottish accent so incomprehensible it sounded like gibberish...until people started to frown at each other and wonder out loud if he was speaking English. Raquel was laughing, her bare shoulders shaking. He only kept up the bit for a few seconds and then slid into his usual thick-but-understandable accent, his eyes twinkling with mischief.

When the officiant pronounced them husband and wife, everyone stood up and cheered as Hamish swept Raquel clean off her feet, held her in his arms as if carrying her across a threshold, and kissed her insensible. "LET'S GET PISSED!" he shouted, while Raquel gazed up at him blearily, as if wondering how they could manage to sneak away and finish what Hamish's kiss started.

And, as the party moved indoors for cocktails and hors d'oeuvres, Hamish and Raquel did indeed vanish together for a good twenty minutes, and when they re-appeared, Raquel was in a short, slinky white cocktail dress and Hamish's tie was gone.

I floated from group to group and table to table for the rest of the evening, picking at small plates of food and avoiding Duncan almost as thoroughly as Hayes was avoiding me.

I really was catching up with my friends, though—two months is a long time to miss out on the comings and goings of people you've hung out with almost every day for four years.

By the time the sun had set and dinner was served, I was pretty well drunk.

And that's when speeches happened.

I found myself standing up with a microphone in hand, scanning the crowd—feeling wobbly, unsteady, and emotional. I locked onto Raquel. "Raquel, Hamish…You guys are couple goals. Your relationship is an inspiration to all of us." I accidentally looked down at Duncan, and his deep brown eyes were carefully blank. "I love you guys. I hope you have a long, beautiful marriage and lots of adorable babies. Congratulations, you guys."

I sat down, proud of myself for sounding coherent.

"Nice speech," Duncan murmured.

"Thanks." I picked at my food and ignored the heat of his gaze on me.

"Rune."

I ignored him.

"Rune, you're being childish. C'mon. Just talk to me."

I pinned him with a glare. "Duncan, just....stop. I told you. There's nothing to talk about."

"But there is and you know it."

I shook my head, which felt a bit sloshy. "I'm drunk, Duncan."

"Me too. So what?"

I looked at him—for the first time that day, I really looked at him, and I realized he was as blasted as I was. Barely holding it together. His eyes swam with emotions I couldn't bring myself to name. "Duncan, *please*." I closed my eyes, tearing my gaze away from his. "I *can't*."

"Won't, you mean."

"Sure. That too. Can't *and* won't."

"Why?"

I shot to my feet, steadied myself with a hand on the chair, and turned away from him. "I need to use the ladies' room."

I bolted like the coward I was, scurrying across the bustling room—I got stopped four times on the way, managed to get away long enough to pee, and then got swept up in a dance-off drinking game on the dance floor. I knew I was in bad shape, so I started slamming water between rounds of shots, because I'm a terrible dancer.

I remember seeing Duncan standing on the dance floor, alone, watching me as my friends swirled around me. He was wearing a tux—which fit him like a glove, and made him look like James Bond. The bowtie had come untied at some point, and his hair, slicked back and gelled to within an inch of its life during the day, was back to being unruly and shaggy, dangling in his eyes. He had his hands in his hip pockets and his deep, dark brown eyes were unreadable, inscrutable, fixed on me as the crowd swept around us, swirling like planets orbiting twin suns.

The shots seemed to hit me all at once, then, and that's when my memory goes dark

—

—Laughter bubbles, a merry tinkle of joy.

A hand, draped on a shoulder. Fingers sliding down an exposed back.

Feet moving, dancing.

Lips touching a cheek, rough with stubble.

Another laugh.

The dance floor bathed in colorful flashing lights, washed in thudding dance music, bodies moving, brushing, sweating. Hand in hand. Hand on hip. Hips against hips, writhing to the beat.

You, me; who are we? No one.

Where are we? Nowhere; everywhere.

Touch is electric. Eyes spark with fire. Rocket fuel burns in my veins, scorches in your gaze.

Your hand grazes my cheek, and I remember with shocking clarity the way you sounded as you came, and I can't remember anything but this moment and that sound—your groan, my moan, our mated breaths and the soft slide of skin on skin.

The music pounds, pounds, pounds. Bodies bump into us as we glide together, eyes locked and warring. The myriad unspoken things hang between us, but we say nothing. Mouths are not for speaking, not in this wild glut of chaos and chemistry.

Mouths are for tasting sweat, stealing kisses as hips gyrate and grind, as hands clutch and palms press.

Lips are for stuttering against stubble, not speaking; tongues are for tangling, not talking.

You sweep me away from the crowd. A quiet corner near

the buffet table hosts a fraught moment, the titanic freight of unspoken sentiments boiling between us—it's too loud in here to hear, but you see the things we've not said coruscating between us like lost and fallen stars, just as I do. They glow like neon signs—my feelings, your need, our rightness, our wrongness; it's all there, prose written in the lingering looks, poetry scribed in stolen touches.

There's the bride, dancing with her husband, her slender brown fingers interlocked behind his neck, toying with his red hair, her eyes blazing her wild love. He gazes down at her, and for them, there is no one else in all the world but each other.

Do you want that?

Do I?

A surge of humanity finds our quiet corner, and we're parted.

I find you alone outside beneath the rose-wreathed arch, moonlight silver on your skin.

The silence is crushing.

Eyes gleam in the starshine.

Still, there is nothing to say if only because there is too much to say and our throats burn from too much alcohol and from the weight of the unspoken.

Sidewalk squares pass underfoot. It's blessedly cool after the humidity of breath and the heat of sweat and the crush of dancing and drinking and eating and merrymaking.

Your hand is in mine. It feels right.

The hotel rises before us, doors swish open, ghost closed; the lobby is silent.

The elevator is slow.

You stare at me as we wait for it.

Your eyes burn, goddammit. Like galaxies and quasars, they burn.

—Don't look at me like that.

—Like what?

There's no reason to answer—you know. I know.

The hallway distorts, morphing into a miles-long tunnel of swirling light from rotating sconces. The floor tilts, an Inception-*like twist of reality, and then there's a wall at my shoulder and you drop the keycard on the floor. You fall over trying to retrieve it.*

Our room is dark. Silent. Still. It still smells faintly of our sex.

You open the blinds and starshine bathes the planes of your face, illuminates the heat in your eyes.

—I'm going to kiss you.

Your warning is too little, too late: I'm already closing the distance between us.

The blinds rattle as I push you against them.

Clothes fly this way and that. A bowtie hangs from a lampshade. A thong drapes over the handle of the room's telephone. A tuxedo jacket is stained by the pink of a dress; a male sock is wrapped around the white loop of a bra strap.

Hot flesh begs for touch.

You kiss me, and I forget how to breathe. Is your heart pounding like mine? I press my hand to your chest and feel your pulse—it pounds and pounds like the music on the dance floor, pounds like mine, erratic and wild.

The mattress welcomes us.

For a long moment, we only kiss. That moment is a glorious forever; it's the kiss that will always be.

Just you, just me, just a kiss.

It should have stopped there.

But it didn't.

It wasn't ever going to.

The moment we locked eyes on the dance floor, we both knew how this was going to go.

The kiss becomes something else.

It's a fusion of souls.

But it's just a kiss. Just a stupid kiss.

Hands cup aching flesh. Lips suckle, tongues taste rivulets of sweat. Thigh against thigh, sliding and crushing. Fingers entwine, palm to palm, squeezing tightly as we find each other.

You move slowly over me. You do not look away from me, and I cannot even blink. Cannot breathe.

I am lost.

I taste your heartbeat in the instant before we crash into each other. We cling to one another, gasping, mouth to mouth, breast to breast, heartbeats shattering in unison, flesh mated and moving.

You kiss my eyes as we come together.

—That's just sweat.

You don't believe me any more than I believe myself.

But then, your cheeks taste of salt as well. I kiss them and kiss them and taste your tears.

You're inside me; it's endless; I'm breathless.

But then, I'm inside you, too.

It lasts forever. We move and we dance and we don't say a word.

You devour me.

I envelop you.

You come, shuddering and silent.

Who knows the rhythm of the hours we spend, tangled in the bedsheets? I don't. You don't. There is no clock, only the stars fading and the moon receding to a dim silver sliver as black sky becomes gray and gray becomes pink.

I gasp against your lips once more, our orgasms synchronized and endless, and I'm weeping and you're seeking the truth in my soul through the windows of my eyes, and I hear the words I won't let you say and I hear my own words like ghosts in a graveyard, my own truths hidden in the rampant chaos of my pulse as we come together, and you shake and you tremble and you cling to me.

Dawn is red and orange and pink fire in the sky as our last night on earth comes to a close.

What if—

Those two words hang between us. Did I say them? Did you?

Nothing follows them. There is nothing.

Nothing.

I'll always remember the way your heartbeat sounds as I fall asleep.

I'll always remember the taste of that last kiss, stolen in the final moments before sleep takes us both—

—Sunlight burned hot and yellow on my eyelids. My throat burned, and my mouth was scorched. My head pounded. Sand was gritty in my hot, throbbing eyes.

Groaning, I cracked one eye open.

Anchorage.

Hotel.

The wedding.

Dancing. Talking to my friends.

Duncan.

Oh, fuck.

Duncan.

I scoured my mind for clues, but it was all hazy and vague.

I heard him beside me, grunting in pain.

I cracked open one eye again, rolled my heavy, throbbing skull to face him. He was naked, his bare ass facing the window. The blinds were open—it was still relatively early.

I was naked, too.

Shit, shit, shit.

No, no, no.

Panic. Immense, immediate, blazing panic. It occluded everything else in my brain and left me with one thought:

ESCAPE!

I slid out of bed as quietly as possible, threw on a pair of leggings and T-shirt—no bra, no panties, which says a lot about how panicked I was, because I never go commando—shoved everything into my bag, and left.

I didn't tie back my hair, I didn't relieve my screaming bladder, nothing. I didn't pack—makeup, phone charger, dirty clothes, everything just got shoved into my suitcase and zipped up.

No note.

I stopped in the restroom in the lobby and then caught a taxi to the airport, snagged coffee and breakfast there, and flew back to Seattle, where my car was waiting for me in the long-term lot.

Finally back in the Lower Forty-eight, I sat in my idling car, radio off, windows down to let out the old, stale air, and tried not to cry.

Why was I weepy?

I slapped my cheeks. "Get it together, Rune," I told myself out loud. "You're fine."

My phone rang: *Duncan*.

Dammit.

I sent it to voicemail and responded with a text message: *Had to catch my flight. Thank you for a great weekend, and for everything you did for my friends. Sorry it had to be this way. Goodbye, Duncan.*

I watched the blue bar creep across the screen, pause a quarter inch from the right side of the screen, and then the bar jumped to the end with the "bloop" of the message being delivered. A second later, it changed from 'delivered' to 'read.'

Three jumping dots…gone. Jumping dots…gone.

Nothing for over a minute.

And then he liked the message.

I waited another minute, but it was clear that's all there would be.

I didn't blame him; how could I? I knew he had feelings. I just...I can't go there. Not with him, not with anyone. But especially not with him—there is not a single part of me that wants to move to fucking Alaska. It was nice enough to visit, but live there? No.

Was there more to my resistance to the notion of being with Duncan? Probably. It likely had something to do with Hayes and the other assholes I've dated. They've all been uniformly terrible.

I don't trust myself.

I don't trust men.

Sure, Duncan *seems* great, on paper. He's hot as fuck in the face, has a great head of hair, incredible eyes; his body is to fucking die for, powerful, lean and hard, shredded, muscular.

That dick.

His mouth.

THAT DICK.

God, the sex was next level.

My vagina ached just thinking about it.

Something niggled in the back of my brain, a worm of doubt, a seed of worry.

What if—

Nope.

My phone rang again, and I cursed it out loud. "Stop fucking calling me, Duncan, Jesus. You're not changing my mind." And then I looked at the screen, realized it was Lindsey, and answered it. "Hi."

"Where are you, bitch? Duncan said you're not in your room, your stuff is all gone, and you sent him some blow-off text?"

I sighed. "I'm in my car in long-term parking at Sea-Tac. And it was not a blow-off text."

"What did it say?" she asked.

"Linz—"

"Read it to me, if it's not a blow off."

I read it to her. "See? Not a blow off."

She just snorted. "It's a blow off."

"How? What was I supposed to say, Linz?"

"You were supposed to stick around and talk to him face to face like a fucking adult!" She snapped. "You owe him that much, at minimum, for everything he did for Raquel and Hamish…which you and I both knew he did for *you*. The man agrees to be your fake date to a wedding for people he doesn't know. He uses his own personal contacts and resources to help *your* friends save their wedding. He gives you multiple orgasms, which you yourself say are the best you've ever had. He gives you the dicking down of a lifetime. And what do you do? You ghost him the morning after and give him a shitty, immature blow-off text. Seriously, Rune, 'thanks and sorry' doesn't fucking cut it."

My eyes burned. "Whose side are you on?" I hissed. "I thought you were my best friend. You're supposed to have my back. You of all people should understand how I'm feeling, why I'm…." I shook my head. "You know what? Never fucking mind. If you think Duncan Badd is so great and wonderful, *you* fuck him. You have my permission. Go for it. Move to fucking Alaska for him."

"Rune!" she gasped, audibly hurt. "I love you. But friends call each other out when it's necessary."

"I have to go. It's a long drive back to LA. Tell Raquel I'll call her later. Bye."

"RUNE!"

I hung up on her. I almost blocked her, but opted to silence her alerts instead. It was a temporary solution to my hurt and anger at my best friend's betrayal.

Fuck this.

I plugged my phone in and turned on a playlist of loud, aggressive, breakup songs—the same ones I'd listened to on repeat after fleeing LA and Hayes's infidelity.

Was that only two and a half months ago? It felt like I'd spent a year in Alaska. Like I'd had a whole, brief life there with Duncan and his family and their bars.

I set my GPS for home and left Sea-Tac.

I drove straight through, stopping only for gas and fast food. I made it home in twenty-three hours flat.

My condo felt weird.

Empty.

Silent.

The last time I was here, I was breaking up with Hayes. Now, I have Duncan on the brain.

Hayes is absent from this place, thank god. His trophies, his clothes, that stupid fucking stuffed beaver he insisted just *had* to sit on my bookshelf for reasons he never fully articulated. His toiletries were gone from my bathroom, his clothes from my drawers and closet. On the bright side, I have my closet space back.

Why do I feel so flat and empty?

When I left LA all those weeks ago, I had this secret fantasy that I would come home feeling renewed and whole, with a new zest for life and a zeal for singlehood. I'd be ready to take on the world. Find my dream job. Meet the perfect guy at a cute little coffee shop around the block from my corner office that I'd somehow already have at my brand new dream job.

The reality of my homecoming is…slightly different.

I don't feel any better about myself. About life. I have no fucking clue what my dream job even is. That's the reality—I have a degree in business management and no clue what to do with it. I enjoyed the classes, mostly. I liked the theories and concepts, and I excelled in pretty much every aspect of college. I'm a 4.0 student, an achiever.

But…now what?

Business as a concept is one thing. But now I'm

out here in the real world with a diploma and a hell of an expensive education and not a fucking clue what to do with it. What business am I supposed to be in? Marketing? Management? How do you get into management? That's not even a field, that's a rank, a position. Film? Music? Tech?

Do I just scour the want ads? Go on Indeed or whatever? Send out my resume at random?

I'm already in the throes of an existential crisis, and I've been home all of twenty minutes. I haven't even unpacked.

"Get it the fuck together, Rune," I said, talking to myself out loud for the second time in one day like a real crazy person.

I unpacked. Started laundry. Put new sheets on my bed—and threw away the old ones on which I'd had who knew how much sex with Hayes. Called my parents and spent a good hour on the phone with them, filling them in on the wedding—without mentioning Duncan, of course.

At the end of the conversation, Mom said her goodbye, ending with a strict order to come over for dinner tonight. Dad, however, lingered on the line.

"You need something else, Dad?" I asked.

He sighed, a gruff half-growl. "Hayes was never good enough for you, Sweet-Pea."

"You can say you told me so, I'm a big girl, I can take it," I said.

"I don't need to—you just said it for me. And I'm

not trying to, like, rub anything in your face, honey. I just…you deserve a *man*. Someone who will take care of you."

"I can take care of myself, Dad."

"I know. And the man who deserves you will know that too, and he'll still take care of you. He'll do it *because* you can take care of yourself. Hayes Willoughby is a needy, whiny, sad sack of shit who couldn't find his asshole with both hands, a map, and a goddamn flashlight. It's no secret I never knew what you saw in him. I ain't a twenty-something girl, so maybe he really is hot or something. I dunno. Or maybe he's got a really big you know what."

"DAD!" I screeched. "WHAT THE FUCK?"

"Well? I don't get it. What did you see in that simpering fuckwit?"

"You really want the nitty-gritty details, Dad?" I snapped. "Yes, it was mostly the sex. Okay? He was good-looking. Not, like, scorching hot, but that's the point. The hottest guys are always the biggest assholes. Hayes was good-looking but not a player. We were physically compatible. And yes, his you-know-what is—"

"I TAKE IT BACK, I DON'T WANT TO KNOW," Dad cut in, loudly enough I yanked the phone away from my ear.

I cackled. "I didn't think so."

"But he is a player, isn't he?"

"No, he's just a cheating fuckwit."

"I just don't get it. I don't get cheaters, especially ones who cheat with someone uglier than the person they're cheating on."

I laughed. "Dad, you don't know who he cheated on me with."

"Yes, I do. I was behind them in line at Costco a couple weeks ago. I recognized his voice before I realized it was him. He didn't know I was there. He and his girlfriend were talking, and I gradually realized from the contextual clues that the girl he was with was the girl he fucked around on you with. They talked about you."

"Whoa, hold the fuck up, Dad. *WHAT*?" I paused in silence. "He was with her…*TWO WEEKS* ago?"

"Yes."

"And you're *sure* she was his girlfriend?" I asked.

"He had his hand on her ass, so yeah, I'm pretty sure."

"And they were talking about me?"

"I mean, indirectly. He referenced his ex, and she said something along the lines of 'that girl with the weird name who threw trophies at you.'"

"'The girl with the weird name who threw trophies at you,'" I echoed. "Wow. And why didn't he bring her to the wedding, I wonder?"

"Oh, she had a work trip."

I laughed. "Dad, how long were you eavesdropping on them? Jesus."

"It was a long-ass line and they weren't being discreet."

I groaned. "He was still acting like a sad sack of shit at the wedding. He was all jealous and angry, like I was the crazy one for being mad at him for cheating on me. But he's still with her? What the fuck?" I shook my head, sighing. "I don't understand him, Dad. At all."

"Don't even waste your brain power trying, Sweet-Pea. He's not worth it. He never was. Now you focus on you. Your future. Your career. In time, you'll find the right guy."

"How will I know if he's the right one, Dad?"

He laughed, a sighing chuckle. "Oh, honey. That's the oldest question in the world, and one fathers dread getting. Because the real answer is I don't fuckin' know, baby-girl."

"How'd you know Mom was it for you?"

He cackled. "I didn't, at first."

I pulled the phone away and stared at it in stunned silence.

"Rune?" His voice came from the speaker, tinny and distant and small. "I lose you?"

I put it back to my ear. "No, I'm here. I just... what? You love Mom. You would never, ever cheat on her."

"I'd cut my dick off first."

"No, *I'd* cut your dick off, first," I heard Mom say in the background.

"Am I on speaker?" I asked.

"No, she just knows what we're talking about." He sighed. "Listen, Sweet-Pea. You *don't* know. Not for a hundred percent sure. Not about anything, ever. The only absolute in this life is that there are no absolutes. I knew I was in love with your mom. But did I *know* for sure she was the only woman I'd ever love, that we were meant to be together until we're old and gray? No! I was twenty-two, she was gorgeous, smart, and seemed to like me. I know how this is gonna sound, but when we first got together, I felt like she was out of my league and the whole thing was a big mistake she'd figure out at some point and dump me when she came to her senses. So I tried as hard as I could to convince her I was this great guy and she should stick with me. But really, I just knew I'd never, ever find anyone better than her."

I heard a rustle, and then Mom's voice came across the line. "Rune, honey. I don't know what happened in Alaska, but it's obvious it's got you thinking hard. Maybe it was seeing Hayes, maybe there was another guy. You don't have to tell me. What your dad means is that love is always a risk. You won't know, not for sure, if you're making the right choice. Even after your dad and I got married, I wasn't sure we'd make it. We had some really ugly fights early on. Marriage is hard, honey. But I love him, and I'm committed to him. I made that choice and I keep making it every day. That's all love is—choosing someone every day, even when it doesn't always make sense and even when you sometimes want to strangle him in his sleep."

"Mom!"

"That will make sense someday, honey. Trust me."

"So you guys' big advice is…there's no way to know, and I might want to strangle the man I love in his sleep, but that's normal?"

Dad cackled. "You're oversimplifying what we're saying, Rune."

"What's his name?" Mom asked.

"Nice try," I mumbled. "There isn't anyone. I was just asking because I can't figure out how I could have been so wrong about Hayes."

"Can't help you with that one, honey," Mom said. "Hayes was a gumpy twat."

"Mom!"

"I never saw it either, is all I'm saying."

"You never said anything!"

"To what end?" she said. "Like you would have listened? My first boyfriend, when I was nineteen, was a guy named Troy. He was buff, popular, handsome, and drove a cool car."

"And what's Troy doing now? Hmm?" Dad demanded.

"Hush, darling. I married you, not him. Stop being jealous." Mom cleared her throat. "My parents both warned me that Troy wasn't a good person. I didn't listen."

"And what did he do?" I asked.

"Assaulted me in his car after a date."

I was silent. "Mom...*what?*"

"I punched his lights out, but still. My point is, I was young and in love with an asshole, too. I never got the sense that Hayes was *bad*, not like Troy was bad, just...a loser, at best. Not worth your time or attention. But I knew you had to see it yourself. Nothing we said would make a difference. I don't mean this as a dig at you, honey, but it's just a fact of life that you can't tell a twenty-something kid anything, especially not about the person they're dating."

I had to literally bite down on my tongue to keep myself from saying "I'm not a kid," because nothing says that you *are* in fact a kid like insisting you're not.

"Got it," I said, eventually, because I had to say *something*.

Mom just sighed. "Honey, when you're ready to talk about it, let me know. I'll do my best to listen, not judge, and give the best advice I have, even if it's not what you want to hear. But I know you have to come to these things on your own—it took you almost a month before you called us and told us what happened with Hayes and why you left town so abruptly with no immediate plans to return."

"I had to process it on my own," I said. "Plus, I had to stop being so mad. If I'd have told you guys about it right away, I wouldn't have had the self-control to not let Dad wring his neck."

I heard Dad laugh in the background. "Smart girl.

Took a hell of a lot of self-control to not wring his neck at Costco as it was."

Mom sighed. "Sweetie, we get it. Just know that we're here for you, always. We love you, and we support you. And I know we're your parents, but we're also humans who have been through a lot of stuff."

"I know. I love you guys, too. I think I just need time to sort through things before I can really talk about it."

"And you don't have to talk about it with us, honey, just know that you *can*," Mom said. "Okay, we've kept you on the phone long enough. I'm sure you're tired. Just come see us soon, okay?"

"This week, I promise," I said.

I hung up, plugged my phone in, ran a bath, and spent the next two hours soaking, watching mindless reality TV, and definitely *not* thinking about Duncan.

Lies. I totally spent the whole time thinking about Duncan.

Unfortunately, the only conclusion I came to by the time I was pruny and ready to get out was that feelings were stupid, I should never have let Lindsey talk me into the whole stupid 'fake date to the wedding' plan, and I was terribly, terribly confused about pretty much everything.

Also, I think I missed Duncan. Which was stupid.

I desperately wanted another round…or two or three or ten…in bed with him, which was not stupid.

Just problematic. Impossible. Not happening. Never, never, never.

I'm not going back to Alaska. He's not coming here. It's over. Permanently, period, full stop.

I just have to get over him.

I slept.

I deep-cleaned my condo.

Fine-tuned and polished my resume.

Spent the next several days posting my resume on headhunter websites, sending it to various businesses, first and foremost the advertising firm I interned with last summer. I was conflicted about that one—I didn't like the office culture there, and the boss I had directly reported to was blatantly chauvinistic and addressed at least eighty percent of his words to my boobs. But on the other hand, I knew they paid well, I knew they liked my work while I was interning, and I knew they needed someone, so I stood a good chance of getting the job.

A few days turned into a week; I got some hits on my resume and went to a few interviews, but none of the places I interviewed felt like a good fit for one reason or another. I was probably being too picky for someone looking for her first real adult job, but I'd like to at least like the company and people I work for and with.

A week became two, and Duncan was still constantly on my mind, especially alone at night.

I took an interview at the ad agency where I interned and accepted a position in their administrative department—an entry-level job, making copies, answering phones, filing, and things like that. It's not glamorous, but it's a job, it pays pretty well, and my boss is a woman who doesn't stare at my boobs. Win-win.

Two weeks became three—the longest I've gone without talking to or seeing Lindsey since we met our freshman year at USC.

She was the one to break the silence, showing up at my condo a little over a month after the wedding, buzzing insistently at the crack of dawn with coffee and bagels from our favorite place.

I let her in without a word, still in my towel after a shower. She took the lid off of one of the coffees and fixed it the way I like it, and then set out the bagels and cream cheese.

"Thanks," I mumbled, freeing my hair from the towel-turban to air dry.

"Rune, about the last time we talked," Lindsey started

"Let me get some coffee in me first," I said.

"Fair enough."

I sipped the coffee, which I'd watched her fix with one cream, one sugar, the way I've taken my coffee since I started drinking it. Only this time, it just tasted…funny. It made my stomach turn.

I sniffed it, stared into the dark khaki liquid, sipped again, wincing at the off-ness of it. "This tastes weird."

Lindsey frowned, reached for my cup, sipped,

shrugged. "Tastes fine to me." She tried hers, next. "Same. Normal coffee. You sick or something?"

I shrugged. "I dunno. My stomach has been weird the last few days." I shrugged. "I dunno." I sipped the coffee again, but my stomach flipped. "What the fuck? I can't drink it. I don't know what's wrong with me."

Her eyes narrowed. "Try the bagel. Sesame, light spread."

I took a tiny bite, but my stomach immediately revolted, and I had to rush to the bathroom to spit it out...along with the rest of my stomach's contents.

When I returned, teeth brushed *again*, Lindsey's frown was deeper than ever. "Is it a stomach bug going around at work or something?"

"No." I arched an eyebrow at her. "You talked to my parents."

"Mom and Pop Rigby are my second parents. Of course, I talked to them before I came here." She set her bagel and coffee down and stood up. "Hang on. I'll be right back."

"Where are you going?" I asked. "You just got here."

"I'll be right back, I said." Lindsey slung her purse over her shoulder and left my condo.

Less than ten minutes later—during which time I decided I was definitely coming down with a bug—Lindsey returned with a plastic bag from the pharmacy on the corner.

I stared at her, shaking my head before I even saw what was in the bag. "No."

She slid the package out of the bag and slapped it against my chest. "Yes."

I looked at the pregnancy test without taking it. "Absolutely the fuck not."

"When was your last period? Are you sick at night? Or any other time of day other than *morning*?" The emphasis on that particular word was not an accident.

I went pale, realizing my period was seriously late—I've been so busy with the new job I didn't even realize it until she asked. "I missed my last period," I whispered.

"Is anyone else at work sick?"

"No, but I could have gotten a bug anywhere else."

She eyed me. "And there's absolutely no possibility you and Duncan raw-dogged it at any point over the weekend?"

"No!" I all but shouted. "We used protection every…." A memory of my panicked escape from Anchorage settled firmly in the forefront of my brain like a ton of bricks. "Oh fuck. Oh fuck. Oh fuck, fuck, fuck, fuck, fuck, *fuck*!"

My eyes burned, tears burning like acid as my stomach flipped, soured, and rose up in my gorge.

Lindsey pulled me to the couch. "Sit down before you fall down and talk to me. You remembered something bad, I take it?"

"The night of the wedding, Duncan and I left a little early."

Lindsey snorted. "I know. You cost me five bucks."

I sniffled, frowning. "What?"

"I bet Raquel you'd leave after an hour, but she said you guys would stay at least two. You left after two and a half hours." She shook her hands. "Never mind. What happened?"

I shook my head. "I don't know, that's the problem. I have vague memories of that night, and vague is at best. All I really remember is waking up naked next to him."

"Which means you guys got hammered and fucked like porn stars all night," Lindsey said.

"Yeah. But…did we use condoms? I don't know. I don't know! I ran, Linz. I shoved all my shit into my bag and left. I didn't even pee in the room—I peed in the lobby restroom."

Lindsey snickered. "You know you're making the walk of shame when you don't even pee after waking up."

"LINDSEY!" I shouted. "This is no time for jokes!"

"Who's joking?" she said, ripping open the box and pressing the test into my hand. "It's time for you to pee on a stick, *ma'am*."

I held the test in my fist, shaking all over. "Linz, I'm scared. I can't be pregnant! I just got a job!"

Lindsey sighed. "Girl, I know. But you can't avoid reality, either. You ran away from Duncan to avoid the reality of your feelings for him. But you can't run away from this. If you *are* pregnant, it's not gonna be any less real or true if you don't find out."

I trembled like a leaf in a long autumn wind. "Linz, I can't be. I *can't*."

"You don't remember *anything*?"

I shrugged, shook my head. "Not really. I...." I closed my eyes, dashing away tears with the heels of my palms. "I know we had sex. And a lot of it. I remember my vagina being super sore that day and the next. Plus, I woke up naked, and you know I never sleep naked. Even after sex, I usually at least put on underwear before going to sleep."

Lindsey sighed wistfully. "I miss having so much sex my pussy hurts the next day. It's been so long I've thought about joining a nunnery."

"You mean a convent?" I said.

"I like the word nunnery better. Convent makes me think of conventions, and conventions make me think of Dalton."

"You liked Dalton. I never got why you broke up with him. He was a nerd, but you said he had a nice cock and he was good in bed, once you'd broken him in." I frowned. "Also, what is it with you and guys whose names start with D?"

Lindsey frowned. "Weird. I never realized that." She groaned. "And for one, don't say 'broke him in' like he's a horse or a pair of shoes."

"You said it first when you started seeing him!" I argue.

"And I shouldn't have."

"Why did you break up with him?"

She blushed, shaking her head. "Reasons."

"Such as?"

"Such as go pee on that stick, Rune. Dalton telling me he loved me after two months and making me freak out like a crazy person isn't going to distract me from the reality that you are, in all likelihood, pregnant."

I stared at her. "That's why?"

"Yes, okay? And he was...he was serious. He really did love me, or thought he did, and I just couldn't handle that. He was sweet, cute, and unexpectedly well-endowed for a guy who was a buck-forty soaking weight at six feet tall. But I didn't love him. I honestly don't know if I'm even capable of being in love, at this point."

"Linz—"

She shot to her feet, grabbed my wrists, and physically hauled me to my feet, shoving me toward my bedroom and the en suite bathroom. "Go take the test, Rune."

"I don't want to," I said, resisting her pushing. "I'm scared."

She kept pushing until we reached the bathroom, turned me so my ass faced the toilet, yanked my towel off, and physically forced me to sit down on the toilet. Then, diabolically, she turned on the faucet.

It worked. Urine squirted out of me, and she

uncapped the test and handed it to me. "Do it, Rune. No excuses."

I peed on the stick, re-capped it, set it on the sink, finished, wiped, washed my hands, and then wandered in a daze to the living room. Lindsey followed me, test in one hand, her phone in the other; she had a timer set, counting down the minutes and seconds until I found out whether I'd fucked up my life.

We sat on the couch with the test on the coffee table in front of us, her phone beside it, silently counting down to doomsday.

We didn't have to wait the full 2 minutes—the word PREGNANT emblazoned itself in the window almost immediately.

I lurched to my feet and threw the thing across the condo; it clattered against a cabinet in the kitchen and then to the floor. "No! God, no. No, no, no." I collapsed to my butt on the floor, sobbing. "What do I *do*, Linz?" I asked in a ragged whisper.

"Well, you call your parents, and you call Duncan." She paused, shook her hands. "Wait, scratch that. First, you call in to work. Second, you and I go to your parents' house and tell them in person. And *then* you call Duncan."

"Mom's got a lecture today, and Dad has classes. They're not home."

Lindsey sank to her butt beside me, blonde razor bob swinging, blue eyes sympathetic and full of love. "I'm sorry I was so harsh, Rune. That's what I came to say. I don't take back what I said, because it was true and I still feel that way. But I was harsh in the way I said it, and I apologize."

I sagged against her, and her arms went around me. "You're right, it was harsh, but I forgive you. And you *were* right." I sniffled tears. "I don't know how to do this, Linz."

"I've got you, babe. You and me, ride or die. Let me make you some tea and we'll come up with a plan, okay?"

"I hate tea."

"I know."

Thirty minutes later, I'd taken two more tests, each of which only confirmed my terrifying new reality:

I was pregnant.

THIRTEEN

Duncan

I SET THE TILL DRAWER BACK DOWN ON THE DESK, ONLY JUST barely stopping myself from throwing it through the fucking wall. I'd counted it four times and came up with four different numbers.

Elias came in as I sat down and scraped my hands through my hair with a series of vicious curses. "You good, boss?" he asked, tossing the liquor inventory checklist onto the desk.

"No. This fucking drawer won't balance. I've counted it four times and I've gotten four different numbers."

Elias chuckled, dragging over the other chair. He slid the drawer onto his lap and counted it with the swift precision of a man who's done it countless times. He wrote the number he got on a Post-It and counted it twice more, getting the same number three times—dead on. "Your head ain't in the game, kid."

"No shit," I mumbled. "Haven't been sleeping well."

He chuckled again. "Gee, I wonder why that is?"

I blinked at him with lifted eyebrows. "Oh? Why's that?"

He counted the day's take, answering without looking at me. "Well, the reason is about five-eight, has black hair and blue eyes, and ghosted you."

"Shut up."

He flipped me off as he put on readers to gather the credit card receipts and send the batch over. "Don't shoot the messenger, sweetie."

"Sorry, I just…it's not her. I'm just not sleeping well."

He just laughed. "Sure, sure."

"Elias—"

He set the receipts down and removed his readers, sighing. "You've been off your A-game since that weekend, Duncan. I don't think it's a coincidence."

"I have not."

He snorted sarcastically, rifling through previous reports until he found the one he wanted, and showed it to me. "Just last week, you had to comp not one, not two, not three, but *five* different meals because *you* fucked up. Not judging, just saying. You miscounted the register this past Monday and I only noticed it because I'm a type-A lunatic who double-checks everything. You bitched out Casey, our new line cook, for what seemed like no reason at all. I can go on. Do I need to?"

I groaned, covering my face with both hands. "No."

"Just admit you miss her and that you're pissed off she ghosted you."

"Fine," I grumbled. "I miss her. But she didn't ghost me—she just snuck out and sent me a shitty blow off text."

Elias blew a raspberry. "If you ask me, a blow off text is almost worse than being ghosted. Scratch that— it *is* worse. I'll take being ghosted over a blow off."

"You're married, Elias."

"Yeah, *now*. I wasn't always, though, obviously. I've been ghosted, blown off, and dumped in just about every way you can think of. It all sucks, but to me it always felt worst when he took the time to make a bullshit excuse. At that point, just be honest, right? But no, the shitty excuses. The lies. The paper-thin reasons, or worse yet, no reason, just a vague apology."

"That's what I got—thanks, and I'm sorry."

He didn't answer until he'd finished the credit card batch, sliding his readers back into the pocket of his short-sleeved button-down and turning to look at me. "That sucks. I think what's bothering you, though, is that you're denying how hurt you are. It's making you a pissy-ass bitch because you're hurt and won't recognize it. That shit festers, Dunc. I know you're all macho and alpha, just like your daddy, but you still have feelings.

And also, for the record, your daddy is way more in tune with his feelings than I think you recognize."

I opened my mouth, said nothing, and closed it again. "I...I've never once considered whether my dad is in touch with his feelings or not."

"Well, he is."

"And you know this how?" I asked.

"I've been tending bar for Sebastian Badd for almost twenty years, kid. I know the man. We've had a lot of deep talks while closing up shop."

"Are you upset that I got the GM job and you didn't?"

He sighed again, tapping a pen on the desk. "No, I'm not. Mainly because we talked about it. If you want a war movie metaphor for it, you're the young buck fresh out of West Point with no experience who gets tapped to lead a unit into battle. I'm the grizzled old non-com who actually knows what the fuck he's doing." He laughed, grinning at me. "I'm here to help you learn the ropes, Dunc. I could get a job managing just about any bar I wanted, anywhere in the world. I'm damn good at my job. But I like your family. I like the way you do business. I'm here because it's where I want to be."

"I see."

He patted me on the back. "Go home, Dunc. I'll finish here. Sort your shit out, okay? Get that girl out of your head, however you have to do it. She's gone. If she wanted the same thing you did, she'd be here. Yeah, I guess you're right," I said. "You sure you're good?"

He nodded. "Just put up the chairs for me. I got the rest."

"Thanks, Elias. I appreciate you."

He winked at me. "Don't you forget it, sweetie."

I put up the chairs and left through the back, heading home with my head swirling.

The house was silent as I let myself in through the garage—not unusual, these days. Mom and Dad go to bed early, Delia and Emerson have both moved out, and Dane has early classes at the community college, so most nights I'm the only one up when I get back from closing shifts.

I grabbed some chips from the pantry and sat at the island in the kitchen, eating chips and salsa and sipping a beer, considering Elias's advice about Rune.

"Chips and salsa at three in the morning?" a voice said, startling me from my thoughts.

"Mom! Jesus, you scared the shit out of me. What're you doing up? Did I wake you?"

She was standing in the hallway at the entrance to the kitchen, wearing one of Dad's button-downs, her hair frizzy and held back by a pink silk sleep mask, legs bare, eyes squinting sleepily. "Nah. A mama knows when her kids need her."

"I'm good," I lied.

She barked a laugh. "Okay, sure. Pull the other one, Dunc, it's got bells on."

"I don't know what the hell that means, Mom."

"It means I don't believe you." She rubbed at her eyes as she shuffled into the kitchen. "When was the last time you had real food? As in, a decent meal?"

"Mom, I'm fine. You don't need to cook for me." She just gave me the Mom-stare until I groaned. "It's been a while. I've been living at work, lately."

She leaned over the island and cupped my cheeks, rubbing her thumbs under my eyes. "And not sleeping, either, I see." She tapped my nose. "Talk to Mommy."

"Only if you never refer to yourself in the third person as Mommy ever again."

She laughed. "No promises, but I'll try. Now, spill the tea, bubbie."

"I'm sure someone has given you the tea about that whole…wedding business that happened a month or so ago?"

She nodded, pouring a can of tomato soup into a pot and heating a frying pan. "Yeah, your Uncle Brock said he flew you and some girl you met and her friends to Anchorage. Apparently you were so upset when he picked you up that you didn't say two words to him the whole way home."

I groaned. "I don't think I ever said thank you to him. Guess I owe him an apology and a thank you."

"No, you didn't, and yes, you do." She slathered two slices of bread with butter, added sliced cheese, and set the sandwich into the pan. "He's redoing their deck this weekend. A good way to thank him would be to show up and give him a hand."

"I will."

"So. The girl?"

"It honestly doesn't matter, Mom," I said. "And not just because I don't want to talk about it."

"But you're gonna!" Mom said, singing the words far too cheerfully for a woman woken up at three a.m. to counsel her grown son.

I sighed. "The Sparks Notes version is that she showed up wanting a date for a wedding. Her friends were having a destination wedding here in Ketchikan and planned to party at the Kitty after. Her ex, who cheated on her, was going to be there."

Mom nodded knowingly. "And she wanted my handsome boy to make her ex jealous."

"Mom," I groaned. "Don't be cringe."

"Too late for that, kiddo. One of a parent's primary jobs when their kids get older is to embarrass them by being as cringey as possible."

"Well then, you're killing it," I said.

She narrowed her eyes at me. "Watch it, bub. I'm making your food."

"I'm kidding."

She rolled a hand. "So? Destination wedding, cheating scumbag ex, and a plot to make him jealous. Then what?"

"Then the Old Toby burned down. They'd rented

out the whole thing for their friends. Their whole wedding plan went up in flames, literally."

"Ahhhh," Mom said, stirring the soup. "So you called your sister and got them the back room up in Anchorage, and got Brock to fly you guys there."

"Yep."

"And she wasn't appreciative?"

"No, it wasn't that."

Mom poured soup into a bowl, plated the sandwich, cut it with the spatula, and sent both in front of me, and then came around to sit beside me while I ate, occasionally stealing a bite of sandwich or soup. "So? You're living at work and not sleeping or eating. Something happened."

"We…" I sighed, finding it hard to put into words, especially to my mother. "She just left."

Mom barked a laugh. "You skipped a bunch of stuff in the middle, I think."

"We hooked up," I said, snapping it with more frustration than I'd intended. "Sorry, Mom. I just… yeah, things happened. She was clear from the get-go that she was leaving after the wedding, and that us getting together was only for the weekend."

"But you thought there was something more there?" She guessed.

I nodded. "I don't *think* there was, I *know* there was." I shook my head. "It's weird talking about this with my mom."

"You know the story of how I met your father, don't you?"

Puzzled by the non sequitur, I shrugged. "I mean, sort of? I'm fuzzy on the details."

"You're an adult, now. You can hear the whole thing."

"Okay?"

"I was about to get married."

"When you met Dad?"

"No, silly. Before. I was engaged to someone else." When I looked surprised, she just laughed. "Newsflash, bubbie, your father wasn't my first sexual or romantic partner."

"Oh god, can we not?"

She sighed. "Duncan, grow up. I'm your mother, but I'm also a person. A woman. And I have a point in bringing this up, so quit acting scandalized as if it's a shock to you that I had a life before meeting your father."

"Fine," I mumbled around a bite of grilled cheese. "Just no details I don't need to know."

"I'll try to protect your delicate sensibilities," she drawled, teasing. "So, anyway. When I say I was about to get married, I mean I was at the church, in my wedding dress, with guests in the pews, about to walk down the damn aisle with my dad."

"Oh dear. Seeing as you're married to Dad and not that guy, I take it something happened?"

"You could say that." She gathered the plate and

bowl as I finished eating and leaned over to set them in the sink. "He was fucking my bridesmaid."

I choked, coughed, and spluttered. "Jesus. Like, you *saw* it? *At* the wedding?"

She bobbed her head from side to side. "Sort of. I was freaking out a bit and wanted to talk to him. I wanted him to reassure me, y'know? Like fiancés are supposed to. But instead, I found his friends—the groomsmen and bridesmaids—all watching a video."

"Oh boy," I muttered.

"They'd filmed my fiancé fucking my bridesmaid. Well, *a* bridesmaid, not *my* bridesmaid. I didn't even know her—I didn't have a big social circle down there, so *our* friends were really just *his* friends, not really mine."

"These people recorded your fiancé, their friend, fucking their other friend, who was standing up in your wedding?"

Mom nodded. "Yup." She popped the P at the end.

"That's trashy in so many ways," I said.

"They were all shockingly shitty people, looking back. My dad never liked Michael, so when I ran from the wedding, he was all too happy to help me get away. He took me to his favorite dive bar near an airfield out in the middle of nowhere, and I got absolutely shitfaced."

I laughed. "Nice. Is there any other way to handle that situation?"

"No, there is not. But then, I got a wild hair up

my ass, decided I couldn't possibly stay in Seattle another second, and got into an airplane about to take off. The pilot agreed to just fly away with me, since I was a drunk, spurned bride in the throes of an emotional breakdown. I ended up here in Ketchikan, walked into Badd's Bar and Grille, and met your dad."

"And the rest is history," I said. "What's that got to do with me?"

"I fought my feelings for him for a long time, Dunc. I fought them hard. You take after your father in that sense—he knew what he felt and accepted it before I did." She tipped her head side to side. "Well, sort of. It was a whole back and forth thing. Whatever. The point is, I fought my feelings. I did stupid things in an effort to get away from how I felt for him, and he did the same thing. But I…" she sighed. "He did something that hurt me, the details of which are one of the things you don't want to know about. The important thing is that he hurt me, emotionally, and I tried to run. The only thing that kept me here was that I couldn't find a way to physically leave Ketchikan before he found me. Which he did."

"Mom…what's this got to do with my situation?"

She rested a hand on my forearm. "The point is that I understand where she's coming from. If she had a cheating ex, I'm guessing she's had more than *one* cheating ex. And that does a number on you. Makes it really hard to trust. And not just men—it makes it hard to trust yourself." She touched my jaw and made me look at her. "We all know what a good guy you are, Duncan. You're not perfect. I'm sure if we interviewed your previous girlfriends and…um, *paramours*…they'd have things to say about you. But you're not a cheater. You're not abusive. You're good. You're kind. Right?"

I shrugged, uncomfortable. "I hope so? I try to be."

"Right—you *try*. And you succeed more than you don't. But she doesn't know that. You spent how long together? A few days?"

"Yeah, but—"

She gave me a look that shut me up. "I'm not denying that you can develop very real feelings for someone you haven't known very long, Dunc. I developed very strong feelings for Bast within days of meeting him, and that's what freaked me out. My question was more about her state of mind. Maybe she *did* feel things for you, but like me, she wasn't ready to accept it. Maybe your feelings were just you, maybe you saw or felt something she didn't. The only way to know is to ask her."

"She snuck out while I was asleep and didn't text me until she got back to Seattle," I told her. "And then she *texted* me, basically saying thanks and goodbye. It was very clearly a 'don't call us, we'll call you' thing, but without the 'we'll call you' part."

Mom winced. "Oof. Yeah, that's tough, bubbie. I'm sorry." She rubbed my shoulder. "You must have really felt like there was something big there if you're this upset about it a month and a half later."

"I don't know how to put it," I murmured, almost whispering.

"Bluntly."

"It was supposed to be just a fun weekend. A hookup. But then when we actually…you know…it was…" I shook my head. "I felt connected to her on, like, a spiritual level, Mom. No joke. It was incredible. Then there was the wedding itself and we got drunk and when I woke up the next morning, she was just gone. No note, no goodbye, nothing. Just gone. And all I got from her was thanks, goodbye, and sorry it had to be like this. I don't care about the thank you, honestly. I just…I wanted more from her, even just a face-to-face goodbye."

"And what I'm telling you, baby, from experience with almost exactly this kind of situation, is that she may not have been *capable* of giving you that. She was dealing with big-time hurt from her ex. You don't just get over that. And then she meets a guy like you and feels something? But she's in Alaska, on vacation…"

I nod, sighing bitterly. "Yeah, I see that. It still sucks. And I don't know how to—"

I cut off because my phone was buzzing on the counter next to me—a call, not a text. And except for Elias, no one would call me *or* text me at this hour.

I frowned at the screen: RUNE.

I looked at Mom. "It's her."

Mom frowned at the clock on the stove. "At almost four in the morning? Answer it, son. She wouldn't call at this hour for no reason." She got up to leave, intending to give me privacy, but I clapped a hand on her shoulder, feeling like I'd need her support for whatever was coming next. "Stay? Please?"

"Of course, baby." She sat back down.

I swallowed hard, dragged the phone across the counter, hesitated with my finger on the slider, and then accepted the call, putting it on speaker. "Rune? You okay?"

Silence.

"Rune?"

Nothing.

I was about to chalk it up to a butt dial when I heard a faint, distant sniffle. "I'm here."

"Uh, hi. You…you know it's, like four in the morning? I don't mean to be rude, Rune, but…did you need something?"

Another sniffle. "I have to tell you something and I don't know how."

My blood ran cold. My hands started shaking. "That sounds ominous." I meant that as a joke, sort of, but it fell very, very flat. "What is it? Just say it, whatever it is."

"I'm pregnant."

Mom gasped, clapping her hand over her mouth, eyes flying wide.

"Who was *that*?" Rune asked.

"My mom. I was talking to her when you called."

"Oh god. Fuck my life." A pause. "Hi, Mrs. Badd.

Um. God, Duncan. You have me on speaker with your mom beside you?"

I shook my head. "Rune, I…are you—"

Mom put her hand over my mouth, then, silencing me. "Duncan, pro-tip from a woman, don't ask that. If she's calling you at four in the morning to tell you she's pregnant, yes, she's sure."

Rune actually laughed at this, a sniffly laugh, but a laugh nonetheless. "Exactly. And it can only be yours, to answer what I imagine is your next question."

"I wasn't going to ask that."

"But it's in your head, so I'm answering it."

I stood up, the chair scraping loudly across the floor. "I…I don't know what to say. How to feel."

A long, thick, burning, tense silence.

"Duncan, I…I just wanted you to know. Okay? I don't expect anything from you. I'll sign anything you want absolving you of any responsibility. I just…you deserve to know. That's…that's all."

"Rune, whoa, hold up. I'm not saying—"

"And *I'm* saying you don't *need* to say anything. To be honest, I don't really know what there is *to* say. We fucked up. The night of the wedding, we…"

I go back in my head to that night. "We were wasted."

"Right," she whispered.

"We obviously didn't use protection," I said.

"I don't remember, but clearly not."

"Me neither, but clearly not, no."

She sniffed a laugh. "I guess I feel a little better that I'm not the only one who doesn't remember that night."

"It's all pretty fuzzy for me," I admitted. "Unfortunately. I've got a feeling it's a night I wish I could remember."

"Dunc, god. Don't. Just…don't."

"Rune, I'm not gonna just ignore how I feel. Especially not with this news."

"And then what, Duncan? You're moving to LA? Giving up your job at your family company? Leaving everyone you know and love to come live with me and my parents?" A bitter snap of laughter. "Or I move up there? Because neither of those makes any damn sense, Dunc, and you know it."

"I *don't* know that. But I'm not gonna—"

"I was calling as a courtesy, Duncan." Her voice was hard. "I'm not asking you for anything. You're off the hook."

"Rune—"

The line went dead. I stared at the screen for a second, and then called her back.

It rang once and went to voicemail.

I called again, and it went straight to voicemail.

"She blocked me," I growl. "FUCK!"

I went to hurl the phone across the room, but a powerful hand grabbed my wrist. "Destroying a thousand-dollar phone ain't gonna help none, son," Dad's voice said.

"Dad?" I turned to see him, shirtless in a pair of shorts, standing behind me. "How long've you been there?"

"Long enough to hear the news," he said. "You know she's just trying to protect you, right?"

I let out a wordless bellow of sheer overwhelmed emotion, yanking at my hair as I paced across the room and threw myself onto the couch.

Dad followed me, perching on the ottoman a few feet away, elbows on knees, eyes tired but full of fatherly compassion and commiseration. "Close your eyes and take a breath, son."

"How the fuck is calling me at four in the morning and then shutting me out protecting me?" I asked.

"She's trying to absolve you of responsibility," he answered. "I'm only guessing here, obviously, but I doubt I'm wrong. She's thinking that only one of you has to have your whole life upended, and since she's the one who's pregnant, it may as well be her."

"Well, that's bullshit," I snapped. "What kind of a man does she take me for? She wouldn't even let me get a word in edge-wise."

Mom settled on the ottoman beside Dad, and they tangled fingers without so much as a look at each other, as if it was blind instinct or second nature. "Because she's scared out of her damned mind, Dunc. She was probably worried you'd try to change her mind."

"Uh, yeah, because I'm going to." I sat up and faced them. "I can't just let her shut me out of this.

It can't be all on her—we both are part of it, and one way or another, that's my child, too." I heard the words come out of my mouth and groaned. "What a fucking mess."

Dad gripped my knee and squeezed. "First thing you gotta do is get some sleep. You're no good to anyone an exhausted disaster. And then you go find her. You talk to her face-to-face, and you figure it out."

"I just...what's the solution? She lives in LA, I live here. I can't move there, and it doesn't seem like her moving here is an option either. And neither is going back and forth. I just...I don't know what to do."

"One step at a time, honey," Mom said. "Like your dad said, get some rest. And then tomorrow come up with a plan, okay?"

My eyes burned. "I really fucked up."

"Takes two to tango, bub," Dad said. "This is life. Shit happens, you deal with it, and you make the best of it. I don't know this girl. Seems like you barely do yourself. What I *do* know is that we raised you to take responsibility for your actions."

"I will, I swear," I whispered. "I just...I gotta figure out how to get her to let me."

"We've got your back, son," Dad said. "We're here for you, and for this girl. What's her name?"

"Rune," I answered. "Rune Rigby."

"Cool name," he muttered. "Just try not to be mad at her for the way she's handling this, yeah? She's scared out of her mind, and fear makes people do crazy, stupid shit."

"Like run away from me without so much as a how do you do," I muttered. "And then drop a bomb on me at four a.m. And then shut me out."

"Duncan," Mom said, her voice low and soft. "You gotta move past that emotion. You have to think about *her*. This is gonna change *your* life one way or another, that's a certainty. But for Rune, this changes literally *everything*. Her body, her mind, her emotions, her hormones, her career, literally every single aspect of who she is will be permanently altered by this. I don't know if there's a way forward in this for you two to be together, but no matter what, you have to start thinking about her and putting her first, whether she lets you love her or not."

I sighed, scrubbing my face. "I hear you."

"Good." She moved beside me and wrapped her arms around me. And for a moment, I was a little boy again, safe and content in my mother's arms; I let myself have that moment, breathing in the warmth and security of my mother. "We love you, Duncan. No matter what. Always."

"I love you guys too," I said. "I'm glad I have you. I don't know what I'd do without you."

"You don't have to find out," Dad said. "Love you, kiddo. Now get some rest and face the fuckery in the morning."

Mom whacked him on the arm. "Sebastian Badd, do *not* refer to a human life as fuckery."

"I mean the situation as a whole, Dru."

I sighed. "I'm too tired and drained for you guys' shenanigans. I'm also too tired to get up. I'll chill here for a minute and then go to bed."

"You need anything, son, you know where to find us," Dad said, getting to his feet.

"I will," I said. "Thanks. Love you."

Mom got up too and preceded Dad toward their room. I heard Mom shriek a laugh—Dad goosing her butt. I stuck my fingers in my ears to block out the sounds of them cackling and whispering to each other on the way to their bedroom. It's a double-edged sword, growing up with parents who are still as hot for each other after twenty years as when they got together. On one hand, you never doubt their love for each other because you see it every day. But on the other hand, you *see* it every day. They grab each other, make out in the kitchen, make jokes about having just had sex just to gross us kids out, or disappear into their room for half an hour and come back out grinning like fools.

I want that for myself. I always have.

But how do I get there from here?

I pondered the situation on the couch for a while, but got nowhere, and then my eyes started to droop, so I went to my room and collapsed in bed.

I dreamed of Rune.

FOURTEEN

Rune

LINDSEY FOLLOWED ME INTO MY PARENTS' HOUSE IN THE Hollywood Hills. It was Saturday afternoon, two days after finding out I was pregnant. I'd called Duncan that night, alone. I knew Lindsey's feelings on the subject: I was an idiot for pushing away a man who seemed to be one of the very few truly decent ones left in this world. I just…there was no way forward. There was no point. We'd had our fun, and it was over. Sure, there was chemistry. Sure, there'd been a moment or two where I'd considered the notion of more with him. But reality had other plans.

For example, me being a single mom.

Nausea roiled my guts at that thought.

I heard my parents' voices in the kitchen and headed in there. They were finishing breakfast at the island, Mom scraping the last yogurt out of a container while Dad polished off his bacon.

Dad saw me. "Hey, kiddo! Not a word about the bacon. It's that turkey bullshit."

Dad had high cholesterol, and the doctor had recommended he reduce his bacon intake from absurd to merely inadvisable.

I held up my hands. "I wasn't going to." I leaned into his side and hugged him with one arm, kissing his cheek. "Good to see you, Dad. Missed you."

He rubbed his beard against my cheek, as he'd done my whole life, eliciting a squeal from me as it always did. "Missed you too, Sweet-Pea." He searched my face and must have seen the heaviness somewhere in my features. "Uh-oh. This ain't just a social call."

Mom tossed her spoon into the sink and threw away the yogurt cup, and then pulled me into a hug. "Hi, baby-girl."

Mom and Dad were polar opposites, physically and in just about every other way. Dad was massive, six-foot-six and built like a tank even in his late fifties, with arms the size of my legs and thighs bigger than my waist. He had buzzed salt-and-pepper hair—I'd gotten my thick black hair from him—and a long, bushy salt-and-pepper beard. He was rough but sweet, bluntly honest to a fault, and brutally sarcastic, especially with those he loved. Mom, on the other hand, was tiny. Barely over five feet, trim and slender—although despite her diminutive build, she had a pretty decently sized peach, which she'd given me, along with the piercing blue eyes and a penchant for being violently independent. She was soft-spoken, but don't let that fool you; she could pop off with a spicy attitude that even my brawny, Strongman-winning, BJJ-black belt dad was scared of. She just did it in a sweet, quiet voice that she never, ever raised, even when she was tearing you a new asshole. Being their child, I'd been…a handful…as a kid, and had been on the receiving end of her tongue-lashings quite frequently.

I wasn't afraid of their reactions—they loved me and would never push me away. But what child wants to deliver this news to their parents?

Not I, said the cat.

Mom and Dad both greeted Lindsey with hugs and kisses—Lindsey was basically family at this point. Her own parents were long divorced and lived several states away from each other, meaning she was alone in LA.

"So," Dad said. "Why the long face?"

I glared at him. "I'm in no mood for horse jokes, Dad," I muttered.

"I wasn't gonna make one, but thanks for galloping to conclusions."

I groaned. "You're the worst."

He set his plate in the sink and lumbered to the den, settled his bulk on the couch, and patted the cushion beside him. "Come sit, Sweet-Pea, and tell your ol' dad what's bothering you."

Mom and Lindsey followed me into the den, Mom sitting next to me, Lindsey in the easy chair across from us. "You brought Linz for support, so it must be serious."

"I…" I sighed, my eyes burning already. "I don't know where to start."

"What, did you get knocked up or something?" Dad asked, obviously joking. When I didn't answer, my eyes going wide and filling with tears, he sank back against the couch, letting out a long, slow breath. "Oh. I see."

Mom just stared at me for a moment. "Rune, really? You're serious?"

"Why would I joke about that?" I snapped.

Mom, uncharacteristically, let my snapping at her go. "We have questions, Rune."

I sighed. "I know. His name is Duncan. I met him in Alaska. He basically single-handedly saved Raquel and Hamish's wedding."

"Raquel's and Hamish's," Mom corrected automatically. "Sorry, sorry, habit." She knew I hated it when she nitpicked my grammar.

"We're…not together," I said. "And I've already told him. I also told him I don't expect anything from him."

Dad shot to his feet, shaking his head and rolling his massive shoulders. "Why would you let the punk off the hook like that, Rune? He knocked you up. He doesn't get to just scoot away, scot-free. Also, I thought we taught you to always, always, use protection unless you were trying to have a baby with a man you loved."

"He's not a punk, Dad." My voice shook, and I hated it, but it wouldn't solidify, no matter how hard I tried. "He's a good guy. We *both* messed up, not just him. We were drunk. I know it's no excuse, I just…it's what happened."

"Then why let him off the hook that easily?" he pressed, turning to look at me, hands laced on his head.

"He lives in fucking Alaska, Dad. What's he gonna do, fly down every weekend?"

"If he's any kind of man, yeah, if that's what it took."

"Dad, if you say one word about him marrying me, I'm out. I'm not doing that. I know you're all old school and whatever, but that's not happening."

Dad held up his hands. "Wasn't gonna—I know better. I may be old school, but I know that forcing two people who accidentally got pregnant to get married is a recipe for misery and divorce."

"Same thing," Mom muttered. Louder, to me, then. "Rune, I do agree with your father about letting this Duncan guy just skate away from his responsibilities."

"I doubt he's skating anywhere," I said, reluctantly. "He wasn't exactly happy when I told him I wasn't asking him for anything and didn't want anything from him."

Mom and Dad traded looks, at this.

"Wait, wait, wait," Dad said. "Explain how this conversation went."

"It was super late, or early. Like four, I think. He works at a bar his family owns and closes most nights, so I knew he'd be up. And I...I told him." I sighed heavily, grimacing at the memory. "He had me on speaker and his mom was next to him."

"At four in the morning?" Mom asked, surprised.

I shrugged. "I dunno, I never met his parents. I guess they were talking. You'd have to ask him."

"I'd like to," Dad muttered. "But I've never met the guy."

"Thomas!" Mom scolded. "Quit muttering imprecations."

"I'll show you an imprecation," Dad growled.

"Guys," I grumbled. "Not the time."

Mom gestured at me. "Continue."

"I...there's not much else to say."

Lindsey chose that moment to utterly betray me. "He's in love with her."

My jaw dropped open and I stared at my now former best friend. "*LINDSEY!* What the hell? You don't know that."

"Oh, please." She rolled her eyes at me. "You know it as well as I do. Or you would if you'd give the guy a fucking chance."

Dad sat down again. "Rune, the truth. Is there any chance that this guy actually does have feelings for you? Like, this wasn't just a one-night stand?"

"It wasn't a one-night stand," I muttered. "I was in Ketchikan a week before the wedding. I met two of his uncles and a cousin. We spent a good bit of time together, actually."

"And?" Dad said, obviously not about to let me off the hook that easily.

I sighed, covering my face. "Yes, there's a good chance he has feelings of some sort."

"And what about you?" Mom asked. "You don't?"

"Oh, she does," Lindsey said, in yet another betrayal. "She just refuses to admit it even to herself. Duncan is a great guy. And while I wasn't there for that conversation," and here she glared at me, "I would wager dollars to donuts that our girl Rune here dropped the bomb on him that she was pregnant, told him she didn't want anything from him, and then hung up on him. And probably blocked him."

"We're not friends anymore, Lindsey Snelling," I hissed. "Done. D-O-N-E. Done."

She just laughed. "You're just mad because you know I'm right, and I've been right from the beginning. My guess is Duncan Badd is pissed all the way off. I wouldn't be totally shocked if he just showed up here."

Ding...Dong.

Lindsey spluttered a laugh. "No! There's no fucking way. If that's him, I should get an award of some kind."

Dad rose to his feet. "I'll get it. We're not expecting anyone or any deliveries, so I don't know who it could be."

Trembling, I drew my knees up to my chest and

wrapped my arms around them, refusing to look toward the door, even though I could see it from here.

I heard the latch click as Dad pressed it, and then
the rattle of the storm door as the air pressure tugged
it against the frame.

"Can I help you?" Dad's voice said.

"Uh, yes, sir. Is…is this the Rigby residence?" That
voice.

No.

NO!

He's *here*?

NOW?

I glared at Lindsey, feeling nearly homicidal at this
point. "You did this!"

She held up her hands, eyes wide. "I didn't! I swear
to god, Rune! I didn't call him, I didn't text him, email
him, Snapchat, TikTok, nothing. I didn't contact him in
any way, shape, or form, directly or indirectly. I swear
to fucking god."

Mom frowned at me. "Well? Go greet him, Rune."

"Hell no." I shot to my feet and quite literally ran
out of the house into the backyard, fully aware of how
immature and childish I was being.

I went to my secret hideout, the place I've gone
my whole life when things got to be too much; it's not
much of a hideout, to be honest, but it's my safe place.
It's a spot where a six-foot-high retaining wall made of
giant boulders near the back of our property meets the
living wall made of impenetrable shrubbery, creating a

triangular nook shaded by a nearby massive spreading oak tree. A large boulder protruded from the top of the retaining wall to create a little roof so I could hang out under it even in the rain. I even get Wi-Fi out here.

I resumed my knee-hugging huddle, feeling ridiculous, overwhelmed, panicked, scared, angry—at myself, at him, at us, at the world.

I heard feet on the grass overhead. "Go away."

"Rune?" Duncan's voice—it shot straight to my heart, rocking my gut and rattling my already frayed nerves.

"I said go away, I'm hiding from you." My voice was muffled because I had my face in my knees.

He thumped to the ground beside me and sat a good three or four feet away, facing me. "We need to talk."

"No, we don't. There's nothing to talk about."

"Unless you're not pregnant, yes there is."

"I don't want or need your help, Duncan," I snapped, finally stealing a look at him.

I hated how damnably attractive the man was. Even visibly exhausted, stressed out, hurt, angry, and frustrated, he was just plain gorgeous. His eyes shone brown in the shade, his hair catching a streamer of sunlight to gleam reddish. He was dressed in faded denim, battered Nike trainers, and a plain black T-shirt, the arm of a pair of rainbow mirrored shield-style sunglasses hanging from the neck of his shirt.

Those stupid arms, gah.

I shut my eyes. "Just take the hint, Dunc. I can handle this on my own. I don't need you."

He shifted closer and then rested a hand on the middle of my back. "I know you can handle this on your own, Rune. I know you don't need me."

I glanced at him, furious as hell at the way my eyes burned, tears I refused to spill threatening like heavy stormclouds all along the lower rim of my eyelids. "Then why are you here?"

"Because you're getting me anyway. I'm gonna be here for you no matter what."

"I didn't ask for that," I whispered.

"I know." He ran his hand in slow, gentle circles on my back—and damn him, but it did soothe me, for some reason. "But you didn't have to. I'm gonna take care of you, Rune."

"I don't love you." The words tasted acidic in my throat, left a bitter ghost on my lips—the flavor of lies.

"I didn't say we were going to be together," he answered, his voice even and steady.

This got him a look from me—curious, despite myself. "If there's no sex in it for you, then what do you want?"

He frowned. "At what point did I give you the impression that all I cared about was sex, Rune?" He sounded angry.

"I...you..." I shook my head, mouth flapping. "Dunc, I just—"

"No, I want to know," he said, as close to fury as

I could picture him getting. "I told you I had feelings. You didn't care. I showed you I had feelings. You *still* fucking ghosted me with a spectacularly shitty blow off text. You know how that felt, Rune? To wake up and find you just fucking gone? And then, hours later, get *this* text?"

He shoved his phone in my face, showing me the text I'd sent him.

I turned my face away. "Duncan—"

"I respected your decision, Rune. I didn't hound you. I didn't call you or text you. I let you go. And then you call me at four in the morning and tell me you're pregnant, but refuse to let me get a word in? And then you fucking *block* me?"

The tears escaped, then. "Duncan—"

"And now..." he shook his head, laughing in disbelief. "Now, I come here to your house to *make* you talk to me about this very big deal that affects us both, and you act like all I give a shit about is sex? Fuck that. And honestly, fuck you for saying it. Clearly you don't know the first goddamn thing about me."

Sobs escaped, then, wracking me so hard I was forced to curl into a ball, shaking and snotting and shuddering. "I'm s-s-sorry!"

"Oh god, Rune." His voice softened. "C'mere."

His strong arms went around me, and I found myself settling onto his lap. And damn me, I let it happen.

It just felt so damned *good*.

He smelled amazing—soap, shampoo, spicy,

woodsy cologne, and that indefinable but undeniable male scent.

His arms cradled me to his firm chest, wrapping around me, knees at my chest and all. "Let it out, Rune. I've got you."

"B-b-but...wh-why? Why comfort me after I've been so shitty to you?"

"Because I'm pretty sure I'm in love with you."

This made the sobbing stop, albeit temporarily, as shock forced me to pull away and look at him. "What?" I whispered. "What did you just say?"

He held my gaze, his deep and brown and wild and calm and sure. "I said I'm pretty sure I'm in love with you."

"Pretty sure?"

He shrugged. "I mean, yeah. It's hard to know for sure since you keep pushing me away."

"We barely know each other, Duncan," I said. "Love takes time."

He shrugged again. "Ehhh, I dunno about that one, babe. My parents both claim they fell in love after only a few days of knowing each other. It took longer for them to both quit fighting it and accept it, but the feelings were there."

"We have great chemistry," I said. "I can't deny that. But that's not love. That's just physical, sexual compatibility."

"There's more to it and you know it, Rune," he said.

"Maybe I *don't* know that, Duncan."

"You would if you let yourself." He pressed his cheek to the top of my head and breathed in my scent, sighing heavily as if trying to absorb the reality of my presence. "You wouldn't be fighting me so hard if you felt nothing."

"I'm not fighting," I argued.

He barked a sarcastic laugh. "Okay, Miss Un-self-aware."

"If you're trying to woo me, you're not going about it very intelligently," I said.

"This isn't me wooing you, Rune," he said. "You'd know it if I was."

"Then what is this?" I asked, shifting so I was sitting sideways on his lap; I didn't dare to examine too closely the fact that I was still on his lap at all.

"This is me trying to make you understand that I'm not 'off the hook,'" he used air quotes around the phrase I'd both heard and used far too many times in the last few minutes. "I don't *want* off the hook. This isn't all on you. You're not alone, Rune." He paused, thinking. "I mean, obviously not—you have your parents and Lindsey, and the rest of your friends. But you've also got me."

I sniffled. "Duncan, I…" I wiped at my eyes with my fingertips. "I don't know what I'm doing. I don't know what I want. I don't know anything right now."

"You don't have to. I'm not asking for anything,

Rune. Except, maybe, for you to be honest with your-self and with me about your real feelings."

"To what end, Duncan?" I asked, sounding exas-perated, even to myself. "You're gonna give up your whole life for me?"

"I don't know. Maybe."

I barked a bitter laugh at that. "Right. Uh-huh, sure."

"If you told me that you do in fact care about me and do want to have a romantic, committed, long-term relationship with me, but the only way it could happen is if I moved to LA, then yes, I'd consider it."

I stared at him, not expecting that. "You…would? For real?"

He nodded. "Yes, I would. I mean, yeah, it would be hard. I've never been away from home or my family for more than a few weeks in my life." He laughed. "I realize this may be the kiss of death, here, admitting this, but I still live with my parents."

"Because it's cheap and convenient, or because you're not ready to be on your own?" I asked.

"The first one," he answered. "I mean, mostly. I could afford a place on my own, and I've considered it, but what's the point? What do I have to prove? I'm saving money so when I am ready, I can buy a house. I live with Mom and Dad because I can save money and because it's convenient, yes. I contribute—I clean, I do my laundry, I feed myself, I buy my own grocer-ies, I mow the lawn. I pay for my cell phone, my car, my insurance. I just…don't pay rent." He shrugged. "I mean, I don't know what your relationship with your parents is like, but I'm super close to mine. I like being there. I like hanging out with them, and with my brother. Who's here, by the way. He flew down with me for moral support."

"He is?" I asked. "You didn't leave him alone with Lindsey, did you?"

He laughed. "Is he safe with her? Or is she, like, gonna eat his head?"

I rolled my eyes. "She's not a praying mantis, Duncan. I was joking."

"So was I. Clearly she's not a cannibal." He shook his head, shoulders shaking with laughter. "He's with your parents. And don't worry, Dane can handle a conversation with them. Lindsey is a different story, but I suspect she can take care of herself."

"Yeah, she can." I sighed, shifted off his lap, and sat cross-legged facing him. "I don't care if you live with your parents. I mean, I think it is sweet. Also, why were you talking to your mom at four in the morning?"

He laughed. "You know, I still don't know why she woke up. I'm always pretty quiet when I come home late. She just…I dunno. She said that a mama always knows when her kids need her."

"And you needed her?" I asked.

He shrugged, looking away. "I guess."

"Duncan?" I touched his hand.

He rolled a shoulder. "Don't worry about it."

"Duncan, c'mon. What?"

"I was…I'd been having a hard time. After you left, and all that. I guess she just…felt it. I dunno. Or she had some sort of motherly ESP about you calling me with your news."

"So when I called…"

"Your ears must've been burning."

I sighed. "I'm sorry I hurt you, Duncan."

"But?"

I shook my head. "No, I really am. I didn't handle the situation right in a lot of ways."

He waited, but I didn't say anything else—my mind was racing a million miles per hour and I didn't know where to start.

"Rune…" he looked away, then back at me. "If you hadn't freaked out and left, we would've realized we hadn't used condoms, and we could've gotten you Plan B."

"I know," I said, miserable, having considered that…oh, a billion times at this point. "Trust me, I know."

"Are you…" He gnawed on the inside of his cheek, thinking. "I don't know how to ask this."

I swallowed hard, met his eyes. "Am I keeping it?"

He nodded. "Yeah."

I shrugged. "I don't know, Duncan. I really don't. I've only known for a few days. And to be honest, I've spent the majority of that time having what amounts to one continuous panic attack. I haven't taken a full breath since I took the first test."

He nodded. "I suppose that's understandable."

"We should go back to the house," I said. "As much as I'd rather stay in my hideout and pretend none of this is real."

He grinned, looking around at my little nook. "Sweet hideout, though. Dane and I would've put up walls and tried to get a PlayStation down here."

I snickered. "Boys. You can't just enjoy something the way it is—you always have to try and *improve* things."

He laughed at this. "That's facts, though. But for him and I, it was more about the fact that we were seriously addicted to gaming."

"Shocking," I deadpanned. "And you're not anymore?"

He shrugged. "Nah, not really. Hard to be when you work the hours I do. We'll play a few rounds when we're both home, but Dane is taking classes at the community college and working for a landscaping company, so he's as busy as I am."

He stood up and extended a hand to me; I took it and let him pull me to my feet. He yanked a bit too hard, though, and I stumbled forward into his chest.

"Oof," he huffed as I collided with him; his deep, rich brown eyes met mine, sparking and fraught with a billion emotions. "Hi."

My hands went flat against his chest, and his

grazed down my back, stopping at the base of my spine, just above my butt. All I could see were his eyes, all I could smell was his scent, and with his hands on me and his arms framing me, for a minute I could almost believe it would all work out.

In that moment, looking up at him, I wasn't afraid.

"Here they are!" Lindsey's voice shattered the moment. "Her secret hideout. Told you she'd be here."

I peered up at Lindsey, who grinned down at me, her smile widening as she took in my proximity to Duncan, the placement of his hands. Another face appeared—Duncan's brother. He could be his twin, and very well might be—all Duncan said was that Dane is his brother. He had the same auburn hair, the same deep brown eyes, similar facial structure. He even had the same knowing, devil-may-care, charm-your-underwear-off smirk.

"Dunky-punky," the brother said. "You left me alone with your girl's family. How do I explain to them that I don't need to be adopted? I think Kelly is about to knit me a stocking for their mantel."

Lindsey arched an eyebrow at me. "Is your twin always like this?"

Duncan sighed, nodding. "Yes, he is, unfortunately. Also, we're Irish twins, not real twins." He flipped his brother off. "And I've told you a zillion fucking times, fuck-face, don't call me that. Unless you like shitting teeth."

Dane sputtered derisively. "Okay, fuck-monkey. Come up here and try."

I eyed Lindsey, who widened her eyes at me, flicked them at Dane, and then wiggled her eyebrows suggestively.

Oh boy.

Duncan has a brother who's every bit as hot as he is, and possibly even more ridiculous.

Dane turned to face Lindsey, crossing his arms over his broad, muscular chest. "Eyebrow wiggling? Really? You *have* heard of peripheral vision, have you not? I'm not a piece of meat, *Lindsey*. If you want to ogle me, woman up and do it to my face."

"I wasn't ogling, *Dane*. I was…communicating. With my friend. And what I was communicating is none of your beeswax."

He cackled. "Wow, I haven't heard 'beeswax' in a hot minute."

Lindsey ignored him, giving me a serious look. "Your parents sent us to find you."

"Great," I muttered. I glanced at Duncan. "C'mon, let's get this over with."

Duncan frowned. "Should I be worried? Your dad could give my Uncle Bax a run for his money in the huge and intimidating department." He shot a specu-lative look at the view beyond our property line, which dropped away precipitously. "I could take my chances that way?"

I grabbed his hand and led him around the

retaining wall and up toward the house. "I'm the only one allowed to run from this situation."

Duncan looked at his brother over his shoulder. "If I don't make it, you can have my PlayStation games collection."

Dane adopted a pious expression and crossed himself. "Go with God, my brother. Peace be with you."

Lindsey cackled. "Not even gonna back him up, huh?"

"Hell to the fuck no! I saw that dude. He could rip my arm and beat me to death with it, and I prefer my limbs attached, thanks very much. I'm here for moral support, not backup if things go wrong." Dane shoved his hands in his pockets. "Plus, Dunc got himself into this mess, he can get himself out. Life lessons and all that."

Duncan looked at me. "See what I have to deal with?"

I just shook my head. "Dad isn't going to hurt you. Stop being ridiculous. We just have to have a very serious conversation that I *really* don't want to have."

"In all seriousness, Rune, we really do have to figure this out." He pulled me to a stop and took my other hand so he was holding both, facing me. "I'm not going anywhere. You can't shut me out of this. If you really don't want to even think about being with me, fine. That sucks, it's not what I want to hear at fucking all, but I'm a big boy. I can handle it. What I won't allow is being shut out entirely. Okay?"

I swallowed hard, yanking my hands out of his and stalking angrily toward the house. "One thing at a time, Dunc. I'm barely hanging on to my sanity as it is. I can't even think about you and me right now. Let's get through this talk with my parents and go from there, okay? Please?"

Duncan trotted after me, catching up. "Fine. I get it."

"Great." I didn't look at him—I couldn't.

I knew I was still being massively unfair to him—this wasn't his fault. Or, it was, but it was equally mine. I had no right to punish him with the attitude I was giving him, I just couldn't seem to stop myself.

We reached the patio with its rose-garbed gazebo, where my parents were sitting side by side on a wicker outdoor couch.

Dad, a mug of coffee looking like a toy teacup in his colossal paw, gave me the look I hated more than any other—disappointment. "Duncan, I need a word alone with my daughter." His gaze caught briefly on our joined hands, then flicked to me.

I took a seat on the loveseat facing them. "Just say what you need to say, Dad."

Duncan looked a little panicky, looking from Dad to me and back. "I, uh…I don't mind giving you guys privacy to talk, Rune."

I grabbed his hand, yanked him to the loveseat, and hauled him down to sitting by his belt loop. "I don't need privacy. I need to get this over with. So just say what you need to say so we can all move on."

Mom patted Dad's knee, silencing him before he could answer me. "Rune, you really need to check yourself, honey. This negative, combative attitude isn't helping anyone." She shifted forward off the couch and knelt in front of me, taking my hands. "I know you're scared, upset, and probably pretty angry. I get that. But being petulant and lashing out at everyone who is just trying to help you and be there for you isn't doing you any favors."

My damned stupid eyes burned all over again, and I tipped my head back, sniffing hard and groaning. "Gah! I'm so sick of crying."

Mom squeezed my hands, shockingly hard. "Rune, sweetie, you *have* to stop fighting your feelings. It's *okay*."

"It's not okay!" I shouted, yanking free of her and rocketing to my feet. "Nothing is okay!"

Duncan was there before anyone, dragging me against his chest—his scent enveloped me and his strong arms surrounded me and my breath whooshed out of me and the strength left me. "She means it's okay to feel what you feel. This situation feels impossible—I get that. And I mean I *really* fucking get it, Rune." He pulled away enough to meet my eyes, brushing my wild, flyaway hair out of my eyes with his middle fingertips. "You're clenching your butthole, figuratively speaking."

I cackled, pulling away. "Wow, that was absolutely not what I expected you to say, Dunc."

He didn't let me go, hauling me back to him. "I know. It's crude, but true. You're all tensed up and closed off. You're self-isolating. You don't have to lean on me—I'd love it if you did, but I'll understand if you're not there. But your parents, Lindsey, whoever else you have in your life—you can lean on them. You can open up and let go. You're not alone."

I shook my head, tears welling, blurring my vision. "Stop, Dunc. Just stop."

"No." He held the back of my neck in a gentle hand. "Let go."

"I can't," I whispered.

"You can."

I shook my head, struggling to get away. When I thrashed violently against his hold, he was forced to let go. "Leave me alone!"

I staggered away into the grass, unable to see through the blaze of tears, throat hot and tight, lungs a solid block of stone, thoughts and emotions a chaotic, violent hurricane within me.

Strong arms wrapped around me yet again, and I thrashed. "Leave me alone, Duncan!"

Dad's voice rumbled softly in my ear. "It's me, Sweet-Pea. Take a deep breath for me."

"I c-c-can't!" I wailed.

He inhaled slowly, counting. "With me, Rune. One…two…three…four…"

My lungs wouldn't cooperate. "I c-c-can't!"

He exhaled slowly, through pursed lips, counting. "Out for one…two…three…four."

I fought him. "I don't want to fucking count my goddamn breaths!"

"Gimme all you got, Rune. Yell. Scream. Hit me. Curse me out. Get it out, Sweet-Pea."

It wasn't tears that came out, it was gulping, gagging, throat-searing sobs. "I'm not ready! I don't want this! I didn't ask for this! Any of it! Why couldn't Hayes just have *loved* me? Why did I waste so much of my life on him? What's *wrong* with me, Dad? Where did I go wrong? What am I so bad at choosing men? Why is this my life? I just started getting my life together and now *this*? I don't *want* it. I don't want *any* of it. I want to wake up. I want this to be a bad dream. I'm *not* pregnant. My life isn't over."

Mom's soft hands framed my face. "Your life *isn't* over, honey. You have choices to make and you're not making them alone. We'll support you through this. So will Linz." Her voice dropped to a whisper. "And honestly, baby girl, I think you ought to give Duncan a chance."

That got through. I looked up at her through tear-glazed eyelashes. "Wh-*what*?"

Mom was crouched in front of me, Dad sitting cross-legged in the grass with me on his lap like I was five all over again, arms around my middle, pinning my arms to my sides, his chin on my shoulder, sucking in slow, soothing, deep breaths.

"You should give Duncan a chance," Mom repeated. "I have a good feeling about him."

"Can't believe I'm saying this, but I agree," Dad rumbled. "He's here. He wants to be part of this. He's not making any demands, but that you give him a fair shake. And even to me, it seems pretty obvious that he has feelings for you."

"That's because it's obvious to anyone with eyes, Tommy," Mom muttered.

I let out a shuddery breath, wiggled away from Dad and to my feet, shaking my hands out and taking a long, deep, bracing breath. "Okay, okay," I said, wiping at my face with my palms. "Enough of the dramatics, Rune," I told myself. "Time to get your shit together."

I turned in place, and my eyes instinctively and immediately sought out Duncan. He was leaning against one of the gazebo's upright supports, hands in his pockets, one foot propped on its toes, crossed against his ankle. My stomach flipped at the expression on his handsome face: pure, patient, unadulterated affection.

Love, even?

Fuck.

I paced across the yard and stopped a couple of feet away from Duncan, my heart in my throat, stomach doing somersaults, hands shaking. He stayed as he was, waiting—I imagined—for whatever crazy, out-of-pocket bullshit I was about to send his way.

"I'm an idiot, aren't I?" I whispered. "I am. You can agree with me."

He grinned lazily, shook his head slowly. "Nah." He pushed off the post, a smooth, lithe movement that put him in my space, close enough to put his hands on me, his lips on mine; he did neither. "You're not an idiot, Rune. You're just scared."

My stupid, stupid, stupid eyes went all hazy and watery again, dammit. "I'm not just scared, Dunc, I'm fucking *terrified*."

"Why?" he asked. "What are you so afraid of?"

"Everything!" I hissed. "Being pregnant. Having to…to decide."

"Between what?"

"A life and my future."

"Why is that the decision?" He pressed. "Being pregnant doesn't mean your future and your dreams are gone, Rune. It may look different than you were expecting, and I one hundred percent understand that it's not my body and not my life we're talking about, here."

I shook my head. "You don't understand."

"No," he agreed. "But I'd like to. So try and help me understand, Rune. There are options for us. For you. And…for us, as in us being an *us*."

I turned and glanced over my shoulder—Mom and Dad were watching openly, and toward the back of the yard, Lindsey and Dane were deep in conversation, heads together, their eyes casting toward us now and then.

"Everyone is watching us," I whispered.

Duncan nodded, his eyes not wavering from mine. "I know." He stepped into me, pressing his hard body against mine. "Let them watch this."

"Duncan," I breathed, heart palpitating wildly, "I don't know—"

"Shut up and kiss me, woman," he growled.

"Well, when you put it like that," I murmured.

We kissed, then.

His lips met mine, questing against mine not exactly hesitantly but rather giving me every opportunity to stop it, to turn away, to tell him no.

But how could I?

Why stop a kiss when it turned the flutter of butterflies in my stomach into a murmuration of starlings swirling and coruscating in mathematically impossible configurations?

My palms rasped against the stubble on his jawline, cupping him closer, keeping him where I wanted him, where I needed him. He hummed wordlessly as my mouth opened for his, growled when my tongue swept against his.

When we parted, I was panting, chest rising and falling rapidly, pressing my breasts against the hard wall of his pecs, my forehead resting against his chin.

"I think I love you too," I whispered, finally letting the truth I'd been denying for what like a lifetime escape past the prison of my teeth.

"I know," he answered.

FIFTEEN

Duncan

I WAS NOWHERE NEAR AS CALM OR CONFIDENT AS I HOPED I seemed. My heart thrummed in my chest, pulse pounding loudly.

Rune's fingertips slid along the line of my jaw, came to rest on the pulse point at my throat. "Dunc, your heartbeat."

"You're not the only one who's afraid," I said. "I want you to want me. I want to do this with you. I've been fucking miserable since you left."

Rune sighed. Brought her silken, warm cheek against mine, lips ghosting near the shell of my ear, her words barely a whisper. "Wanting you isn't the problem, Dunc."

"What is?"

"Everything else." She exhaled slowly, shakily. "C'mon, we need to talk somewhere more private."

She pulled away, her sapphire eyes flicking up to mine. "*Talk*, Duncan. Just talk."

"I'll try not to rip your clothes off," I deadpanned.

"You joke," Rune said, "But with us…"

I chuckled. "Yeah, you're not wrong. We don't have a great track record when it comes to restraint."

She took my hand and led me toward the sliding glass door, glancing back at her parents, who were sitting on their butts in the grass, watching us with open curiosity. "We're going up to my room to talk."

"Should we run an errand or something?" her dad asked, eyebrow arched.

Her mom whacked him on the arm with the back of her hand. "Tom! Inappropriate!"

He frowned at his wife. "Quit hitting me, woman. It's a perfectly appropriate question. She's a grown adult woman, not a fifteen-year-old girl."

Rune rolled her eyes, huffing. "No, Dad, you don't need to leave. We're talking—just talking. It's the not talking that got us into this in the first place."

Her mother bit her lip, stifling a laugh. "It's always the not-talking that gets us into trouble, isn't it?"

Rune shook her head. "Like you would know. You and Dad were married when you had me."

Something made her stop, and we both glanced at her parents, who were trading glances.

"Wait," Rune said, turning to face them. "Weren't you?"

Thomas Rigby was smirking. "Not great at math, are you, Sweet-Pea?"

"What are you talking about?"

Her mother, Kelly, was grinning also. "You weren't exactly planned, Rune."

She pulled me back toward her parents. "What the *hell* are you talking about?"

"I was almost six months pregnant with you when we got married," Kelly said. "I had my dress custom-made to hide my bump."

Rune stared at them, one parent and then the other.

"Not even my parents knew," Kelly added.

Tom chuckled. "They were pretty confused when you gave birth three months after the wedding."

Kelly took to her feet—generously and helpfully assisted by her husband's hands on her butt. She batted at his hands with a comically cat-like hiss. "Hands to yourself, you dirty old man."

Tom just lounged back on one elbow, idly plucking at blades of grass. "Nope."

Kelly crossed to Rune, looking from her to me. "It's not something we felt was important, Rune. You may not have been planned, but you were welcomed with joy."

"I was scared shitless," Tom offered. "Definitely didn't feel ready to be a parent."

Kelly rolled her eyes. "You were barely taking care of yourself at that point, Tommy."

He nodded. "You ain't lyin', baby girl. I was a fucking disaster."

Rune shook her head. "I feel like you're shaking my worldview right now. What are you even talking about?"

Kelly took her daughter's hands. "I'm saying, this situation you're in is sort of like history repeating itself, honey. Your father and I had only been together for six months when I came up pregnant. Your father was living in a frat house with like ten other guys, and each of them was more of an animalistic, irresponsible man-child than the last, regardless of which order you put them in."

Rune looked to her dad for confirmation, and he nodded. "Don't look at me—she ain't wrong. I owned, like, three outfits, no underwear, worked part time, was failing all my classes, and spent pretty much every spare moment I had in the gym."

Rune frowned at her mother. "Then…what did you see in him?"

Kelly cackled at this. "*Who he was,* sweetheart, that's what. I saw his kind heart. I saw how he treated the people in his life." She glanced at him over her shoulder, a tender smile on her lips. "One of their roommates had Downs. His parents lived close and checked on him every day, but Tommy was his best friend. He took such amazing care of him, Rune. It was so sweet to watch. That, as much as anything, was what convinced me that there was a lot more to him than met the eye."

"And you liked what met the eye, eyyy, baby?" Tom quipped.

She rolled her eyes again. "Yes, I did. But if I hadn't been willing to look past you dressing like a hobo, being broke, and prioritizing lifting over your education, it wouldn't have mattered."

"I prefer the term vagabond to hobo," Tom muttered. "And the lifting ended up paying the bills, if you care to recall."

"*The point is,*" Kelly said, loudly, "I wasn't even sure I was in love with him when I found out I was pregnant with his child. And like you, honey, my first instinct was to run. You get that from me, I'm afraid."

"Had to chase her fine ass from California to Rhode Island," Tom added. "She didn't make it easy. Still doesn't, come to think of it."

"Hush, you grumpy old bear." Kelly framed her daughter's face in her hands. "I wasn't ready. I was scared. I thought everything I'd worked for my entire life—getting my degree, my research, my career—was over. I didn't want to be a mother. Not yet, at least."

"Sounds familiar," Rune muttered.

"Right? That's my point." Kelly smiled, kissing each of Rune's eyes tenderly. "I'm not going to lie and say it was easy. It wasn't. I told you already, your father and I almost didn't make it, those first few years. Having a kid while being barely more than kids ourselves, your father trying to make a go of it on the strongman competition circuit while I studied? It was really, *really* hard, and we wouldn't have made it without your father's parents taking care of you while I was in class." She paused, sighing. "But we did make it. We committed to each other and to you. We worked at it. We forgave each other constantly."

"*You* forgave *me* constantly, you mean," Tom said. "Your mother was a saint, those early years. I never cheated, but anything else I could've done to lose her, I did."

Kelly smiled at him. "You were trying, honey. And I saw it. You worked yourself to the bone taking care of us." She turned back to Rune. "We made it, baby. And I've had a pretty decent career, I think. I know you're facing a scary prospect. I get it—that's why I'm telling you this. I know exactly how you're feeling. And what I'm telling you is that you *can* do this. You just have to decide what you want and what's important to you."

"Guess that's what I need to figure out," Rune said.

She patted Rune's cheek. "Go talk. But Rune?" She held her eyes. "You have to be honest with yourself, okay? You're a lot like me, and I have a tendency to twist myself in circles trying to avoid the truth when I don't want to admit it."

Rune sighed. "Yeah, I do that a lot." She looked from one parent to the other. "Any other secrets I should know about?"

Tom shrugged. "Nothing comes to mind."

Kelly glanced at him, then at Rune, her face clouding. "I had a late-term miscarriage when you were two. The doctors told me it was too risky for me to get pregnant again, so I got my tubes tied and your father got a vasectomy. That's why we never had any more kids."

Tom's face shuttered. "That's not a secret, just hard to talk about. And you being conceived out of wedlock wasn't a secret either, just not relevant until now."

"Wedlock, Thomas?" Kelly asked. "Really? It's not the Middle Ages."

Rune kissed her mom's cheek. "Thanks for sharing that with me, Mom. It...it does help to know. If you can do it, maybe I can, too."

"There's no doubt in my mind, honey," Kelly said.

Rune drew me away, then, inside and upstairs to her room, which was an eclectic reflection of the various periods and phases of her life—treasured stuffed animals from her girlhood decorated her bed, band and movie posters plastered the walls, bookshelves featured dogeared romance paperbacks, high school textbooks, dictionaries, a thesaurus, and nearly two dozen black and white comp notebooks. A delicate, antique white desk under a window held a framed photograph of Rune with her parents at what I assumed was her first day of college, another of her as a preteen in front of the Grand Canyon in a Vanna White *ta-da!* pose, and a third showed Rune and Lindsey in matching sorority

T-shirts, faces painted in USC colors, grinning like fools in the SoCal sun.

Rune perched on the edge of her bed and slid back to put her back to the wall, grabbing a floppy-eared, well-loved stuffed rabbit. "I feel like I need to hold Babbitt for moral support," she said. "No jokes from the peanut gallery."

"Y'know," I said, lounging on the bed beside her, our feet hanging over the side, "I was talking to a customer a couple weeks ago about that phrase, and she told me it actually has racist connotations."

Rune looked at me in surprise. "Really? How? I thought it just meant unsolicited opinions or something like that."

"That's what I thought too," I said, "but apparently the peanut gallery meant the cheapest seats, which were pretty much always reserved for Black people, back during segregation."

Rune blinked at this information. "Huh. Guess I won't be saying that anymore. I had no idea."

"Me either, until she told me." I took her hand. "So."

She slapped her other hand on top of mine. "So."

"You're pregnant."

She nodded. "Yup."

"You said you're planning on keeping the pregnancy?"

She nodded. "Yeah. I...I guess I never really

considered any other option." She looked at me. "Do you...do you have any thoughts on that, Duncan?"

"I mean, I feel like I don't really get an opinion, Rune. It's not my body, it's yours. I support any decision you make."

"I appreciate that, but what's your personal opinion?"

"That *is* my personal opinion. Men shouldn't have any say in what women do with their bodies, legally or otherwise." I shrugged. "I believe life is precious, but so is bodily autonomy. And while there are circumstances where there just may not be any other choice but to terminate, this doesn't seem like that kind of a situation to me. But, it's not my life, not my future, and not my body."

She nodded. "Your mother raised you well," she said.

"And my dad. He raised Dane and I to respect women." I laughed. "Plus, my sister is kinda scary."

Rune sighed. "I'm keeping it. Like I said, I've never really considered anything else."

"That's settled, then. I just...I guess I felt like I had to get that question out of the way so I know we're on the same page."

"How does this work, Duncan?" she asked, looking at me. "You and me." She touched her belly. "This."

I shook my head and shrugged. "I don't know."

"Well, in a perfect world, what would it look like for you?" she asked.

"Rune, I…"

She drew her legs up to sit cross-legged, turning to face me. "Answer the question, Duncan. And be honest."

"Thinking selfishly, you mean?" I asked.

"Yes," she said.

"In my selfish, perfect world, you'd live in Ketchikan with me. We'd come back here as often as possible. It's a five-and-a-half-hour flight. Not nothing, but not crazy, either. Doable for a long weekend, easily." I shrugged. "That's my honest, selfish answer."

"I'm an LA girl, Duncan," she said. "I'm worried Alaskan winters would kill me."

I laughed. "Rune, I think you're falling victim to a common misconception about Ketchikan. We're actually located in a temperate rainforest region. Our winters are actually more like Seattle's. People from the Lower Forty-Eight think of Alaska and they think every city in Alaska gets forty-six feet of snow and is dark year-round. The reality in Ketchikan, though, is that most winters we get more rain than snow, and it tends to stay above freezing for the most part. Yeah, thirty-eight will be cold as hell to a SoCal girl, but it's not the Arctic Circle. It's not Gnome. When you think 'Alaskan winter,' that's what you're envisioning—the sun setting in November and not rising until January, temperatures in the teens, and tons of snow. It's not like that where I live."

She frowned thoughtfully. "Really? You're not making that up to trick me into moving there?"

I snorted. "That would be a pretty stupid trick, Rune. You'd make it to Christmas and find out I'd lied to you. And then what?"

She laughed. "True. I still don't know if I believe you."

"Fine," I said. "Pick anyone from my family. I'll call them right now, and you can ask."

"Your mom," she said immediately.

I got out my phone and FaceTimed Mom. It burbled a few times and then Mom appeared on screen, her hair in a high, messy bun, dirt smudging her cheeks. She was holding a gardening glove in her hand as she swept a wrist over her upper lip. "Hey, baby boy. How's LA?"

I pivoted the screen and leaned closer to Rune. "Say hi to Rune, Mom."

Mom squealed. "Duncan Badd! Give me a warning before you spring your girlfriend on me! I'm all dirty from gardening."

Rune laughed. "It's totally fine, Mrs. Badd. It's good to meet you, sort of." She frowned. "I, um... about the first time we spoke. I...that's not how I'd have wanted that to go."

Mom didn't answer right away—the screen showed blue sky shifting and rocking as she walked somewhere, and the back of the house hove into view as she took a seat in one of the chairs around the fire-pit in the backyard.

"It happens," Mom said. "And believe me, I get it. It's okay."

"You've raised a wonderful son, Mrs. Badd. I don't know what's going to happen with Duncan and me, but I can say that Duncan has made me realize that maybe not *all* men are cheating assholes. Which is how I felt when I met him."

Mom cackled. "Oh, honey, that's a hell of a compliment. I *do* know that feeling, trust me. I found a good man, and we've done our best to raise good men."

"You have," Rune said. "I mean, I only met Dane briefly, and while he might be a bit of a lunatic, if he's anything like Duncan, he can't be too bad."

Mom laughed even harder. "Dane is definitely a bit of a lunatic, but we love him for it."

"Most of the time," I muttered.

"Oh, hush, you," Mom said. "The women are talking."

"Oh, well ex-*cuuuu*-se me," I said, chuckling. "Carry on."

"So," Mom said, in between sips of water from a big pink insulated tumbler, "to what do I owe the pleasure of this unexpected call?"

"Duncan is trying to tell me that the winters there aren't that bad," Rune said. "I said I wasn't sure I believed him."

"Oh, well, he's not wrong. I mean, I grew up in

Seattle, and it's not *that* different. It gets cold. There's snow once in a while, and blizzards rarely. Gets dark early. It'd be an adjustment for someone who grew up in the perpetual summer of LA, for sure, but it's not Antarctica."

Rune sighed. "Great."

I frowned at her. "Why do you say it like that?"

"Because you're making a pretty decent case and I'm not sure how I feel about that," Rune said. "Winters aren't the only hold-up, though."

Mom dragged the heel of her palm over her forehead, mixing sweat with dirt in a long brown smear. "Rune, honey, there'll always be hangups and holdups and worries and fears. You don't ever know if you're making the right decision. All you can do is make the best choice you can with the information you have, and then make the best of it. I know my son is a good man. I know that no matter what you decide about you and him, he'll be there for you—and not just because he knows his father and I will kick his ass if he isn't."

"Mom!" I protested. "Unnecessary."

Mom ignored me. "Follow your heart. But listen to your head, as well."

"What if they're telling me different things?" Rune asked.

"What can you live with? What *can't* you live with? You're pregnant. You're gonna need support. But support can look like a lot of different things. Just speaking from a purely selfish standpoint, here, we'd *love* to have you in our lives." She grinned. "And not just because snuggling grandbabies is one of my favorite things in the world."

Rune sighed. "The more people I talk to, the more confused I get."

"In the end, no one can decide what's best for you but you, Rune. Not me, not Duncan, not your parents or your best friend. Only you."

"Thank you for talking to me, Mrs. Badd," Rune said.

"Please, call me Dru. And please don't take this as me trying to sway your decision one way or another, but I really do hope we get to meet in person sooner rather than later." Mom looked off-screen for a moment. "Bast is calling for me, so I have to go, but Rune, whether you end up with my son or not, you're having my grandchild. If you ever need *anything*, I'm here for you, no matter what."

Rune's eyes misted. "Thank you, Dru. That means more to me than I can express."

"Okay, gotta run. Love you, Dunc."

"Love you too, Mom. Talk to you later."

"Bye!" Mom waved at the screen, and then the call ended.

Rune slumped back against the wall with a heavy sigh. "Your mom seems amazing."

"I mean, I think she's pretty cool," I said. "But then, your parents are pretty cool, too."

She smiled at me, then went back to staring at the

ceiling, which still featured a constellation of greenish-white glow-in-the-dark stars and crescent moons. "I don't know how to make this decision, Duncan," she whispered.

"Well, what's the decision?" I asked.

She glanced at me. "You, and me? Where I'm going to live?"

"Oh."

She frowned at me. "Oh? That's all you have to say?"

I laughed. "Rune, what am I supposed to say to that? I'm in love with you. I want to be with you. I've told you what I want—I want you. I want us. I want to be a couple and raise this kid together. And yeah, selfishly, I don't want to leave Ketchikan. I love it there. I love seeing my giant, crazy, weird family all the time. Get-togethers are wild, and we have them all the time."

She glanced at me, at this. "You do?"

I nodded. "Oh yeah. Not just holidays. If any of the family who lives out of state comes into town, we all get together, all seventy or eighty of us."

Rune shook her head. *"Eighty of you? Jesus."*

"I told you how many cousins I have. I'm telling you, babe, Badd Clan shindigs are a fucking hoot."

"I see Dad's brother and his wife maybe once a year at Christmas, and they never had kids," Rune said. "Mom's sister and her husband come over for Thanksgiving, and we go there for Christmas Eve."

"Do they have kids?" I asked.

Rune nodded. "Yeah, but I don't get along with them."

"No?"

"Nope. They're rude people. Mom's whole family is just…weird and rude. Aunt Kathy is cool, but her husband is a dick, and their kids were fucking half feral, growing up. They'd come over for Thanksgiving and trash everything. When I was seven, I had a big Barbie dollhouse that I loved. I'd just gotten it for my birthday a couple months before. My cousins totally fucking destroyed it the first day they were at our house and Aunt Kathy did nothing about it."

"Fuck that," I said. "If we ever broke anything that belonged to another cousin, we were expected to replace it. I broke Jax's Nerf gun once, and I spent a month doing extra chores to pay Mom and Dad back for having to replace it."

"Jax is…?" Rune asked.

"Uncle Zane and Aunt Mara's oldest son." I eyed her, hesitating. "And he's actually how I found you."

She arched an eyebrow at me. "I was wondering that."

"He's, um, sort of a hacker? He used your phone number and somehow got your parents' address. I dunno how."

"And your Uncle Zane is where in the pecking order of your twenty-nine billion uncles?" she asked.

"Second oldest after Dad," I answered. "He's the Navy SEAL."

She only nodded at this, staring at nothing. After a moment or two, she looked at me. "What if I told you I couldn't do it?" she asked. "Move to Ketchikan, I mean."

I tried to ignore the acid in my gut her question created. "I would understand." I swallowed hard. "I'd probably move down here. We do have a location in West Hollywood."

She searched me carefully. "But you'd be doing it for me. You really don't like the idea."

"No, I don't." I shrugged. "But you don't like the idea of Alaska, either. I just…it just sucks that for us to be together, one of us has to move."

She looked around her room, her gaze coming to rest on the photographs on her desk. "Duncan, how do we decide?"

I hesitated. "You said earlier that you think you're in love with me. You meant that?"

She softened, nodding, taking my hand. "Yes, Duncan. I fought it as hard as I could for as long as I could, but I can't deny it anymore."

I sighed, relief flooding through me. "Then we'll figure it out. We can't necessarily solve it all right this moment. I don't know that we need to, either. Maybe we split our time. I don't know. I'm not trying to drag you away from your home and your family, Rune. I want you to be happy."

There came a knock on the doorframe—we had

the door open. "Rune, Duncan?" It was her mom. "We need to talk to you guys downstairs, please."

Rune slid off the bed immediately—perhaps a little glad to be escaping the conversation. "Right behind you."

We gathered in the living room, including Lindsey and Dane—between whom I detected some sort of tension. Tom and Kelly sat together, waited for us to all sit, and then Tom cleared his throat.

"So, Rune, your mother and I have some news that may help inform some of your decisions." He glanced at his wife and then continued. "Your mom has decided to take a sabbatical."

Rune blinked. "I...I'm not entirely sure what that means, honestly."

"A leave of absence from the university," Kelly responded. "I'm taking at least a year off and your father and I are going to do some traveling. It's something we've been talking about for a long time, and I actually just got the approval from the department just now while you guys were talking. I've got a new book I've been working on, and this sabbatical is going to be partly research and partly some much-needed time away together."

Rune was silent for a moment. "What does that have to do with me?"

"Well, we know you've been worried about leaving. Being away from your mom and me." Tom rested his elbows on his knees, meeting his daughter's gaze.

"We've also been talking about selling the house. Possibly leaving LA altogether."

Rune blinked. *"What?"*

"We've been here for almost thirty years, honey," Kelly said. "We're ready for a change of pace. Not retirement, exactly, but just…something different." She rested a hand on her husband's knee. "Rune, baby, you need to do what's right for you. No matter where you are, we'll find ways to be together. If you were, just for example, to move to Ketchikan, it's not *totally* out of the realm of possibility that your father and I could spend summers up there with you guys."

"The fishing around here sucks balls, if nothing else," Tom muttered.

Kelly shot him a nasty side-eye glare. "Sucks balls, Thomas? *Really?*"

I couldn't help a laugh. "Blatant plug for my own interests, here, but my uncle Ramsey is an outdoor guide. He and Papa Lucas run trips to the interior all the time, as well as day trips to fishing spots all along the Passage. So if you like fishing, we've got you covered, Mr. Rigby."

Tom's eyes lit up. "See? It's all coming together."

Rune laughed. "Ah yes, fishing. The real reason for me to move to Alaska."

"Sweet-Pea, I was just—"

Rune cut in over him. "I'm teasing, Dad." She let out a breath. Glanced at Lindsey. "Do you have any thoughts, dearest friend of my heart?"

Lindsey blew a raspberry. "Do I have thoughts? Do ducks shit in the water?" She barked a sarcastic laugh. "Yes, Rune, I have thoughts. I could give a PowerPoint presentation, if I didn't loathe presentations and if I knew how to make a PowerPoint presentation."

Rune sighed. "Linz?"

"Right, right. I'm off topic." She gestured at me with both hands. "Reason number one why you'd be an idiot not to move to Alaska—the fine hunka-hunka burnin' love beside you. The man came all the way down here just to tell you he loved you."

I opened my mouth to tell her that that wasn't the primary reason for my visit, but she glared me into silence.

"I know, I know," she said. "You came down to express your support. But really, you came down to tell her you love her and to try to get her to admit that she loves you back."

Rune covered her face. "Lindsey."

"What? You do and you know it, hooker-beans! You just can't—"

"I told him I did, Lindsey!" She yelled. "Move on, please!"

"Oh." She looked from Rune to me and back. "Cool, cool. Moving on. Reason number two: LA traffic. It sucks. There are barely even roads in Alaska, let alone four-hour traffic jams straight out of Satan's butthole."

When I opened my mouth to protest the Alaskan roads comment, she once again glared me into silence.

"I know, I know, Alaska *has* roads. Just…you shushy-time." She let her expression go serious, then. "Rune, all jokes aside—which you know is hard for me—you belong with Duncan, and Duncan belongs in Alaska, ergo, you belong in Alaska. He even *looks* weird here. He's clearly a fish out of water. His inner light is dimmed by the oppressive Angeleno heat and smog."

Rune sighed. "I thought you said it was all joking aside."

"Who's joking? Look at him!"

I frowned. "I'm…fine? What are you ever talking about, woman?"

She frowned back. "Don't woman me, man. I'm trying to help you."

I held up both hands, glaring at Dane, who was having trouble containing his laughter.

"Look, Rune," Lindsey said, "I'm serious. If your parents are leaving LA temporarily, maybe even permanently, what's keeping you here? I hate LA. I've been looking for an excuse to move literally anywhere. If you move to Alaska, maybe I will too. You'll need a buddy to keep you company during what I hear are some super epic Badd Clan parties." She glanced at Dane sidelong for some reason, and then back to me. "Don't stay here for me, or for your parents. If you move, we'll come to you. Maybe not permanently, but regularly. You love Dane—I mean, Duncan, sorry. You love Duncan. He loves you. You belong together."

"What about my job?" Rune asked.

Lindsey stabbed a thumb downward, raspberrying again. "You mean your entry-level job that in no way uses your degree or offers any kind of job security or advancement? The job that has you literally making copies and taking notes? That job?"

Rune frowned. "It's not that bad."

"Do you love it?" Lindsey asked. "Does it fulfill you?"

"I mean…it could. In time."

Lindsey rolled her eyes. "It's a job, babe, not a career." She got up and crossed the room, jamming herself between Rune and me. "Go sit with your brother," she ordered.

"Yes, ma'am," I muttered, going over to sit beside Dane.

"So, Lindsey?" I whispered to Dane.

"If it were me," he stage-whispered back, "I'd be more focused on the conversation that very well might dictate my entire future."

"But there's a thing," I said.

"There's not *not* a thing, but don't worry about it." He pointed at Lindsey and Rune. "Pay attention."

"Rune, I say this with love, but you've never had a very clear idea what you wanted for your future," Lindsey said. "You majored in business because it was an easy path. You're good at school. But you know as well as I do that you had a whole vision for your future that had nothing to do with where you worked."

Rune dropped her gaze. "Linz, don't."

"I'm gonna, babe, so pucker that butthole."

"Gross."

Lindsey took Rune's hands. "Your vision for your future was all about Hayes. The house. The kids. I know you remember the conversation we had about that as clearly as I do."

"We were drinking when we had that conversation, and I hadn't realized what a cheating puddle of pond scum he is," Rune said.

"You're missing the point, Rune," Lindsey said. "I think you had the right vision, just with the wrong guy."

Rune blinked hard. "Linz, I—"

"Rune, *listen* to me. When you found out about Hayes cheating on you, you treated it almost like a death."

"It felt like one," Rune admitted.

"But why? Who died? Can you really sit there and tell me that you loved Hayes *that* much?"

"No," Rune admitted, her tone small and miserable. "The more time passes, the more I..." she looked at me, then. "The more I realize what being in love really means, and the more I realize I didn't love him at all. I *wanted* to love him. I *wanted* him to love me."

"So what was it you were mourning?" Lindsey pressed.

"You obviously have a theory," Rune said, "so share it. Stop trying to drag it out of me."

"What use is a psychology degree if I can't use it on my friends?" Lindsey asked. "But fine. You were mourning the death of the life you really wanted. You went into college wanting to meet a guy, fall in love, get married, have kids…"

Rune pulled away from Lindsey and paced in circles, raking her hands through her hair. "It kinda sounds like you're saying that deep down I want to be a stay-at-home mom."

"Yes, and?" Lindsey said. "Do you have a problem with that?"

Rune groaned. "Not on principle, but—"

"But what?" Lindsey shook her hands. "Just…put that aside. Forget all that for a second. What do you want, right now? Close your eyes and think about. Really think about it."

Rune closed her eyes, went still, and tipped her head back. She was quiet for a long time.

When she opened her eyes again, they found mine. "You. I want you. I want us. I don't want to do this alone." She cast her gaze from Lindsey to her parents. "I don't mean alone, I know I have you guys. I just meant—"

"We all know what you meant, Sweet-Pea," Tom rumbled.

I stood up and went over to her, threading my fingers with hers. "Just putting this out there, Rune. But, um, you may be aware that my family sort of owns a business. And you have a business degree. I know Alaskan bars ain't exactly the glamorous business world of Los Angeles, but there's always plenty to do, and I don't mean waiting tables or pouring drinks. We need a dedicated administrative director, for one thing. Delia is wearing, like, sixty different hats on the admin side of the Badd's Bar stuff and could really use someone competent, and preferably in the family, to take some of that load off. So, if you're willing to take a risk on me and on Ketchikan, I can promise you that you won't ever be bored. And if it's not a Badd's bar, there are plenty of aunts, uncles, and cousins with businesses to go around. Do you like the idea of working in real estate? Mama Livvie runs a brokerage. The art world? Aunt Eva runs galleries in three states. I can go on."

Rune laughed. "Okay, okay. I get it."

I ran my thumb over her lips. "I really want to kiss you right now, but I won't." I smiled at her. "I just want to be with you, Rune. Whatever that looks like, wherever it is. Here, Ketchikan, Timbuktu—wherever the fuck that is—it doesn't matter. We'll work it out, one way or another. I just want you to know that you have options. I'll do everything I can to make sure you're happy and fulfilled. If that's working with us in the bars, great. If it's something else, great. If it's staying home with our kid, great. I just don't want you to think that you're trapped or limited. You're not. And if you don't know exactly what you want yet, that's fine too."

For a moment or two, she just looked into my eyes, searching me. Thinking. Deciding.

"I think…" she trailed off, started again, a smile spreading across her face. "I think I'm moving to Alaska."

SIXTEEN

Rune

THE LAST TWO WEEKS HAVE BEEN INSANE. DUNCAN AND I have been working like crazy to merge our lives, but in so doing, have barely seen each other. Mom and Dad needed help getting ready for their sabbatical—Dad stepped away from his BJJ classes, but was re-entering the Strongman world again, doing some comps that lined up with some of Mom's planned stops throughout Europe, researching for her next book. This meant helping them sort through things at the house, since they were now seriously considering making Ketchikan their home base once I've moved there; I've also had to pack my condo, ship things to Ketchikan, and get the condo sold. I needed money, though, so I've also had to keep working.

I've been back to Ketchikan twice since that con-versation in my parents' living room, and we've looked at a few places together, but until we find the right place, the plan is for me to stay with Duncan at his parents' house. Which is gonna be weird, but his parents are awesome. Bast was a little scary and intimidating at first, what with the six-four frame and giant muscles, growly voice, and the tattoos, but once I got to know him, I realized he's a lot like my own dad—gruff, rough, and intimidating, but sweet and loveable once you get past that.

Today was my first official prenatal doctor's visit… in Ketchikan.

Duncan sat beside me, knee bouncing a mile a minute, while he picked at hangnails on his left thumb. I grabbed that hand and pressed both of our hands down on his knee, which was thumping so loudly the whole waiting room was vibrating. "Duncan," I whispered. "Relax. It's a standard prenatal visit. There's nothing to be nervous about."

He sucked in a deep breath, held it, and let it out slowly. "Sorry. I have a totally irrational dislike of doctor's offices."

I gave him a confused frown. "Why? Did something happen?"

He snorted. "No, thus my use of the word 'irrational.' I just…" he let out a sighing, self-deprecating laugh. "It's stupid. I just feel like if I go to a doctor's office, I'm gonna get bad news. It's ridiculous and I know it is, but every time I'm in a waiting room, my stupid brain spins all sorts of absurd worst-case scenarios. And now it's not about me—it's about you and the life inside you, and the irrational fear is even worse."

I squeezed his hand. "Everything is going to be fine, Dunc."

He nodded. "I'm sure it is. Try telling that to my frantic monkey brain."

I laughed, leaned close and whispered in his ear. "I think I know what your frantic monkey brain needs."

He growled quietly, a sighing rumble. "Rune, we haven't had a moment alone in months. I haven't even gotten to see you naked since we decided to do this together. And now you're trying to distract me with horny thoughts in the middle of the waiting room?"

I nuzzled his jaw with my nose. "Yup. Is it working?"

His gaze burned with arousal. "Yes. It is." His hand gripped my thigh, high up, teasingly close to my sex. "I'm about to haul you into an exam room and play doctor with you."

"And I'm about to let you," I said. "How can we find even thirty minutes of privacy?"

He glanced away, his vice-grip on my thigh unrelenting. "I dunno, but I'll figure something out."

"You'd better or we're gonna end up doing something bad somewhere very inappropriate."

"Like the back of a Volkswagen?" he said.

I frowned at him. "Huh?"

"*Mallrats*?" he asked, but then waved a hand at my blank expression. "Nevermind. Just a movie quote."

I opened my mouth to respond, but a nurse

emerged to stand in the doorway and called my name: "Rune?"

I got to my feet, and Duncan followed me, wiping his hands on his thighs. He really doesn't like doctors, does he? Weird. Not much else seems to bother him.

We're brought to a dark room, where after a ten-minute wait, one nurse takes my vitals, and then we wait another ten minutes, and a different nurse has me lay on my back. She slid my shirt up and my leggings down, tucking a large square of blue paper into the waistband and squirting jelly all over my belly, and then pressed the ultrasound wand to my skin.

I spent as much time watching Duncan as I did the screen—for the first minute or so, there wasn't anything discernible or recognizable to see or hear, and then she found the location and angle she wanted.

A rhythmic whooshing noise filled the room: a heartbeat.

"There's Baby's heartbeat, Mom and Dad," the nurse said. "Strong and healthy."

Duncan's hand went to his face, covering his mouth. "Holy shit, it's real," he breathed. His eyes went to mine, wide and emotional. "You can't tell if it's a boy or girl, yet?"

The nurse smiled at him, shaking her head. "No, not yet. It's about the size of a plum, right now. He or she has visible limbs, most major organs, eyes, nose, and mouth, but sexual organs can't be reliably determined until about eighteen to twenty-two weeks. That's when your next visit will happen, and we'll do the gender scan then."

"The heartbeat is so fast. Is that normal?" Duncan asked, taking the words out of my mouth.

"Oh, yes," the nurse answered. "A hundred and forty to a hundred and seventy bpm is normal for this gestational age. It slows down after about week twenty-six."

Duncan's eyes met mine again. "Holy shit."

I couldn't find words. My eyes were wet and my throat was tight. "Dunc," I whispered. "We have a healthy baby."

"It seemed…kind of abstract till now," he said. "This…seeing it, hearing the heartbeat…it makes it way more real."

"It really does," I agreed, grabbing his hand and squeezing it hard. Tears dribbled down my cheeks again. "Gah, I'm *so* sick of crying all the time."

The nurse spoke while cleaning off my belly and putting away the wand. "That's totally normal, Mama. There are a lot of hormones flooding your system right now, and also, it's just an emotional thing. You're creating a human being inside you. It's a big deal and it's absolutely normal to feel a wide range of very strong emotions, most of which tend to express themselves through crying."

I nodded. "The months leading up to this were pretty emotional, too, so I'm just…I'm tired of being weepy all the time."

She just huffed a soft laugh. "Unfortunately, I don't know if that's going to change much for a while. My advice? Don't fight your emotions. Let yourself feel them. It's okay." She looked at Duncan. "Your job is to support her, Dad. Don't be afraid of her big feelings, okay? And also, speaking from experience, try not to take it personally if weird stuff you do or say sets her off. Most of the time, it's not you, it's just hormones and emotions. Don't minimize what she's feeling, just... don't take it personally."

Duncan nodded, examining me with wide, thoughtful, emotionally-fraught eyes. "Is it...it safe for us to... be together? I mean for the baby. And for her."

"Absolutely," she answered immediately, understanding what Duncan meant. "Totally safe. You're not gonna hurt the baby, or her. Just for informational purposes, Mom's libido will fluctuate throughout the pregnancy. It's normal during this first trimester for her libido to be a bit lower due to exhaustion and nausea. But you're right about twelve weeks now, so you might start noticing an increase in libido. The third trimester is pretty hit or miss as far as sexual urges go, though, and varies a lot by individual. Some women want it but find it difficult or uncomfortable, others have no drive whatsoever, and others have a higher drive than ever... like I said, it really varies from woman to woman." She looked from Duncan to me and laughed. "Something tells me I should wrap up this appointment, huh?"

"That might be smart," Duncan said, with no trace of humor whatsoever.

I laughed as the nurse's eyes widened and she shot to her feet, shoving the ultrasound machine aside. "You're all set," she said, "just make your follow-up appointment with the desk. Good luck, Mom and Dad!"

She left and I did a more thorough cleaning of the ultrasound goo from my skin, righted my clothes, and headed for the door.

A hand shot past me and shut the door. He grabbed my hips and turned me in place, pressing me back against it. "Where do you think you're going?" he growled.

I laughed breathily, playfully attempting to push him away. "We can't actually have sex here, Duncan."

"I know," he murmured. "But I can do this."

His mouth slanted across mine, his tongue slashing past my lips. I gasped at the sudden intensity of the kiss, and then melted into him, welcoming his lips against mine, his tongue against mine, his breath tangling with mine.

"I need to be inside you, Rune." His words were barely a breath, felt as much as heard. "I don't want to be apart from you anymore."

I whimpered as he ground his erection against me. "Take me somewhere, Daddy."

He growled a laugh. "Um….not sure how I feel about that one."

"Maybe you'll feel differently about me calling you

daddy when you're buried inside my tight…hot…wet…pussy." I breathed the words in his ear, rubbing against him, feeling his erection grow.

His hands gripped my ass, and he scooped me up, slammed me hard against the door, and kissed the everloving shit out of me.

And then he damn near dropped me, whirling away with one hand scraping through his hair. "Fuck, Rune. Jesus." He turned again to look at me from across the room. "My control is in shreds right now. If you don't turn and walk out of this room right the fuck now, I'm liable to fuck you right here against the door."

I grinned at him, gnawing on my lower lip, my body throbbing with need. "That wouldn't be so bad," I breathed.

"Rune," he snarled.

I opened the door and stepped into the hallway before we did anything that could get us arrested. I felt Duncan behind me, radiating sexual arousal. We reached his tricked-out Wrangler in what had to be record time, and yet despite his obvious hurry to get me somewhere private, he still took the time to not just open my door for me but buckle my seatbelt.

He also drove so carefully it would have been infuriating if it wasn't so obviously motivated by a sweet and touching concern for my—our—safety.

I glanced at Duncan as he drove—his forearm muscles rippled as he gripped the steering wheel, his eyes constantly raking the road ahead as well as his mirrors;

his jaw ticked and pulsed. He reached up and scratched the back of his head, and that made his bicep bulge... fuck, that was sexy. Even the way he glanced at me with heated eyes was unbearably sexy.

"Looking at me like that isn't helping, Rune," he muttered. "Barely keeping it together."

I reached across the space between our seat and rested my hand on his thigh. "Are we almost there?"

We hit a red light, and Duncan hissed. "Yes. Less than five minutes."

"I don't know if I can make it five minutes without touching you, Dunc," I whispered, sliding my hand toward his zipper.

The light turned green a moment or two later, and he gunned the engine so his tires barked as we bolted forward. He sped to the limit and then five over, constantly feathering the throttle in an attempt to stop himself from speeding too far over the limit.

My fingers danced over his zipper, and my own arousal rushed through me in a hot gush, soaking my underwear and making my nipples pebble into hard, sensitive points as his cock slowly unfurled against the confines of the zipper.

"Rune?" He growled through clenched teeth.

I flipped open his jeans and lowered the zipper millimeter by millimeter. "Duncan?"

He let out another low sighing groan as I traced my fingertips over the swell of his burgeoning cock, only the thin barrier of his underwear between my touch and his flesh.

He squealed around a corner and then gunned it, flying past mailboxes and driveways, helplessly pushing into my hand.

"Fuck," he snapped, impatiently furious—a UPS truck was blocking the whole road as the driver jogged a package to the door.

"Fuck this. I need you," I whispered, and dove my hand beneath elastic to grip hot flesh. Duncan growled wordlessly as I fisted his cock, and I echoed his growl with a needy whimper of my own.

"Hurry," I breathed.

I've never felt such need. Not ever. I needed Duncan. I needed his kisses. I needed his hands on my curves, I needed him to claim my body—my very soul.

"Dammit," Duncan groaned, "can you take any fucking longer, jackass?" The big brown delivery vehicle finally trundled past us, and Duncan mashed the gas pedal. "Fucking finally."

"How much longer, baby?" I whispered. "I need you inside me so fucking bad."

His cock pulsed at my words. Fuck, I needed him.

I whimpered at the throb of him in my hand, and needed…more. Just more.

"Fuck it." I released my seatbelt and bent over him, took him in my mouth, groaning long and loud as his hot, hard cock filled my mouth, the lush tang of his precum smearing on my tongue.

"Jesus, baby," Duncan gasped. "Careful or it'll be over before it starts. I haven't even jerked off since the last time we were together."

I whined desperately as I took more of him, greedily pumping his root with my fist and cupping and massaging the plump weight of his balls.

Gravity pulled at me as he drifted around another corner, and then the engine howled as he gunned it up their long, winding driveway. I was thrown forward against the steering wheel as he braked to a tire-barking halt, and he pulled at me. "Stop, sweetheart. There's no one home."

I didn't want to stop. I wanted his release. I wanted to taste him. I wanted to feel him lose control and give me everything.

He had other plans.

He physically pulled me away, his cock popping out of my mouth nosily. His palm cradled my cheek as he drew my face to his, lips moving against mine. "Feels great, Rune, but it's not what I need."

He was out of the car before I knew what was happening, draping his T-shirt over his crotch as he rounded the hood. My door flew open, I smelled his cologne and felt his heat as he leaned in and scooped me up in his arms.

"I can walk, Duncan," I whispered. "I'm twelve weeks pregnant, not handicapped."

He ignored this as he strode toward the garage's side door, which unlocked with a thumbprint. The garage was dark and empty, motion sensors kicking on the lights as he carried me across the vacant space. Content to let my man carry me, I busied myself with tasting his skin, knotting my fingers in his hair, and exploring his throat, jaw, mouth, temples, eyes—anywhere I could find to kiss.

My man.

My Duncan.

I heard a door shudder as he kicked it open, and then the loud slam as he kicked it shut. Two steps, and then he deposited me with reverent gentility on his bed. I reached for him, but he was busy multi-tasking—toeing off his shoes and unlacing mine, peeling off his shirt with one hand while dragging my leggings down with the other, taking my panties and socks with them. I ripped my T-shirt and sports bra off—my breasts had enlarged a full size over the last few weeks, and none of my regular bras fit anymore.

By the time I had the two garments off, Duncan was naked and draping himself over my thighs.

"No, Dunc," I whispered. "Please. You can eat me out to your heart's content later. Right now, I just need you inside me. I need you to make love to me."

"One taste," he murmured, the words lost against my thighs as he buried his face in my sex.

"Ohhh—f-f-fuck!" I cried as his tongue slipped against my clit, sending a pulsing blaze of arousal boiling through me. "Dunc!"

The sound he made, then, was beyond

description—a feral noise that was purely male, entirely sexual, demanding, and appreciative. "Rune," he whispered. "Sweet as fucking honey."

Heat billowed in ravaging waves as he devoured me, putting the lie to his claim of just one taste—I was rocking on the edge within seconds, arching off the bed with my heels scrabbling at the comforter, hips pivoting to grind my greedy pussy against his hungry mouth.

"Duncan! Oh Jesus, Dunc. YES!"

"Come for me, Smokeshow."

His command acted as a trigger. Or maybe it was just my body releasing when it was ready. Either way, I came the moment he told me to, a loud cry ripping from my throat as I clutched at his head and spasmed madly, shaking and shuddering and wailing as my orgasm tore me to pieces.

The moment I could move or form words again, I dragged him up to me. "Come here, Duncan. Now. Please."

He prowled up my body, and his gaze locked on my breasts. "Holy fuck, Rune." he knelt over me, cupping one breast, rolling a thumb over my erect nipple. "Did...did your tits get *bigger*?"

I nodded. "Yes," I breathed. "And more sensitive."

He bent down to suckle my nipple, and I nearly came again just from that, jerking and gasping. "Holy shit, you're not kidding."

I reached down and grasped his cock, pumped his length, moaning as he continued lavishing attention on

my breasts. "Please, Duncan. I need you inside me."
I drew him closer, and then he was nudging my seam
with his broad tip.

He hesitated, however, searching me. "We don't
need…"

I shook my head, hooking my legs at his ass
and pulling at him. "No, honey. I can't get any more
pregnant."

I gripped his thick shaft and wedged him inside
me, then cupped his face and mated my mouth to his.
His arms snaked under my neck, and my head was
pillowed in the crook of his arms. There was another
drawn-out moment of hesitation as we kissed, and then
I thrust my hips against his at the same time that he
drove into me, and I was forced to break the kiss as a
wail of ecstasy sheared through me at the aching stretch
of him filling me.

"Duncan!" I gasped. "Oh my god. Oh my god.
Oh my god."

He was bare inside me, and nothing had ever felt
better. The world, time, worries, needs, fears, everything fell away.

Duncan groaned as he pushed deeper, inch by inch,
slowly. "Rune! Fuck—you feel…oh god, Rune."

"I know," I breathed. "I know."

When our hips met, I locked my legs high around
his back, tipping my hips up to keep him deep. He
rocked against me, moaning.

"Rune, I…" he rocked again, and I felt his cock

throb and pulse, thickening inside me. "I'm sorry, I can't—fuck, fuck, you feel too good, Rune. I won't last long."

I whimpered as I felt him thrust as deep as he could physically go, speared to the root within me and rocking there in small, rolling thrusts, and I knew he was trying like hell to hold on, to hold back.

I squeezed around him with my inner muscles, scraping my nails down his back to claw at his iron-hard ass. "Don't hold back, Duncan. Come for me. Come right the fuck now."

He shook his head, trembling with the effort to hold back. "Not yet, Rune, I want—I've barely—"

I rocked against him, squeezing and squeezing and squeezing around his cock, pulling at his ass, pumping my hips to take him in grinding thrusts. "Just come, Dunc, baby. I want you to. Please. Please come, my love."

He gasped, a sound that was nearly a whimper. "Say that again."

I brushed his wild hair out of his eyes and brushed my thumb over his lips and kissed his eyes and thrust against him again and again, forcing him to meet me, to match me thrust for thrust. "Don't look away, Dunc." I kissed his mouth, sucked his tongue into my mouth and then ghosted my lips against his ear. "Come inside me, my love. Right now. Please."

"Oh fuck, Rune!" He drew back, hesitated, and

then pounded into me, and I felt him come, then felt him release inside me.

I felt the flood of his cum fill me, and he thrust again, slowly, tenderly, his mouth shaking against mine. "Rune, oh god, Rune! I love you, oh god Rune, I love you so fucking much."

I found my own release in his declaration of love, my legs clenching around his waist, my fingers clawing into his back and raking down his spine as I rocked with him, and I bit into the hard ridge of muscle at the top of his shoulder and screamed and screamed and screamed as I came. His cock split me open and pierced me, penetrated me, filled me with thrust after thrust, and I felt his cum spreading through me and spilling out of me, and Duncan groaned through our mutual release, his face nuzzling my throat as he surged against the soft, welcoming cradle of my thighs.

I felt him spasm once more and go limp, and I nipped his earlobe. "I love you, Duncan. I really, *really* fucking love you." He started to shift, but I locked him in place with my arms and legs. "Don't move. Not yet. Just…stay here. Just like this, my love. Let me hold you."

His shoulders shook, though he was silent. "You love me."

"Yes," I breathed. "So much. I always did. I was just scared."

"Of what?"

"Everything," I answered. "How much I cared about you, so damn fast. I think some part of me always knew it'd be you. I think that part of me somehow subconsciously knew we'd end up here, one way or another, at some point, and that scared me because I didn't trust you."

"Do you trust me now?" he asked.

I caressed his face and turned it so he was looking at me. "Yes, Duncan. I do. I trust you. You've been there for me. You were there for my friends when you didn't know me and didn't owe anyone anything. You didn't let me push you away when that would've been the easiest way out."

He huffed. "Never done anything the easy way."

Duncan rolled us so he had me on his chest; I lost him inside me and felt a seep of seed down my thigh. I didn't care. Messes could be cleaned up—this moment was too important.

I traced abstract lines and arabesques on his chest. "We're going to be parents," I whispered. "I'm going to be a mom."

"You'll be an incredible one, too," he answered. And then: "We haven't talked about getting married."

I froze. "Duncan, we don't have to."

"I want to."

"Duncan, honey, please listen to me." I lifted on an elbow and held his gaze. "I don't want to get married—"

He opened his mouth to protest, and I covered his mouth with my hand.

"Hold on, let me finish," I said. "I don't want to

get married just because we're having a baby. I want to get married because we love each other."

He reached a long arm out, opened the top drawer of his nightstand. "Well, then, in that case…" he rolled me to my back and leaned over me. "Marry me, Rune. Because I love you. Because I can't handle being away from you. I want you to be mine forever."

He put a ring in front of me—it was small and simple, a half-carat diamond solitaire on a white-gold band.

Once again, tears sprang to my eyes—these of joy. "Yes, yes, yes," I whispered. "I'll marry you."

He slid the ring onto my shaky hand. "Lindsey told me your ring size. She wasn't sure what kind of diamond setting you liked, so—"

I shut him up with a kiss, sobbing even as I kissed him. "It's perfect. You're perfect."

"Hey, that's my line," he said, grinning against my mouth.

I held my hand up so the sun streaming through the window caught the diamond and sparkled. "It's beautiful, Duncan." I looked at him. "Lindsey didn't know what kind of ring I liked because I've honestly never thought much about it. I guess I always just wanted to be surprised." I palmed his face and kissed him. "And this is definitely a surprise. I love it, Duncan, truly."

"I know it's not much, but I figured I could upgrade it for an anniversary—"

I shook my head. "No. It's perfect, Duncan. Even if you had a billion dollars to spend, I wouldn't want anything else. You chose this for me. You put it on me. I don't want or need some five-carat rock. Just…you. All I need is you. Our little family. Our future together."

He let out a shuddery breath. "I was so worried you wouldn't like it. That it would be too small, or you wanted a princess cut or—or—"

I laughed, touching his lips with my fingertips. "Stop, baby. It's perfect. When did you even have time to think about this, let alone shop for it? And how did you afford it?"

He shrugged, and then slid down and rested his head on my chest. "I made time. Elias watched things for me so I could run over to Mr. Katzenberger's shop."

"Mr. Katzenberger, huh?"

"Just about every single ring the women in my family wear has been made by Isaiah Katzenberger," he told me. "As for how I afforded it, well…that's part of the other surprise I have for you."

"A surprise?" I felt my heart pitter-patter. "You better not have bought a house without asking me, Duncan. I'll be so mad, I swear to god."

He shook his head. "I didn't buy anything, I promise. I would never make a big decision like that without you."

"Then what—" I started.

He pulled me on top of him, and I felt his erection prodding my entrance.

"Oh," I gasped. "I see. I like this surprise." I held his gaze as I slid him inside me, sat up on my knees, and then drove down to impale myself on his cock, gasping as he crushed deep inside me.

"This..." he groaned, head thrown back, eyes rolling back in his head. "Oh fuck, honey—you feel incredible. This isn't the surprise."

He lasted a whole hell of a lot longer, this time. We fucked for an eternity, moving together in synchrony, each gasp mated, each moan muted by mouths, laughing as we came in perfect unison.

Finally finished, sweating and gasping, I rested my chin on his chest and gazed at him. "So? What's the surprise?"

He patted my ass. "Let's get cleaned up and I'll show you."

His version of us getting cleaned up meant I lay where I was and let him clean the rather shocking mess we'd made of my thighs and sex, each touch gentle and tender and reverent. Only then did he let me get dressed.

He drove us to the original Badd's Bar location on the boardwalk overlooking the Inside Passage. Being late afternoon on a Wednesday, there were only a few die-hard regulars at the bar, which was being tended by a middle-aged woman with light brown hair laced with silver.

She lit up as we entered. "Duncan! And I finally get to meet my newest niece-in-law." She swept out from behind the bar and embraced Duncan, gave him a light kiss on one cheek, and then, to my shock, did the same to me—after the cheek-kiss, she held me by the arms and looked me over. "My god, you really are gorgeous. I mean, you've definitely got the preggo-glow, but you're just stunning."

I wondered if she could tell the glow was more of a 'my fiancé just fucked my brains out twice' glow. Unthinking, I brushed a lock of hair out of my face with my left hand, and the woman—who hadn't been introduced to me yet—squealed like a teenager and clapped a hand over her mouth. "No! You're *engaged*?"

Duncan laughed. "Yeah, and you're the first know, so don't spill the beans. We want to tell Mom and Dad."

She mimed zipping her lips. "I won't say a word." She took my hand and examined the ring. "You did good, nephew, I'll say that. It's beautiful. Just like your bride."

Bride.

That hits different. Bride…mom…I've got a lot of new titles coming my way.

"So, Aunt Kitty—' Duncan started.

"Oh!" I exclaimed. "*You're* Kitty? The one the bar is named after?"

She rolled her eyes. "I've been annoyed by that for twenty years. But yes. I'm Kitty Badd. Sorry—we're not great at introductions, sometimes."

Duncan huffed. "Sorry, babe. Yeah, this my Aunt Kitty. Aunt Kitty, this is my fiancée, Rune Rigby."

"Now that we've got introductions out of the way," Duncan said. "I was hoping—"

"Right this way," Kitty said, cutting him off. "It's been professionally deep-cleaned after the tenant moved out. And I'll say, it'll be a relief to have family in there again. It's been weird having strangers live above this place."

I frowned at Duncan. "What's going on? Why are we here?"

He just grinned. "C'mon, I'll show you."

"It's unlocked," Kitty said. "I'll be up after you, I just gotta top off a couple beers."

Duncan led me across the bar to the kitchen, but instead of going through the doorless entryway into the kitchen, he opened a door next to it marked "Private" and held it for me.

A set of stairs led up; the stairwell, while steep and narrow, was clean and well-lit, and none of the stairs creaked as we ascended them. The door at the top was also unlocked, and Duncan pushed through it. I followed him into a surprisingly expansive and well-lit great room. A bank of windows let in buckets of natural light, bathing an unfurnished living room, opposite which was a kitchen—recently remodeled by the look of things. Beyond the kitchen and living room was a long hallway with three doors, two on one side, one opposite. Another small window at the end of that hallway let in more light.

"What is this place, Duncan?" I asked.

He grinned at me. "Home."

I gasped. "What?"

He nodded, showing me keys he had in his pocket. "We own the building—my family, I mean, not you and me. Dad and my uncles grew up here, and Mom and Dad lived here with a various assortment of uncles. When all the aunts and uncles had houses and kids, they rented it out. The lease just ran out and the tenant didn't want to renew it. We need somewhere to live that's not with Mom and Dad, so…voila. Home."

I looked around again, envisioning it with my furniture, maybe a few new pieces we picked together. "Duncan. Really? It's ours?"

He nodded. "Aunt Kitty wants to step back from managing this place, and Elias is way overdue for a promotion, so I'm taking over here, and Elias is stepping up at the Kitty."

"I'll still be around if you ever need help," Kitty's voice said from the top of the stairs. "Not that you need it. I'm just ready to hang out at home with Rome. Maybe take a few longer vacations and wait for our kids to give us grandbabies. I'm jealous of Dru, you know. She's already got one, and now she's getting another? Donovan needs to step up his game."

Duncan barked a guffawing laugh at this. "Don't hold your breath, Aunt Kitty. I'm not sure Donovan has any plans to settle down any time soon."

She shrugged. "Yeah, well, neither did you, and now look. Engaged *and* having a baby!"

I grabbed Duncan's hand. "I *love* it."

He grinned. "Me too! I was hoping you'd like it, because this way, we can keep saving money and live close to work. If Dane ever moves out, he may want one of the rooms, but I don't see that being a problem, do you?"

I shook my head. "Nope, not at all." I elbowed him. "Speaking of Dane, did you notice any weirdness between him and Lindsey?"

He nodded. "Yeah, but he won't talk to me about it. Just says don't worry about it. Lindsey say anything?"

I shook my head again. "No, same story. Something's up with those two."

Kitty just laughed. "Leave 'em be. If there's something going on, they've got to sort it out themselves. And if they need their family and friends, they'll let you know."

I set the question of Dane and Lindsey aside, already imagining paint colors, a new couch, a bedroom set...a rocking chair.

I have a home.

A fiancé.

A healthy baby growing inside me.

If you'd told me six months ago that this is where I'd be in life, I'd have laughed you out of the room.

Yet here I am.

And I couldn't be more excited. A little nervous about being a mom—okay, scared, too, maybe, but I've got a huge support system in my family and Duncan's.

What more could you want?

Not a damn thing.

EPILOGUE

Dane

I HONESTLY CAN'T QUITE BELIEVE THIS IS HAPPENING. MY BIG bro, Duncan, is getting married.

What a tool.

I mean, look—Rune is fucking great. I like her. I love her for him. I love them together. Honestly, I do. She inspires him to be better—and he is.

But my god, what a try-hard.

Twenty-three and you're getting married *and* having a baby *and* moving out of Mom and Dad's?

I have no interest in any of that. Marriage, babies… nah. Not for me. I have no problem with marriage and children as, like, an idea. But for now, at least, it's just not for me.

And I really don't understand how all this happened so fast. One second he was hanging out with some random tourist chick, hooking up and being the bro

I know. And then suddenly he's all serious and *in love* and moving in with her and she's fucking *pregnant*…

Sure, I might be projecting my own issues onto Duncan. I'm in no way ready for or interested in a serious relationship, let alone the fast and furious assault of adulthood he's going through.

You can miss me with that shit.

A certain memory nibbled at the edges of my awareness, but I pushed it away as I stood next to Jax at an angle near the altar in our backyard. *Our* being Mom and Dad's, the place I at least still call home. Delia's moved out, Emerson's moved out, and now so has Duncan, which means I'm the last one still living with my mommy and daddy.

It's fine. I'm fine.

The subject of said memory stood opposite me, and my damned eyes were having a hell of a time staying away from the wondrous vista that is Lindsey Snelling's epic cleavage.

The woman has incredible tits.

Her ass is divine.

Her hips that definitely do not lie.

Legs for days.

Snatched waist.

In a word, she's fucking gorgeous.

Piercing sapphire eyes, platinum blonde hair cut with razor precision at her shoulders, swinging loose around her perfect, heart-shaped face.

And yet, after what happened several months ago, she still won't even look at me.

Her eyes were fixed on Rune as she wafted gracefully down the aisle in her white wedding dress, which was an admittedly amazing piece of fashion, being created almost entirely of a spiderweb of sheer lace, with a stripe of silk covering her from chest to thigh, highlighting rather than hiding her belly bump. The result was sexy as hell. Rune's hair was loose around her shoulders, her bangs braided back and held in place with a strip of blue silk donated by Mom as something blue, according to that "something borrowed, something blue" business.

Duncan, unsurprisingly, has eyes only for his about-to-be wife, and his eyes were shining. Uncle Canaan, Uncle Corin, Aunt Aerie, and Aunt Tate form a four-piece band playing the wedding march. Opposite Jax, Rune's other best friend, Raquel, was positively beaming.

Lindsey…also beaming. But every so often, her eyes flicked to me, and her expression went carefully blank.

I still don't understand what happened.

I pushed that out of my mind yet again—as I've done multiple times a day every day since that incident occurred. She won't talk to me about it, and I'm stuck in some sort of limbo, wondering if I'm the asshole for reasons I'm not self-aware enough to understand, or if there's something in Lindsey's past that created the situation.

It's put a serious cramp in my style, to be honest.

I hooked up with a girl a few weeks ago—or tried to, but I kept thinking about Lindsey and what happened, and had to pull the cord on the poor girl I was with. She was understanding and didn't seem too upset about it, which was cool of her, but it's messing with my head. I haven't been able to even think about being with anyone since.

Fuck—I'm spacing out at my brother's wedding. Focus, jackass.

I put Lindsey out of my mind as best I can—a big ask, considering she's standing a few feet away wearing a pale blue dress that cups her epic tits, hugs her killer hips, and leaves bare her fucking endless legs.

All of which I've had the immense privilege of having seen naked. And can't stop seeing…

I daydream about her. I dream about her at night and wake up hard as a damn rock.

"And now the bride and groom will exchange vows," Papa Lucas said. "Hit it, Dunc."

I shook myself like a dog in an attempt to clear my wandering brain. It mostly worked, and I tuned into Duncan's vows.

"…To say the events of the last few months have been unexpected is an understatement," Dunc was saying. "I definitely didn't have 'meet the love of my life, get engaged, and find out she's pregnant' on my bingo card, especially when things didn't exactly happen in that order."

This got a smattering of laughter from the gathered

audience—the entirety of the extended Badd Clan, plus Raquel and Hamish, Lindsey, Rune's parents, and a handful of Rune's social circle from USC, most of whom were just up here for Raquel's wedding a few months ago.

"I wouldn't trade any of it," Duncan said. "My life was on a specific track, and this…none of it was in my plans. And I honestly couldn't be happier that my plans got derailed when a certain black-haired spitfire with the bluest eyes I've seen asked me to be her fake date for a wedding, specifically for the purpose of making her douchebag ex jealous." His eyes flitted to Ricky, Raquel's brother, who was said ex's best friend. "Sorry, Ricky, but he's a cheating jack-hole."

Ricky just held up his hands in a gesture of surrender, laughing. "Hey, I told him he was making a mistake when he first started flirting with that chick. He didn't listen, obviously."

"I don't think we need to go there, Dunc," Rune said, laughing.

Duncan just grinned. "I've never been so glad to be anyone's fake date. That weekend changed my life in so many ways. I can't imagine my life without you, Rune. I'm excited for our future together. I know being young parents won't be easy, but we've got a hell of a support system in place. I love you with every last part of myself, and I vow to you in front of everyone we know and love that I will spend every moment of the rest of my life trying to be worthy of your love, making you feel cherished, supported, and protected.

I promise that I will always try to put you first. I probably won't succeed at that all the time, but I sure will
try. You're the best thing that's ever happened to me.
I love you. You're my everything." He sniffed, shook
his head. "Um, yeah. That's it. Do I say, like, amen?"

"No, you doofus," I said. "You're not praying."

"Dane Badd, you cannot call your brother a doofus while he's getting married," Mom hissed at me,
while Dad endeavoured to not look like he was stifling laughter.

"Do *not* encourage him, Sebastian Badd," Mom
snapped at Dad.

"Guys," Duncan muttered, narrowing his eyes at
me, Mom, and then Dad. "Can we not?"

Rune's shoulders were shaking with laughter, and
she wiped a tear out of her eye—tears of laughter, tears
of wedding emotions? Who knows.

Feelings are not my speciality.

Papa Lucas sent a warning glare at us offenders,
and then gestured to Rune. "Now that my family is
being rude, it's your turn, Rune, my dear."

"Thanks, Papa Lucas." Rune takes a deep breath,
focusing on Duncan. "Dunc, my love. Falling in love
with you was definitely not in the plans, but it's absolutely the best thing that ever happened to me." She
covers her slight bump with one hand. "Becoming a
wife and a mother were always someday goals for me.
But life has a funny way of throwing twists and turns
at you, and now, suddenly, I'm getting to be both of

those things, and I could not be more excited. We get to discover life together, Dunc. I'm so incredibly grateful to have found you." She looked to Lindsey and then Raquel. "Linz, you encouraged me to stop hiding and running and get back out there after certain things took a very wrong left turn. Raquel, if it wasn't for you and Hamish planning your wedding here, I'd never have met Duncan."

"Good thing the Old Toby burned down then, eh?" Hamish called, to much laughter.

Rune took another deep breath, held it, and squeezed Duncan's hands. "I promise to love you as hard as I can, Duncan. I promise to always forgive you when you're a jackass, and I promise to never run when things get hard. Or, if I do, I promise to at least let you catch me again." More laughter. "I can't promise to obey you all the time because I've never been good at that, but I'll definitely try to listen to you. I love you, Duncan Badd, and vow, here and now, in front of everyone we know and love, that I will spend the rest of our lives learning how to love you more perfectly."

"If anyone has reason to object," Papa Lucas said, with a dramatic pause, "keep it your damn self. These kids are gettin' hitched. Now. Rune. Do you promise to love, honor, cherish, and at least try to obey Duncan for the rest of your days, no matter what?"

Rune sniffled, nodded. "Yes. I do."

"Duncan, grand-nephew, do you promise to love,

honor, cherish, and at least try to obey Rune for the rest of your days, no matter what?"

"Absolutely I do," Duncan said, blinking hard.

Oh god, he's crying.

Shoot me.

I glanced at Lindsey, and I guess I must have rolled my eyes or something because she was glaring daggers at me. Or maybe the glaring-daggers was for some other reason. I honestly wish I knew.

Maybe I can corner her fine ass and get some answers out of her at some point this evening.

"Well then, by the powers given to me by the good ol' internet and the great state of Alaska," Papa Lucas said, with a big old grin, "I now pronounce you two beautiful kids married as hell. Kiss'er, kid."

Duncan yanked Rune against his chest, hooked one arm around her waist and the other around her shoulders, dipped her backward, and kissed her stupid.

I couldn't help myself. "Get a room, you two!"

"That's the plan," Duncan said, lifting his wife to her feet. "But first, we party! Let's get it, Badd boys and girls!"

Cheers erupted and white roses were thrown at the couple as they walked down the aisle together toward the Passage, Aunt Eva snapping roughly a hundred photos every few seconds. As choreographed, Lindsey and I were next, meeting at the front of the aisle and pausing so Aunt Eva could get a portrait of us together. At the very last second, as my aunt was crouching to get the right angle, I snagged Lindsey's hand and stepped closer to her, angling my body toward hers as if we were not just standing up in the wedding together, but actually were together.

"Aww," Aunt Eva crooned as she snap-snap-snapped. "You two are adorable together! Lindsey, sweetheart, turn toward Dane a touch. There you go. Perfect!"

Aunt Eva stepped out of the way and snapped again as we walked hand-in-hand toward where Duncan and Rune were waiting.

Lindsey, the second Eva turned to focus on Raquel and Jax, yanked her hand out of mine. "What the *hell* was that?" she hissed, sounding absolutely furious.

"I don't know what you mean," I said, trying to sound innocent. "Just posing for the photos."

"You made it seem like we're together," she said, still hissing her words with serpentine venom. "We are *not* together and you know it."

"We aren't?" I said, faking shock—gasping and clapping a hand to my chest. "My god, if only I'd known…. oh wait, that's right." I snapped my fingers. "We fucked exactly once, after which you freaked the fuck out, bolted without a word, and haven't so much as acknowledged my existence since, let alone offering me some kind of an explanation."

She stomped with blatant fury radiating from every pore. "Maybe it just wasn't that good," she snapped, "and I'm just not interested in a repeat."

"And maybe you're full of shit." I leaned toward her.

"It was goddamned fantastic and you know it, Lindsey. You owe me an explanation."

"I don't owe you shit," she answered, now speaking through gritted teeth as we reached Duncan and Rune. She left my side and hurried to Rune. "Congratulations, bitch. I can't believe you're married *and* pregnant!"

The girls embraced and I sidled over to Duncan, wrapped an arm around him, and shook him. "Congrats, I guess." I bumped my head against his. "For real, bro, I am happy for you. You snagged a winner."

He turned into me and pulled me into a hug. "Thanks, Dane. I know I did." He put his mouth near my ear. "When are you gonna tell me what the actual fuck is going on with you and Lindsey?"

I blew out a frustrated breath, squeezing him closer and embracing him hard. "Soon as I fuckin' know, man. She won't talk to me."

He laughed, the bastard. "Ah. So...what'd you do?"

I frowned at him. "Why do you assume I did something, asshole?"

"Because you're my little bro and I know you. You'll shoot yourself in the foot before you even know you're holding a gun and then put that foot in your mouth."

I shoved him away, laughing even as I bitterly recognized the nugget of truth at the center of his teasing statement. "Shut up, jackass."

"For real, though, man, what happened? I know something happened."

I shook my head. "Not the time or the place, Dunc."

I clapped his shoulders. "Today's about you and Rune. We'll talk later."

He nodded. "Heard, bro." He playfully shoved me. "So, you gonna be lonely all by yourself up there. Last kid in the house."

I snorted. "Yeah, I think I'll be okay."

Jax and Raquel joined us then, and the opportunity for private talk was gone as we were ordered by Aunt Eva into roughly forty-seven billion different poses and configurations with the wedding party—which consisted of me and Lindsey, Raquel and Jax, Mom and Dad, and Tom and Kelly Rigby. Why Duncan and I had to pose with Tom and Kelly, I wasn't sure, and neither did they, I didn't think, but you didn't argue with Aunt Eva. She was the sweetest, most soft-spoken woman you'll ever meet, but my god, she had a core of pure titanium. I mean, she'd been married to Uncle Baxter for something like twenty years, and god knows that man is more than a bit of a handful. Takes a hell of a strong woman to tame a man like Baxter Badd as much as she has.

While photos were happening, several party buses were transporting the rest of the wedding guests to Badd's Bar and Grille for the reception, and then a stretched limo took the rest of us once photography was over.

The irony of the reception was that Duncan, in solidarity with his pregnant wife—that's gonna take a while to get used to, my big bro being *married*—didn't drink any alcohol.

Nine months without drinking? Yikes.

I, obviously, didn't have that hindrance, so I went after it. A DJ had been hired so Canaan, Corin, Aerie, and Tate could enjoy the reception rather than provide the music, and I spent a lot of time dancing with my various cousins, doing shots, and avoiding Lindsey.

Avoiding didn't mean I didn't think about her, though. Or, more specifically, her claim that the sex hadn't been that good.

My response had been automatic—I'm pathologically incapable of filtering myself. But after the fact, it was haunting me.

My memory of that night was crystal clear. After Duncan and Rune had gone upstairs to Rune's room to talk, Lindsey and I, having spent the better part of the day flirting, had gone to dinner together. Dinner had led to drinks at a bar near her apartment in West Hollywood, and drinks had led to us going to her apartment.

The sex, according to my memory, had been goddamn spectacular. I know for a fact that she'd had at least one orgasm—unless she was faking it, but she'd need to be an Oscar-winning actress for that to have been faked. I *felt* her pussy spasming while I was inside her, for fuck's sake. I don't know how you can fake that.

We'd passed out together. Woke up. Pillow talk about nothing in particular. And then I'd gone down on her. Eagerly. For a very, very long time. And skillfully, I like to think. I certainly have never had any complaints.

And again—unless she was a world-class actress, she hadn't faked the orgasms I'd given her.

Once she'd recovered, she started returning the favor. Now, admittedly, we'd had a good bit to drink, and I was a bit hazy from that and having just woken up in the middle of the night. But I definitely don't remember doing or saying anything that could be construed as pressuring her to do *anything*. I wouldn't. I may be a horny jackass and bona fide hookup artist, but I'd never pressure a girl to do anything. Lindsey had gone down on me of her own free will.

And then, after I came—and I gave her plenty of warning beforehand so she could choose how to let me finish—she freaked the fuck out. Rolled away from me, hyperventilating, locked herself in her bathroom, and screamed at me to get the fuck out.

I remember being confused as hell. Like, what just happened? Did I do something? I've scoured my memory of that night obsessively, and I can't think of anything. I hadn't held her head down, hadn't forced her down or anything like that, and I gave her lots of lead time before I let go. I hadn't begged or demanded or insisted or cajoled. The second I'd finished making her come, she'd seemingly eagerly moved to suck me off. Great, I love it. But if she had some sort of an issue with it, I'd *never* have let that happen.

In the words of a somewhat overrated hero, I may be an asshole, but I'm not a hundred percent a dick.

With no other option, since she just kept screeching

for me to get the fuck out, I'd gotten dressed and left, going back to the hotel Duncan and I were sharing.

She'd refused to speak to me since. She blocked my number. Didn't answer texts, didn't return voicemails. I even talked to Rune about it privately—without explaining what happened, just asking her to have Lindsey get ahold of me—and had been told that Lindsey wasn't talking to her about me either.

She'd shut everyone out when it came to me.

Which made me think that whatever had happened in her head wasn't about me.

But it just doesn't seem fair that I get punished for it.

Fuck, I'm thinking about it again.

I took a fresh bottle of beer through the kitchen, pressing the dewy, icy-cold bottle to my sweating forehead and cheeks. I'd long since lost my suit coat and tie, had my sleeves rolled up and my shirt undone so my tank top peeked through the gap of my open shirt.

I emerged in the alley behind the kitchen, taking a long slug of beer. Which, honestly, should have been water, considering I was pretty tipsy. But fuck it. Your brother only gets married once.

I hope.

I leaned against the brick wall next to the door and held the bottle against my cheek, trying to quiet the chaos in my mind.

I'm ADHD, so that's a losing game, but right now, the crazed squirrel on a treadmill that is my brain is going a little haywire, and I needed a moment alone in the silence to bring down the noise in my head.

Which is when I heard it.

A sniffle.

A shuddery sob.

And damn me, but I recognized the voice, somehow.

I looked left and saw Lindsey in her baby blue bridesmaid dress, leaning against the wall a few feet away, head tipped back, weeping.

Fuck.

"Um, hey," I said. "Uh, you…you good, Lindsey?"

She snorted. "Yeah, Dane. I'm peachy. I'm out here bawling my eyes out for fucking fun."

"Jesus, dude, I was trying to be nice. Fuckin' shoot me for having the teensiest bit of compassion, even though you won't fucking tell me what the fuck I did wrong."

"*NOT EVERYTHING IS ABOUT YOU!*" She shrieked, and collapsed to her hands and knees.

Stunned by the outburst, I stood frozen for a moment, and then went over to her and knelt beside her, recognizing an emotional breakdown when I saw one.

"Hey, whoa, Linz. Take a deep breath, okay?"

She shook her head, hyperventilating. "C-c-can't."

I rested a hand on the smooth warm skin of her back just above her shoulder blades. "Keep trying. Take a breath. Slow it down."

"Don't—d-don't…don't *touch* me," she hissed.

I removed my hand immediately and sank to my ass on the dirty ground beside her. "Okay, no touching."

"Go away."

"No."

"Dane. Fuck off."

"When you can stand up and breathe normally again, I'll leave you alone. Not until then."

"I d-d-didn't a-a-a-sk for your h-h-h-help."

"Too damn bad, Killer. You got me anyway."

So I sat next to her as she knelt in a quasi-fetal position on the dirty alley ground, her sobs and body-wracking shudders slowly subsiding.

Eventually, she stood up and began pacing back and forth. I remained on the ground, sipping my beer and watching her pace.

She came back to where I was, and leaned against the wall. Didn't look at me as she spoke. "I don't owe you any explanations."

"I disagree. I've spent the last several months trying to figure out what I did to make you freak out like that. And I've come up empty. I don't think it's too much to ask for you to tell me what I did."

She didn't answer for a very long time, and I waited in silence for her response, sipping beer and occasionally stealing glances at her long, smooth, tanned legs.

When it felt clear she wasn't going to even respond, I stood up, tossed my empty bottle into the dumpster, and paused at the door to the kitchen. "Fuck me. Got it. Well, have a nice fucking life, Lindsey. And for what it's worth, I'm sorry for whatever it was I did. I mean that. I don't expect you to give a fuck, but it's true."

I held my place for another beat, but she still said nothing. With huff and a headshake, I left her there alone and went back to the party.

By three a.m., everyone over thirty was gone, leaving only the younger crowd—my boatload of cousins. And we can fuckin' party. Duncan and Rune had long since left as well, with an encouragement to us to keep the party going. Which we did.

Lindsey rallied, but stuck mainly to Raquel's side, hanging out with the handful of LA kids who were Rune's friends.

By four, I wasn't hammered, but I was pretty damn sloshed, and ready to call it. Rune and Duncan had taken their honeymoon to Hawaii—a last getaway before she was too pregnant to fly, which I hadn't realized was a thing, and before they had a baby and wouldn't be taking any vacations for a long damn time.

Which meant the guest room upstairs was open— Duncan had given me blanket permission to crash there when I needed, as long as I understood that they weren't going to be quiet on my account.

Noted.

Fortunately, they were on the flight to Hawaii, and I wouldn't have to hear them boning.

Thank god for that.

I shuffled, dizzy and unsteady, upstairs. Bounced off half a dozen different walls, found the guest room. Took a five-year-long piss in the en suite bathroom, stripped out of my clothes, and collapsed in the bed.

I woke up wrapped around a soft, warm, naked female body. Her bare ass was pressed against my groin, which was throbbing with a giant boner.

Um.

I went to bed alone. I *know* I did.

I cracked an eye open, saw a tangled haze of blonde. She shifted, and I caught a glimpse of a medusa tattoo at the base of her neck, usually hidden by her hair. She flung her arm aside, showing a semicolon tattoo on the inside of her wrist.

Lindsey.

Confused, I rolled to my back, away from her.

She twisted, rolling to follow me, and put her head on my chest. Huffed, nuzzled.

My heart clenched, flipped. What the fuck was going on?

I held still, frozen by sleepy indecision and confusion.

Her hand slid up my chest, found my mouth, and covered it. "Don't," she mumbled. "Just…shush."

"I…"

"Dane," she whispered. *"Please.* Don't say anything. I need this. Just this. Please."

"Okay, Linz. All right."

I kept still, my arm around her shoulders, her soft breath slowly evening out as she fell back into a deep sleep.

I was a lot longer in returning to slumber.

I dreamed of Lindsey screaming, "GET OUT!" Dreamed of her on her knees, shaking, crying, but refusing to let me so much as touch her.

I dreamed a memory of that night we spent together—silver moonlight streaming through her window, bathing her naked body in quicksilver light, highlighting her lush curves, glinting off of her eyes as she smirked up at me while slipping sensuously down my body, mouth opening as she neared my aching cock…

The dream ended then, and I woke up with a start, seconds from coming.

"FUCK," I snarled, covering my face as I dragged myself back from that edge.

When I had myself under control, I glanced at the space beside me.

Empty.

On the pillow was a sheet of paper towel, scribbled on in neat, female block letters with a Sharpie.

There were three words: *It wasn't you.*

Wow, what a relief.

I'm saved from my obsession.

Not.

I'm more confused and worried than ever, especially after her meltdown last night, or this morning.

I had to find her and figure out what was going on.

My phone rang—I slapped at the nightstand blindly, found my phone, stabbing at the answer button without reading the caller ID.

"H'lo?"

"Dane?" It was a female voice I didn't recognize.

"Yeah? Who's this?"

"Raquel. Rune's friend?"

"Oh, right," I said, sitting up, confused yet again. "Uh, what's up?"

"So, Lindsey never came back to her room last night."

"She, uh, slept here with me. Not *with* me, with me, but with me." I slapped my forehead. "She was here last night. She's not here now, though."

"Shit. Her phone's going right to voicemail."

"Well she's had me blocked for months, so I dunno."

"Dammit. I'm worried about her. She's not been herself lately."

I cleared my throat. "Honestly, I'm worried too. She, uh, she had a bit of a breakdown last night, around three."

Raquel was silent for a second. "She…she did?"

"Yeah. Big one. Hyperventilating, crying, the whole nine yards. Wouldn't tell me shit, but what else is new."

"Not good," Raquel said. "Not good at all."

"Where would she go?" I asked.

"That's just thing—I dunno. But we have to find her."

"Let me call my cousin, Jax. He can help."

"He can? How?"

"Well, he's my Uncle Xavier's protegé, which means he's sort of a world-class hacker. He can find her."

"Is hacking even a thing anymore?" she asked.

I laughed. "Y'know, that's a good question. I dunno. I just know he can do just about anything that involves a computer. He can help find her."

"Can you guys meet us at our hotel? We're at the new Old Toby."

"Yeah," I said. "We'll be there ASAP."

Well…shit.

This isn't good.

ALSO BY
Jasinda Wilder

Visit me at my website: **www.jasindawilder.com**
Email me: **jasindawilder@gmail.com**

If you enjoyed this book, you can help others enjoy it as well by recommending it to friends and family, or by mentioning it in reading and discussion groups and online forums. You can also review it on the site from which you purchased it. But, whether you recommend it to anyone else or not, thank you *so much* for taking the time to read my book! Your support means the world to me!

My other titles:

Forbidden Fruit

Wild Ride: Biker Billionaire

Delilah's Diary

Big Girls Do It:
Big Girls Do It
Married
On Christmas
Pregnant
Rock Stars Do It
Big Love Abroad

The Falling Series:
Falling Into You
Falling Into Us
Falling Under
Falling Away
Falling for Colton
The Ever Trilogy:
Forever & Always
After Forever
Saving Forever

From the world of *Wounded*:
Wounded
Captured

From the world of *Stripped*:
Stripped
Trashed

From the world of *Alpha*:
Alpha
Beta
Omega
Harris: Alpha One Security Book 1
Thresh: Alpha One Security Book 2
Duke: Alpha One Security Book 3
Puck: Alpha One Security Book 4
Lear: Alpha One Security Book 5
Anselm: Alpha One Security Book 6
Sigma
Gamma

The Houri Legends:
Jack and Djinn
Djinn and Tonic

The Madame X Series:
Madame X
Exposed
Exiled

The Black Room (With Jade London)

The One Series
The Long Way Home
Where the Heart Is
There's No Place Like Home

Badd Brothers:
Badd Motherf*cker
Badd Ass
Badd to the Bone
Good Girl Gone Badd
Badd Luck
Badd Mojo
Big Badd Wolf
Badd Boy
Badd Kitty
Badd Business
Badd Medicine
Badd Daddy

Goode Girls:
For a Goode Time Call…
Not So Goode
Goode To Be Bad
A Real Goode Time
Goode Vibrations
Dad Bod Contracting:
Hammered
Drilled
Nailed
Screwed

Fifty States of Love:
Pregnant in Pennsylvania
Cowboy in Colorado
Married in Michigan
Christmas in Connecticut

Billionaire Baby Club:
Lizzy Goes Brains Over Braun
Autumn Rolls a Seven
Laurel's Bright Idea

Club Sin:
Rev
Kane
Chance
Silas
Saxon
Solomon

Blood Heir:
Blood Heir
Blood Bonds
Blood Reign
Blood Bonds

Three Rivers:
Into the Light

Standalone titles:
Yours
The Cabin
The Parent Trap
Wish Upon A Star
Big Hose

Non-Fiction titles:
You Can Do It
You Can Do It: Strength
You Can Do It: Fasting

Jack Wilder Titles:
The Missionary

JJ Wilder Titles:
Ark

To be informed of new releases and special offers,
sign up for
Jasinda's email newsletter.